TAKING POWER

ALSO BY DAVID LEWIS STEIN

Scratch One Dreamer

Living the Revolution: The Yuppies in Chicago

My Sexual and Other Revolutions

Toronto for Sale: The Destruction of a City

The Hearing

City Boys

The Golden Age Hotel

TAKING POWER

A NOVEL BY

DAVID LEWIS STEIN

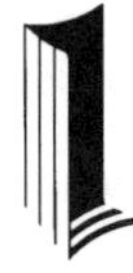

LESTER

PUBLISHING

Lester Publishing Limited acknowledges the financial assistance of the Canada Council and the Ontario Arts Council.

Canadian Cataloguing in Publication Data

Stein, David Lewis, 1937–
Taking power

ISBN 1-895555-26-4

I. Title.

PS8537.T45T3 1992 C813'.54 C92-093038-7
PR9199.3.S74T3 1992

All of the characters in this book are fictitious, and any resemblance to actual persons living or dead is purely coincidental.

Design: Gordon Robertson

Lester Publishing Limited
56 The Esplanade, Toronto, Ontario M5E 1A7

Printed and bound in Canada.

92 93 94 95 5 4 3 2 1

For Alison

with all my love

ACKNOWLEDGEMENTS

In memoriam, Harry Tepperman, with whom the last line of this book began, over a regular Friday-afternoon lunch at United Bakers, and without whom none of this would ever have been possible.

I would like to thank Marian Hebb for her years of friendship, support, and good counsel.

I would like to thank Jules Newman for his generous offer of help at a time when it was most needed

I would like to thank John Honderich, who gulped hard and then arranged for me to take a sabbatical year.

I would like to thank Susan Walker for her sensitive and thoughtful editing, and the following people who were kind enough to read parts of this novel in manuscript: Peter Cheney; Robert Harlang; Marvin Horwitz; Harvey Kotler; Joe Leigh; Peter Newman; Kate, Ben, and Alison Stein; Dave Truster; and Colin Vaughan.

I would like to thank Jack Tannenbaum, who provided the shoes; the Morning Runners, who provided the typewriter; and Martin Stone, who brought the wine to Arnprior.

CONTENTS

1

LIVING TOGETHER: 1969

In which five friends undertake to make repairs to their lives and, along the way, to stop an expressway and save the city

PROLOGUE

IT IS OCTOBER 1969, and in the City of Toronto a young lawyer named Harry Margulies has just discovered the secret of life. It radiates out to him now from the shimmering squares between the woven threads of a linen dishtowel he holds on his lap. He can hear it in the empty spaces between the notes of the desperate Jefferson Airplane song floating through the stereo speakers—"...you both stand there, long hair blowing, eyes alive and minds still growing, saying to me..." Harry understands it all. Light and sound, rocks, plants, human beings, stars and distant galaxies—all the same process, all becoming...

"Field...," Harry says. He struggles to get all the words out in their proper order. "Unified..."

Dane Harrison, who is sitting beside him on the floor, picks up the dishtowel and wipes Harry's forehead with it.

"You're not Einstein," he says gently.

Yes, true, but if Einstein were alive today, Harry Margulies would help him out. The poor guy spent the whole last half of his life trying to fit everything together in one unified-field theory. But he could never see that there is no real difference between living things and things that are not supposed to be living, animate and inanimate matter. What holds molecules together to make up things big enough to be seen and touched? What holds mighty galaxies in their place? Exchanging energy, that's what! So, what holds people together, eh? They give it different names, according to the different circumstances in which it happens to them—fear, anger, religion, love—but what they are really doing is just bumping into each other, exchanging energy. Human beings are only bits of matter floating through the universe.

Harry sees his own life clearly now. So what if they never make him a partner at Carlton and Boggs! Something else will happen. Someone else will bump into him. Harry has freed himself from five years of slavery. Six, if you count his year as an articling law student. He has freed himself from a million years of superstition and fear.

Harry turns to his wife, Doreen, who is sitting on a couch under the window, her long legs folded beneath her. He can see the anger in Doreen's face, and it shouldn't be there. She should be happy for him. Doreen is thin and pale and has heavy black hair that falls below her shoulders. She has a long, pointed nose too, and a small lower jaw, and sometimes Harry thinks of her as a sensitive forest animal, like a young fox, that he has captured and is holding prisoner. Harry hasn't the strength to cross the room, but he blesses his wife with the penitent-little-boy grin Doreen likes so much. Don't be mad at me, honey. I was just trying to protect you. Doreen was terribly eager to take one of the LSD tabs Dane brought home, but Harry pointed out to her that she has a seven-year-old son to think about. What would happen to Gordon if his mother went on an acid trip and never came back? Harry insisted he must try the stuff first, and if it's all right, then Doreen can have some too and Harry will stand guard for her.

"Are you all right, Harry?" Annabel asks.

"I'm fine. Just leave me," Harry says.

The luminous crystalline structure Harry has been working on is beginning to darken. It's Annabel's fault. She is sitting on the floor across from him. She should back up, give him more room. Annabel has a heavy, raw, worried face. She is wearing a full blue skirt and an embroidered white blouse. She looks like a revolutionary from the hills of Mexico with bandoliers of bullets criss-crossing her chest. Harry understands her anger now. He would like to help her, but she'd never listen. Let it go, Annabel. You can't control me. You can't control anybody. It's just people bumping into each other. He struggles to see the holy light pulsating again between the threads of the dishtowel. It is taking all his will-power…

The front door bangs open.

Harry jolts upright as though hit with an electric shock. His face fills with fear. Annabel grips the blanket on her knees and gets ready to throw herself on top of Harry.

The four people in the living-room listen to the tapping of high heels coming down the hall. Vivian Billinghurst, the fifth person who lives in the house, reaches the door of the living-room and stops. Harry cries out, "Get her away!"

Vivian just stands there, staring at Harry Margulies and the other people in the room.

"Get her out of here!" Harry screams. He cowers against the wall.

"What the hell?" Vivian says.

"It's nothing to worry about," Dane says. "He just took a little acid."

"A paranoid-schizophrenic reaction—very common," Annabel says soothingly. "It'll pass."

"Is he okay?" Vivian asks. She can just see what's coming. They'll have to rush Harry to the Clarke Institute, and the resident head-shrinkers will demand to know what in the world he took, and word of what has been going on in their house will get around—you can't keep things like this quiet—and her husband, Trevor, will come after her, demanding that Vivian send the girls back to him. How could the people she has chosen to live with do this to her?

"Get her away! Help me!" Harry bawls.

"He'll be all right in the morning," Dane says to Vivian. "Please, just go now. We'll take care of him."

Vivian turns away and climbs the stairs.

On the second floor, Vivian checks to see if the children, at least, are all right. The boys' room is an appalling litter of old clothes, plastic toys, and comic books. It smells of candy and urine-soaked bed sheets. Vivian doesn't even bother to go in.

In the girls' room at the end of the hall, Vivian's daughters, Sasha and Paola, sleep soundly in the double bed they share. Vivian has promised that when she has a little more money, she will get them single beds. But right now, they look so sweet together she is not sure she could bear to separate them. Sasha and Paola lie surrounded by brown bears, dusky lions, and grey and white rabbits. Vivian had to leave most of her former life behind when she walked out of her home but she did, at the last moment, grab the stuffed animals. Vivian lifts a blanket and pulls it up around Paola, her youngest.

On the third floor, the roof slopes and a person can stand upright only in the centre of the room. The air is beginning to be chilly. Vivian plugs in the little space heater even before she takes off her duffel coat. When the coils are glowing red and she can feel the heater having some effect, Vivian takes off all her clothes and stands with her back to a mirror, her head turned over her shoulder, studying her body.

Then she studies the drawing on the easel in front of her. Yes, it's true, she is putting on weight. Vivian is tall, five feet ten inches and she has long, well-formed bones; so, with her clothes on, the extra pounds probably do not show very much. Annabel insists on whomping up huge platters of spaghetti and shepherd's pie because she says these are the best kinds of food when so many people are coming and going. Still, it's annoying to think Vivian's body is punishing her for the choices she has made.

One Sunday morning, back in another lifetime, Vivian threw her clothes and the children's things into the back of a station-wagon and took off for her sister's house. Her sister asked her, Why drag the kids into it? Vivian said she wasn't going to leave her girls behind, caught in a life she herself was running away from.

Vivian told her husband that she just needed time. She knew this wasn't true, even then. But at least by pretending the door was still open she thought she could get Trevor to agree to monthly payments. It worked, but dear old Trevor always has an angle. What he finally agreed to turned out to be just barely enough for Vivian to pay the rent and to keep herself and the girls fed. She knows Trevor thinks that, after a little taste of the real world, she will be happy to come back to the studio he had built for her. It is on the sunny side of the house, overlooking the glorious maple trees of the Don Valley and the Billinghursts' kidney-shaped swimming pool.

But Vivian, in turn, outsmarted Trevor. She went to Annabel Warren, the old friend from Havergal College who had dropped out. Listen, Vivian said, if kids strung out on dope and crazy politics can start communes and live together, then it ought to be a snap for mature adults.

Annabel liked the idea. She said being with other people right now might help Dane, the man she has been with for the last couple of years. It was Annabel who then brought in Doreen, the anxious young woman who had been stuffing envelopes in the Student Peace Campaign offices. And it was Annabel who found the old house on Landrigan Street with the wide, wooden porch and high peaked gables over the windows. It was in a block right beside where the city is building a new expressway, so they were able to get it for only $275 a month.

With three families contributing to household expenses, Vivian can live without having to find a job. She can spend her time going to classes at the Ontario College of Art and know there will always be someone at home with her daughters. Given the state of her life right now, Vivian feels perfectly justified in being outraged at Harry Margulies. She has always thought of him as a stuffed shirt; now he is upsetting everything she has worked for just so he can fool around with drugs that are already going out of style.

In the room directly below where Vivian stands, studying her body, Gordon Margulies flails his arms, hollers something that sounds like "Yark!" and turns over—all without waking up. He is deep in wheezing, childish sleep, completely unaware that Annabel is standing beside his bed and has, with a gentle pull on his arm, saved him from falling out of his top bunk.

She looks at the face of her own son, Paul. Unlike Gordon, who heaves and groans as though demons were chasing him through his dreams, Paul sleeps curled into a gentle ball. Out of habit, part of her nightly ritual, Annabel studies his pale cheek. There is no hint of the blue tinge in the skin that Dr. Kernohan has warned her about, the sign for her to panic. She does not have to rush her son to the hospital tonight. But it could happen any time. The tiny weak spot in the internal chamber of his heart—smaller than a pin-point they say—could suddenly give way. Love, which Annabel has in abundance, will not be able to save Paul then.

The doctors have told her they cannot fix her son's heart until it is fully formed. But if Paul lives to about the age of seventeen, they can cut into the heart and replace the damaged tissue with a fabric patch. The prospect is terrifying but Dr. Kernohan has assured Annabel that for a young man, open-heart surgery will be no greater strain than having an appendix removed—if Annabel can just keep Paul alive until he is ready.

Annabel yearns now to slide in beside her son. But she is wide and the bottom bunk is narrow, and most likely she would wake Paul up rather than comfort him. Instead, she retreats to her own room, her long, red-flannel nightgown flapping around her feet.

Annabel adjusts her little steel-rimmed reading glasses and settles down to do the crossword puzzle in the *New York Times Magazine* and try to keep herself calm and reasonable. But, goddamn it, Dane should be up with her, doing his husbandly duties, instead of looking after stupid Harry Margulies. Annabel has checked her cycle and body temperature; her unreliable reproductive organs are not at optimum, but very close. Nobody knows better than she that calculations of fertility are not precise, but tonight is at least within the range of time when she might conceive. Dane should be in bed, helping her to make a baby, instead of playing nursemaid to a fool. If Harry Margulies were left to Annabel's care, she'd take his pants down and give him a good spanking. Annabel thinks of herself and Dane as survivors of a war, and now they are being made to live through battle scenes again just because Harry Margulies and his frozen little goody two-shoes wife think maybe they missed something.

Annabel could tell them they didn't miss a fucking thing—if only they'd take the trouble to ask her. She has done it all: played field hockey in the green and secluded fields of Havergal College; hung out in the smoky, grungy folk clubs on Yorkville Avenue; fallen in with the ragged clumps of hippie kids panhandling in front of the elegant stores on Bloor Street, two blocks away, trying to get enough for food—and more dope. Her own sister walked right by once and didn't even recognize her. Annabel has balled more men than she can remember—sometimes for fun, sometimes for love, and sometimes just for a place to keep warm at night. Doreen and Harry may have fantasies about the hippie days, but Annabel was there and she could tell them, if they asked her, that she felt ill through most of that time. And in the end it cost her a marriage and may well cost her a son.

The doctors have told her it was pure chance, a role of the genetic dice, that weakened Paul's heart. Annabel knows better. She has seen too many wiped-out, burned-out people to believe that our bodies do not pay us back for what we do to them.

Dane should be here now, helping to fill her up again. When she decided to live with Dane, she said to herself, "This is the last time. From now on, this is my man." But, instead of a man she can rely on, Dane is turning into a zombie.

Seventy-six down: what's a three-letter word for "bitter vetch?"

In the largest room in the house, a second-floor bedroom, Doreen Margulies feels Harry sliding in beside her and pretends to be asleep. Her body curled stiffly away from him, she really does want to be left alone but she realizes her husband is not fooled by her attempts to simulate deep breathing. She left him downstairs more than an hour ago. Dane said it was all right for her to go. But she couldn't fall asleep by herself in the big bed, and now she feels Harry's hand making circles on her back, and then reaching around her to cup her breast, and his lips tenderly touching the back of her neck. She hears his vibrant, expressive voice whispering that he's all right now and she is definitely going to take acid next because acid is, really, magnificent, and they were foolish to be so afraid of it all these years. Doreen is not fooled. She is never going near the stuff. She's never going to let herself be turned into a drooling lunatic, even if acid does promise to give her visions.

Doreen is sure now she should not have listened so eagerly to Annabel. Annabel made the commune sound as though it would help Doreen's life with Harry. They would live with interesting, artistic people. Doreen and Harry would become a part of these people's lives.

Doreen feels her nightgown being gently tugged up. She rolls over to receive her husband. She is too honest. She cannot pretend any longer. She is moving with Harry. But she still struggles to hang on to her anger. She begins to cry. Everything slips away from her. It's not fair! Doreen has no sanctuary. Harry bends his head down to her and kisses her damp cheeks. "So beautiful...," he says, laying his head beside hers on the pillow.

When night loses its power, birds begin to sing in the heart of the city. Dane Harrison sits at the kitchen table, listening to their shrill, nervous little yodels. How many times has he been still awake at this hour and why has he never heard the singing before? Because, Dane tells himself ruefully, he was too busy mouthing off himself. Now he has nothing more to say to anyone and he can hear the birds at sunrise. What the hell could they be? Robins? Cardinals? They must be on their way south, the last stragglers before the snow falls. Dane pours himself more vodka and wonders if he will finally start to feel sleepy before he reaches the end of the bottle.

How he envies Harry Margulies! It is all new for Harry; he has only to swallow a bit of acid and the whole world lights up. Dane can still recall the wonder of his first trip. Through the night Dane has watched Harry's raptures and thought that when Harry finally crashed, he might take a tab himself. After all, Dane's the one who brought the stuff home. An old comrade from the Student Peace Campaign came into the restaurant where he works and offered him three tabs of California Sunshine for just ten dollars. But no, Dane has had too much experience with dope. It's not smart to drop acid when you are depressed. It will just make you feel worse.

Dane remembers a silly little song his father used to sing, and begins to sing it again to himself, adding a verse of his own.

I used to work in Chicago,
in a department store…
I used to work in Chicago,
I did but I don't any more.
A lady came in for some steaks one day,
I asked her what kind she came for
Strip, she said…so strip her I did…
I did but I don't any more…
My friends and I went to Chicago,
to tell them to end the war.
I worked for peace in Chicago.
I did but I don't any more…

Dane had believed devoutly in the power of non-violence. War only begets more war. Even a superficial reading of history teaches that much. Dane went farther. He studied the works of Thoreau and Gandhi and A. J. Muste. He saw that if you met those who opposed you with love instead of anger, you could turn aside, or at least absorb, their wrath, and they would come to love you in return. Dane joined the Student Peace Campaign. And when he graduated, he devoted all his time to the fight to end nuclear weapons.

But, then he went to Chicago, to the great Festival of Life organized by the Youth International Party. From all over North America, people were answering the call of the Yippies to come and demonstrate at the convention of the Democratic Party. Dane wanted to be there because he thought it was going to be one of those pivotal moments in history. They would force America to end the war in Vietnam. They would show the world that nonviolence and love were the way of the future. A new generation was going to take power in Chicago, and Dane Harrison was going to be part of it.

But the demonstrators for peace became a howling mob. Dane still does not know quite how it happened. But he found himself rushing towards the Hilton Hotel, where the delegates who supported Hubert Humphrey were supposed to be staying. The shrieking demonstrators filled up the whole intersection in front of the hotel, and no cars could get through. The police charged into them, swinging nightsticks. Dane was hit in the head, but there was no pain, only a thud and the feeling of blood running down his face. He made his way to the doorway of a store, where other people had taken refuge. A policeman with a plexiglass riot mask pulled down over his face stepped into the doorway with a little aerosol can.

Slowly, deliberately, he pressed down the plastic tab and sprayed stinging Mace into the faces of the people in the front row. They screamed and dropped to their knees. The police picked them up and threw them into the back of a blue and white patrol wagon.

Dane knew he must stand there without flinching and let this policeman spray his face with searing chemicals and then he must fall to the ground and submit to being taken to jail. But Dane could not make himself feel any love for the policeman with the can of Mace. He felt only murderous hatred.

Dane managed to wriggle free from the tangle in the doorway. He started running down the street, and as he reached the corner, he passed a cop going the other way. The man was as big as a football player with full pads on. He was still in his civilian clothes, but he was pulling on a blue fibreglass helmet as he went. He must have been recalled for this special duty. Running past him, Dane could see anger and fear on the policeman's face, despite his enormous size. He had pulled a blackjack—it looked like a steel eggplant—out of his pocket. Dane turned and watched him.

He saw then what the policeman saw: the main intersection of Chicago packed with punching, kicking, clawing, screaming people. He watched the policeman plunge into the crowd, swinging his blackjack. And he thought, If I was that cop, I would do exactly what he is doing. I'd try to kill people to save my own life.

He got his haversack from the church where he had been staying and caught the next bus home. The Canadian border guards sniffed at the bandage on his head, but they let him through without trouble.

Once he was safely back in Toronto, Dane quit all the political groups he belonged to. Some people tried to hang on to him. Dane Harrison is a leader, they said. He must give at least an accounting. Dane pushed all his old friends away.

He knew he was hurting Annabel terribly. The peace movement was her life too. But Dane had to be honest. Annabel said she would stay with him. She said she loved him. But Dane knows that she turned to him after her husband drifted away because she thought Dane was so dedicated to his principles and so strong in spirit. Dane does not believe he will ever be that way again.

He has taken a job at a lunch counter. He has told Annabel he is going to enrol at George Brown College and learn to become a proper cook. Preparing the daily bread for people is a healthy, sacramental act.

The birds have finally stopped. Sunlight pours in through the kitchen window. The morning paper lands with a thud on the front porch. Dane drops the empty vodka bottle in the garbage pail. Dead soldiers, that's what his dear old daddy used to call empty liquor bottles. Dead soldiers. Dane climbs the stairs to bed. He holds on to the banister to steady himself.

1

FROM a column by Bobby Mulloy in *The Daily News:*

Suddenly, the game has come alive again.

The Citizens Against the Berryman Expressway had been pushed back to their one-yard line with one minute left to play when they intercepted a pass and started streaking for the other end. The mind boggles.

Those noisy folks who want to stop the Berryman Expressway from ploughing through the Grove lost all the political fights and it was time to send in the bulldozers. But just as the engines were revving up, the politicians ran out of gas.

The drain brains in the roads department had budgeted $75 million to extend Berryman Avenue for two miles up to Woodhurst and the northwest suburbs. But that was back in 1960.

Now we find out that the estimated cost has jumped to $140 million. The city and regional councils cannot take that kind of money out of petty cash. The politicians are going to have to sell bonds. But, before they can take on more debt, they have to get approval from the Ontario Municipal Board.

That little problem turns the game over to CABE.

Until now, this patchwork of indignant university professors, leftover flower children, and mortgaged-right-up-to-the-eyeballs white-painters along the expressway route has made little headway.

But the law says anyone can go before the Municipal Board and argue against a new bond issue. So CABE has hired J. Arthur Quinn to fight their case.

Our political leaders are in a state of shock. Quinn has been off the scene for some time now, recuperating from a heart attack, but he is still highly respected as the mouthpiece for the kind of developers who like to chomp big cigars and sport diamond pinky rings.

The Berryman Expressway is absolutely crucial to the future of Canada's most important city. We've got Highway 401 going across the north, the Gardiner Expressway on the South, and the Don Valley Parkway on the east. But we still need the Berryman on the west to complete the circle, or more accurately, the rectangle. With the Berryman completed, the city can construct a series of smaller expressways and give us a complete network. But without the Berryman, the whole thing falls apart. We've got nothing.

This winter, the shootout at the OMB is going to be the best show in town.

It's more than a fight over an expressway. This is a struggle for the soul of Toronto.

Remember, you read it here first.

2

"HARRY, are you busy right now? Could you haul your ass over here for a minute?"

"Yeah, sure. I guess so."

Harry Margulies hangs up the phone, leaves his windowless cubicle in the centre of the thirty-seventh floor of the International Trade Centre, and strolls nonchalantly east, passing the double row of desks where crisp, all-knowing legal secretaries are already bent over mounds of paper and whispering electric typewriters. He turns right at the corner and passes a row of outer offices that are slightly larger and more comfortable than his own and have windows looking out on downtown Toronto. These are occupied by lawyers, some no older than Harry, who have already been accepted as junior partners. Harry envies these people, and fears them too. How much room can there be in the officer class? The folk wisdom of Carlton and Boggs is "Five or out." If they haven't made you a partner in five years, you'd better start looking for somewhere else to practise law. Harry Margulies is in the seventh month of his fourth year with the firm. At the far southeast corner of the floor, Harry comes to a stop in front of the office of Charlie McConnachie, chairman of the firm's powerful Promotions and Compensations Committee. Harry is waved in by McConnachie's private secretary, a motherly blonde who knows Harry well and likes him.

McConnachie is not at his desk. He is seated in a leather armchair with half a dozen thick blue folders laid out on a glass-topped coffee table.

"Siddown," he barks, and waves Harry to a leather couch beside him. Harry does as he is told.

"You will not believe the bullshit that is flying around here this morning. We got a routine meeting of the Management Committee and all of a sudden, in the middle of his bran flakes, Artie Quinn announces he's got a real hard-on for you."

Then, a quick jab: "You know anything about this, Harry?"

"It's news to me." Harry's diffident shrug conveys the message that this is not even very interesting news.

McConnachie is studying Harry. McConnachie has a slick, hard face and thick red hair that is just beginning to turn dull grey in spots, like fine pewter. "Ye-a-ah," McConnachie says, drawing the word out so that it sounds as though he does not quite believe Harry. "So it looks like the old fart's finally figured out you're the smartest young guy we've got in land use. He must think you're going to save his ass."

"You're kidding"—which is what Harry says when he doesn't know what else to say.

"Now, you didn't ask me but I'm going to tell you anyway, because nobody else around here will level with you," McConnachie says. "Stay away from Quinn. He's bad news."

Harry's stomach begins to feel unsettled. Picking a side in a power struggle is not his idea of a smart thing to do.

"Your name's coming up and you know what the Promotions and Compensations Committee looks at?" Charlie McConnachie says. "They don't care how many clients you've sucked off, or how many clients you've pissed off. They just want to know how much money you've brought in. And you know how many billable hours you'd get out of this expressway shit? Sweet fuck all, Harry."

"Yeah, I can see that," Harry says.

McConnachie smiles. For a small, compact man, he has unusually large teeth. They radiate health and cleanliness. Harry feels uneasy with McConnachie's beaming patronage; he turns to look out the senior partner's windows. He reminds himself how pleasant the rewards for success at Carlton and Boggs can be. The International Trade Centre is a fifty-nine-storey, black Mies van der Rohe monolith, and up here, on the corner of the thirty-seventh floor, McConnachie has made himself a sleek little command post. Looking east, Harry can see factories and warehouses that line the railway tracks leading into downtown, and then the wide, wooden boardwalk that runs beside the Beaches neighbourhood all the way to the eastern border of Toronto. To the south there are the seething, grey waves of Lake Ontario running down to New York State.

"People talk a lot of shit about the practice of law," McConnachie says. "And in some ways, it's all true. But there's one thing they always forget. A firm like this is a business like any other business. We've got to pay our rent in this fucking mausoleum. And the guys who get ahead at Carlton and Boggs are the guys who bring in the bucks."

"I understand," Harry says.

McConnachie reaches out and clasps Harry's knee and gives it a friendly squeeze.

"I knew I wouldn't have to spell things out for you," McConnachie says. "I liked you right from the time we decided to take you on as an articling student. We could have had that little wop who won the gold medal, but I told them Margulies was a Carlton and Boggs kind of guy. Keep in touch, Harry. Let me know what's happening with you."

3

MARTA PERSOFSKI is more interested in the woman beside her than in the man in front of her. The woman is older than the other people in the class, a fleshy, well-used blonde in tailored pink wool slacks and a heavy white cable-knit turtle-neck sweater. Doesn't it bother her to be so obviously overdressed in a room where everybody else is in blue jeans and sweat-shirts? The man in front of Marta is naked, lying on his side on an old couch. One hand hangs idly down in front, not exactly covering his sexual equipment, but at least putting it into a bit of shadow. What a jerk! Does he think this coyness makes him more attractive, less like an inanimate object, a bowl of fruit or a pile of blocks? So stupid. Human bodies are blotchy, sweaty, smelly. Everybody who has ever had anything to do with physical love knows you have to get over the disgusting functional utility of the human body before you can feel any pleasure with another person. So why do they fuss and coo over pictures of naked men and naked women? From a purely aesthetic point of view, what's the big difference between men and women anyway?

If Marta took off her clothes and lay down on the couch, she would not look much different from the model. Like him, she is thin but muscular; like the model, whatever his name is, Marta has even features and short brown hair. Her breasts look only slightly heavier than his pectoral muscles, especially when she is lying down. Except for the fact she does not have such obvious hair on her torso and, of course, none of that ugly reproductive stuff hanging outside her body, Marta Persofski, the art student, and the naked man she is supposed to be drawing are essentially the same.

So why would anyone want to look at a picture of either of them? Power, that's what makes people go ape-shit over nudes. The spectators get to keep their clothes on while the person—the thing!—up there is compelled to stay naked. The spectators get to play in complete privacy with any stupid, cruel thought that comes into their heads. If there were some kind of reciprocity, if people had to strip before they could look at nude pictures and statues, there'd be a lot less nakedness in art—that's for sure.

"Excellent work," the instructor says, studying Marta's easel. He has been patrolling the room, coaching people as they work. "You could do a bit more modelling on the quadriceps, but you've got an excellent feeling for shape there."

"Bullshit!" Marta says. She does not sound angry or truculent. She is simply delivering a basic truth.

"Yes, well, keep it up...keep it up," the instructor says with a sigh, and turns to Vivian Billinghurst.

"You're still giving me too much technique," the instructor says. "That's like a blueprint for a man, not a drawing of a living person."

Vivian stares resentfully at her charcoal drawing. What the hell? She doesn't see anything wrong with it.

"I'll tell you a little trick," the instructor says. "Think about your own body when you're trying to draw. When you're doing a stomach or a leg, think about your own leg or stomach. Work your own muscles."

He moves on, leaving Vivian holding a piece of charcoal at arm's length, staring at her drawing over the point of it.

"I'm getting out of here," Marta Persofski says. It is a quiet announcement to herself, but Vivian hears and turns to look at her.

"I've had it," Marta says. "You want to go for lunch?"

Vivian is astonished.

"The class isn't over yet," she says.

"It is for me," Marta says. She begins packing up her equipment.

Vivian watches and then says, "Okay." She stuffs her own boxes of charcoal and drawing pads into a knapsack and follows Marta out the back door of the classroom. The other students, still concentrating on their easels, don't even seem to notice.

In the cold, bracing air, Marta strides past the grimy little Chinese stores on Dundas Street. Vivian has to rush a little to keep up, but Marta takes no notice. She turns in abruptly at a steamy glass door leading into the Pearl River. The restaurant seems gloomy and still after the bright sunlight of the street and so narrow there is room for only one row of small booths. Vivian has trouble understanding what all the dim sum names signify so Marta volunteers to order for both of them: spring rolls and har gow, shiu my, and dai bow, which turn out to be delicious little dumplings stuffed with pork, chicken, and shrimp.

"I didn't expect you to come with me," Marta says. She rests her long legs on the seat, letting her feet protrude carelessly out into the aisle.

"I was hungry too," Vivian says. "I just hope he doesn't make a big fuss about it on Wednesday."

"Won't bother me," Marta says. "I won't be there. How old are you?"

She watches the flash of anger and then the awkwardness as Vivian turns her eyes down to the table, clumsily trying to avoid a straightforward answer.

"I'm twenty-two," Marta says. "Last year I earned $16,786 doing freelance photography. Now you know my age and how much money I have—the two things no one ever wants to talk about."

"I'm thirty-three," Vivian says. "I'm Vivian Billinghurst."

She pushes her hand out over the table. Marta hesitates: people do not usually introduce themselves to her with such stupid gestures. This woman really is from another world. But then Marta reaches out and clasps Vivian's hand firmly. She is surprised at how dry and fearful Vivian feels.

"I'm Marta Persofski," she says. "I was watching you. You were as pissed off as I was. What are you doing there, anyway?"

"The same as everybody else. Studying art."

"Bullshit," Marta says. "Nobody studies art. You can do it or you can't. Period. I can do it. I don't need those assholes."

With a shrug Marta leaves the college and the whole tradition of Western art behind. Now she is free to enjoy this strange creature she has dragged in her wake. The woman is tall and determined, but she has fear in her face. She looks like she has been wounded many times. She is wearing a fat gold wedding ring set with chips that look bright enough to be real diamonds. Does she like her husband? She likes humping, that's for sure. And she's not getting enough of it. That message rolls off her, sweet and strong.

"So if I'm such a shit-hot artist, why was I was there myself, eh?" Marta says. "Because of my father, that's why. He was a total asshole, but he managed to mess up my life pretty good before he kicked off. He was a violinist—he was first violin—and I drove him crazy because I never had to learn how to use a camera the way he had to study to play the violin. I was born knowing how to take pictures. I compose the shot in my head. I'm a natural. But my father used to practice five, six, seven hours a day. You could hear him all over the street. 'No pain, no gain,' my father used to say. I really felt sorry for him. He went through all that pain and he never got any better anyway.

"You want to know something really funny? My father had seven kids. I was the last and I was obviously a mistake, but they went ahead and had me anyway. So you'd think, with seven kids, my father must have liked humping, right? But how could he, because it's supposed to be a pleasure and my father didn't believe in doing anything just because it made you feel good. And I know for sure my mother didn't like it very much, so he couldn't have had much fun screwing her. In fact, come to think of it, screwing my mother must have been pretty awful. So maybe the real reason he kept at it was so both him and her could suffer. I think my father had a Presbyterian dick. That's an interesting idea, eh? A Presbyterian dick."

"I guess so," Vivian says. "I think I'd better get back to the school."

"You don't like the way I talk, do you? You should come to my encounter group. You'd learn how to open up, be honest about yourself. You wouldn't be so uptight."

"I am not uptight," Vivian says quickly.

"Yes, you are."

"I really must get on my way now," Vivian says.

She was only curious. Vivian just wanted to know a little more about how a person could be so self-confident she would just walk out of an art class. But Vivian has no intention of getting into a long discussion of her own life. She is certainly not going to try to explain herself to this arrogant young woman.

"This is for my share of the lunch," Vivian says and lays a two-dollar bill on the table.

But there is a terrible finality about exchanging money.

"Are you going to be at the class on Wednesday?" Vivian asks.

"I was going to quit," Marta Persofski says. "But if you're going to be there, maybe I'll come again."

4

HOW DO YOU TELL a mother to do things that could bring about the death of her own child? Jim Kernohan contemplates the boy on his examining table. There is nothing physically wrong with Paul Warren; his height and weight, three feet eleven inches and forty-four pounds, are a little below normal. But the note from his pediatrician, and all the lab tests that have been done, show the kid is in good health. Except that he has no health at all. Just look at him, in his underpants, sitting on the edge of the table, listlessly waiting to be told what to do next. His body has no bounce to it. Blow on him, and he'd fall over.

"I've got everything I need from you, Paulie. You get dressed now and go out to the waiting-room," Kernohan says, hoping his professional cheerfulness will mask his real feelings. "I just want to have little chat with your folks."

What a pair they are! The woman's built like the proverbial brick shithouse. The guy looks like a fairy, skinny as a broomstick and face as pale and fine as a young girl's. As a doctor, Kernohan is angry. But, as a man, he feels pity for them. These two were right at the heart of the great whirligig party of the 1960s; now they are waking up with one hell of a hangover.

"...so the way I see it," Dr. James Kernohan is saying to Dane and Annabel, "we've got to put some muscle on Paul. That way, when we're finally ready to do the procedures on his heart, he'll have something in the bank to draw on."

"What if his heart caves in?" Annabel cries. "What will you say to us then?"

Kernohan faces her, eye to eye, doctor to patient. "I don't know," he says, and shakes his head. "All I can tell you is that what you are doing now isn't working. The boy's too frail. He's not going to make it this way."

"Are you trying to tell us he's not going to make it at all?" Dane asks.

"Paul's heart can go any time. Just like that!"—Kernohan snaps his fingers loudly in front of Dane; Annabel flinches—"When he's crossing the street. In his sleep, even. Keeping him under wraps isn't going to protect his heart."

"But isn't it more likely to happen if he's out there pushing himself?" Dane asks. "If he's out playing hockey or football, isn't that going to put a big strain on his heart?"

"Oh, for sure," Kernohan says. "But would it do him in? I don't know. Would to God that I did. I can't tell you where the line is. But I think—I firmly *believe*—that if we can get Paul active, it will tone up his whole body and it should make the heart stronger. Because the heart is, when all is said and done, only another muscle."

"If it was your son?..." Dane asks.

Kernohan has been expecting this.

"If it was my son, I'd get him into sports."

"I can't do it," Annabel says. She is starting to cry.

"For God's sake, look at the boy!" Kernohan is both exasperated and pleading.

"I don't care," Annabel says.

Kernohan slumps into his chair, wishing he could sink behind his desk and be freed from these people. James T. Kernohan is a cardiologist, not a goddamned priest!

"I'm sorry, Mrs. Warren. The last thing in the world I'd ever want to do is hurt you. But Paul is my patient. I have to do what I think is best for him."

"We understand," Dane says. He wraps his arm protectively around Annabel. "We appreciate your honesty."

Kernohan watches them go out to the waiting-room. Paul looks up in anticipation, and then in fear, as Dane and Annabel approach. How will they explain to the boy why his mother is crying?

Kernohan thinks about the bottle of vodka in the bottom drawer of his desk. It's 12:30; the sun is over the yard-arm. A quick shot wouldn't do any harm.

5

J. ARTHUR QUINN's office is at the southwest corner, as far away from Charlie McConnachie as it is possible to get. Quinn's secretary is a white- haired, prim little woman. Her downy upper lip curls with distaste. Without saying a word she makes it plain she will never understand how people as crude as Harry Margulies ever get through the front door at Carlton and Boggs.

"Good morning, Mr. Margulies. So good of you to come by," Quinn says, graciously, and rises to extend his hand across an enormous, antique monstrosity of a desk.

He seems astonishingly soft and plump for a man who is renowned for having such a sharp mind. His skin looks thin and pink, and might be taken to be as fresh as a child's except for the webbing of dark purple veins on his cheeks. Strands of listless grey hair have been combed directly across the top of his head to disguise, without much success, the fact that Quinn is nearly bald. His eyes are blue and friendly, but they are a little too close together, and he has rimless, antiseptic-looking glasses of the kind Harry always associates with doctors and dentists. Then there is the nose. It is long and pointed, much sharper than the nose Harry's wife, Doreen, is so self-conscious about. Quinn's nose is a genuine beak. The star of Carlton and Boggs looks like a giant penguin.

"I'm pleased to see you here, after all the times I've imposed upon you over the telephone," Quinn says.

"Me too," Harry says.

"I've got something to offer you at last," Quinn says.

While Quinn explains to him what Harry already knows, Harry takes the time to look around his office. Quinn's floor-to-ceiling drapes have not been drawn back to display the magnificent view, and the overhead fluorescent fixtures have not been turned on. The only light here comes from two large brass standing lamps. Harry feels distinctly uncomfortable; he begins to long for fresh air.

The walls are covered with paintings of fishermen out in dories being almost swamped by huge white-capped waves, and tall three-masted sailing ships racing into the wind. Quinn's vast desk is coated with satiny red lacquer and has carvings of dragons and other animals on the front and sides. The desk looks like something that might well have been brought back from China more than a century ago, during the days of the tea clippers. But Harry also notes that sitting on a brass tray beside Quinn's desk blotter are four bottles of pills, two red, one white, one yellow. Harry wonders what the different pills are supposed to do and how often Quinn has to take them.

"So you can see the expressway appeal is going to be the fight of a lifetime," Quinn is saying. "There are twenty-seven people in the Region's legal department—some of them very fine lawyers, as I have good reason to know. They'll be able to hire all the experts and planning consultants they need. You and I will not have enough to buy a box of paperclips. We'll be like a couple of gunslingers in an old western movie, trying to hold off the lynch mob."

"I'd love to," Harry says quickly. "It's a real challenge, Mr. Quinn. But I've got more on my plate right now than I can handle."

Quinn smiles benignly.

"Is that what Charlie told you to say?"

Harry stiffens, but does not reply. The smile fades from Quinn's face. He leans across his desk to speak earnestly to Harry.

"I don't envy you," he says. "You have a tough choice to make. Old Blake Edgar's finally gone to his reward, a condominium in Palm Beach, and now the Carlton and Boggs breakfast club is about to pick a new managing partner. Charlie wants to be boss, but I'm not going to let him."

Harry feels cold and lonely. Why in God's name did these guys have to choose him to play their games with?

"I'm just an Indian," Harry says. "I don't try to get into the tepee with the chiefs."

"If I win this," Quinn says, "and you're with me, you'll be a partner in this firm the next day."

"There are sixteen other guys in land use," Harry says. "Why pick on me? I'm no genius."

"I don't know them," Quinn says. "And I do know you, and I know you've got a good head on your shoulders. Besides, you're the only Jew in the joint."

Harry knows he has heard it correctly, but he wants to hear it again.

"I'm the what?"

"The only Jew at Carlton and Boggs."

Harry knows he should be sensible. This doesn't mean anything, and the old bastard's on his way out anyway. But Harry remembers his father's heroic stories about the riots at Christie Pits, the night the Jewish boys from Berryman Avenue went after the anti-Semitic gangs from the west end with baseball bats.

"Mr. Quinn, I have been at this firm almost five years, six if you count my articling time," Harry says slowly, emphasizing each word. "And in all that time, you are the first person who has even mentioned my religion. So, you know, Mr. Quinn, what you can do with your expressway appeal."

"You are not the first person this morning to make that suggestion," Quinn says. "Wouldn't you like to know why your religion interests me?"

"Because you are a first-class, grade-A prick!" Harry says.

"Quite possibly," Quinn says, without anger. "But if you are the only Jew to get taken on at Carlton and Boggs, then I figure you must be just a little bit smarter than any of the well-connected, private-school goyim we normally hire."

Harry laughs. He doesn't really want to give Quinn the satisfaction, but he can't help himself.

"I never thought of it that way before," he says. "But you are probably right."

"Do you like my office?" Quinn says. "It's as phoney as a six-cent nickel. But I come from Nova Scotia, and people up here think everybody from down east must be a sailor. So I do a little song and dance for them. The truth is I grew up on a stinking sheep farm, and the first, and last, time I ever saw the ocean was when I went to Halifax to get the train for Upper Canada. And my name isn't Quinn. It's Duhamel. My grandmother was a Quinn. When I first came up here people with French names did not get taken into big Bay Street law firms."

"Okay! I get the message," Harry says, holding up his hands in the classic gesture of surrender. "And I know what's in it for me. What I don't understand is why you're putting your ass on the line."

"A comeback," Quinn says bluntly. "When my ticker gave out, I almost went down for the count. A lot of my old clients started making telephone calls to other lawyers. If I win this one, against all the odds, they'll come back to me."

"I wouldn't be so sure of that," Harry says. "I hear a lot of the big guys have been buying up land on the expressway route. If you win this thing, those guys are going to lose a ton of money."

"The ones who get it up the ass will be lining up outside my door," Quinn says. "Cardinal rule: if somebody is smart enough to give you a screwing, make sure you've got him on your side next time out. Mr. Margulies, if I stop that expressway, I'll be rolling in clover. And those fortunate few who stick with me will be able to write their own tickets."

"Yes...well...you certainly make it sound interesting, Mr. Quinn. But what happens if we lose?"

"Ah, yes, if we lose," Quinn says. He sinks back in his chair and contemplates his fingertips, which have come together like a church steeple in front of him.

"If we lose, Charlie McConnachie takes over and I get squeezed out of Carlton and Boggs. They'll let you stay if you want, but they'll never let you become a partner. You'll be the office bum boy."

"Yeah," Harry says. "I can see that, all right. I'd like to think about this."

"Of course," Quinn says. "Take all the time you need."

He settles back in his chair to wait for Harry's decision.

Harry has a sudden urge to punch him in the mouth. What right does the old bastard have to crowd him like this? Every right in the world. If Harry ever gets to the top in this firm, he will probably lean on people and exploit people just the way Quinn is using him now. The right to exercise power is one of the rewards that hard work and using your brains can bring.

But what if what Harry learned, or thinks he learned, when he took acid is also true? What if what happens to you depends as much on who bumps into you as on anything you do for yourself? Harry understands luck, but he has never depended on it. You're so stiff, Doreen is always saying to him, Why do you have to be so uptight? Why can't you just let things happen to you? Well, things are certainly happening to Harry Margulies today. This decision he dedicates to his wife. Never again will Doreen be able to say that she is married to a man with a dead soul.

"If I come with you, I'm a damned fool. That's the truth, isn't it?" Harry says.

"I try to avoid putting things into rigid categories," Quinn says. "But yes, if it matters to you, you could find many people in the firm who would agree with that statement."

"Well, I'm coming anyway," Harry says. "I'm your man, Mr. Quinn."

"I am delighted to hear that," Quinn says. His mouth curves upward in a broad, benign smile that makes him look like a statue of the Buddha. Buddha the Shark, Harry is thinking.

"Harry, I think we will do better if you begin to call me Arthur," Quinn says. "And now let us get to work, my friend. We have seven weeks left to save the city."

6

ELI, THE CANTOR, likes to say that the synagogue in the little house at the bottom of Landrigan Street lives on miracles. To that, Morry Weiss is thinking, should be added the quality of pure, unadulterated selfishness that some Jews like to sanctify with the Yiddish word *chutzpah.* At ten-thirty, Saturday morning, the congregation of Anshei Torah, people of the Torah, is still one man short of the ten that are needed, according to the law, to take out the Torah scrolls and read from them. Eli pleads with Morry to go out and find somebody. If Morry cannot complete the minyan, they will have to cancel the service and disperse to their homes. Morry hates himself when he performs this chore. But it's true; he does know a couple of old men still hanging on in neighbourhood rooming-houses.

Morry resents being made to put the arm on these old guys just because he's given them a few bucks now and then. Even more, Morry hates to feel he is letting other people take advantage of his good nature. Still, Morry reminds himself, this is Eli who is asking. Eli is a saint, and Morry goes back with him a long time, all the way to kindergarten. Most of the Jews they grew up with, the people who used to live in the Grove, have long since moved up north, to the barren suburban streets and the synagogues that look like Miami Beach hotels. But for the few religious people who still live downtown—the rough, half-mad survivors of the Holocaust, pious young university students, odds and sods like Morry himself—Eli and his friend "Doctor Joe," keep the shul alive. Morry sighs, pulls on his quilted ski jacket, and goes out into the street.

He steps out the front door and—a miracle! Eli was right. Coming up the street are a man and a woman, young, bright, perfect. Morry plants himself in front of them.

"Please," he says. "We need a minyan. It won't take very long."

"What makes you so sure I'm Jewish," Harry Margulies says, laughing at him.

"Please, just for an hour. You'll be doing a real mitzvah."

"I'd love to help you, my friend, but..." Harry holds up bulky shopping bags. The young couple are on their way home from the Harbord Bakery.

The man is dressed in an expensive suede windbreaker and smirking as though he cannot believe this encounter on the street is really happening to him. Morry is furious. Listen, buddy, he would like to say, I am not a funny character. I am not part of the local colour. I am the same age as you are—well, a little older maybe, but close enough. I know what's what.

"Please, Harry..." The woman puts her hand on her husband's arm. Morry turns to her, seeing Doreen Margulies really for the first time. He finds her dangerous. Everything about the woman says she is desperate for help. But she is so self-absorbed and so naturally elegant she probably doesn't even know what messages she is sending. Very gently, Morry says to her, "This shul where I want to take you is very nice. You'll like it there, I promise." The woman smiles, and the tremulous lengthening of those taut, beautiful lips says to Morry that the woman has decided in an instant to trust him—as well she should, because he would never do anything to hurt her. So before the husband can open his mouth again, Morry has taken over the shopping bags and he's got a firm grip on the guy's elbow, and he's leading Harry into the converted little house with the brick front that serves as his synagogue.

Eli honours this stranger who has come to their rescue by asking Harry to read one of the blessings over the Torah. The fellow looks confused and a little desperate, so Morry whispers to him, "Don't worry," and tactfully slides a card in front of Harry so that he can read the English transliteration of the blessing, which begins, "*Barchu es Adonai Ha M'vorach*...Blessed is the Lord, the Blessed One...

Eli bends over the unrolled scroll of the Torah and begins to sing out in his wonderful, poignant voice the story of Jacob disguising himself as his brother, Esau, and stealing in to see their father, Isaac, in order to claim the paternal blessing that should have gone to Esau. Morry leans back against the railing of the bima, the small square platform where the Torah reading is taking place, and looks down into the women's section, where the stranger's wife is sitting. Frail little Mrs. Kolodny is delighted to have a second woman in her row and she has opened the bible for the woman at the right page. It's clear the stranger cannot follow the Hebrew and has no comprehension of what is going on. But still, she is smiling up at him.

He smiles back, trying to make her feel welcome without becoming overbearing about it. The woman has a thin, perfect face. Not even the long nose can spoil it. Her skin is clear and taut; it shines with care and good health. But these are common, ordinary features, Morry is thinking. You can find them on a million well-fed, overly protected Jewish princesses—and on goyisha princesses too, for that matter. A man can hardly tell the breeds apart any more. It is the woman's eyes that really hold Morry. They are so restless and fearful. They tell Morry that the woman is sensitive not only to beauty and to pain, but to pleasure too. Morry suspects that, just below the jittery surface, this is a very powerful person. Does her husband know how deep she goes? Is that why the guy is so wound up himself? Maybe he already knows he can't control her. But, then, what the hell business is this of Morry's?

7

CLINGING TO HARRY'S ARM as they march up Landrigan Street, Doreen finds her attention divided between a feeling of longing for the joyfulness she experienced in the little white-walled synagogue and a desperate struggle to keep up with her husband. Harry shouldn't be angry. He did a good deed, and the people were grateful. Did Harry think if he stayed around too long they'd surround him and refuse to let him leave unless he promised to return the following week? Doreen would like very much to go back.

But she'd be so out of place by herself. How could she fit into this little group of wrinkled-up old men who look like her grandfather—older than her grandfather, in fact? She can just imagine what a quarrelsome, hawking and spitting gang they must be when they get going. Yet, when they were all on their feet, singing out, Doreen felt she was sharing a deep, communal experience, even if she could not understand any of the Hebrew words they were using.

The only person she felt she could talk to without being embarrassed by her sentimental feelings and lack of knowledge about her own religion was the man who accosted them in the street. But, Doreen has to concede, he was one of the strangest-looking people she has ever encountered. His face was delicate and unlined, like a little boy's face. But his hair, although thick, was an old man's hair, completely silver, like a wig made out of crumpled aluminum foil. His face looked so refined one would naturally have expected his body to be thin and ascetic too. Instead, his body looked chunky and powerful. Doreen found she was embarrassingly curious.

After the service Harry tried to make a quick exit, but the pious-looking cantor caught him at the door and invited him to come upstairs for the Kiddush. Harry immediately started making excuses, but Doreen surprised herself by saying yes, the two of them would love to come. The strange man, whose name she discovered then was Morry Weiss, had been standing beside the cantor, not saying anything, but Doreen could tell he, too, wanted them to come upstairs.

A long trestle table had been set up, covered with a white paper tablecloth. The cantor poured rye into shot glasses and said a blessing, and everybody drank up their whisky and sat down. They nibbled herring and gefilte fish from paper plates, and then Eli spoke on the passage from the Torah they had just read, about how the question was asked, how could Jacob, our father, cheat his brother, Esau, out of his birthright? The sages teach us that Jacob knew Esau would be a terrible leader for the Jewish people and he had to replace Esau, even though Jacob knew that God would punish him for his trickery. So we learn from this that sometimes we have to do things we know are wrong and accept punishment in order to bring about something that serves a greater good. Doreen felt she was participating in what synagogue life must have been like in the little villages of prewar Poland that both sides of her family had emigrated from.

Harry said he was starving and he took advantage of how slowly the old people extricated themselves from the table after the Kiddush to hustle Doreen downstairs, grab their bags of bread and bagels, and escape out the front door.

"Hey, wait up! Just a minute." Doreen turns back. It is Morry Weiss from the synagogue. He is walking quickly, almost running, up Landrigan Street. Doreen yanks Harry's arm to hold him back.

"Hello. I just wanted to say thanks...you know...personally," Morry says when he is facing them. "I'm afraid I really cut into your morning."

"We loved it," Doreen says.

"Yeah," Harry says. "It was very interesting."

He lets the words hang in the air. His body is so tense, he looks ready to sprint down the street. Doreen feels sorry for her husband. Poor dear. He had such a nice day all planned. He and Doreen would walk to the Harbord Bakery and get all the bread for the house, and then he would whip down to the office and spend the rest of the day working on the expressway case, and then he was going to take Doreen out for a fancy supper, just the two of them, because they are off tonight. Vivian will be putting their son, Gordon, and all the other children in the house to bed. But now it's already almost 1:30 and Harry is undoubtedly going to tell her his whole schedule has been shot and he will probably have to spend Saturday night at the office—again. He can't blame Doreen for this, but he will. Harry made all the decisions but in his mind, Doreen knows, it is her fault when things don't work out because she never keeps track of what they are supposed to be doing.

She turns to Morry Weiss now and, embarrassed by Harry's awkward silence, which is growing into outright rudeness, she says to Weiss, very politely, "It was a very sweet place. Do you go there all the time?"

"Just since the last year. Since I moved back downtown. That's me over there." He points across Landrigan Street and a bit to the north. The porch of one house has been torn away and a glass storefront has been built right to the edge of the sidewalk. The rounded white and black porcelain letters on the window say: "Weiss's Kosher Style Poultry."

Doreen, still holding to Harry's arm, can feel him relaxing a bit and she is relieved.

"You don't look much like a chicken flicker," Harry says, "if you don't mind my saying so."

The man smiles at Harry and shrugs his shoulders.

"So nu? Tell me, what does a man who pulls feathers off chickens look like?"

"I'd take you to be a lawyer," Harry says. "Or a doctor. Or a social worker —some kind of professional man, anyway."

"You don't win the big cigar, but you're close," Weiss says. "I was in real estate. My mother got sick about a year ago and I came down to the old store to help her.

"Say," he adds brightly, turning to Doreen and she understands, with a pleasure she takes care to hide, that seeing her again is the real reason Morry Weiss has come chasing after them, "how about letting me take you guys to lunch? I feel I really owe you."

"No, no," Harry says desperately. "Some other time. I've got a day's work to do yet."

And Doreen, still holding on to Harry's arm, is pulled beside him up Landrigan Street.

8

IT IS TEN O'CLOCK at night and Vivian is with Marta Persofski's support group, in a storefront on Dupont Street, called "Charlie's," after Charlotte Whitton, the social worker who became the first woman mayor of Ottawa. Vivian is looking around the room, wondering how many of these people are laughing at her. She cannot remember an occasion when she has felt so stupid.

For almost an hour they have all been listening to a dumpy little woman named Moira complain about the terrible-tempered Lannie.

"...yeah, like, what you guys are telling me all sounds great, but whenever I try to bring up any of this stuff with Lannie, you know, just talk about it, it turns into another fight. So I don't say anything, because, like, what's the point, eh? I don't want to get yelled at. But not saying anything doesn't help either. Because you can only keep swallowing it so long and finally you just blow..."

Tears begin to trickle down the woman's face and she is whimpering, it seems to Vivian, like a little kid after a licking. Indeed, being in the "hot seat," as they call it—an old armchair covered in flowered chintz—is not unlike getting beaten up. The other members of the group, seven more women, sit in a circle on the floor, and they are supposed to ask questions and make helpful observations. Marta said this was a loving group, but some of the things these women have said to each other seem downright cruel. Vivian is sure she can still teach them a thing or two.

"Well, I'll tell you something that used to work for me," Vivian says to Moira. "When I thought I couldn't talk to my husband, I'd write him letters. I'd put down everything that was bothering me, even things about sex. My husband would blow his stack sometimes, but even when he did, he was all by himself. I wasn't around to get into a fight with. Then he'd settle down and we could have an honest talk. Why don't you try that with Lannie? Write him a letter. See what happens."

The other women look at the floor, at the ceiling, at anything to avoid facing Vivian. What's wrong? Were visitors not supposed to speak up? To hell with that, Vivian thinks. These people could use a good dose of common sense. Moira leans forward in the chair to talk some more but this time she directs everything to Vivian as though they were the only two people in the room.

"I like that—a letter," Moira says. "I think Eleanor's real trouble is her work, not me. Eleanor feels she has to always be defensive and sarcastic with the men lawyers in the clinic, and I don't think that's true at all because, like, I've met some of them and they are really nice guys. But Lannie thinks they're all making cracks behind her back, calling her a 'dyke,' and all that. So, when she comes home at night, she's all wound up and she goes after me over every little thing. So maybe you're right, if I could put all this in a letter and Lannie could read it and take it in, then maybe we could just talk about it like normal human beings."

"Yes, well, it sure worked for me," Vivian says quickly. She closes down, withdrawn from the conversation. "But I've got to tell you, I'm not with my husband any more."

Vivian is furious. How could her friend do this to her? But, then, how could Vivian have been so stupid? When she thinks back on it, Marta has been sending her messages right from the first time they had lunch together. But Vivian was too much the nice lady to pick up on them.

At the end of the session, all the women stand up and join hands. "Affirming," they call it. Vivian studies the other faces. How many more of these people are queer? It's hard to tell; they come in all shapes and flavours. But Vivian is still pretty sure she is the only normal woman in the bunch. She grabs her coat and hurries out the door.

She feels Marta coming after her, and she speeds up. Marta calls out, but Vivian drops her head into the collar of her old muskrat coat and pretends not to hear. Finally, Marta lays her hand on Vivian's shoulder and Vivian has to turn around and face her.

"I'm sorry," Marta says. "I thought you understood...Sometimes I forget..."

"Don't worry about it," Vivian says. "I had an interesting evening."

"I've got some wine. Would you like to come to my place?"

Vivian cannot think of anything to say that would not sound mean and petty. For three weeks Marta has been coming to life-drawing classes and they have been going out to lunch together and spending afternoons at the Art Gallery or prowling through the antique stores on Queen Street. Vivian thought she had found a friend; Marta thought she was starting a love affair. The misunderstanding is Vivian's fault. She's older and she should have been more in control.

"I'm sorry," Vivian says. "I'm just not...I mean I'd like to be friends, but..."

Marta has gone. She is disappearing into the dark streets of the Grove. Vivian starts after her. She can't just send Marta away like this.

Now it is Marta's turn to keep silent. Vivian stays with her until they get to a large, gloomy old house. Marta's only acknowledgement is to sign with a finger to the lips that Vivian must be quiet while they are climbing the narrow stairway to a fourth-floor attic.

The room impresses Vivian. There is hardly any furniture, just an old wooden desk and chair, and a mattress covered with a messy tangle of sheets and blankets. There is an old steamer trunk that is meant to serve as a dresser but clothes are scattered everywhere. So are books, magazines, and dozens of photographs. This is obviously the room of a person who cares little about appearances and everything about art.

Marta opens the window and takes a bottle of wine off the ledge. It's open, but she has covered the top with aluminum foil. She fills two tumblers and, instead of turning on one of the lamps, lights two candles. Marta courteously sits against the wall that slopes right to the floor and leaves Vivian the wall that is straighter, where she can be upright. But this means Vivian is sitting on Marta's bed, and this makes her uneasy all over again.

"Do you think I'm going to make a pass at you?" Marta asks.

"No, I don't." Vivian delivers this statement so heavily it sounds like an order.

"I might, you know. You're a real turn-on in some ways. I might decide to attack you."

"You could try…" Vivian says. She is taller and heavier than Marta and quite sure she could handle the girl physically—if it came right down to that.

"I have a brown belt in karate," Marta says. "A blue belt, anyway. I know how to really hurt you. I could make you do anything I want."

"Oh, cut it out," Vivian says. "I'm tired of these stupid games."

"If you don't want to play games," Marta says evenly, "why did you come up here with me?"

"It had nothing to do with you…personally, I mean. I came for myself. Because I was afraid to come up here. Because I was afraid to be with you alone."

"I can relate to that," Marta says.

Vivian sees that she is not explaining herself very well. She reaches for a better answer. She finds, to her surprise, she has picked up the confessional spirit of Marta's support group.

"Because I'm tired of being afraid all the time, okay? Because, when I look around me and I try to understand what makes most people the way they are, I think the only thing that drives them is pure, naked, fucking fear. And I don't want to live like that. Not any more, anyway. So I'm here. And I'm not afraid of you. Okay?"

“Okay,” Marta says. “You don’t have to get hot about it...Do you want some more wine?”

“No, I’d better get going. It’s almost midnight.”

“What would you do if I came over there right now and kissed you?”

Vivian stiffens. She can’t help herself.

“I don’t think it would do anything for me,” she says.

“But you don’t know, do you? Wouldn’t you like to find out?”

“I don’t think so,” Vivian says. “I think I should get going now.”

“Goodbye,” Marta says. Vivian has been dismissed. She makes no move to show her guest back downstairs.

Vivian pauses by the door. Marta is slumped into the angle of the wall, watching a candle she has set in saucer in front of her burn down into a pool of blue wax. Vivian wonders, will Marta now finish the bottle of wine by herself?

“Will you keep coming to life classes?” Vivian asks. “Will I see you again?”

“Why would you want to? Knowing what I am...and what I want?”

Vivian laughs at her then. The kid is a delight. She never gives up. “I’m a big girl,” Vivian says. “I can take care of myself.”

9

ANNABEL WARREN’S SON, Paul, is discovering that, lonely and small though he is, racing down the ice, hockey stick ready to score with, is not so difficult after all. Paul can feel the blades of his new skates tilting inward a little and probably they shouldn’t be like that, but Dane has done the laces up good and tight and his ankles feel firm, even if they are starting to ache. But what’s really important, the only thing that matters, is that when Paul pushes back with one foot and then the other, he moves forward. It’s so easy. Anyone can do it. And the harder he pushes, the faster he goes, and all he has to do now is turn, because he is getting to the end of the hockey cushion and his chest is going into the boards and he is going over and he can hear the crack when his head hits the ice and it hurts, like the worst headache you could ever imagine. The thing about stars that you see in cartoons is really true. Coloured lights, red and blue, are flashing in front of his eyes.

"Pauly! Are you all right?" Dane is bending over him. So is the coach, Henry Delamere, with his long hair and the big moustache drooping like a black snake around the sides of his mouth.

"I'm okay," Paul says, but his voice sounds off-key and unconvincing, even to himself. Henry has him under the arms and is helping him to his feet. The effort dislodges Henry's military-looking postman's cap and it slithers over the ice.

"Paul, do you want to go on?" Dane is bending over him, blocking out the sky, whispering urgently, and in code, to hide their secret from Henry.

Paul hesitates. He bends his head towards his chest. Nothing is happening in the worst place. He gives his head a little a shake. The pain is still with him, but it has left the place behind his right eye, where bad headaches concentrate. He's pretty sure it's going to go away. He pushes out his stomach to see if it's getting ready to heave. That often happens with a headache, and it would be horrible, out here in front of all these people. But his stomach is not doing anything either.

"I'm okay," Paul says. "I'm having fun."

"Good boy," Henry says. He puts his hand on Paul's shoulder. "You just keep doing lengths. But you gotta remember to bend your knees. And when you want to turn, you come down, almost like you're going to go into a squat"—he demonstrates; he is able to turn the long blade of his hockey skate with the grace of a figure skater—"and then take the weight off the foot that's turning and use your ankle to point the whole skate in the direction you want to go."

Paul looks wistfully over at the other side of the rink where Gordon Margulies and members of the team Henry coaches are taking turns charging in on their goalie and trying to shoot the puck past him.

"You'll be doing that soon enough," Henry says. "Right now, we got to work on your balance."

Paul dutifully sets out for the other end of the rink. He holds the stick out in front again, but this time he keeps his head up so he can see when he is getting close to the boards. And he doesn't try to go quite so fast.

Dane and Henry Delamere return to the side. Dane climbs over the boards. He feels awkward being on the ice in galoshes, especially beside Henry, whose hockey skates look like scimitars fastened to black riding boots.

"Dane, that kid is never going to be a hockey player," Henry says. "Not in a million years."

"Are you going to cut him, then?"

Henry shakes his head. "These are house leagues, Dane. Any boy that's eight years old and can lace his skates up gets on a team. But I've got to tell you, your kid is going to get himself killed out there."

"That could be truer than you know, Henry. Paul's got a bad heart. He could go any time."

"What?" Henry turns to look at Dane, holding on to the boards to keep his balance—just as Paul had been doing. "What the fuck are you doing to me, Dane?"

"Nothing," Dane says. "I'm not doing anything to you, Hank. There's permission sheets, aren't there? Like, I sign and it says you're not responsible for anything that happens to the kid, right?"

"Are you his father?"

"I live with his mother."

"No good, Dane. For this you got to be a parent. Or a legal guardian, at least."

"I'm neither. And I don't think I could ever get his mother to sign. That's why I came to you, Hank."

"You came to the wrong guy. I don't know what you're up to, but I don't want any part of it."

Dane explains about Paul's heart and why the doctor wants to build him up.

"His mother sits on him. She's afraid to let the kid out of the house. But the heart man says if Paul doesn't get out and get a little muscle on him, he'll never make it through the operation."

"So you're going to take it on yourself to make the kid an athlete?" Henry sounds incredulous.

"Something like that."

"You are out of your fucking mind," Henry says, and to keep from losing his temper, he skates off to where his boys have been practising shooting and are starting to flag. Dane is presuming too much on an old friendship.

In the old days, Dane Harrison and Henry Delamere were a great team. Dane was the cool, brilliant organizer. Henry Delamere was his deputy, the crazy who made things happen. Everybody loved Henry because he lay down in front of the air force trucks when they picketed the missile base in Cromwell. Yeah…yeah…but all that was another life. Everybody is doing different things now. Henry Delamere is a postman. People sneer, but he's outdoors most of the time and he's not earning his living by exploiting other people.

Henry calls his boys for a body-check drill: two lines, skate at each other, keep your hands behind your back and your shoulder out. Try to knock the other guy on his can. The kids are delighted. They love banging into each other. Henry skates back across the rink to where Dane is still keeping his lonely parental vigil, watching Paul struggle up and down the ice.

"Dane, even if I was to listen to you—which I am not!—there is no way you can come out ahead, eh? If anything happens to that kid, you're responsible. But even if nothing happens, your old lady is still going to go after your ass, right?"

"You got it."

"Okay, so lay it on me, Dane. I know I'm stupid, but tell me anyway."

"I want to give the kid a chance to live," Dane says. "That's not so strange, is it, Hank? If he's got to go—and there's a better-than-even chance that he will—at least he'll have done some things. He keeps telling me he wants to be a hockey player. I'm trying to give him a few good times."

"You mean like we had?" Henry says. He skates back to his team. He warns the boys again to keep heads up and stay alert when they are throwing a body check. If you let the natural fear instinct take over and close your eyes when you are coming in, the other guy'll dump you for sure. He watches a couple of exchanges to make sure the boys are at least trying to do what he wants, and then he skates back again to Dane. He wags his finger threateningly in Dane's face.

"You get a helmet!" he says. "And you get a full set of pads. I'll take care of the paper work, but I want that kid protected from his toes right up to the top of his head."

"Done," Dane says.

"It'll cost you a fucking bundle!"

"Don't worry about it."

Henry lets his threatening index finger come down to his side. His face knots up. Dane can see he is struggling to find words that will not sound stupid. Dane cannot help him. He can only grin at Henry in a goofy, helpless sort of way.

"Tell me something," Henry says at last. "Why am I always a sucker for you?"

"I dunno...I guess you were born lucky," Dane says.

"Yeah, that must be it," Henry says, and skates down the rink to Paul. At the corner, he holds the boy's arm, keeping him from using the cushion as a prop for his turn. Paul grapples with Henry and manages, still clumsily, but without falling, to turn around and start for the other end.

Paul is getting tired, but he's not going to quit. The harder he works, the faster it will happen. He'll stop being the person everybody in school laughs at. Paul Warren will become a real boy. He will have real friends. Paul knows he is not going to die just because he is playing hockey. God will protect him. Paul has even spoken to God, although that is not something he would ever tell anyone, not even his mother. And although God has never said anything back to him—you don't hear God; you just feel Him—Paul knows that God wants him to be like other boys. God will not let him die while he is trying to do what He wants.

10

FROM a column by Bobby Mulloy in *The Daily News:*

> ...so the fellow faced Alan Gilchrist, the tweedy leader of Citizens Against the Berryman Expressway, and said to Gilchrist in an accent that I took to be Polish or Ukrainian, that Gilchrist should go to a place which I am not allowed to name in a family newspaper. Because, as far as this gentleman was concerned, the Berryman Expressway is a dandy

idea, just what he needs to get to his job in a furniture factory which is in one of those new industrial parks way out past Woodhurst. I got the distinct impression that if Gilchrist did not retreat immediately from his front door, the householder was going to punch him in the snoot.

But up stepped Victoria Sommers, the glamorous housewife from the Grove, and she said to the gentleman, who looked a bit like Yul Brynner, only shorter, "Do you want to be living across the street from an expressway ramp? Do you want your neighbourhood wrecked just so you can get to work five minutes faster in the morning?"

Alan Gilchrist is an astronomer by profession but the real star of the CABE crew is turning out to be Victoria Sommers. Gilchrist sounds like he just stepped out of his ivory tower, but Sommers really gets to people.

The gentleman didn't say anything at first. He just kept staring stonily ahead. But when Sommers held out a leaflet, the gentleman took it. And then he said to her, "Thanks, lady."

The next house was what you could call the cliché of the future. The front porch had been torn off, and the bricks had been sandblasted, and there was even—I swear this—the regulation, instant-antique brass coach lamp.

So you'd have thought this house would be easy picking for the zealots from CABE except for one thing: the householder had filled up his lawn with black asphalt so he could park his Volvo station-wagon on it.

Sommers and Gilchrist walked right past.

The third house had one of the now familiar red and black cardboard "Stop the Berryman!" signs nailed to a wooden stake on the front lawn, so you might have expected the CABE team not to waste time preaching to the converted. But I guess even crusaders need a little hugging from time to time.

And that is literally what happened. The fellow who answered the door and Gilchrist took one look, and the next thing you knew, they had their arms wrapped around each other.

It turned out that, years ago, the two of them had been out doing a sit-in at the front gate of a Bomarc missile base up near Cromwell. The learned astronomer said that his pal, whom he introduced as Dane Harrison, was the best leader the student peace movement ever had. But Harrison just looked like he wanted to be somewhere else. He led our little party into the house, where some women and children were cleaning storm windows and a chap in a flowery apron was down on his hands and knees, scrubbing the kitchen floor.

As soon as Harrison introduced Gilchrist, the fellow jumped to his feet and, throwing up his hands like an old black-face minstrel, started crying, "Yassuh, dere boss! I'm really working for ya dere, boss."

Besides being in excruciatingly bad taste, this little song and dance totally bewildered the people from CABE.

But Harrison explained that the fellow in the apron is actually a lawyer and he is helping J. Arthur Quinn prepare for the OMB hearing.

So then there was a lot of handshaking and everybody talking all at once, and it was turning into a love-in—until Sommers stepped forward again.

"How many of you other people are also helping us stop the Berryman?" Sommers demanded to know.

There was much shuffling of feet and looking around the room. Sommers then delivered a lecture about how it wasn't enough to leave stopping the expressway to lawyers; CABE needs people to get out and build public support for saving the city.

Gilchrist turned to his old buddy and said, "We could really use you, Dane," and I felt sorry for the poor man. Everybody else turned to him too. You go in for us, buddy. Win this one for the Gipper.

But Harrison was not having any.

"I'm sorry," he said. "I'd like to help you but I'm involved in other things now."

The learned astronomer said that was quite all right, he completely understood, and there was another round of handshakes, but the goodbyes were noticeably cooler than the hellos had been. Then the CABE team moved off down the street and I came back to the News office to write this column.

Now, this was not anybody's idea of a scientific survey, but sometimes a morning out on the street can provide an accurate snapshot of how things are.

It looks like the success of the stop-the-expressway movement still depends on the skills of J. Arthur Quinn and that guy in the apron on Landrigan Street...

11

PROBABLY NOTHING would have happened had it not fallen to Doreen to do the shopping. So Doreen is thinking that what is going on now is not really her fault—although she knows it is. Annabel had put three chickens on the list, and after loading up at the supermarket it made sense to Doreen to drag the bundle-buggy a couple of blocks back over to Landrigan Street and Weiss's Kosher—or, at least, "Kosher Style," as it says in the window—poultry. Chickens from such a quaint, homey shop were certain to be fresher and probably cheaper than anything she could get at Loblaws.

So there she was, standing behind this little Chinese woman, who was all dressed in black and having a long talk about nothing with Morry Weiss, and it suddenly struck Doreen that what she was feeling was mortally dangerous. A woman with nine years' experience of being a wife, a woman who has gone through all the pain of childbirth and has a son to raise, does not suddenly watch a man she doesn't know at all wrap a stack of scaly yellow chicken feet in old newspapers and think to herself, Dear God, yes, that is the person I want. But Doreen loves Harry Margulies. She wanted the marriage more than he did. Three chickens, please. Yes, whole, not cut into pieces—we want to roast them. Thank you.

Morry hardly recognized her. Doreen was not tense and beautiful the way she had been that Saturday morning when Morry had pulled her into shul. She was wearing blue jeans and a scuffed plaid coat, and her head was wrapped, bubbie style, in a black wool kerchief. Her face, what showed of it, was sallow and puffy. She was probably having her period. There were foggy half-moons under her eyes, and those eyes were overflowing with fear and confusion. Morry told Doreen he needed to get out of the store. He hung a "Closed" sign in his window, locked the door, and took her out for a long walk.

Morry started off by talking about himself. He told her that all he really wanted to do in life was read Byron and Blake because these were the poets who actually invented the romantic pose, the artist alienated from society. Doreen said she didn't know that.

Morry told her about the apocalyptic morning when he walked out of his PhD oral exam. He had been answering their questions without much difficulty because they were really stupid questions and suddenly he had this vision of himself, twenty years in the future, attacking some English scholar the way they were attacking him. So he just stood up and said, "Gentlemen, good morning," and left the room. He told her how he had set out to make a fortune in real estate so he could spend the rest of his life just reading and studying. He had been so close, he said. He had twenty-three houses all fixed up and ready to put on the market. Then the market began to turn. The bank called his loans.

"I could be bitter," Morry said. "That's the greatest danger for people my age, eh? I'm forty-three. When your great schemes don't work out, you can start eating yourself up alive."

A car pulled up beside them, an old Buick with a grill like a mouthful of chromium teeth. A man opened the door and stood half in the car and half in the street.

"Hey, Morry, I was just at the shop," he said in a raw, loud voice. "You retired now?"

"I'm just getting a little fresh air, Joe; they tell me it's healthy. Here"—Morry took a key ring from the pocket of his leather jacket and tossed it to the man—"Leave these in the back. In the flower pot."

"How is she?"

"Better, Joe. I think... Who the hell knows?"

"Yeah," the man says, sighing and shaking his head dubiously. "Yeah, well, we'll see."

He slides down into the car, pulls the door closed, and drives off. That is the famous Joe Greenberg, Morry explains, the last doctor in the whole world who still makes house calls. Dr. Joe is trying to keep Morry's mother at home as long as possible. Joe always says that hospitals are no place to be when you're sick.

Doreen told Morry how much she was beginning to hate living in the house on Landrigan Street. Doreen didn't really want to talk to anybody about her troubles but how could she hold back when her new friend had been so open with her? The trouble with a commune is that you are living right on top of people, but you have no way of getting through to them. If you grow up with brothers and sisters, you all know each other well. You don't have any choice, really. And if you're married...well, obviously you're intimate with the other person. But in a commune you're with people constantly and you're not intimate with them at all. The weird thing of it is, Doreen said, is that you can be right in the middle of all these other people...Annabel keeps insisting they are a tribe...and you can feel lonelier than when you were on your own.

They had reached the bottom of Landrigan Street. The decaying old row houses leaning into each other and the patchy little lawns had given way to the deadly roar of cars, trucks, and buses churning east and west on College Street. Morry led her across the wide street, holding her by the elbow—his hand felt like a steel clamp, the sensation not unpleasant—and into a restaurant called, simply, The Bagel, which Doreen had never been to before. It was warm and smelled of chickens and frying onions. Doreen felt it was like being back in her grandmother's kitchen. The owner, a bald, mournful-looking man named Benny, came to their table and told Morry he was feeling much better now and maybe he would go to Florida this winter. Morry said that was the first smart idea Benny had ever had. Benny brought them cups of coffee.

"My husband's trying to save this neighbourhood," Doreen said proudly. "He's a lawyer. He's working on the OMB case."

"Yeah...well, that's good, I guess."

Doreen was surprised and hurt. She had been counting on Harry's good works to establish her own credentials.

"Don't you want to stop the expressway?" she asked.

"I don't have any big thing about the old neighbourhood," Morry said. "Most of the people I grew up with moved out a long time ago."

Doreen had just assumed that every one of her generation and social class must be against the Berryman Expressway. But, of course, Morry is not her age; he's more than a whole decade older!

On the way back up Landrigan Street, Doreen finally began to talk about her husband. She was not disloyal. She told Morry about how brilliant Harry is. Everybody says it now, but Doreen knew it the first time she met him, at a Sigma Alpha Mu dance. Harry is kind. He adores their son, Gordon. Harry is always supportive. He came into this commune just to help her.

"Help you what?" Morry asked abruptly.

"I..."—Doreen paused, thinking of how to explain it. She knows she has already babbled on far too much. Harry would be furious—"To be a better person. To be a happier person, I guess."

"Yeah, that's what we all want," Morry said.

They were at Weiss's Poultry. Morry unlocked the door. Doreen followed him inside. She watched him wrap her chickens in brown paper and tuck them into the top of the waiting bundle-buggy.

"Well, this has been a really nice afternoon," he said. "Thank you."

She leans forward. She puts her hand on his. She brushes his cheek with her lips. The salty stubble surprises her. It occurs to her that through all their talk Morry has said nothing about his own status—married, single, or divorced. But why should he? She draws away. She is kissing him on the lips. His lips are so wide. This is a man who is not her husband. His arm is around her. She is reciprocating. Somebody called Morry Weiss is kissing her and pressing her to him. And she wants to stay. Then she is out on Landrigan Street, going home, lugging the overladen wire bundle-buggy behind her.

12

IF IT WERE ANGLOS, if it were Jews even, out here in the semi-detached, split-level houses of the northwestern suburb of Woodhurst, Alderman Vito Alcamo could tell you exactly what would be going on. The Berryman Expressway would be built and filled with cars. But because it is on the edge of the city, right up against North York, and it is mostly Italians, with some black people and a bunch of dismal welfare cases piled into public-housing projects, the seventeenth ward always gets screwed.

Vito Alcamo understands better than most people how parliamentary democracy is supposed to protect minorities. He used to teach history at Woodhurst Community College. Just fifteen months ago, the Liberal riding association said they would back him if he ran for alderman. And eleven months ago the people elected him. Vito thought he was setting an example for immigrants of all kinds. Now he knows better.

Vito sits in the back office of the Gold Star Travel Agency, listening enviously to his best friend and former campaign manager, Alfredo Spinelli, talk to the president of the Barese Community Club. They are planning a three-week holiday that will include a visit to Rome and a tour of the Dalmatian coast. Al is telling them not to worry, he will handle everything. Leave it all to your dear friend, Alfredo.

Vito and Al were together from grade three to the end of university. Vito said they should go out and make something of themselves; Al just laughed and went into his father's travel agency. Why fight the Anglos, Al said, when you can do just as well staying with your own people? Alfredo Spinelli is barely thirty and if he isn't already a millionaire, he soon will be. So how is Al's best friend doing?

Vito Alcamo is supposed to be at the beginning of a brilliant political career. The St. Cuthbert Liberal riding association welcomed Vito. He was their first honest-to-God Italian. They made him secretary-treasurer, and, a year later, vice-president. But it wasn't all dull meetings. The St. Cuth's gang were famous for their parties. When Vito met Gillian, a beautiful, knife-thin, blonde visitor from the cake-eating Moore Park Liberals, and began to go out with her, his friends in St. Cuth's did not turn up their noses and they did not take him aside for a little talk. Instead, the guys gave a stag for Vito that people still smile guiltily about, and they rented striped trousers and cutaway jackets and stood up for him as ushers. The St. Cuth's gang are like a family. But Vito is beginning to understand why these English people always come out ahead.

Because now that he is in City Hall, Vito has come to realize that there are two city governments, not one. Out front, you see politicians getting elected and passing laws. The Anglos are happy to let anybody in on that. They still control the back office. The Anglos still run the administration, that grey thicket of municipal bureaus, commissions, and boards that surrounds everybody from the time they get up 'til the time they go to bed at night. Look at the names of the city's top civil servants and the people appointed to run the hospitals and the libraries and the zoo and the museum and the parks and the community centres and a hundred other important institutions people depend on. Not an Italian in the lot, not a

Polack, not a Chink, and hardly even any Yids. The administration is pure lily white. And that's how the people in the Anglo Establishment keep control. They lock the doors and they take what they want.

Now a handful of Anglo university professors, pampered and overpaid compared to community college teachers like Vito, figure they can manipulate the administration to cheat the immigrants yet again. Alan Gilchrist and his gang can bring in big Bay Street lawyers and get a city council decision overturned and the rules of democratic government changed just to protect their crummy little neighbourhood. Then all the Italians who bought houses out in Woodhurst expecting their property to go up in value when the expressway was completed will lose out. They will be living in an instant slum. What Gilchrist and these anti-expressway nuts are trying to do is just like stealing the food from people's tables.

Vito Alcamo is not going to let them get away with it.

His friends are already drifting into Al's back office. These are the homeowners Vito has patiently organized into ratepayers' associations. Then there are Peter Singh, who has the bakery, and Mr. Rizzo, who has the furniture store; they are from the Crockford Street Business Improvement Association. Vito organized the BIA and helped the store owners get money from the province for sidewalk benches, trees in concrete pots, and new lamps. The people in the seventeenth ward respect and love Vito Alcamo. Before he came along, they say, they didn't know anything.

"Thanks for coming this morning," Vito says. "The OMB case is only a week away. And we got to make sure that we win. I am going to tell you now how we can do that..."

13

WHO IS seducing who? Or whom? Vivian is allowing her clothing to be slipped off her a piece a time, and this must be a sign, surely, that she wants this to happen. She is in Marta's chilly attic. So many times she has come here and nothing has happened. She should go home now. All she wants is to go home. So Trevor, bastard, Trevor! Why don't you help your poor wife? She is letting herself be a victim again. The lips of another woman are flavourless and messy, just the way the lips of a man are. She should tell Marta she is wasting her time. Vivian has never been a kissing person, not with Trevor and not with any of the other men she has known. So if nothing is happening to her, Vivian should feel happy not sad, eh? Because that means Vivian is a normal woman, doesn't it? She is letting Marta do whatever Marta wants now. Vivian isn't afraid any more. Her mind is filled up with the old joke they used to pull in her college residence: Hey, listen, if I fail this exam, I can always go sell my body on Hanover Street. Yeah, somebody else would crack, but what if nobody buys? Marta is naked now, too, but Vivian cannot see her; she can only feel Marta pressing against her. The lumps pressing into her must be Marta's breasts. The beast with two backs also has two fronts. They will be burned for witches. Vivian has gone too far. She left Trevor because he was manipulating her life too much, and now she is manipulating Marta. She does not love this sullen young woman, she does not even care about her particularly; Vivian is using another human being to explore her own feelings. She is using Marta the way she has herself been used so many times. Vivian should be shot. She should be whipped. She should stop this.

The feelings are definitely beginning now. It is not like with a man. There is no sensation of being mounted, of being driven. The feelings are like sweet, clear water. They come from far off, they gain speed, they flow through hidden channels, they come together and overflow; they burst into a morning-fresh garden. Dandelions and wild orchids—Vivian giggles and then puzzles at the thought. Why do these two flowers, so dissimilar, spring so immediately to consciousness? She must put them into one of her paintings. Marta pours her a glass of chilly, golden wine. Marta is sitting in front of her, chin resting on her knee, watching her with that same insolent smile that started it all. Vivian has a great desire to smack her behind, and she tells Marta so and Marta turns obediently on to her stomach and stretches out on the floor, daring Vivian to hit her. Vivian does, but the sight of her red finger marks on Marta's skin and the sudden spurt of violence inside herself frighten Vivian and she lies down beside Marta and kisses her, and they smoke one of Marta's rich Gauloise cigarettes together.

14

"YES, HELLO. I'm Doreen." Doreen Margulies stands fearfully at the door of the dim hospital room. "She's smiling at me, Morry."

"Yeah, she's pleased. You're the first person besides me that she's seen in days."

But the effort exhausts Morry's mother. She falls back into the large bed, and her waxen hair spreads out on the pillow. She surrenders to the thick plastic tube rising out of her nose. Clumps of stuff that look like black muck are bubbling up through the tube. Poor woman, does she know she's dying?

"Thanks for coming down here," Morry says. "I didn't think anybody even knew where I was."

"I had to see you."

"I'm glad you came."

"I have to talk to you."

"You don't have to talk to me."

"Morry?"

"Yeah, I know."

"I can't."

"It's okay."

It had been a week ago. Doreen had said she was just passing by and saw the light on over the store. She had just been walking her husband to the subway, she said, because he was going back to the office. She was laughable. But Morry found he couldn't just shrug her off. The woman was so jittery she couldn't even sit down. Rejection would have destroyed what little self-esteem she had left.

All that is true. But Morry Weiss knows perfectly well he wasn't just trying to be compassionate. He wanted Doreen Margulies, selfishly and ruthlessly.

Doreen told herself she was there only out of curiosity. She had started an interesting story and she wanted to know how it would come out. She watched Doreen Margulies take her clothes off and lie down in a bed that was not her own, in a room where the black wallpaper held enormous pink peonies and the air was stale and warm and touched with salty spices from the chickens barbecuing on an electric spit downstairs. Doreen noted that being with Morry was completely unlike being with Harry. Harry is really two people, one clever and subtle, and the other angry and harsh. With Harry, even when things are really good, she can never escape the worry that he is going to hurt her.

Everything Morry did with her was easy and gentle and so understanding of women. Doreen forgot all about being afraid. Afterward, he held her damp face between his hands and kissed her on the forehead. That kiss meant as much to her as the lovemaking did.

"My mother's going to be out for a while," Morry says. "Let's get a bite."

He walks beside her now, not touching her, hands jammed into the pockets of his leather windbreaker, navy blue watch cap not quite covering his strange silver hair. What will happen to him now? They have walked together and they have talked and they have known each other, and now Doreen is going to be one more person who has hurt him. But what else can she do? Doreen is no good at games and deceptions. She is much too much like Morry Weiss himself.

There is some relief, at least, in despising Morry's wife. How could a woman do such terrible things? When Morry's little real estate empire went bust, he still had enough left after paying his debts to start over again. Instead, he paid off the mortgage on his home. Then, into the house Morry had paid for, his wife brought another man to raise Morry's children, and they told Morry to stay away because cutting him off from the kids was the way she and her new husband were going to create a family of their own.

Why do people inflict such pain on others? But who is Doreen Margulies to look down so haughtily on Morry's wife?

He leads her away from the brooding hospitals of University Avenue and down into the noisy stores of Chinatown with their glistening, watery neon signs. She is wearing grey trousers and a white turtleneck sweater, and a light grey Persian lamb coat. She has brushed her thick black hair and put on lacy silver earrings. She is performing now for Morry, the way she was performing for her husband the first time he met the two of them and pulled them into Eli's shul on Landrigan Street. Morry accepts the offering gratefully. Everything this woman does seems to Morry to express a simple, unlaboured elegance that has always been beyond his reach.

Morry orders supper for the two of them. They do not talk. Morry wonders whether this is because they have nothing to say to each other or because they have too much to say. But between them now there is only the sharp clicking of chopsticks.

I am forty-three years old. That thought eradicates all else, pounding away with the melodrama of a piston. I am forty-three years old. Bitterness is only one of the temptations that come with middle age. There is also self-pity.

"This just hit the spot," Doreen says. "Thank you. I guess I should get going."

"Yeah, me too. I should get back to the hospital."

"How long will it be?"

"God knows. A day, a week—every doctor tells you something different."

"I'll try to come again."

"If you want to. Yeah, that would be good. She doesn't respond too much, but she knows when there's people in the room."

"Goodbye, then." Her hand brushes Morry's hand.

"Goodbye, Doreen."

She is down the steps and out on Dundas Street, hailing a cab.

15

J. ARTHUR QUINN really should be moving on. But he is enjoying himself so much out here under the stars that he can't bring himself to go. Ta-ta-ta-tum...ta-dee...ta-tum. Quinn sings along with the vaguely Viennese waltz. The chirpy music comes out of loudspeakers placed around the rink in front of City Hall. The doctors have told him he must exercise to rebuild his damaged heart, and Quinn has taken to skating here as often as he can. Despite his heavy body and his long black overcoat and the thick black attaché case he must keep with him at all times, clutching it now in his right hand even while he is on the ice, Quinn still manages to move along quite smoothly. He takes a childish delight in being in the company of the vigorous young men, and the lithe young women in their brief figure-skaters' skirts.

Quinn is not disturbed at all by the thought that while he is out here enjoying the cold early-evening air, Harry Margulies is back at the office waiting to confer. Quinn has had a hard day too. But when Quinn reaches the thirty-seventh floor of the International Trade Centre and sees Harry Margulies's face, he is struck by remorse. There are purple half-moons under Harry's eyes. Quinn brings him around to his corner sanctuary and invites his junior colleague to help himself to a scotch while he hangs up his overcoat and skates.

"Two days!" Harry moans. "Jeezuss! We are not ready, Arthur. We are just not fucking ready!"

"I know," Quinn says. "I don't think I've ever gone before the OMB feeling I was properly prepared. But we open Monday morning, Harry. Tell me what you've got."

"Okay. Okay, then. Okay, here it is. There are two possible lines of attack, maybe three. You've got to make a choice. I've got 'em in separate books, eh? Three separate books! You've got to decide, okay?"

"Yes, I understand. Would you like some water with that?"

"I'm okay. What are you drinking? Aftershave?"

"This is Armagnac, Harry. Prune brandy. Go on."

"Okay. So, this thing goes back to the forties. But they never actually got around to putting the whole expressway grid into an official plan until 'fifty-nine. And—this is the beautiful part; this'll kill you!—they never sent it up to Queen's Park. I have checked, up, down, and sideways, and there is no fucking reference anywhere to this plan ever going up to the Ministry of Municipal Affairs. So, what these guys are operating with is a fucking official plan that is not official. How do you like them apples!"

"Not bad," Quinn says. "What else have you got, Harry?"

"Wait! The fun is just beginning! Originally, they had this whole expressway grid. And the key to it was the Crosstown Expressway. The Crosstown was going to run through the middle of the city and connect the Berryman to the Don Valley Parkway. The idea was that half the cars coming in from the suburbs would get onto the Crosstown and then they'd build smaller expressways to distribute them all across the city. But this

Crosstown Expressway was going to cut right through Rosedale. They had a cloverleaf in there that was going to take out half of the richest neighbourhood in Toronto!

"So, the good burghers of Rosedale screamed bloody murder. Those folks got clout. Suddenly there's no more Crosstown Expressway. That's when they should have stopped. They should have said, 'Okay, there's no more grid and now we've got to rethink the whole goddamned thing.' But they never did. They just started work on the Berryman. So, cars coming down the valley and the ones that are supposed to come in on the Berryman got nowhere to go but downtown. Instead of a reasonably sane grid of expressways, what they're trying to give us is two huge superhighways funnelling thousands of cars into downtown streets where the traffic is already so heavy nobody can move."

"Yes, that looks a little better. But what about the money, Harry?"

"The money! You wouldn't believe the money! Like why else are we here, right? Originally, when they first started, they said the whole grid, five expressways, was going to cost a hundred and twenty million dollars. Shit! They spent almost half that just building the Don Valley and the Gardiner. But they never went back and changed their estimates. They've been playing all kinds of bullshit games with operating and capital budgets. Only now they can't do that any more. They've got to go down to New York and peddle bonds. They're out in the open and we nail them."

"Yes," Quinn says. "And cities are required under the Municipal Act to balance their books every year. They can't borrow for operating expenses the way the province and the feds can. But, from what you are saying, it sounds like they may have been disguising some of their operating expenses as capital expenses. You'd better check it out, Harry. Before Monday."

Harry looks stunned. He and Doreen are going to watch Gordon play hockey and they are supposed to have supper with two of Harry's old pals from Sigma Alpha Mu fraternity and their wives on Saturday night. On Sunday he and Doreen were going to spend the morning in bed.

"You had plans for the weekend, Harry?"

"Nothing definite. I mean, nothing that can't be changed." Harry hates himself for saying this.

"I don't want to interfere with your private life, Harry. As long as you've got it for me by time we open on Monday morning, that'll be fine."

"You'll have it, Arthur," Harry says emphatically. "No problem."

Harry has been pushed to the edge. He decides he has earned the right to be treated as an equal.

"Arthur...what do you think?"

"About what?"

"Our chances."

"I wouldn't hazard a guess, Harry. All I know is that you and I are doing the Lord's work. And, win, lose, or draw, I expect the Lord to reward us."

16

SOMETIMES, dreams really do come true. Paul Warren is alone behind his blue line, too much in awe of Henry, the coach, to abandon his defenceman's position and go charging up the rink to get in on the play, too embarrassed to look up into the stands to see where his mother and Dane and the other people from the house are supposed to be sitting. Maybe they are not there at all. But wait! Look! Something's going on in front of their goal. It's a breakaway. The two teams are in Varsity Arena where the pros play. Whoever wins this game goes on to the all-city round-robin playoffs. But the score is tied. Only one minute left in the game. He's coming right for Paul. There is no one else around. Paul braces himself, leans into his stick. He closes his eyes. It's more of a collision than a body check, and the shock of it almost knocks him over. But the other guy's flat on his back. The puck has landed on Paul's stick. He takes off. Instinctively he keeps to that long clear alley close to the boards. One of their defencemen comes slinking out to stop him. Paul dekes right, scoots left. He turns, he's closing in on the goal. They're all coming after him now. There's an opening, he can see it, up near the top of the net. He shoots! He scores! Just listen to that crowd. They're going wild.

He could have died. That other boy hit him right in the chest, Annabel is thinking. So, if she is a good mother, she will do exactly what she told Dane she would do: she will go down there and haul her son away from this madness.

When Dane told her they were not just coming to see Gordon Margulies tonight, but that Paul was on the team too, she was so outraged the only thing she could think of was to walk out on him—and she told him so!

"You lied to me. You told me you were taking Paul to a pottery class. Stupid old Annabel. Who the fucking hell do you think you are? The only man entitled to make any decisions in Paul's life is his natural father, and that little prick isn't around any more. So I'm in charge. He's my kid, you lying piece of shit! You never were anything in your life and now you're not even Annabel's man because I can't trust you any more. So what the fuck use is Dane Harrison to anybody?"

Now it is time to snatch her son away. But the other boys are surrounding Paul, clapping him on the shoulder, patting him on the behind. The announcer is booming his name through the cavernous arena: Paul Warren, nineteen-oh-three of the third period. And it was, Annabel has to say this, a beautiful goal.

She squeezes Dane's hand. If there is no way out, Dane said, if Paul really has to die before his time, then at least let him have a full life while he is here. We should be trying to give him good memories. Annabel digs her fingernails possessively into the soft flesh of Dane's palm.

Beside Dane, Harry Margulies is thinking that winning and losing will not be abstract concepts for his son. After a season on a hockey team, Gordon will understand why his father has to keep rushing back to the office every night. What Gordon's friend has just done is exactly what Gordon's father and J. Arthur Quinn are being called upon to do—score in the final minute of the game.

Beside Harry, Doreen Margulies is appalled by the brutality. These children are sent out onto a rink that is really much too large for them and then they are ordered to smash into each other. This is not what Doreen Margulies wants for her son. She is not going to be an old witch right now, but this is the last hockey team Gordon Margulies is ever going to play on. His mother will see to that.

Next to Doreen, Sasha Billinghurst is reflecting sourly on how power is shifting in the house. When everybody first moved in together she had the power, even though the boys made up their own club. She was still older, and they still listened to Sasha and did what she said. Now, Sasha can see, keeping her power is going to be very difficult.

Beside Sasha, her six-year-old sister, Paola Billinghurst, is starting to whimper. Her mother promised a box of Smarties if she was good. It was a dumb bribe, but Paola went along anyway because the hockey game was a chance to stay up, for once, with everybody else. But now it's really late and the air in this big arena is just as frosty as outside and all Paola wants is to go home and go to bed.

Beside Paola, Vivian Billinghurst is lost in sad memories of Paola's father, Trevor Billinghurst. How splendid Teddy looked on skates. She remembers the sleek, young lord who could pick up the puck behind his own net and take off, twisting and turning through the entire other team, finally to charge the goal and send the puck singing into an uncovered corner—much like little Paul Warren has just done, although Paul has none of Trevor's grace. Poor Trevor. He wasn't a bad person. He just didn't understand anything.

Beside Vivian, her new friend and lover, Marta Persofski, sits with her arm surreptitiously but possessively around Vivian's waist, fingers thrust lasciviously into the pocket of Vivian's grey flannel slacks.

Twenty rows above the little group from Landrigan Street, Dr. James Kernohan sits in the darkness at the top of Varsity Arena. Dane called him about the game but he is not going to say hello to the family because he doesn't want the woman thinking her doctor and her boyfriend are conspiring against her. Besides, Dr. Kernohan is afraid they might see the tears pushing out of the corners of his eyes. But that is one hell of a good kid down there.

17

HARRY MARGULIES started the day furious. He had landed in hostile territory, and this was not supposed to happen. Alan Gilchrist and the steering committee of Citizens Against the Berryman Expressway swore they would pack the hearing-room. Harry wanted the three members of the Ontario Municipal Board to walk in the first day and find a room full of clean, handsomely dressed, passionately concerned young citizens. Their anxious scrutiny was supposed to encourage the board members to do justice, walk humbly, and save the Grove. But, instead, the board is looking out on solid rows of lumpy middle-aged women, most of them slouched timidly into cloth overcoats, and stocky, weather-worn, suspicious men in windbreakers and ill-fitting blue suits. These are the sullen, immigrant workers from the Woodhurst neighbourhood who are supposed to suffer if the Berryman Expressway isn't built up to their front doors. Right in the middle sits their hero, Alderman Vito Alcamo. The bastard must have spent all weekend phoning people who don't go to work on Monday mornings—housewives, pensioners, construction workers with wrecked backs living out their lives on workmen's compensation. Alcamo's crowd filled the corridor a full hour before the doors to the hearing-room were even opened. By the time the CABE contingent finally arrived, every seat was taken.

Quinn gets to his feet now. Harry can feel the tension running through the crowd behind him. This is Quinn's first attack on a witness. The hearing-room is laid out like a court. The three board members sit on a dais, like judges. The witness is in a chair beside them. In front of the board members are tables for the lawyers, the City's team on the left, CABE's counsel on the right. Standing between the two sides is a sturdy wooden lectern. Quinn leans over the lectern now and smiles at the witness.

The witness beams back, so full of confidence his smile is almost a smirk. He is William Ferrier. Willy, as everyone, including Quinn, calls him, has been regional planning commissioner for twelve years. He is tall, grey-haired, distinguished. He wears a thick tweed jacket with leather elbow patches. Urban planner? Bullshit, Harry is thinking. This guy looks like an English country gentleman.

"Mr. Ferrier, I would like to show you something," Quinn says courteously. He reaches into a cardboard box Harry has placed beside the lectern and takes out a book of about forty loose pages held together by a plastic binding.

"Would you please read the title for the benefit of the board?" Quinn asks.

"Official Plan, Borough of Cedarbrae."

"Yes, thank you. And, course, I don't have to tell anyone here that Cedarbrae abuts the northern border of the city and is one of the seven boroughs making up the Urban Region...Now, Mr. Ferrier, may I direct your attention to page thirty-six of this document."

Ferrier turns to the page. Harry can see he's getting a little nervous. He hasn't figured out yet where Quinn is trying to take him. Good. Beautiful.

"Would you tell the board what you see on page thirty-six?"

"It's just a map. The official plan for Cedarbrae."

"And the date?"

"Nineteen fifty-five."

"Yes, and when did you start work on the regional plan?"

"Nineteen fifty-seven."

"So this borough plan existed before you started your regional plan. Now, would you tell the board whether this borough plan looks familiar to you?"

"Yes, of course. I've seen it many times."

"Yes, I'm sure you have." Quinn speaks with just the faintest hard edge to his voice to let the board know he has reached the point he wants them to pay attention to.

"And one of the places you have seen this Cedarbrae plan is on your own regional master plan. In fact, it's identical isn't it? Would you agree with me, Mr. Ferrier, that if we took this borough plan for Cedarbrae and put it on top of your regional plan, it would be an exact fit?"

Ferrier does not reply. His horsy, snobbish face knots up. Harry is delighted. Ralph Kopinski, the Region lawyer, jumps to the lectern, taking over the other half of it from Quinn.

"Mr. Chairman, I don't wish to inhibit my friend," he says. "But, if Mr. Quinn is going to ask you to make comparisons between planning maps, I think he should be putting them up where we can all see them. So, I would request a day's adjournment so we can have the proper visual aids brought to this hearing-room."

Quinn instantly agrees. They make an interesting contrast, the two lawyers occupying their respective sides of the lectern. Quinn is large, fat really, and soft, but he always looks neat and composed. Kopinski is thin and hard, but he is one of those awkward men whose suits will never fit him. He always looks grey and untidy. But don't let appearances fool you, Quinn has warned Harry. Kopinski is very smart.

"I certainly support the request of my friend," Quinn says. "But I may be able to save the board some time. I am simply trying to establish that the regional plan incorporated the official plan for Toronto and all the surrounding boroughs that make up the Metropolitan Region. If Mr. Ferrier feels that he can agree with me on that, we can move ahead."

Kopinski cannot be seen in the hearing-room openly telling his witness what to say, but all his anguished body language is warning the guy to shut up. Ferrier refuses to pick up the signal. He's such a serenely confident little prick. These guys have spent so many years testifying at public hearings they think nobody can touch them.

"I don't know what Mr. Quinn is trying to prove, but I would not dispute his point. Yes, the regional plan does include the planning that was done in the boroughs before we began our work. We didn't think it was necessary for us to reinvent the wheel."

"Yes, and now I am going to hand you a copy of the Planning Act for the province of Ontario and I would ask you to turn to page fourteen and read what you find there."

Ferrier's ingratiating smile flicks off. He can see what's coming now. In a cold, diffident voice he reads, "In the making of an official plan the municipality shall; one, conduct a thorough survey of the region's existing land-use patterns; two, project the future land-use expectations; three, produce a preliminary plan—"

Quinn cuts him off. "You don't have to read farther, Mr. Ferrier. There are fourteen requirements. We are interested only in the first two. Would you tell the board if you did, indeed, survey the land-use patterns in this region and then project these into the future?"

"That work had already been done. We did extensive computer simulation studies. I might add, Mr. Chairman, we were the first municipality in North America to make use of these sophisticated programs for predicting traffic flow."

"But not the last," Quinn cuts in quickly. "The truth is the region kept growing and changing, and you never changed or updated your computer studies. When the time came to make an official plan, you just took everything that had been done in the past and pasted it together. That is really what happened, isn't it, Mr. Ferrier?"

"I object." Kopinski is on his feet again and this time he looks genuinely angry. "Mr.Chairman, my friend is trying to get Mr. Ferrier to repudiate twenty years of regional planning and I don't think that is the purpose of this hearing."

"I have no further questions of this witness," Quinn says benignly. "Thank you, Mr. Ferrier."

Kopinski makes a good comeback in the re-examination. He leads Ferrier into saying he consulted with the local planners and never accepted what they had done unquestioningly. But Quinn has still scored. Those board members aren't stupid. They know what's been going on.

By the end of the week, though, Quinn and Harry are losing ground.

Kopinski brings in the deputy minister from Municipal Affairs. He says the province put money into the first two expressways and that means the province gave de facto recognition to the expressway grid and the regional plan.

Never mind that the regional council never took the final plan and asked the Municipal Affairs minister to go over it and put his seal on it and make it "official." The minister is familiar with the plan and he knows it has been approved by the regional council, and as far as the Province of Ontario is concerned, the plan expresses the will of the people of the region.

18

SPOUSES AND CHILDREN are responsibilities we take on voluntarily, even if we say, later, we had really no idea what we were getting into. But by what right does anybody outside this immediate circle make demands upon us? Dane cracks two eggs and uses the spatula to keep the whites from spreading across the crackling silver grill. Once you decide that you are not, personally, going to make any difference in the history of the world, you wield Occam's razor and eliminate everything outside yourself that makes demands upon your time. Dane has chosen Annabel, or, to be more accurate, Annabel has chosen him, and Dane has certainly chosen to make certain commitments to Annabel's son. But no one else has the right to say to Dane Harrison, "You must help us!"

Dane is rehearsing these arguments because, in the back booth of the Imperial Restaurant, Alan Gilchrist and his friends are waiting for Dane to bring their orders. Dane is sure that what they would like to get, along with their coffee and tuna salad sandwiches, is the soul of Dane Harrison.

He focuses his mind on an easy, controlled turn of the wrist so that he can get the eggs flipped onto their yolks without breaking them. Being a good counterman requires the grace of a ballet dancer. Dane Harrison has become an honest craftsman. Not too many other people in this alienated backwater of Western civilization can still say that.

He brings Gilchrist and his people their food and leaves them while he makes sure everyone else in the restaurant is taken care of. Then, because there is nothing else he can think of to do, he pours himself a coffee and sits down with the Citizens Against the Berryman Expressway.

"We won't take up too much of your time, Dane," Gilchrist says. "Our problem is quite simple, really. We don't want to turn everything over to lawyers. We are trying to build a movement that will save the whole city."

Sitting beside Gilchrist, Victoria Sommers leans towards Dane as though the pure force of her righteous ardour ought to be enough to make him sign on. Dane is thinking, I know you, lady. Get away from me. Victoria Sommers is painfully, obviously a product of the old-monied Upper Canada upper class—the sleek chestnut hair falling straight to her shoulders, not a lock out of place; the fearless blue eyes; the huge, gleaming teeth. She is a living example of the classic simplicity that wealth, marrying for three generations within its own social circle, and a good, private-school education can produce. Dane spent the first half of his life with her kind, and the second half getting away from them. Now she thinks she is going to work moral blackmail on him?

"Listen, you people have already got a political party," he says coldly. "You don't need to go to all this trouble."

A worried, frail-looking chap beside Dane responds for the group. His name is Don McPartland and he has the kind of dry, scratchy voice that Dane recognizes as coming out of tobacco-farming country in western Ontario. But McPartland has been introduced to him as chief actuary for an insurance company.

"The NDP can't relate to urban issues," McPartland says. He sounds as though he feels personally responsible for this failing. "They're social democrats; they believe in centralized planning. But CABE is trying to save the city a block at a time. I've been part of the New Democratic Party since it began, but they can't understand what CABE is about. They tell me I'm wasting my time."

"I can understand where they're coming from," Dane says. The restaurant is beginning to fill up again; he should be getting back to work. "If you want a political movement, you've got to organize around class interests. Your group is trying to organize people around a single issue: stopping an expressway. It never works. As soon as the issue's resolved, everybody goes home."

"So? You think because we are from the middle class we are so uncultured, so incurably greedy we are not worth bothering about. Am I correct?"

Dane recognizes the speaker's accent and decides he is not going to get drawn into any arguments with this fellow. He has been introduced as Peter Strassner. He has thick black hair, sad, sunken eyes; and the kind of long, sharply hooked nose that undoubtedly inspired the Nazi anti-Semitic caricatures.

"I try never to discuss politics with people who have come through the Holocaust," Dane says. "They are in a different dimension of experience from me."

"You think I am Jewish?"

"I would assume so, yes."

"Catholic. And, surprisingly enough, still a practising Catholic. But you made a not-bad guess. I am from Europe and my accent is German. Sudeten German. My father stood out on the street and cried, 'Heil, Hitler!' when the Nazis marched in. Now, ask me what I do."

"Okay, I'll bite," Dane says. "What do you do?"

"I teach moral philosophy. At Francis Xavier College."

Dane laughs, and Peter Strassner laughs too.

"You teach ethics to Jesuits?"

"I teach them ambiguity," Strassner says. "Who needs ambiguity more than Jesuits? Now...you are going to say to me that the middle class is so amorphous it cannot be defined and, even if it could, the people are so obsessed with consuming everything in sight it is inconceivable they should ever work together to pursue a class interest. I am right, no? Yes!

"So now I am going to say to you, 'What is it these terrible middle-class people want?' To be safe in their own homes. To eat, to drink, to do a little screwing with their mate, and with somebody else's mate if they can get away with it. They want to raise children. They want to be happy. What is so bad about all that? I say to you, my friend, that the middle class expresses the noblest desires of all mankind. That is our class interest."

Dane is charmed. He hasn't had the pleasure of this kind of self-conscious conversation in a long time.

"You folks are way ahead of the game," he says. "What do you need me for?"

"Not just because you were a student peacenik," Sommers says quickly. "But because you've kept the faith. You've been involved in every important movement for the last ten years. People trust you. They look up to you."

"If I were that important, you'd be talking to me in jail," Dane says.

"We want continuity," Strassner says. "We need to pull people from outside the downtown neighbourhoods. If you will excuse me for using language which has bad historical connotations, we want to create a 'popular front.'"

"You want me for my symbolic value?"

"Don't laugh. How many people get to be symbols in their own lifetimes?"

"Hey, Dane, come on, eh? It's supper!" Jimmy, the owner of the Imperial Restaurant, has come out of the kitchen and has picked up Dane's work behind the counter.

"I've got to go," Dane says. "But, okay, I'll tell you what I think—for what it's worth. You can't build an ongoing political movement around neighbourhood issues because they keep getting resolved. Every time you win, you lose. And you can't get middle-class people to act out of class interest because no matter how much you and I might agree on what they ought to do, they're just not used to acting collectively. So, all you've got left is shared experience. If you want a political movement, you've got to start by building a community."

Dane is thinking about Chicago now. Would these people be so eager for his help if they had seen him running down the street to get away from the riot in front of the Hilton Hotel? Ah well, it would take too long to explain all that.

"If it was up to me," Dane says, "I'd take my people and I'd sit down in the middle of Berryman Avenue. Stop all the traffic. I'd make a human wall."

McPartland shakes his head sadly. Alan Gilchrist looks embarrassed. Victoria Sommers looks like she wants to slap Dane in the face.

"This is not exactly what we were expecting," Strassner says.

"If you want to blockade Berryman Avenue, I'll come with you," Dane says. "Otherwise, there's nothing I can do for you."

19

FOR DAYS NOW, the other side has been salivating in anticipation."The 'Poole Report' is coming! Poole's going to knock your socks off," the young lawyers who work with Kopinski have been whispering to Harry Margulies down in the basement coffee shop where both sides go during breaks. Their killer witness has turned out to be a plump, pink, little man who speaks with the relentless enthusiasm of a summer-camp director. He has been introduced as Dr. Norman Poole, head of the economics department at the University of Western Ontario, and a founding member of the Economic Round Table of Canada.

"Dr. Poole, I think we can agree that one point…uh, one point…," Quinn is saying.

Poole rushes to help the famous lawyer.

"One point seven three four!"

"Thank you, Dr. Poole: one-point-seven-three-four billion dollars' worth of new apartment blocks and office towers would be beneficial to the city."

"And plazas. I'm projecting two large indoor shopping malls. These wouldn't be regionals, but they'd certainly be in the neighbourhood of five hundred thousand square feet."

"That's a pretty impressive neighbourhood. By all means, let us include shopping malls too. I had no intention of leaving them out."

"These are only projections, of course. Best estimates, if you want."

"I understand, Dr. Poole. And nobody is trying to hold you to these figures. But you have told the board that your studies show we will get almost two billion dollars' worth of new buildings beside the Berryman Expressway."

"That is correct. That is what I said."

"Yes…well, now, what will happen if the Berryman Extension is not built?"

"The Region will lose all that tax revenue, for one thing."

"But the Region will have to pay for building the expressway, won't it?"

"I have estimated that, allowing for variables in interest rates at the time the bonds are put on the market, tax revenue from new buildings along the expressway route could begin to service debt on the expressway bonds within twelve years."

"But what about additional sewer capacity for new buildings beside the expressway, Dr. Poole? What about the widening that will be needed on streets leading up to the expressway? What about new schools for the children of all those new people who are going to live in all those new buildings you tell us are going to go up along the Berryman Extension? I don't see those cost projections anywhere in your report."

"I do point out that new services will be needed. But no one can say at this time how many new people will be involved. Therefore, it is not possible to estimate with any degree of accuracy the full extent of the new services that will be needed."

"But we do agree the expressway will require new municipal services and that these will cost money?"

"Yes, certainly."

"Mr. Poole, do you think that if we took the new tax revenue you project and we set that against the cost of building the expressway and the cost of the new municipal services, the region would probably just about break even? Do you think that is a fair statement?"

"Yes, I do. But let me answer a question you haven't asked, Mr. Quinn.

What about the new commerce and new jobs that are created by development along an expressway route? Let me tell you something I tell my first-year urban economics students: a city is a living organism. Once a living organism stops growing, it starts dying."

"Dr. Poole, something that keeps growing without control is called 'cancer.'"

"Mr. Quinn, you are twisting my words!"

"Dr. Poole, let's get down to specifics. How much do you estimate your clients will lose if the expressway is cancelled?"

"I am engaged by the Canadian Real Estate Institute."

"But your institute is made up of individual members, isn't it? One of your vice-presidents, William Shannon, owns three lots on the corner of Glenwillow and Berryman Avenue. That shopping mall you were talking about will be built by Premier Developments, won't it? Donald Morton, a dentist, owns the corner of Berryman Avenue and St. Clair. I am going to enter these certified copies of deeds as exhibits, Dr. Poole. I can, if you wish, enter documents which will show that just about every available site along the route has been purchased by members of the Canadian Real Estate Institute. Will that be necessary, Dr. Poole?"

"No, I don't think so."

"So you are not here just to tell us about how much the public is going to benefit from the expressway, are you? Is it not true that you are here to protect the interests of speculators who bought land along the expressway route and hope to make a lot of money?"

"I object to the term 'speculator,' Mr. Quinn. Many members of CREI are syndicates and public companies rather than private individuals. Many people with investments on that expressway route are your pensioners and your archetypal little old ladies."

"Dr. Poole, if a little old lady gets into a crap game, do you think the government is obligated to protect her?"

"These people invested because the government said it was going to build an expressway. The government should be consistent."

"Not too long ago, Dr. Poole, it would have been consistent with government policy to say women should not be allowed to vote. Do you believe governments should have remained firm on this issue?"

Kopinski is on his feet, flushed and furious.

"I object. Mr. Chairman. My friend has lost touch with the purpose of this hearing. He is bullying the witness."

Quinn looks surprised and hurt. He leans over the lectern.

"Mr. Chairman, I am sorry if I have been overzealous with this witness. Mr. Poole, please accept my apology. You and I are not involved in a personal dispute here, and I greatly appreciate your patience..."

"I understand, Mr. Quinn," Poole says magnanimously. But his hands keep sliding back and forth along the railing of the witness box. Harry is delighted. Poole no longer looks like an upbeat camp director. He looks more like a camper who has been caught playing with himself.

"I have no further questions, Mr. Chairman," Quinn says.

Quinn steps away from the lectern and returns to his seat at the CABE table. Harry can hardly resist hugging him. When the hearing adjourns tonight, he is going to take Quinn up to the roof bar of the Park Plaza Hotel. They will step out of the elevator onto the thick broadloom and sit by the window overlooking the lights of the city, and Harold, the waiter, will bring them Chivas Regal doubles. The roof bar is where all the guys go when they have a case running and they think they are winning.

But, at four o'clock, with barely an hour to go, Kopinski puts Vito Alcamo on the stand. This is what his claque has been waiting for. They clap for their handsome hero so boisterously the chairman has to threaten to clear the room.

"Look at these people! These are not speculators," Alcamo says in response to questions from Kopinski. "These are just ordinary working people. They are not trying to make big profits. They are just trying to get to their jobs in the morning."

The alderman speaks so plainly and so sincerely that even Harry has to concede the bastard is having an impact.

"These are New Canadians," Alcamo says. "They may not speak English very well, but they do understand what it means when the government makes a promise. You cannot break faith with these people!"

When Alcamo finishes, the cheering of his admirers is so loud it drowns out the chairman announcing that the hearing has adjourned for the day.

Harry does not even suggest going up to the Park Plaza roof. He and Quinn return to the office and work until three the following morning, preparing for the next set of witnesses.

20

VIVIAN BILLINGHURST is embroiled in a lovers' quarrel, which is ridiculous because she is not in love with anybody. But she is standing now in a chaste white slip, at the centre of the barren room on Landrigan Street she calls "my studio," and listening to Marta Persofski go up one side of her and down the other— as Vivian's mother used to say. But Marta is telling her the truth. Vivian cannot deny it.

"The truth is, Vivian, you never left home. Oh, yeah, sure, you walked out on your husband, but where did you go? Back to a big family with a fat woman playing Mommy. You're even afraid to come home too late at night. Annabel might ground you."

Vivian does not even know the meaning of the word *love*, Marta tells her. Vivian thinks it means feeling protected and knowing every day exactly what is going to happen the day after. For people who give themselves up to love, tomorrow is a million years away. Real lovers are tightrope walkers. Real lovers cling to each other and tell the rest of the world to go fuck itself!

That's where art comes from too, if Vivian really wants to know. All those classes Vivian keeps going to are just wasting fucking time. It's like going to business school. It's like learning to type and then telling people you're a writer.

"Art comes from way down, deep inside, Vivian. Art comes from putting yourself way out on the edge and knowing that if you fall, baby, you just keep right on falling forever and ever. No support payments, Vivian. No house on Landrigan Street to hide out in. No fucking nothing, Vivian!"

Vivian just point-blank refuses to look inside herself. She's scared to death she might find something there she can't handle. It's not that Marta cares about Vivian not being really gay. Marta has been with lots of bi women. People should do whatever feels right for them. But Vivian just won't go into that part of herself.

"The truth is, Vivian, you spend three-quarters of your energy just holding yourself in. You're stiff as a board. You spend all your time on a power trip—a power trip over yourself! And it's killing you. Because, right now, all those paintings you keep calling 'my work' are pure shit!"

Finally, it seems that Marta is beginning to wind down. Vivian asks her quietly why she is doing this.

Marta says that Vivian knows perfectly well why. Marta has offered three times to come with Vivian. She will give up her own place, which she really loves, and she will move into somewhere new, with Vivian. She has offered three times to give Vivian her whole life, and Vivian keeps stalling.

"And I am fucking sick of it. So, you better make your mind up who you are and what you want. Because, even if I am crying now, it's only because I am so angry. Marta Persofski is an all-or-nothing person."

21

HARRY MARGULIES has never attended a boxing match, but now the metaphors of the ring seem the only language appropriate to describe the state of the Berryman Expressway hearing. J. Arthur Quinn and Harry Margulies are in the thirteenth round. They may be ahead on points, but this is a title bout.

"Now, Mr. Sissons, as a responsible financial officer, when you saw that inflation was pushing the cost of expressway construction up higher than anyone had ever dreamed, did you not think it your duty to sound the alarm?" Quinn is saying.

Norval Sissons, treasurer of the regional municipality, has been playing shamelessly to the board members. He is a sombre, athletic-looking man in a rich, dark, three-piece blue suit. Kopinski, the Region's lawyer, had him open his testimony about financing the Berryman Expressway by telling the board he is a certified public accountant and a major in the Toronto Highland Regiment and he has been in the service of the Region for twenty-two years. So, even though Mr. Sissons has been affable and patient, he is not about to let J. Arthur Quinn, or anybody else for that matter, cast aspersions upon his integrity.

"Every year," Sissons is saying, "I issued a five-year forecast of capital expenditures. This included the revised estimates for construction of the Berryman Extension."

"Are these the forecasts you are referring to?" Quinn holds up a stack of green booklets.

"Around City Hall, those are known as 'Green Hornets,'" Sissons says. Harry takes a weary pleasure in watching Quinn expose a bit of the man's vanity.

"Let me give you the five-year forecast for nineteen sixty-nine, the most recent of your 'Green Hornets.' Would you open it to page thirty-seven, 'Capital Expenditure, Roads and Traffic Department,' Item seven: 'Berryman Extension.' Would you kindly tell the board what the estimated total cost is?"

"One hundred and forty million dollars."

"Now would you show the board where in this report it says that the original estimated cost of the expressway was seventy-five million dollars."

"That's not in this report."

"Why not?"

"This is a forecast, not a retrospective audit."

"Mr. Sissons, would you agree with me that unless a person knew what the original estimated cost of the expressway was ten years ago, it would be impossible to learn from your five-year forecasts how much those estimates had increased? Isn't that the case, Mr. Sissons?"

"Not at all. The regional chairman was well aware of the upward revisions. So were all members of the regional council. My five-year forecasts were discussed in open council meetings and I was questioned—quite closely, I don't mind telling you, Mr. Quinn—about several items in my report. The media were there. I think it is fair to say, Mr. Quinn, that the public has been well aware of all revised estimates."

"Mr. Sissons, how much do you think the Berryman Extension will increase in cost this year?"

Kopinski is on his feet again.

"I object. The witness is being asked for conjecture."

"I am merely asking the treasurer of the regional municipality to do for the board what he does every year for the regional council."

The board chairman nods in agreement.

"Go ahead, Mr. Quinn."

But the witness has picked up the cue from his lawyer.

"You are asking the impossible. Until I have a good idea of the rate of inflation and the increase in the cost of labour and material, it is impossible for me to estimate the cost of the expressway."

"Mr. Sissons, if you can't tell us how much you think the Berryman Extension will cost if we start work on it next year, isn't it fair to say that you don't know how much it is going to cost when it is finally completed?"

"Mr. Quinn, there is not a responsible financial officer in the whole world who could tell you what the final cost of a public facility as large as an expressway will be."

"So when you ask this board to approve a bond issue for the expressway, you don't know how much money you have to raise, do you? There is a good chance you will be back here next year and the year after that, asking this board to approve still more bond issues. Is that not the case, Mr. Sissons?"

"Perhaps it is. But you should also let the board know, Mr. Quinn, that we have always been able to pay for capital expenses out of current revenues."

"Yes, and how have you accomplished this?"

"Through taxes."

"Yes, taxes. Through raising the tax on property, am I right?" Quinn draws out the word *raising*. "Now would you be good enough to tell the board how large a tax increase you will need to service the debt on these bonds you want the board to authorize?"

"Mr. Quinn, the board knows I cannot do that with any degree of accuracy. Until we know interest rates at the time bonds are issued, we can only guess at what we'll need to pay them off. The best I could give you would be a box-car figure."

"I am sure the board is not interested in box-car figures, Mr. Sissons."

"Mr. Quinn, you should tell the board that expressways are not just capital expenditures. They generate revenue."

"Yes, we've heard all about the new buildings we can expect along the expressway route. Thank you for your patience, Mr. Sissons. I have no further questions."

Quinn yields the lectern to Kopinski, who takes his witness through "re-examination," trying to dispel any doubts Quinn may have raised.

Quinn sits down at the table beside Harry. Harry feels he ought to be giving Quinn a rub down and squirting water into his mouth. All that jabbing must have tired the old man.

But, the next day, Quinn is up and jabbing again. Kopinski's final witness is Clair Lipsett, the regional roads commissioner. Lipsett, a thin stooping man with heavy horn-rimmed glasses is supposed to clinch the case. Lipsett certainly looks like a scientist, a man who works with figures and is not moved by transient passions.

Kopinski takes Lipsett through seven years of cordon counts. Lipsett has been keeping track of the cars coming into downtown. There is no doubt traffic has been getting bad. If they don't have the expressway, it is going to get one whole hell of a lot worse. Common sense would tell you that, but just in case there is any doubt, Lipsett has the hard figures to prove it. Vehicles entering the downtown have been increasing at a rate of three-point-eight per cent a year for the last five years.

"Mr. Lipsett, you are aware, I would think, of the modal split for downtown?" Quinn asks.

"Yes, of course I am."

"Would you please describe that modal split for the board?"

"Seventy/thirty."

"Mr. Lipsett, the board may not be as aware of transportation terminology as you and I are. Would you kindly elaborate for them?"

"It means seventy per cent of the people coming downtown use public transportation—streetcars, buses, and the subway. The other thirty per cent use cars. But it's not just cars we need the expressway for, Mr. Quinn." Lipsett is beaming maliciously now.

"There's trucks, Mr. Quinn! Everybody talks about cars, they forget about all the trucks that have to get downtown. What about them, Mr. Quinn?"

"Mr. Lipsett, if there were more public transportation, another subway perhaps, more people would leave their cars at home and, therefore, would there not be more room for trucks on the existing streets?"

"There is no way to know that. We have no figures."

"But would you agree with me that it is at least a possibility?"

"I couldn't deny that."

"Would you then also agree that building an expressway is not the only means open to us for solving our traffic problems."

"No, I would not agree with that statement."

"Thank you, Mr. Lipsett. I have no further questions."

More points for Quinn. But again, in the re-examination, Kopinski goes over those scary cordon counts. Harry worries that board members will go home and have nightmares about hordes of cars desperately trying to creep through the downtown streets.

"What more have you got for me?" Quinn asks Harry.

They are up on the roof of the Park Plaza. Harold has brought them double scotches. They should be back at the office, working, but they are too bone tired. They have decided they will go home, get a few hours' sleep, come to the office at four in the morning. The hearing doesn't begin until 9:30. They will have time to prepare.

"I've got an environmentalist who's going to talk about all the shit cars put into the air," Harry says. "And a stockie who's going to say another bond issue could knock back the city's triple-A rating."

"Not bad," Quinn says. "But will it be enough?"

"You bet it will!" Harry says enthusiastically. "We're really hurting them now. You just stay in there and keep punching away."

22

DANE THOUGHT he had got rid of them. But now the leaders of Citizens Against the Berryman Expressway have returned to the back booth of the Imperial Restaurant. Alan Gilchrist says grimly that media reports of the hearing are turning the public against CABE. They need a dramatic gesture. They are going to blockade Berryman Avenue.

"You said anything else was a waste of time!" Victoria Sommers says. "Those were your exact words."

"Yes, I remember," Dane says.

"You said you'd come with us," Don McPartland, the small, worried-looking actuary, says.

"I remember that too," Dane says quietly.

He does his best to frighten them. They will go where there is a traffic light so at least the cars will be stopped when they sit down. But there is always the possibility that when the light turns green, some crazy bastard will try to run over them. And even if nobody is that nuts, they can count on people getting out of their cars and trucks, yelling abuse, and quite possibly assaulting the demonstrators.

"So we are really stupid people?" Peter Strassner says.

"I didn't say that," Dane says.

"Yes, you did. And you are absolutely right. We are very stupid people. Politics is about power and money, eh? Not about ideas. And never, ever, not in a million years, is politics about doing good. All politicians are corrupt, and city politicians are absolutely corrupt. Who doesn't know that, eh? They run for office only so they can steal. These local aldermen, they're all in the pockets of the big developers. There is no way they are ever going to pay attention to stupid little people like us. Yes?"

"Those are your words, not mine," Dane says.

"But it's true!" Strassner says. "And, listen, it gets worse. We have the same interests as the people we are fighting against. We own houses, at least most of us do, and when we say we are saving the neighbourhood, they can turn around to say to us, 'You are just afraid the expressway will lower the value of your property.' So why do we think we are better than anybody else?"

"Okay, I'll bite," Dane says. "Why are you better than anyone else?"

"Two reasons: one, because nobody, no matter how saintly they want to be, can avoid doing something for themselves once in a while. And, on the other hand, nobody, no matter how selfish they want to be, can avoid doing something for somebody else once in a while. So everybody is a little bit dirty and a little bit clean.

"So yes, we want to keep our houses, but also these old streets have oak trees and maple trees and these streets are good places for everybody to walk in. They are good for the soul. So we are doing everything we can to keep these old neighbourhoods from being turned into an expressway cloverleaf.

"But how do we know this is going to make any difference in the world? The answer is: we don't know. All we can do is hope for the best. So now we are ready to sit down in front of the cars. We are going to put our soft, white, middle-class asses out there on the front lines. As my Jesuit friends from South America would say, we are bearing witness. That has to be worth something too.

"You know, I think...now that I think about it...I think I have given you, maybe, two and a half reasons."

"I lost count," Dane says.

"What counts is whether or not you are coming with us," Victoria Sommers says abruptly. "Because, if you're not, there's not much point in us talking to you, is there?"

But before Dane can answer, Jimmy comes stomping out of the kitchen. He is angry and he doesn't mind at all showing it front of Dane's friends. Five people are sitting there, waiting to give their orders. Is Dane working here or not?

Poor Jimmy, Dane is thinking. Does he have any idea how perfect his timing is?

"I'm sorry, Jimmy, I really am," Dane says. He removes his white counterman's apron and hands it back to the owner of the Imperial Restaurant. "I guess it's time for me to move on."

23

THROUGH THE NIGHT, while earnest telephone conversations rattled across the city, there was talk of three hundred, maybe even five hundred people marching into the middle of Berryman Avenue. But, in the clear, chilly light of a Thursday afternoon, only thirty-seven people have gathered in the basement of the Landrigan Street United Church.

But these are the faithful. Dane Harrison tells them a little story about an old friend of his in New York, Igal Roodenko. Roodenko organized the first demonstration against the war in Vietnam. Roodenko's little War

Resisters League went out to picket the hotel where Madame Nhu, the wife of the Vietnamese dictator, was staying, and all they could get was twenty people. Only a couple of years later, there were five hundred thousand people marching around the Pentagon.

Annabel feels so proud. Dane rests one hip on a table, lanky gunfighter–style, and lays out for these nervous straights what they are getting into. This is the old Dane, the man who leads by quiet conviction. This is the man Annabel chose for herself. If you're attacked physically, roll into the famous foetal ball. This is the best way to protect your vital parts, especially if someone is kicking you. When the cops come, go limp. If we're going to have any impact, we can't be seen on television just marching meekly into the paddy wagons. Make the cops drag you away. Do not, under any circumstances, respond to violence by getting violent yourself. We don't want any brawls out there.

These people are, for the most part, teachers, social workers, business consultants, engineers, even a few ministers in black shirt fronts and white turned-around collars. It comforts these people, Annabel can see, to know they are being led into this extraordinary activity by a man who is also a professional in his field.

"Don't let the cops know if you're hurt, even if you think they've done it deliberately. They'll just charge you with resisting arrest. Good luck, keep cool, and as Dick Gregory said to us just before we set out on the march in Chicago, 'May the good Lord have fun with you.'"

They move out of the church basement, carrying hastily painted placards saying "Stop the Berryman" and "Save Our City." They march through the streets to the anthem of the American civil rights movement, a solemn spiritual they have heard so many times on television but never dreamed they would one day be singing themselves: "O, deep in my heart, I do believe...we shall overcome some day."

Doreen Margulies holds tightly to Annabel's hand. People on the sidewalks are moving aside and then turning to look at the straggling line of demonstrators. Some faces are hostile; most are indifferent; a few are smiling and friendly, wishing them well. Doreen envies them all. They can stay where they are and be safe, but Doreen is being dragged along. She can't remember ever feeling so frightened.

Doreen should not even be here. Harry said the last thing in the world he needed right now was for the wife of the CABE lawyer to be arrested. But the wife of the CABE lawyer has allowed another man to touch her, and make love to her. Harry said the media boys would go into a frenzy if Doreen got taken in. Harry is probably right. But Doreen can no longer listen only to her husband; she needs to be cleansed and made whole again. Doreen has to do that for herself.

They are at the intersection now. The light has turned green. They are marching out into the middle of Berryman Avenue. They are singing, "Deep in my heart, I do believe, we'll walk hand in hand…" Dane is at the front of the line. He sits down. The singing stops. In the sudden, isolating silence, the others follow Dane and sit down in front of the cars. Dane looks down the line of demonstrators. Some have already linked arms. Good…beautiful! Just stay peaceful, folks. This isn't going to last too long.

Dane looks up. Holy shit! He is in front of a goddamned diesel tractor-trailer. The fucking thing is huge. If Dane stood up now, he would not reach the hood ornament. The bastard is racing his motor. It's possible he cannot even see the man sitting in the lotus position in front of his right wheel. The cocksucker can say he never knew anyone was there. The light is orange. The light is turning green. The diesel motor begins to grind.

Dane Harrison is not moving. It's a little difficult under such circumstances to analyse one's own reactions, but Dane decides there are two reasons why he is keeping his legs folded exactly where they are. One, he wants the approval of the people he is with. They are hardly brothers; they are not even comrades. But, in Chicago, he had been alone and he ran away. Nobody was watching; nobody knew but Dane himself. Here he has been introduced to people as a leader. Maybe inside of every brave, reticent hero there is an egomaniac struggling to get out. Be that as it may, Dane will not let them down. Two, he really believes in what they are doing out here. Just a small group of people trying to save a few blocks of the city, but just imagine the world if everybody made their own turf a little better place.

The diesel truck in front of Dane growls and thunders. Fuck you, buddy. The twin exhausts in back of the cab snort oily black smoke. The wheels strain against the asphalt. The thing is getting ready to charge. Dane starts an old union song that became a peacenik song; the others pick it up.

"We shall not, we shall not be moved…we shall not, we shall not be moved…just like a tree that's standing by the wa-ah-ter, we shall not be moved!"

The police have arrived. They have begun to haul people away. Doreen gets angry at them. Why can't they take her first? She has got separated somehow from Annabel. Why can't the police pull Doreen away to safety right now? She is so alone in the midst of this crowd. These other people want to stop an expressway, but Doreen is sitting out here in the name of love. She told Morry Weiss she didn't want to see him again, but he didn't believe her. She didn't believe it herself. But tonight, on the six o'clock news, Morry will see her being dragged away in the name of the cause Doreen's husband is serving. He will understand that Doreen Margulies has thrown in her lot with her husband. With one private and public act of sacrifice, Doreen Margulies is putting her life in order.

A policeman is wrapping his arms around her upper body. She slumps over her knees, as instructed. The policeman's arms are as thick as tree trunks. The slick hardness of his nylon winter jacket rubs against the back of Doreen's head. A bright light is shining in her face. The TV people are really here. Harry was wrong to be afraid. The world will see that the wife of the CABE lawyer is just as committed to the cause as he is. But somebody has grabbed her by the bum. A policeman has hold of her bum and he is lifting her off the ground. His fingers are digging right up into the crotch of her blue jeans. Ow! Ow!…It hurts like hell! Policemen are not supposed to do things like this! They are thrusting her forward. Doreen is on all fours on the metal floor of the patrol wagon. She tries to look around, but the door is closing behind her.

24

HARRY MARGULIES smashes his fist into a wall. The force of the blow rattles the walnut barometer and the paintings of straining fishermen that adorn the office of J. Arthur Quinn.

"We could get her out, you know," Quinn says mildly. He has his legs slung up on his desk, a yellow legal pad resting on his knees. They have come back to the office to collaborate on his final address to the Municipal Board. The witnesses have all been heard. Tomorrow the lawyers will make their final pitch.

"What do you mean, get her out? A fruit-cake with a hacksaw in it?"

"Harry, this is a very old and well-established law firm. Some of our former colleagues are on the bench..."

The possibility of actually rescuing Doreen distracts Harry for a moment from his anger. But how could Doreen have done this to him? Just when he should be concentrating all his energy and intellectual strength on the final battle at the OMB, he has to turn away and start worrying about a wife who has no more common sense than God gave geese. Doreen is lucky she is in the can tonight. If she was right here, right now, by God he'd throttle her.

"Sit down, Harry. Have a cup of tea."

"It's no good," Harry says roughly. "The others'll blab, for sure. Great story, eh? CABE lawyer pulls strings to get wife out."

"You'll have to be there in the morning, Harry."

"You can't send me to magistrates' court." Harry's voice becomes a whine. "The media guys'll be all over me."

"I know. But I can't go myself, obviously. Don't worry about the press, Harry. We'll win this one—or, quite possibly, lose it—on the strength of our arguments, not because of anything our asinine clients have taken it upon themselves to do."

"What time are they coming up?"

"God knows. You may be there all day."

"Shee-it!"

Harry punches the wall again. The shock travels from his arm right up to his head; his knuckles are turning red and one of them is bleeding. Harry slumps down in a chair and accepts a Royal Doulton fluted white and gold porcelain cup filled with smoky Darjeeling tea.

"Tomorrow," Quinn says, "I figure we should start heavy: the official plan that was never made official; the expressway that was never formally approved. Your guy who said they never considered alternative routes'll be a big help there. Then we hit the environmental stuff—noise and the poisoned air. We finish up pounding on the finances, how they're just making it up as they go along."

"No good," Harry says.

"Why not? What's wrong with it?"

"It's what Kopinski's going to do. Chapter and verse; he says it's justified. You say it's not justified. That's not enough. We're the outsiders. You've got come up with something bigger, Arthur."

"What, exactly, do you have in mind, Harry?"

"I don't know! I wish I did. All I can tell you is I've been sitting there for days, watching the faces of those three bastards, and we haven't got through to them. They know damned well that if they step in and stop that expressway, every alderman from here to Hudson Bay is going to be after them...an appointed tribunal overruling elected politicians...dictatorship from Queen's Park. The board's waiting for us to show them how they can cover their asses. So far, we haven't done that."

"You think the whole of our case is less than the parts?"

"I guess that's what I'm saying, Arthur. And I'm the guy who put it together, right?"

"Hmnn...you may have a point," Quinn says. He stares into the legal pad on his knees as though it were a crystal ball.

Harry waits anxiously. Quinn takes a large white pill from a bottle on his desk and yellow capsule from another bottle. It frightens Harry when Quinn starts gulping his heart medicine like this. Harry is thinking that if Harry Margulies were really smart, he would keep his mouth shut now and let the great J. Arthur Quinn do things the way he has always done them. If Quinn loses this one, and it looks like he is going to, Harry Margulies may well be able to cover himself by keeping as much distance as possible between himself and Quinn. But Harry has decided, to hell with it. If Quinn is going to get rapped for this one, Harry Margulies is going down too. Harry thinks of himself and J. Arthur Quinn as being in this together, a pair of warriors. Which is proof positive, Harry knows, that he is not at all as smart as some people think he is.

"What you are really urging on me," Quinn says at last, "is the 'Uncle Mike defence.'"

"What the hell is that?"

"The secret weapon of Carlton and Boggs. One of our colleagues in corporate litigation has an Uncle Mike who never likes to pay traffic tickets. He's figured out that if he waits 'til they haul him into court, nine times out of ten the traffic cops'll never show up and he'll get off. But, one day, they're laying for him. Six cops stand up and give evidence on his back tickets. He's up for a grand or more in fines. So the judge turns to him and says, 'Well, what have you got to say for yourself?' Mike stands up and says to the judge, 'I was in the Canadian army for six years. I went ashore at D-Day. I always pay my taxes and I'm a good Canadian and I love the Queen.' The judge turns to Mike's wife: 'Is this man with you?' She says, 'Yes.' 'Then get him out of here,' the judge says."

"I don't follow," Harry says.

"It's not complicated, Harry. When you can't think of anything else to do, stand up and talk crazy."

"That is not what I am telling you to do, Arthur."

"Yes, you are, my friend. And you are dead right."

25

"TAKE OFF your clothes, please."

Doreen stares at the policewoman. She has been expecting this. Everybody talked about it when they were still at the station house being booked. Nobody seemed too worried about being searched. Doreen never dreamed she would feel so lonely. At the station house, people were divided into groups and then shown into adjoining cells, but the only thing that made it feel oppressive were the bright lights. They were set deep in the ceiling and seemed to increase in intensity as they bounced off the tile walls. But the CABE people were a brotherhood. They joked about getting off the charges by pleading insanity and not being allowed across the American border any more. Even the rough-looking people who had been brought in for real crimes laughed too.

When Dane came back from talking to the police higher-ups, he led everybody in singing "We Shall Overcome," and some people began to cry. Doreen cried a little too. She was so proud of them all, and proud of herself for being in their company. But the police kept the CABE people in the station house too long. Doreen began to feel unbearably weary. All she wanted to do was go home and go to bed. It seemed to take the police forever to get enough patrol wagons to take them to the central jail on Riverdale Avenue.

"Please," the young, honey-blonde, fresh-faced policewoman is saying to her. "You would be amazed at the things people try to bring in here."

Doreen is confused. She still has not done anything about undressing. There are three uniformed policewomen in this plain, windowless room. Resistance would be impossible. Oh well, Annabel must have gone through this too.

Doreen hands over her leather jacket and kicks off her shoes and takes off her blue jeans and her turtle-neck sweater.

The two older policewomen go through the pockets and run their hands all through her clothing.

"Underwear too," the young policewoman says. She seems to be in charge, even though she looks so young.

Doreen does not move. Undressing in front of other women is nothing. But to be ordered to do so is unbearable.

"Come on, let's get this over with, eh?" the young policewoman says. There is menace in her voice now.

Doreen removes her bra and hands it over. Let them feel the padding; everybody has their insecurities. She slips her tights and underpants off and hands them over too. God, how can anybody want to do things like this to other people?

"Turn around, please. Bend forward. Rest your elbows on the table."

The grey-haired policewoman is pulling a clear plastic glove out of a box. This is unbelievable. The sense that it is all unreal, that it is not happening at all, sustains Doreen. It feels no worse, after all, than a doctor's exam. She is beyond humiliation now. She just wants to get out of here and put her head down and fall asleep.

"Take out the tampon, please."

They have gone too far. This is too stupid.

"It's just a tampon."

"I know that," the young policewoman says. "You know what I pulled out of someone last night? Half a pound of high-grade hash."

She holds out a paper towel to Doreen. Doreen would like to be helpful, she really would, because she wants to get out of here. But she just cannot make herself take part in something that is so awful.

The young policewoman gives a sigh of impatience. Doreen feels herself being grabbed from behind again. She kicks out and then her legs are held. She feels the roughness of the paper towel being pressed against her. In an instant, it is done.

She is on her feet again. They hand Doreen her clothes. They give her a pad to stuff in the front of her underpants. She turns her back on them while she dresses. This isn't rape by any means, but surely to God this must be what rape feels like. When she is fully dressed, she turns to the three policewomen, fixing them in her memory, treating them to her scorn.

"You brought this on yourself," the young one says resentfully.

The simple truth stuns Doreen. The words stay with her as she is led to join the others in the cells upstairs. She cannot sleep now. Long into the night she sits up, wide awake, in a corner of the cell, staring gloomily up at the moon through the barred window, listening to the troubled breathing around her.

Everybody, Doreen is thinking, Annabel, Dane, me, Harry—especially Harry!—everybody's doing what they have to do. Just like the cops do what they have to do. But what's the point in it all? Even when you're trying to do something good, like stop a stupid expressway, you're hurting somebody else. So that gives them the right to turn around and hurt you. There's no end to it. That beautiful young policewoman was right: everything that happens to you is your own fault. You make your own troubles. But I don't want to be like this. I don't want to spend my whole life hitting out and then waiting for other people to hit back at me.

26

THE HOUSE feels eerie, off balance, as though it has been uprooted and gone floating down the street. Gordon Margulies lies stiffly in his bed. He tries, but he cannot remember the stages of the dream. It may not even be over.

Someone is running down the hall. Gordon considers his own breathing.

"Gordon! Are you all right?" It's Paola's mother.

"Yeah, I'm okay."

"You called out?"

"I guess so."

She sits beside him on the bed. She places her hand on his forehead. It feels very heavy and wet, not at all like his mother's thin hand.

"Can I go in with my mother?"

"She's not here, Gordy. She and Dane and Annabel have gone away. But they'll be back tomorrow."

"Oh," Gordon says. Below him, he hears Paul snorting as he tries to wriggle into a more comfortable position. Gordon begins to feel better. His friend is still with him. Paul's funny though: he moves around a lot and sometimes even says things in his sleep, but he never gets up.

"You just had a nightmare, son." Harry has come to the door. His large form stands out reassuringly, clearly, in the light from the hall.

"Try to get back to sleep, Gordon. School tomorrow."

His father bends over to kiss him. He is awkward because he has to keep hold of the glass with the ice cubes at the same time. But he smells sweaty and good.

Vivian pulls the covers up around the boy and tucks them in tightly.

"We're right here if you need us," she says. She follows Harry out of the bedroom and down to the kitchen.

"You could have told me you were here," she says angrily.

"I just got back."

"Have you heard anything?"

"Yeah, they're fine. They come up in the morning. I'll get them out."

Vivian helps herself to a scotch from the bottle Harry has set out on the kitchen table. It's almost two in the morning. She was working so hard on her new piece, "Woman Sitting: #29," that she lost all track of time.

"I'm not used to this," Harry says. "It's too quiet."

"That's because nobody's here," Vivian says.

"Yeah. Just us. We're nobody," Harry says. He holds up his glass.

Vivian smiles at him and clinks her glass to his. He really is a goof.

"I'm going to take a bath and try to get some rest," Harry says. "I've got another big day coming up."

"I want a bath too," Vivian says.

"I'll flip you for who goes first," Harry says.

But the same thought has occurred to both of them.

Why not? It's late and it would save time. This is a strange night, anyway. They both want to get to sleep. The others don't have to know anything about it but so what if they do? Aren't the people in this house supposed to be one big family?

Vivian is in the tub first. She is sitting back with water rising up to her shoulders when Harry comes in. He turns his back to her while he takes off his paisley robe and his silly-looking boxer shorts. He slides into the tub, facing her.

"What the hell is that?"

Oh, dear, Vivian forgot. She begins to giggle.

"It's bath oil," she says. "Lily of the valley."

"Oh, that's great!" Harry says. "I'll smell beautiful in court tomorrow."

It's very interesting about Jews. Vivian has heard they have much more hair than WASPS. This one certainly has shiny, vigorous black curls all down his chest and back. It's quite attractive, really. Her husband's body hair was like peach fuzz.

"You want to know something funny?" Harry says. "I was around a little, eh? But, since Doreen, I've never even looked at another woman."

"Well, you're certainly seeing one now," Vivian snaps. "Stand up and turn around. I'll do your back."

Harry does as he is told. She begins working on his thick shoulders. Her mind is filled with thoughts of her lover. Marta said such reckless, hurtful things to her.

"Okay, enough," Harry says. "Now, I'll do you." He turns to face Vivian. He takes the soap from her hand begins spreading the smooth lather over her heavy breasts and down her thighs. Harry knows what is going to happen next. It is so simple and so right, he doesn't even have to think about it.

Afterward, Harry lies with his head cupped on his hands, looking at Vivian's painting of herself on the easel. One whole wall is covered with self-portraits of Vivian in standing and sitting positions. The woman really ought to find something new to work on. She's getting a little stale. Vivian lies beside him on the mattress, snoring contentedly. No whispered confessions and tender cuddling for Vivian. When it was over, she shoved him away and fell asleep immediately.

It was more like a wrestling match than making love. They didn't even look at each other. There have been times with Doreen, quite wonderful times really, when he had the thrilling sensation that they were trying to do each other in. But with Vivian, he felt they were just trying to beat each other up. His back is covered with scratches. He's going to have a fine time trying to keep those hidden from Doreen until they heal.

So, obviously what he and Vivian have been doing together doesn't matter. Harry hasn't taken anything away from his wife. If Doreen had been here tonight, he would have woken her up and done it with her. Harry just needed it. He was all wound up. So how has he hurt Doreen?

How would Doreen hurt him if she did the same thing? It's not very likely, but what would Harry feel if Doreen opened up her legs and let someone else enter that place where only Harry Margulies has ever gone before? Would he be furious? Would he feel rejected? Would he be overcome by an insane need for revenge? None of the above—Harry goes over the possibilities and realizes he would only feel a deep sadness for Doreen. It is the same sadness he feels now for himself. They were both so young when they started going together. It's only years later you wake up and realize what you have got yourself into.

Doreen is still the only person he wants to be with; there is no question about that. Only now, there are going to be more games in their lives. He and Doreen are going to be telling each other a lot of lies. Probably this is the way most people live. But Harry Margulies still loves his wife. And, curiously enough, he feels more protective about her than he ever did before.

27

IF J. ARTHUR QUINN were Ralph Kopinski this morning, he'd at least have some fun. The lawyer for the region builds his case like an old-time carpenter, nailing in one board at a time: every city and regional council decision in favour of extending Berryman Avenue going all the way back to 1943; a stack of plans and consultants' reports, each supporting the expressway; citations of each occasion, year, month, and day, when the province gave de facto recognition to the official plan and, in effect, the expressway network by contributing money to it. If Quinn had all that good stuff to work with, he'd take half the time and put on twice as good a show. But Kopinski will do, Quinn reflects sourly. Kopinski will do. He may be droning on now, but he's getting everything he needs entered in as evidence, and when everybody has gone home, those three unimaginative, suet-faced members of the Ontario Municipal Board will have it all sitting on a table in front of them.

"...and so, as you have heard from the regional chairman, with supporting evidence from the regional treasurer, Norval Sissons, the Region can support the expressway bond issue—and indeed could service a much larger debt if it had to...

"Mr. Chairman, members of the board, the Berryman Extension has the long-standing commitment of all levels of government. The expressway plan is a promise to the people of this region. They are confident you will order that promise to be kept."

The hearing-room explodes with raucous applause. There has been no competition for seats this morning. The CABE people are three blocks away, over in magistrate's court, entering pleas and getting dates set for their trials. Harry Margulies is with them. J. Arthur Quinn feels very lonely. The board chairman has to rap his gavel and call for order several times before he can quell the cheering for Kopinski's speech.

Quinn walks slowly to the lectern. He places upon it a heavy three-ring binder. He opens the binder and begins to flip through pages, apparently seeking the arguments he intends to start with. He finds what he wants. He studies it for a moment. He looks up at the board. He pushes his old-fashioned rimless glasses firmly back from the bridge of his long nose. By the time Quinn has finished, everyone is watching him suspiciously. The room is absolutely quiet.

"Mr. Chairman, members of the board, there is nothing wrong with an expressway," Quinn says—and pauses—"that building another expressway won't cure."

Small eddies of nervous laughter can be heard behind Quinn. Even Vito Alcamo's admirers have to admit that's a pretty good opening line.

"Mr. Chairman, I'm not going to waste your time this morning by disputing the historical evidence my friend has so diligently laid before you—except on one crucial point," Quinn says.

"De facto recognition, no matter how many times it is given, is still not equivalent to the process...including the crucial, all-important opportunity for the public to speak up and be heard...by which a regional municipality makes an official plan and the provincial government approves it, thereby giving it legal force.

"So this board may, if it so chooses, order the regional municipality to stop the Berryman Expressway and go back and take the time to make a proper official plan.

"You need have no fear you are acting beyond your powers and that it will be said an appointed tribunal has overruled the duly elected municipal councillors. You are yourselves appointed by an elected body, the provincial government, and in this respect, you stand today in the shoes of the Minister of Municipal Affairs.

"Under the Canadian constitutional arrangement, municipalities derive the powers they exercise from provincial governments. Municipalities are, as the popular terminology has it, 'creatures of the provinces.' So, it is my submission to you, that it is entirely within your powers to act as my clients are asking you to do."

Kopinski slumps down in his seat. So far, so good. The old fart isn't going to score any points telling OMB members what they already know.

"But why on earth should you take such a drastic action?" Quinn demands. His voice begins taking on depth and colour. He must be about to get into his substantial arguments but Kopinski isn't worried. Kopinski is sure the board members have seen *The Daily News* this morning, the big front-page picture of cops dragging Quinn's clients away from the middle of Berryman Avenue. They must know Quinn is representing a gang of fools.

"I submit that there are good and sufficient grounds for halting the expressway and ordering the creation of an official plan—notwithstanding all the legal and historic precedents my friend has set before you...

"You cannot know the future. You cannot foresee what is going to happen in the city.

"My friend cites consultants' reports predicting a doubling, even a tripling, of automobile traffic downtown within the next twenty years and warning of chaos unless we have the expressway network, but I draw your attention to page thirty-seven of the Rollins-Newkirk study of the Waterfront Expressway, marked exhibit number eighty-one. In nineteen fifty-nine, just one year after the Gardiner Expressway opened, three of the four exit ramps into downtown were already crowded to capacity.

"The only way to get relief for this congestion is to build another expressway. And when that is filled, to build another one. When do you stop, gentlemen? How can you be sure you are doing what the future requires you to do?

"My friend has submitted to you the nineteen forty-three plan as evidence of the historic roots of the Berryman Expressway. If you turn to page seventeen of that plan, you will see that it called for the replacement of all housing below the Escarpment and the Canadian Pacific railway tracks—almost the entire southern half of the city!—with apartment blocks. That whole vast area was considered a slum in the forties.

"There was no way anyone could have predicted that eager young couples migrating in from the suburbs would buy the old houses, renovate and rebuild them and turn the Grove and other downtown neighbourhoods once again into cheerful, bustling communities.

"The future is made up of thousands of individual, unpredictable decisions.

"Just as the civic leadership of the nineteen forties could not have foreseen the rejuvenation of the inner city, so the leadership of today cannot be absolutely certain that automobile traffic into downtown will increase exponentially, as they claim."

Quinn ostentatiously closes up his binder. It makes a loud crack. The whole room knows now that he is through with figures and planning reports. He moves away from the lectern and steps towards the dais where the board members are sitting. Kopinski straightens up and leans across the table, straining to catch every word. Damn Quinn! People forget he spent years doing criminal work. He's talking so fervently and so intimately to the OMB members now you'd think they were the jury in a murder trial.

"My friend has not, for all his numbers and charts, proven beyond the shadow of a doubt the need for an expressway. But there can be no doubt about the impact of extending Berryman Avenue—the destruction of some of our finest neighbourhoods.

"We are told the expressway network is a promise to people in the suburbs and particularly to those who bought homes in Woodhurst. But what about people now buying into new subdivisions just beyond the borders of the region? Will they, too, not soon be demanding new roads?

"One can foresee a hearing at this board in which the issue is whether the lovely old streets in Woodhurst should be sacrificed for a new expressway—an extension of the Berryman Expressway, in fact!—in order to serve a newer ring of suburbs.

"What my friend is asking you to endorse is 'the disposable city.' When one part has become a little used, we simply toss it aside.

"That is the cannibal city, feeding on itself.

"My clients have often been described as 'radicals' and 'extremists.' But notwithstanding their actions yesterday, they are the true conservatives here. They are seeking to preserve the city that already exists.

"It is my final submission to you that building an expressway is an act of faith. Its supporters cannot with facts alone justify ramming a superhighway into the heart of the city; they can only hope the expressway will turn out to be as beneficial as they claim.

"Stopping an expressway is equally an act of faith.

"If you want to build a city for cars, the Berryman Expressway is a good place to begin. If you want to build a city for people, the Berryman Expressway is a good place to stop.

"Mr. Chairman, members of the board, that completes my case."

28

THIS IS the last thing Doreen expected to find. The sign says "For Sale," and over it, a diagonal paper sticker has been added with a cheerful three-word message: "Sold, Gino Emilio." Peering through the window, Doreen can see that the counters and shelves have been taken out. The store is empty. The arch of raised white letters on the window still proclaims "Weiss's Kosher Style Poultry," but everything else is gone. Doreen pounds on the door.

There is no response. She steps back and looks up to the second floor. One window still has curtains. But there are no lights.

There is a narrow, shadowy concrete walk between the store and the home beside it. Doreen calls up what little resolution she still has left and goes down it. She stands on her tiptoes and looks in the back window. There are open cardboard boxes in the centre of the floor, half-filled with crockery and books. Morry is sitting at an old, cracked white porcelain table, his head down on his folded arms.

Doreen knocks on the window. Morry shakes himself and lifts his head. His eyes are watery; his face is deathly pale. The long, beautiful silver hair is flat and lifeless, falling in all directions. Morry pulls himself up and lets her in.

"Morry, why? What's happening?"

"Nothing's happening. We sold the store, that's all. My mother died. My brother and sister want the money."

"Where are you going?"

"I'm going to Israel."

"Why?"

His shoulders hunch, the sad, diffident, shrug. A small, ironic, saintly smile comes to his frozen lips.

"Israel is for refugees. I'm a refugee."

"I'm coming with you."

As soon as she says it, Doreen knows this is why she has come here.

Morry does not move. He has returned to his chair beside the kitchen table. He remains there, watching her.

"You have a son..."

"I'll take him with us—if I can."

Morry nods in agreement. He has been a father before; he can be a father again. That's the easy part.

"It's a kibbutz, Doreen. Up in the north, near the Syrian border. My cousin's there. He says it's pretty rough."

"Morry...take me with you."

His arms feel clumsy around her. She has offered her whole life to a stranger. She must be mad. But she doesn't feel insane at all. Doreen Margulies feels cool and rational. If this is a mistake, she is ready to pay for it. But Morry Weiss is something she never expected to find in her life. Morry is a man who feels the world as keenly as Doreen herself does. Harry will never know that kind of intensity. He can't even imagine it. Morry is gentle and kind too; Doreen is sure of that, although she cannot say she has real proof. All she knows for certain is that she cannot let Morry go to Israel while she stays here, trying to keep up her marriage to Harry Margulies. Beyond that, may God protect her—even if she doesn't know the words to any prayers. She just has to do this. Doreen presses her face against his chest. She has begun to cry.

"I'm not going to say I love you," she whispers. "Not yet."

"I know. It's okay." He bends forward and kisses her on the cheek. "Do you know that line from 'The Family of Man'? 'We two form a multitude.' That's us, honey. You and me. We two are going to form a multitude."

29

FROM a column by Bobby Mulloy in *The Daily News*

> So…after the OMB released their decision on the Berryman, it was a tale of two cities.
>
> In City Hall, there was gloom and doom. When I dropped in on Willy Ferrier, the regional planning commissioner, he said downtown was going to choke to death on cars, and someday they'd realize their faithful servant had been right all along.
>
> I tiptoed quietly out of Ferrier's office. I can't stand to see a grown man cry.
>
> Downstairs, in the big front office, I found the Regional Chairman huddling with his best buddies, Finance commissioner Norrie Sissons and Ralph Kopinski, the Region's lawyer.
>
> "We have not yet begun to fight," the chairman said, or words to that effect.
>
> There are, to be sure, some moves they can still make, an appeal to the provincial cabinet and maybe even going to court and working

their way right up to the Supreme Court.

But my guess is it's the end of the road for the Berryman Extension. The OMB decision doesn't leave much room for manoeuvring. Not only did the board buy all J. Arthur Quinn's arguments, they added a few of their own, stuff about how there was no point in building multimillion-dollar expressways to pour cars into a small grid of nineteenth-century downtown streets designed for horses and buggies.

Over at the roof bar of the Park Plaza, when the Great Quinn stepped off the elevator, there was a such a burst of clapping and cheering, I'm sure it must have been heard all over the city.

Harry Margulies was right behind him. Gossip on the street is that the sorcerer's apprentice is about to get his name on the Carlton and Boggs letterhead.

The party at the Plaza's quiet, old roof bar was a scene not to be believed. It was like carnival time in Rio. The OMB decision came out at 3:00 p.m. and by 3:15 people from the Grove were beginning to gather at the Park Plaza.

By the time I got up there, the bar was packed, and people were filling up the terrace outside. I asked Victoria Sommers how they'd been able to put this bash together so quickly, and she said nobody'd organized it. People just went to the roof because it's their local pub and they wanted to celebrate.

You can certainly understand them wanting to have a bash. Citizens Against the Berryman Expressway came out of nowhere and, against all odds, stopped an expressway and brought the whole regional government to its knees...

30

VIVIAN BILLINGHURST sits alone on the porch, her feet up on the railing, watching the people go by. Those going north are pulling bundle-buggies, on their way to Dupont Street to shop for groceries in the Power Store.

Those going south are holding small children by the hand. They are on their way down to Kendal park, to play on the swings and slides and do exotic things in the sandbox. Vivian gives them all her silent blessing, she wishes them well in their future lives. Summer has come at last to the Grove. The maple trees, the oak and beech trees are thick with dark green leaves. The air is warm and heavy.

Dane and Annabel left yesterday. They hugged Vivian and kissed her and promised to keep in touch. Probably they will, too. Dane and Annabel are conscientious people.

Harry Margulies was the big surprise. Vivian expected him to fight like hell. She couldn't imagine Harry giving up something he thought he owned. But, in the end, he didn't hassle Doreen. He even let her take Gordon. Harry said he just wasn't equipped to look after a kid by himself.

When Harry left, he shook hands with Vivian and kissed her on the cheek. Harry has promised he will do all the paper work for her divorce and go to court for her when she is ready. She knows, without asking, that Harry will not send a bill. Of all the people in the house, the last person Vivian ever thought she would call "friend" was Harry Margulies. But that's the way things have worked out.

A noisy, rusty pickup truck pulls up in front of the house. Two young men get out. They are long-haired and wasted-looking, but they've offered to do the job for twenty dollars, and money is going to be an important consideration from now on. Vivian got their names from a bulletin board in the laundromat.

She takes them upstairs to the back bedroom where the girls are sitting amid their boxes and suitcases, reading comic books. Gordon and Paul were unhappy about leaving the house and hung onto each other. But Sasha and Paola are content with going. In their new home, Vivian has promised, they will have rooms of their own.

The scruffy moving men dismantle the bed and carry it out to the truck. They take all the girls' stuff first, and then Vivian leads them up to the attic to get her paintings, all wrapped in brown paper and blankets, and her old mattress.

It takes barely an hour to load the truck. Vivian pulls the door shut behind them. She drops the key through the mailbox, so the landlord can find it. The house on Landrigan Street is empty now, ready for new tenants.

2

LOVERS: 1971

Vivian Billinghurst, Marta Persofski, and Trevor Billinghurst discover the meaning of success and the truth about art

31

November 14, 10:00 a.m. Subject Billinghurst emerged from house, 310 Kerr Street. Subject holding hands with Persofski. Subject and Persofski proceeded down to College Street. Subject kissed Persofski and whispered in her ear.

November 17, 2:00 p.m. Subject observed walking over hills in High Park with Persofski. Subject observed kissing Persofski seventeen times…

November 19, 8:00 p.m. Subject observed at Troy's restaurant, corner table with Marta Persofski. Subject observed talking with Persofski in intimate manner. Observer believes Persofski and subject maintaining hand contact under table, but this cannot be confirmed…

TREVOR BILLINGHURST imagines the detective sniggering as he types this stuff. Until this report landed on his desk Trevor could honestly say he felt no bitterness towards Vivian—in spite of the terrible things she has done to him. But, by God, he is starting to hate her now. He reads on. He has to know it all, the worst of it.

You can say I'm being stupid and paranoid, but I want my kids back. That's the bottom line. They are not going to grow up calling some stupid dyke bitch "Daddy."

Trevor sighs and turns again to consider the layout he has stayed into the night to work on, a lavish, four-colour annual report for two of Jack

Cowlishaw's umpteen mining properties. The copy is too flowery; it needs a tang of honest reporting, something that will give shareholders some cause for hope but not alarm financial writers who always think Jack is peddling moose pasture. Why the hell does Trevor Billinghurst have to do this? He knows why. Because the nine men and women who work for him are all useless. Outside Trevor's door are the offices for his help, but they've all gone home. Only Trevor works late. Only Trevor cares. The sign on the door says, "Trevor Billinghurst and Associates, Public Relations." Do those assholes out there ever realize that without Trevor there would be no associates, no offices, no jobs for anybody?

Trevor is both the inside man who comes up with the bright ideas and the outside man who brings in the business. Trevor has the crucial connection, Golden Arrow Enterprises. This firm exists only because Trevor Billinghurst is a one-man think-tank for Jack Cowlishaw, the first, the best, and still the fastest moving of the new breed of Bay Street deal makers who have begun to be called "conglomerateers."

It isn't sex. That much I'm sure of. I tried all of those funny things with Vivian, and when it came right down to it, the only thing that turned Vivian on was plain, old-fashioned screwing.

Trevor cannot focus his mind any more. Better to start fresh tomorrow. His sleek grey Jaguar sedan swings on to the Don Valley Parkway. It is two o'clock in the morning and the greasy slush of the afternoon has frozen into patches of black ice. Trevor is frightened by how much he has to fight to hold to the lane in front of him. He remembers the bottle of Swedish vodka still sitting on his desk. His secretary will find it in the morning. To hell with her.

In the apartment houses beside the expressway, windows shine merrily. But liveliness disappears as soon as Trevor peels off the expressway and winds into Woodridge Heights. No lights burn in the two-storey colonial-style house on Edyth Drive. Trevor pauses at his front door. Vivian did this to him.

I earned a good living. We had a beautiful home and two lovely children, and I had a sunroom studio built onto the back of our bedroom so my wife could do her painting. We always had supper together on Thursday nights, just the two of us, candles and a sirloin steak and a bottle of good wine...a little privacy before we got caught up in the weekend and the social rat race. Thurs-

day nights were our time for a roll in the hay. We did it lots of other times too, don't get me wrong. But we always made sure we had Thursdays. We had a good sex life. Hell, I don't know whether it was good or bad, but I never complained. I never went looking for anything else. Then, one day, my wife left. No warning. No big, final fight. Just walked out. Now she's living with another woman. If that's not grounds to give me custody of my children, then you tell me: what the hell is?

32

VIVIAN BILLINGHURST, neat as a pin, looking proper and prim, sits in the front row of the divorce court. She told the boys at Enrico's she wanted to look like a Rosedale lady again. They laughed and said she was selling out. Darling, you'll never look Rosedale; it's just not you. But she told them why, and good-hearted, skilful boys that they are, they did a splendid job. Her wild, golden mop has been washed, beaten, and pinned into a prim chignon. She wears a beige wool suit and a plain, cream-coloured blouse, with a high neckline like a clergyman's collar. Her only pieces of jewellery are gold earrings and a string of pearls.

Vivian despises herself. Marta, in the rows behind, is sending messages of support and encouragement. Vivian can feel them. Marta should be up here, sitting beside her. Vivian should be holding hands with her lover. But Harry Margulies advised caution. Harry is a smart lawyer, and a good friend, but Vivian should never have listened to him.

In the morning, Marta had lain tangled dreamily in the sheets and watched her get dressed. A bra? You're chickenshit, Vivian. And a girdle! I haven't seen one of those in years. You look like my mother, Vivian. Vivian lunged for her. They tussled on the bed. They kissed. Marta bit Vivian's lip. She pulled Vivian down beside her on the bed and held her. Vivian tried to get away, and Marta refused to let her go. She held her arms, pinning her down and kissing her. Vivian began to sob. She felt herself skidding out of control. Marta let her up and Vivian clung to her. Marta kissed her gently and held her until the trembling stopped. Marta is the most honest thing in her whole life. Above them sits County Court Judge Amanda Gill. The judge looks, Vivian decides, a bit like Queen Victoria. She wears a long black robe and a square black cap; her face is round and petulant. Harry actually sought her out. He said they were likely to get a more sympathetic hearing from a woman judge. But, looking up now at those haughty eyes and those descending double chins, Vivian is not so sure. She is beginning to suspect that, in getting her in front of Judge Gill, Harry was once again being too clever by half.

"April fifteenth: Subject observed walking on College Street in company of Marta Persofski. Subject observed holding hands with Persofski. Persofski observed fondling subject."

"Fondling...Fondling?" Trevor's lawyer's voice rises in exaggerated disbelief. People in the benches behind smirk and snicker. They have got bored waiting to place their own lives on the chopping-block. The dyke wife and her snoopy husband provide some comic relief.

"Fondling? What do you mean by 'fondling'? Would you tell the court exactly what you saw?"

"Yes, sir." Peterhouse, the private detective is a dapper, wizened man, impervious to embarrassment. He understands the meaning of loyalty; the person who pays is entitled to the full range of the Peterhouse professional skills.

"Persofski had her hand on the subject's buttocks."

"And was Persofski's hand inside or outside the subject's clothing, Mr. Peterhouse?"

"Let me see..." There is a shading of fish-and-chips Cockney in the private detective's voice. He consults his notebook, showily turning the pages. "Persofski had her hand inside the waist band of the subject's trousers, sir."

Laughter now from the benches behind Vivian; this is great stuff.

"And was the subject, Billinghurst, objecting to this...uhm...liberty?"

"She did not appear to be, sir."

"You were close enough to observe her reaction?"

"I was right behind them, sir."

The picture is delightful. Just the word *behind* is enough now to bring unrestrainable giggles.

"I object!" Harry Margulies has jumped to his feet. "This line of questioning is irrelevant. We are here only to decide on whether Mrs. Billinghurst can provide a better home for the children than her former husband can."

"If my friend will be patient…" Trevor's lawyer speaks plainly now, abandoning for the moment the theatrical game-playing. "My friend will see that I am giving the court an illustration of the unwholesome atmosphere created by his client."

"You are giving us pornography," Harry says.

Judge Gill's head nods slowly and affirmatively. It appears that she appreciates Harry's indignation.

"Would counsel approach the bench." Judge Gill looks down coldly on the two lawyers.

"How long have you been attempting to negotiate a custody agreement between your clients?"

"Almost a year, your worship," Harry says.

"And what are the ages of the children in question?"

"Twelve and eight, your worship."

"I think they are old enough to tell the court what they prefer. Would either of your clients object to the children talking to me in my chambers?"

The two lawyers withdraw from the bench to consult their clients. Vivian's response is instantaneous. She will not force her girls to make a choice. She will risk losing them before she will let them suffer such a trauma. But just as soon as she tells Harry with an impulsive shake of her head, "No!," Vivian regrets her decision. Sasha, the older, might have preened herself in front of the judge; Paola, the baby would have chosen to go with her mother. Vivian could have won this thing with one telling stroke. But the opportunity has gone by, and Vivian is left breathless and furious.

Trevor is eager to send the girls into the judge. The private detective has been a mistake; his evidence is turning the judge against Trevor. He needs to recoup his losses. But what if the girls say they want to live with Vivian? They have always been a little afraid of the masculine assertiveness of their father. Vivian took them with her, stole them really, when she ran away. But that won't count here; the fact is the girls have been living with Vivian for over two years. Going to Trevor now would be a disruption in their lives. If only he could talk to Sasha and Paola before they talked to the judge; he could tell his girls how much he loves them. But will there be time? Trevor cannot face the risk. Slowly, reluctantly, he, too, shakes his head "No."

The two lawyers again approach the bench. Judge Gill is pleased. People who are willing to let a child choose which parent to be with are more concerned about revenge on each other than with the child's welfare. Judge Gill is ready now to make a decision.

"The court would like to award joint custody, but earlier testimony reveals that the parties are not yet prepared to work out satisfactory arrangements.

"The court, therefore, awards temporary—and conditional—custody to the mother for one year. The father is to have visiting rights one day a week, and at his request the children will stay with him one weekend a month. The court directs that a social worker from the Children's Aid will make regular visits to the mother for the purpose of determining whether the mother's living arrangements are having a detrimental effect on the children. The social worker will report to me. One year from today, both parties will again appear in this courtroom to make final custody arrangements..."

"Hillman versus Hillman, your worship," the bailiff calls.

The new lawyers and the new about-to-be-sundered couple have already taken their places at the front tables by the time Vivian and Trevor and their party have made their way out of the little courtroom.

The elevator down from the eighth floor is crowded with lawyers in their black gowns, and worried-looking clients. Marta and Vivian are pressed against the back wall. Marta clutches Vivian's hand. The pressure is not reassuring. Vivian feels desperate. She has extricated herself from Trevor, yes, but can she really call herself free when she has already turned her whole life over to another person?

Vivian and Marta emerge from the side door of the county court. Fresh sunlight bounces off the cold white flagstones of the walkway leading to City Hall square. Instinctively, Vivian turns to look for Trevor. Her eye picks up the strong, square back and the thick brown overcoat as Trevor falls in with the crowds of City Hall employees hurrying past the giant Christmas tree in the square, on their way to lunch.

"You can still catch him," Marta says.

"Don't be a jerk," Vivian says.

"I'm taking you to lunch," Marta says.

She even buys a bottle of champagne. Sweet, reckless Marta. They hold hands under the table. By the light of the candles—candlelight lunches? Vivian can almost hear Trevor guffawing—Marta's face looks childish and uncertain. Marta's fingers probe gently under her skirt and press her thigh. Vivian does not like being handled in such a proprietary fashion, but she does not fight back. She owes Marta a little extra consideration. Her lover has been so sensitive and supportive.

Later, an age later it seems to Vivian, she lies awake, still savouring the events of the day. Marta lies beside her, gently snoring, back turned and legs curled up into herself. The house creaks around Vivian. From the floor below, she can hear Sasha crying out in her sleep. She wishes there were something she could do for her older daughter. It saddens Vivian to think how much the tension of the divorce has infected this child's life. Maybe now that the future is no longer uncertain—Vivian has no doubt she will emerge at the end of the year as a more fit parent than Trevor—Sasha will be able to settle down.

Vivian lights up a cigarette and sinks back into the pillow. How delicious. How naughty. Trevor used to go crazy when he caught her smoking in bed. Vivian draws the salty tobacco down into her lungs and resolves that, from now on, Christmas will have a new and special meaning. It will always be the time she got her divorce. Her new life is her gift to herself. Merry Christmas to me, Vivian says.

33

THIS WAS really Vivian's fault. My troubles began the day she walked out on me. Instead of concentrating on business the way I should have been doing, I was trying to put my life back together. So, even though I could see all the signs and I knew Jack was going down the tubes and I was going with him, I couldn't do anything. I didn't have the strength. I stayed inside my cosy little dream world. And then it was too late. One week after my divorce, the day before New Year's, Jack called me into his office and gave me the bad news. Like I was his fucking secretary and he was dictating a letter. Jack Cowlishaw, my best friend...

Jack Cowlishaw was a scientist. He studied geophysics, which applies the science of physics to the earth. Jack spent three summers half-freezing to death on a glacier in British Columbia so he could drill into the ice and study core samples for his thesis. His patron, the great Tuzo Wilson, expected Jack to join him at the university and further our knowledge of the earth. Jack Cowlishaw had other ideas.

Jack figured mining companies and stock promoters would pay dearly for the kind of information a geophysicist could provide. No longer did the money men have to rely on drunken prospectors or moody geologists who disappeared for months into the bush. J. Cowlishaw, Consulting Engineers, went up in old Dehavilland Otters, floating over thousands of square miles of forest and muskeg bog, bouncing electromagnetic waves through the stony layers of the Canadian Shield down below. The returning echoes were recorded on rolls of graph paper with red, blue, and green pens. Even if the patterns did not actually reveal folds in the rock that might contain valuable ore bodies, the print-outs were so complicated that promoters of mining stock could always claim they at least looked promising. Jack Cowlishaw began to prosper.

But until he hooked up with me, Jack never dreamed of going for the big money. I was writing reports for old H. E. Bates. Jack had my name because he'd picked up a couple of copper claims from some character who couldn't pay his bills and he'd formed a company and was trying to push the stock. There wasn't a hope in hell, and I told him so. But I took him up to the back room at Malloney's anyway and we got plastered. Neither one of us was married then, and we sat in the big chintz easy chairs Malloney's used to have and we just hit it off together. Jack was this skinny, tight-assed guy with a baby face and a snooty English accent. But when you got a few drinks in him, he'd go apeshit. I'm not going to tell you all the things we did in those days. But if you go up to Malloney's even now and you say "Jack and Teddy," you'll get an earful, believe me!

Jack Cowlishaw knew the mining game. Trevor Billinghurst knew Bay Street. Together they were dynamite. Jack Cowlishaw's holding company,

Golden Arrow Properties, quickly established eighteen separate mining exploration companies, two of which actually did own a small piece of one small, producing copper mine. But since all the mining companies owned shares in each other, they could all claim to have an interest in the mine as well as their own properties. Trevor wrote prospectuses, hyped the salesmen, worked the bars of the Granite Club and the York Club and the Simcoe Club, and kept the stocks moving at a merry pace.

Golden Arrow also came to have a controlling interest in seven muffler-replacement garages, three car agencies, and a car-leasing chain, and half-interests in three Montreal apartment houses, a chain of seven laundromats, a chain of twelve discount appliance stores, two suburban shopping plazas, a summer camp to teach hockey to rich kids, and—Trevor's personal favourite—a company that imported socks from South Korea and sold them in Toronto for less than half what it cost to manufacture the same socks in the sweatshops on Berryman Avenue. Trevor liked to say he and Jack had even beaten the Jews at their own game. The money came rolling in.

It was all happening so fast, Jack and I used to talk sometimes about "The Reckoning." We figured we were living through a replay of the 1920s and it was all going to end in another Great Depression. But we never did anything about it.

Jack Cowlishaw was buying up companies with small down payments in cash and large chunks of Golden Arrow stock. Each new acquisition furthered the diversification of Golden Arrow. If they're losing in one place, they'll make it up somewhere else, the smart players said, and people kept pushing the price of Golden Arrow stock up and up. Everybody loved Golden Arrow.

When Jack bought an insurance company in Worcester, Massachusetts; invested heavily in a data-processing outfit in Forth Worth, Texas; and bought a taxi company in St. Louis, Missouri, *U.S. Business* devoted a whole page to him and called him "a Canadian conglomerateer who developed his keen eye for a deal on our last frontier, the Canadian mining camps..." Jack had the article framed and hung behind his desk. He wanted people to be reading it over his shoulder while he was talking to them.

I'll never forget, I came into Jack one day when I was working on the annual reports and I said to him, "Jack, we're in trouble." And you know what he said to me? "It's those crazy fuckers in Quebec; they're driving us to the wall!" If I was smart, I'd've got out then and there.

Jack blamed the FLQ *for all our troubles. He said it was all the fault of those crazy separatists in Montreal kidnapping those two guys and killing one of them. We're not the Sweden of North America any more, Jack said. The big-money people can see what's coming. Quebec's going to fuck off, and the rest of the country won't be worth a shit. But the fact is, after they sent in the troops and they caught those guys, the country settled down, and lots of businesses were doing better than ever. But Golden Arrow was still going down. Jack just couldn't face the truth.*

The truth was, people just stopped trusting Jack Cowlishaw. It was as simple as that.

Golden Arrow was a public company and so were all the companies that Golden Arrow owned shares in. Jack had so arranged matters that not only could people buy shares in Golden Arrow itself, they could also buy shares of individual companies that Jack had set up as holding companies for the shares of other companies Golden Arrow had an interest in. Some analysts complained that there was so much paper floating around it was impossible to figure out who owned what. But others said Cowlishaw had come up with a neat way of helping investors cover their bets. Some analysts said this "sharing of shares" was a brilliant innovation.

But Golden Arrow itself still had to issue financial reports and hold annual shareholders' meetings. Handling all that was Trevor's job.

I was having my own troubles, but that wasn't the reason I couldn't keep it all going. I'm an artist, but even an artist needs something to work with. I had gallons of booze at the annual meetings and all the pâté de fois gras and smoked salmon you could want. I made the meetings into big parties. I even had broads around. And the financial reports were masterpieces, if I say so myself. I had these gorgeous photographs, you could hang them on your wall, and the copy I wrote to go with the pictures could make the shittiest hole in the ground sound like we were just about to strike oil. I kept the hard numbers at the back, but there are always some smart asses who turn to the numbers first. And even though I had an accountant who was genius at coming up with names like 'subordinated annual pretax capitalization' for things, and we tried to keep the really bad news to the footnotes, some people know how to read a report, and they look at the footnotes too. To the people who knew what they were doing, it was obvious. Every company Golden Arrow controlled was losing money.

"I'm no good at counting nickels and dimes," Jack said one night, when he had taken Trevor up to the comforting Victorian elegance of Hy's Steak House for a late snack. They had been reading financial reports and adding up columns of figures and placing telephone calls to company managers. The news they had been getting was all bad.

"You ought to take over operations yourself," Trevor said. "That would give us more credibility on the Street."

Jack only scowled.

"Cut the bullshit, Teddy," he said. "Everybody knows I couldn't manage my way out of a paper bag."

Jack picked up the T-bone and began to tear off the last scraps of red meat with his teeth.

"Then we'd better get somebody to run these outfits," Trevor said, "or we're going to be in even deeper shit than we are now."

"Don't get your drawers in a knot," Jack said. "We've been in tight spots before."

The end came suddenly and swiftly. Trevor got the news just ten minutes before the public announcement. The story in *The Daily News* said: "Jack Cowlishaw announced today that he has sold his interest in Golden Arrow investments to the McKenna Mining and Smelting Company of Tucson, Arizona. This will give the American conglomerate a controlling interest in the Toronto-based firm. In a telephone interview, Mr. Cowlishaw said that with the resources of the American firm behind it, Golden Arrow would be able to 'rapidly expand into new areas...'"

On Bay Street there was considerable amazement that anybody would want to buy a dog like Golden Arrow. Old Jack must have cooked the books, people said. He'll probably wind up in the slammer.

On further reflection, it appeared that the purchase did make some sense. McKenna had not brought in a new producing mine since 1960. The company had survived, as Golden Arrow itself had, by diversifying. With one blow, McKenna acquired one gold mine and two silver mines in Canada, even if they were small, and some interesting real estate and all the other commercial bits and pieces Jack Cowlishaw had put together. McKenna stock rose by eighty-seven cents the day the Golden Arrow purchase was announced.

The only real casualty, it seemed, was Trevor Billinghurst. The Americans made short work of him. The man who called him into Jack's old office wore cowboy boots. He had his feet up on the desk, and Trevor could see that the sharp lines worked into the thick leather were supposed to represent the head of an eagle. It was probably some Hopi or Navajo symbol.

All I could think of was: "What kind of an asshole wears cowboy boots on Bay Street in the middle of winter?" He told me that McKenna actually owned a piece of a public relations company in New York. They had been handling all McKenna's business and they would look after the Canadian operations too. Bye-bye, Trevor Billinghurst. They didn't even want the files I'd built up on Jack's operations. Didn't need them, he said. I was out of there in five minutes.

Jack Cowlishaw left Toronto the day the sale of his company was announced and took up residence at the bar of the Clairmont Hotel, near Nassau. He is sitting now at the hotel bar. On one side, at the pool, in the blinding glare of white tile and blue chlorinated water, shapely young women and shapeless old men lounge soaking up the sun and sipping drinks made with rum and sticky fruit syrup. Inside, to Jack's left, one can hear the soft clickety-click of the roulette tables in the casino. Jack is waiting for his wife. She is negotiating to open a boutique in the hotel, where she can sell imported swimsuits and lingerie. Jack and his wife are going to have supper and then do a little gambling. They love the action.

Jack's wife strolls up and sits down on the bar stool beside his. Elinor Cowlishaw is no longer as thin as she was when she was a figure skater, but she is not heavy either. She looks solid and firm. She is wearing a magnificent gold and dark green emerald bracelet. Her voice is heavy and musical. People feel an immediate intimacy with Elinor Cowlishaw. She has already made many friends at the Clairmont.

Elinor Cowlishaw hooks her arm protectively through Jack's.

"We have to go now," she says. "They'll give our table to someone else if we don't show up on time."

Jack pays for the drinks, and he and Elinor head for the dining-room. They make a handsome couple—the vivid, ardent woman in the lime-coloured pant suit and the stout man in the white dinner jacket and broad-brimmed white panama hat.

Back in Toronto, Trevor Billinghurst has taken a three-year lease on an empty supermarket. He has an idea for a new business which, he says, is going to be better than anything he ever did with Jack Cowlishaw. And when anybody asks, he tells them he is not at all bitter about what Jack did.

Why should I be? I've got capital. I've got the knowledge I gained in the business world. I know a lot of people. I'm ready to go out on my own. Jack did me a favour, if you want to know the truth.

But I'll tell you something funny about Jack. He's got this delicate English skin. Put him outside for ten minutes in the summer and he looks like a boiled lobster. Sometimes, when I'm slogging through the cold and slush, I think of Jack down there in the Bahamas with all those beautiful tropical beaches and afraid to stick his nose out the door. I tell you, I laugh like hell.

34

VIVIAN STRIDES HOME from her figure-drawing class, thinking how splendid it is, how morally uplifting really, that if you have the courage to make changes and take charge of your life, good things do begin to come your way. Her teacher, Brian Bellamy, has just told Vivian that he is impressed with her new work and if she can get a decent array of paintings together, he will take her to Jeremy Richmond and suggest a one-person show. Richmond's little "Galerie '71," on Queen Street, is home for some of the most experimental, and the most successful, painters in the country. If he takes on Vivian Billinghurst, there can be no doubt, anywhere, that Vivian has become an artist too.

Vivian pokes the eggplants laid out on the table in front of the store and picks out four small, firm ones. The girls don't like eggplant, but Marta does. Vivian feels a sense of community with the immigrant women who spend their afternoons trekking through the little grocery stores, meat markets, and fish stores on College Street. The daily struggle simplifies life. It makes women strong and purposeful. For Vivian the goals are clear: art and liberation. What do her companions in their long black dresses and black kerchiefs want? Vivian wishes she could talk to them. But they all seem to speak only Italian and Portuguese. Vivian wonders if the people she sees in the stores even know she is there, in their midst.

The handles of the plastic shopping bags bite into Vivian's cold fingers. She must still carry her heavy load two long blocks over the treacherous frozen snow of Kerr Street. Vivian remembers, a little ruefully, the days when she could drive her station-wagon to the supermarket and, in little more than an hour, pick up enough groceries to last for a week. But Marta has made sacrifices too. She no longer lives in the Grove. To get a house big enough to provide a studio for Vivian, an office for Marta, and separate bedrooms for Vivian's two daughters—so essential to promoting their sense of individuality—they have had to move west of Bathurst Street into a neighbourhood where it seems that everyone else has just arrived in the country and the two women who were born here are foreigners.

But in return for accepting exile, Marta and Vivian have been able to rent the perfect place. It is brick, three storeys, with high, gabled windows and a wide front porch. The back of the ground floor holds the kitchen. Vivian unloads her groceries onto a old wooden kitchen table and sets to work. When Sasha and Paola come home, chattering and stamping their feet to shake off the cold, she has meatballs and spaghetti all ready to put in front of them. Vivian sits down at the table too. This is their time to talk and be together. Vivian takes a small plate of plain spaghetti for herself so she can contribute to her little family's sense of breaking bread together.

"I have to get a present for Megan's birthday party," Sasha says. From the way the topic has been introduced, angrily and without preamble, Vivian understands that her daughter has been waiting all day to talk about this.

"We could go tomorrow after school," Vivian says calmly.

"There's this neat sweatshirt at Morningstar. Pink, with sequins. Meg and me were looking at it Saturday. It's excellent."

Vivian remains noncommittal.

"How much is it?"

"Twenty-seven dollars." The hesitation and longing in Sasha's voice cut Vivian deeply. If they were still with Trevor, twenty-seven dollars would be a piddling amount. Vivian looks over at her other daughter. Paola is methodically shovelling spaghetti into her chubby face, pretending she is not involved.

Where will Sasha be by the end of Saturday's birthday party when

Megan, the social dictator of grade seven, has opened all her presents? The girls in grade seven gain their ranking from how close Megan allows them to get to her. But how in God's name is she going to squeeze twenty-seven dollars out of the household money? A careless slamming of the front door; Marta is home. They listen in silence to Marta kicking off her boots and hanging up her duffel coat.

"We'll go to Morningstar tomorrow," Vivian says quickly. "If this thing's as good as you say, we'll get it." Vivian knows that Sasha is not entirely satisfied. She will not trust her mother until she has this most perfect gift in her own hands. But at least there will be no scenes at the dinner table.

"Hi, folkses," Marta calls out, entering the dining-room. She wears black horn-rimmed glasses and the heavy, olive-green pant suit she likes to put on, like a uniform, for dealing with art directors at magazines and ad agencies. Marta claims it makes her feel like a proper businesswoman, but Vivian says it makes her look like Fidel Castro.

"I'll get you a martini, hon," Vivian says. "Sit down and relax."

"You will never guess what Kenny Shimoya, the boy genius of *Canadian Homes*, has dreamed up." Marta speaks loudly, communicating with Vivian, who is out in the kitchen cracking ice cubes out of the metal tray and turning on the oven to heat up the eggplant parmigiana that has been waiting, a little soggily, for Marta's return.

"He's found these two old farm ladies down in Leamington who take apart old blankets and things and then weave their own stuff out of it. He wants me go down there and shoot them on their home ground. I'll be up to my ass in snowdrifts and cow shit."

"Sure sounds crazy," Vivian calls from the kitchen. Marta looks at the other people around the table, acknowledging them, really, for the first time. Paola, the fat little eight-year-old has mopped up everything on her plate and is waiting patiently for dessert. Marta is fascinated by the child's mass of brown curls. Luis, her hairdresser, would go bananas over a head like that. She must talk to Vivian about taking Paola there one day. Sasha, the skinny one, has hardly touched her food. She is sitting now, looking fixedly at Marta. The kid is spooky. Marta is always catching Sasha staring at her, but the kid never says anything. Marta smiles at Sasha. Marta remembers what it's like to be twelve years old and so desperate for things to happen to you.

"How's it going, Tiger? You have a rough day too?"

Sasha does not respond. Her face is so rigidly fixed Marta cannot tell if the kid has even heard her. Marta gets up from the table and goes into the kitchen.

"You forgot my martini," she says sullenly. The glass with the ice cubes ready is sitting on the edge of the sink. Marta takes the liquor bottles from the cupboard beside the fridge and mixes her own drink. Vivian mutters, "Sorry, hon," but does not turn around as Marta stomps back into the dining-room. Vivian looks so harassed that Marta begins to feel guilty about her.

Vivian serves the children vanilla ice cream and then, when they have scarcely had time to shovel it down, Vivian announces "grown-up eating time." Her daughters dutifully carry their plates into the kitchen and go off to the front room to watch television. Vivian, with a sense of drama and triumph, brings out the eggplant parmigiana and the caesar salad.

"I'd love a glass of wine with this," Marta says.

"We don't have a drop in the house," Vivian says. "I'll fix you another martini."

They talk about how the day has gone. Vivian tells about Brian pushing her to get in with Jeremy Richmond and Marta is properly impressed. Marta has been to three other art directors besides Kenny Shimoya. It looks like she will have enough work to keep her right through to spring. The eggplant is thick, strong, flavoured with tomatoes, salty cheese, and garlic. Vivian is a superb cook. Marta feels contentment spread through her. She used to think of wives, even women who formed permanent relationships in the gay world, as cowards who could not face living alone. Only now, with Vivian, does Marta realize how much has been missing from her own life.

"You don't suppose I could talk you into doing a little posing, eh?" Vivian is casual and tentative but Marta knows she has been waiting all night to ask. Marta is bone tired, and what she would really like to do is fall into bed. She toys with her coffee and melting ice cream, looking gloomily at her Vivian.

"Okay, lover. But you've got to fix me another drink."

Vivian is always fascinated by the way Marta undresses. It is as though she pulls a cord in the middle of her chest and her clothes just fall away from her. Marta puts on the gown Vivian has made for her. It is pink cotton and Vivian has added white smocking across the bodice like one finds on an upper-class child's dress. Marta sits down on the grey aluminum stepladder Vivian has set in the middle of the bedroom.

These times in her studio at the end of the day are Vivian's reward. She has taken care of everyone else. Now she is free to look after herself. In her previous lives she could never get this much space. Trevor was always after her. Even when Trevor wasn't in the house, she could feel him oppressing her. And the commune on Landrigan Street wasn't much better. People there were always making demands on her time. But now Vivian has cut away all extraneous entanglements. She has only two obligations left, her daughters and Marta Persofski.

"I'm tired," Marta says. "Are you going to be long tonight?"

"Ssh," Vivian says. She is studying the half-completed canvas on the easel in front of her. "Just hold still."

"Who made you the boss?" Marta says.

"I did," Vivian says curtly.

She is trying to decide whether to work on Marta tonight or on the background. The bedroom wall behind Marta is stark white. But the wall in Vivian's painting is made of red bricks, chipped and covered in spots with ivy. The bricks are plainly part of an outside wall, but Marta seems to be in a room with a luxurious blue rug and a ceiling with wall-paper of gorgeous dark blue asters. In the painting, there is also a window behind Marta. It looks out on an all-but-impenetrable forest of pine and bushy cedar trees. These trees are coated with snow and ice. An enormous brown grizzly bear is at the window, leaning over the sill, menacing the woman in the pink child's nightgown.

"I want to go bed," Marta says.

"Stop moving your head. It changes the light."

"I've had a hard day."

"So have I."

"If I stood up right now, what would you do? Hit me?"

"Yes."

"Don't try it, Vivie."

"Hold still, damn it!"

Marta stands up. She walks, struts really, towards Vivian, the long pink gown flapping against her legs. She stands insolently in front of Vivian.

Vivian is frozen. The paint brush sticks out from her extended hand. Marta is smiling at her, but Vivian can see there is uncertainty and some fear in Marta's eyes.

Marta takes another step forward and presses her lips on Vivian. Vivian remains rigid. Marta wraps her arms around Vivian and slides her fingers under the waistband of Vivian's pants and down below the elastic of her underwear. Vivian cannot resist any longer. She allows Marta to press and shape her body. Marta's warm tongue explores the inside of her mouth and darts back.

"You want to fight some more?" Marta says.

"No," Vivian whispers back.

"Okay, ten more minutes. I'll be good," Marta says cheerfully. "Then we hit the sack."

35

VALENTINE'S DAY is the very bottom of darkest February. But it's also the time when people are finally beginning to get their Christmas bills paid off. Trevor Billinghurst has figured out that, in spite of the miserable weather and grey streets, Valentine's Day is actually a good time to open a new store. People are ready for a little novelty and entertainment. Trevor uses connections from his old public relations days to put together a fine show for the opening of his new venture, Poor Richard's Auto Parts. A nightclub singer in a red evening gown, a comedian, and a Canadian actor who is the fourth lead in a U.S. network cop show and likes to tell jokes, too, perform at Trevor's front door. The entertainers are enough for Trevor to pull some TV coverage in the evening news and this, added to three days of full-page newspaper ads, gets Poor Richard's off to a running start.

Do you know what one of the biggest sellers was in the thirties? Cigarette-making machines. People couldn't afford to buy tailor-mades, so they rolled their own. They had to have these machines—really just a wooden board and a sheet of rubber slung between a couple of rollers—so they could get the tobacco into the paper without slopping it all over the floor. The guy who had the Canadian agency for cigarette machines made millions when Bay Street brokers were jumping out of windows. I'm applying the same principle to Poor Richard's Auto Parts. Times are getting tough. When people can't afford new cars, they start fixing up their old one. And a lot of them are going to do the repairs themselves. Poor Richard's is a natural.

But the real stroke of genius, if I say so myself is location. I'm just five blocks east of Hanover Street. Six blocks from the corner of King and Bay. I hit people on their way to work and on their way home. I get them coming and going—before anyone else does.

But Trevor quickly discovers a curious fact about human nature. Abundance makes people uncomfortable. Trevor thought he had lucked in when he was able to get hold of an old neighbourhood supermarket so close to downtown. With almost 26,000 square feet of floor space available, Trevor was able to offer people an absolutely splendid range of parts and prices to choose from. But instead of being grateful, people run back and forth between the aisles, dithering over which item is better.

It seems they want to talk to somebody knowledgeable, especially when they are thinking about undertaking difficult and expensive car repairs themselves. But the floor manager at Poor Richard's warns Trevor that he cannot be checking inventories and be on the phone bugging lackadaisical jobbers and do the thousand and one other jobs that managers have to do and, at the same time, stay on the floor, holding customers' hands.

Trevor hires three new people and boasts in his next series of full-page ads that Poor Richard's has a licensed mechanic on the floor at all times to give advice. They'll even ride around the block with you, look at your motor, and give you a diagnosis.

The new men wear wine-coloured blazers and they make a difference, but Trevor has to pay his new help $550 a week, plus commission.

Trevor fires the manager. He unlocks the door himself every morning at six, and most nights he is there until after midnight. Trevor discovers the special agony of the storekeeper. Once you've paid for the ads, after you've screamed your head off in public, there is nothing else you can do but sit in the store and wait.

On one particularly bad Tuesday, when the aisles at Poor Richard's have been empty all day and the four checkout counters have not recorded a single sale, Trevor sits behind the glass wall of his little office, with the phone in his hand. He is going to call Jack Cowlishaw down in the Bahamas—just to ask Jack how his sunburn is coming along. But the person Trevor really wants to talk to is Vivian. Even before he dials, he can hear Vivian being sympathetic and supportive.

Trevor puts the phone down. He cannot bear the thought of being pitied by his former wife.

"The car companies are having their best year since the fifties," Trevor's accountant tells him. "I wouldn't take it personally, Teddy. It's not your fault the economy bounced back."

To cover the salaries of his mechanic salesmen, Trevor has to raise his prices. He makes up for this with another burst of frantic advertising. It seems to help a bit. The store's business seems to go up one week and down the next. But every week, it seems to Trevor, he is sliding farther and farther below the break-even point. He begins to suspect that he is never going to get off the nut.

The worst blow is the realization that he has picked the wrong location. Now he discovers that he is just a bit too far from the downtown office buildings for people to hike over at lunch hour. In the mornings, they are anxious to get to work. In the evenings, they are rushing to get home. Trevor was so sure he had the perfect spot, a neighbourhood supermarket with thirty-seven parking spaces. But the lot beside Poor Richard's remains sadly empty.

The bank is swift, almost merciful. Trevor asks for an extension of his line of credit. There can be no question of that. Indeed, the loan officer would like to know, is Mr. Billinghurst in a position to make a substantial payment on the principal? It is not a question; it is a verdict.

Trevor's best hope is to sell while his doors are still open. But the real estate agent brings back word that Poor Richard's Auto Parts is considered a lemon. Clearly the pros in this business think Trevor has been a fool. Clearly they are right. He does not even have a business to sell. He has only two floors of stock—most of it now classified as "used"—and twenty-seven months of an unexpired lease on a former supermarket.

"Mr. Billinghurst, meet my wife, Gladys."

Trevor looks up from his endless sheet of figures and finds himself shaking hands with a young Chinese woman in a nurse's uniform, a white smock and white slacks.

"Gladys be just off shift," Albert, the elderly Jamaican mechanic says. "We going to supper now, Mr. Billinghurst."

Who would have ever dreamt that an old geezer like Albert would have a beautiful young wife? Albert looks to be at least sixty, a tall, gaunt man who walks the floor of Poor Richard's bent over like a dignified, arthritic stork.

"Well, I'm very pleased to meet you, Mrs. Warner," Trevor says. "Albert's a terrific salesman."

"I move two crankshafts today," Albert says. "I think we be turning the corner, Mr. Billinghurst."

"I think so too, Albert. I think this could turn out to be the best week we've had."

"Well, we got to go now. Gladys been in the hospital all day. She not have anything to eat."

"Well, very nice to have met you, Mrs. Warner."

Trevor extends his hand and Gladys shakes it awkwardly. Trevor can hardly feel any pressure at all from her tiny hand. He is overcome with sadness, watching the two of them button up their coats before stepping into the darkness. The failure of Poor Richard's Auto Parts is going to hurt them too. Trevor calls out.

"Hey, Albert. Gladys. Wait. Come and have dinner with me!"

Albert and Gladys look at each other uncertainly.

"Albert's had a good day; I think it's a sign. Let's celebrate together."

"I would like to do that," Albert says gravely.

Trevor hustles them into his Jaguar and over to Hy's Steak House on Richmond. A couple of scotches, and the awkwardness is gone. They settle comfortably into their deep banquettes. Albert tells wonderful stories about chasing the stowaways and drug smugglers when he was an engineer on the oil tankers travelling from Venezuela. Gladys, whose family comes from Trinidad, says the heavy red, almost funereal, decor of Hy's reminds her of the hotel dining-rooms where her mother and father worked. Trevor insists that they get the twelve-ounce instead of the eight-ounce steaks and orders a $32 bottle of French burgundy.

I don't care whether people think I can afford this or not. I'll put it on Chargex. Let the bastards chase me. This is a celebration. I'm turning in my white collar. From now on, I'm going to be just a working man. I'm right back where my grandfather started out.

36

IN THE PICTURES Marta Persofski takes, the light is sometimes so bad you can hardly tell what is going on. Sometimes—for heaven's sake!—everything is out of focus. Yet art directors love her work. Marta Persofski photographs subtleties of feeling that other photographers miss. Even when she is shooting something inanimate, a newly decorated or newly renovated room, say, for *Canadian Homes*, the angle of Marta's picture and the lighting she sets up catch underlying tensions. It is as though the people who live in this room have left just moments before. Marta Persofski is the hottest young photographer in the country.

But, oh, the cost! Marta has been four days in Montreal, in a hot, airless studio, shooting layouts for a fashion magazine. She struggles off the plane now with the heavy camera bag over her shoulder and both arms wrapped around a bulging, nylon carry-on garment bag. The muscles at the back of her neck are as rigid as cables, a warning that if she does not find some way of releasing them, she will get a terrible migraine headache. This is what happens when you walk onto the scene with every nerve end fearlessly exposed. Marta prowls around her subjects like a hungry wolf, clicking her camera from every angle. At the end of a shoot, Marta is soaking wet and exhausted. So many nights she has sat alone in hotel rooms, convinced that she cannot do this any more, that she is burning out.

But tonight, Marta Persofski feels joyful and eager despite her fatigue. Vivian is waiting for her. She is going to take Vivian out tonight. Vivian won't know it, but they will be celebrating Marta's new understanding of the meaning of love; Marta has been faithful to Vivian, even against her own instincts.

One of the models in Montreal came on to her, a darling redhead with warm, pouting lips. She was only seventeen, and Marta sensed that the kid's obedience to her posing instructions was moving into the slave-to-master adoration that can sometimes happen between model and photographer. Marta knew she could have the kid with the merest nod of her head. She let the moment go by. At first she was furious with herself. Goddamnit she was all alone in the midst of a gruelling job and she was entitled to a little relief. But, then, Marta discovered the deeper pleasure that comes from self-denial. She was thrilled. It was an entirely new experience.

Marta comes through the corridor, looking for a porter or at least one of those little golfcart trains. Nothing. She readjusts the shoulder strap of her camera bag, wraps her arms more firmly around the garment bag, and sets out on the long trek through the endless, dank arrival corridor. Tonight, when she finally gets out of this miserable airport, she is going to take Vivian to Troy's, the restaurant in the narrow old house across from the railway tracks on Marlborough Avenue that makes you feel you are a guest in the home of an eccentric antique collector. They will dine well, drink fine wine, and Marta will lift Vivian's hand from the table and kiss it fervently. Then she will take Vivian to Momma Pippo's. They will dance long into the night. Marta will show off her new lover to her old friends. They will see how absolutely devoted she is to Vivian.

Marta's luck changes when she finally reaches the end of the corridor. A cab is sitting there as though it has been waiting all day for her. Marta gratefully turns her luggage over to the driver and settles down in the back seat. Before the car has wound its way out of the airport and reached the highway into the city, Marta's eyes have closed and she is sound asleep.

37

A CANDELABRA casts romantic light over the dining-room table. The placemats are pink linen, the plates are shimmering white porcelain rimmed with gold. A bottle of red wine is open, mellowing in the air. Marta stands, looking in at the dining-room of her own home, bedraggled and bewildered. She lets the luggage slide from her grip.

"Hiya, lover!" Vivian comes down the stairs and takes Marta in her arms. Marta allows herself to be kissed. It is all she is capable of at this moment.

"You look beat," Vivian says, stepping back. "Go take a bath while I finish up in the kitchen. Sasha's off at a sleep-over and I've just got Paola settled down. We're going to have a fantastic supper."

"I was going to take you out," she says woodenly.

"Aw, I couldn't, hon. Sash'll be gone all night and I could never get a babysitter this late. But, listen, the meal I've got planned you couldn't buy in any restaurant. Believe me. Go have your bath."

She pats the seat of Marta's corduroy trousers.

"Get dressed up. When you come downstairs, it'll feel just like Troy's. I'll be your cook and your waiter. And"—with a lewd, servant's smile—"anything else you want."

"I want to go dancing." It sounds so mean and selfish. But Marta cannot help herself. She feels she is being smothered.

"You've got to give me warning," Vivian says. "I can't just pick up and go whenever I want."

There is no question about the truth of this. But is it Marta's fault?

"I'm going to have that bath," she says. She picks up the suitcase and the camera bag and struggles upstairs with them.

The bath gel starts out a heavy violet globule and gradually diffuses, tinting the water. Marta lies back in the tub, watching liquid climb slowly over her knees and thighs and up her body. The soft, flowery scent soothes her nerves. It is better to sulk a bit like this than to let frustration escalate into a fight. Too bad that little red-headed model will never know how important she became. Marta leans her head against the back of the tub and closes her eyes. The hot, fragrant water has reached the stiffness in her neck. She is half asleep when the door bangs open.

"Hiya, honey. Just brought a little something to help wash away the cares of the world."

Vivian hands her an old-fashioned glass. Marta takes it without a word. A sniff tells her it's a martini. She dutifully takes a sip. She cannot think of a single thing to say.

"You look good, hon. Hard work must agree with you," Vivian says, looking down hungrily on Marta's nakedness spread out under the faintly purple water. After years of living alone, Marta has lost the habit of locking the door when she takes a bath. She tries to think of some response that will not reveal how imposed upon she feels at this moment. She is rescued by the harsh ring of the telephone.

"Don't answer that," Marta says abruptly.

"Honey, I have to. It could be Sash."

The cool bitterness of the martini does make a pleasing, sensual complement to the sweet steaminess of the bath. Vivian certainly knows how to mix a good drink, a holdover from her long years in the bungalow boondocks. What would all the beautiful and passionate lovers who tried—and failed—to get Marta Persofski to move in with them say if they could see her now with Vivian Billinghurst? She drains the glass and holds the ice cube in her mouth. The door opens again, this time slowly and hesitantly.

"It's somebody called Shimoya," Vivian says fearfully. "He says he has to talk to you."

"Tell him I got hit by a truck."

"He says the fate of Western civilization depends on talking to you."

Vivian holds the big bath towel, rubbing Marta's thin back and her muscular thighs. But there is no acknowledgement from Marta. She steps away, pulls on a robe, and goes down the hall to her cluttered little office.

Cooking sweetbreads is so complicated that just to attempt a sweetbread dinner is a demonstration of devotion. All day, Vivian has been changing the acidulated water the two pearly gelatinous masses have to soak in and pulling bits of membrane and other unnecessary matter away from the delicious core. Now she quickly blanches the sweetbreads in boiling, salted water. The risotto is staying nicely warm in the oven, and an endive salad and a chocolate mousse, Marta's favourite dessert, are cooling in the fridge. Vivian lifts the sweetbreads from the boiling water and quickly slices them. She is going to sauté them in a mélange of onions, carrots and celery flavoured with beef stock and Madeira. She is anxious to have everything on the table ready for Marta as soon as she comes downstairs. No wonder the poor girl's been testy since she got home; she obviously hasn't eaten anything all day.

But when Marta comes downstairs she is not wearing the grey blouse and black velvet trousers Vivian had thoughtfully laid out for her. Instead, Marta has on an old tan jumpsuit.

"I've got to get down to *Canadian Homes*," Marta says. Vivian is sure she can detect more relief than regret in Marta's voice. "Shimoya's going apeshit. Two big spreads have gone down the tube. He's pushing my stuff for October ahead to this issue. I've got to get down there and do some printing for him."

"That's not fair!" Vivian can feel tears coming to her eyes and she is furious with herself. Why does she always have to sound so weak and shrewish?

The doorbell rings.

"I'm sorry," Marta says. Her voice is toneless, cruel. "If we'd gone out, Kenny never would have found me."

"So, it's my fault, right? You come marching in here and say, 'Let's go somewhere!' But I can't do that. You know I can't do that."

The doorbell rings again, longer, more insistently.

"I'd better see who that is," Marta says, escaping from the dining-room. Vivian lifts her apron to her face and wipes her eyes. She hears the front door open and Marta greeting someone. The sweetbreads are bubbling away, filling the ground floor with the fragrance of meat stock and syrupy Madeira. She should go and turn them before they get ruined. Marta comes back, and the person she has with her is Mary Ferreira, the young social worker from the Children's Aid Society.

"Hi!" Mary says brightly. "I just happened to be in the neighbourhood. I thought I'd…" She turns and sees the elaborate setting in the dining-room. The candles have already burned halfway down. "Oh, I've interrupted something. I'm sorry. I'll come back another day."

"No," Marta says. "It's all right. I was just leaving. I have to see an art director. An emergency."

Then Marta is out the door, leaving Vivian alone to face the snooping social worker. Vivian wills herself upright. She lets her hand drop from the supportive chair she has been gripping.

"Sasha's at a sleep-over," Vivian says. She amazes herself. She sounds so serene and confident. "Paola's up in her room, reading. She may be asleep."

Paola has indeed nodded off when her mother and the social worker stand at the door of her room. Vivian tiptoes in, removes *The Tale of Jeremy Fisher* from Paola's plump hand, and pulls the comforter up around her shoulders. The room is delightful: pink teddy bear wallpaper, a little white bookcase with a row of stuffed animals, a child-sized desk with a toy sewing machine. Vivian has clearly re-created on shabby Kerr Street all the secure luxury of the suburban bedroom she took Paola away from.

"She looks great," Mary says. "I'd better get going now."

Vivian has a sudden vision: the front door will close and she will be left all by herself to eat the lovely dinner she has prepared.

"Hey, you must be hungry," Vivian says. She can see by the sudden, unguarded flicker in Mary's eyes that she is right. The poor kid has had a rough day too.

"Come on. Marta won't be back 'til God knows when. It's a sin to waste good food."

Mary has never tasted sweetbreads before. She pronounces them "squishy," but very good. Vivian strives to put everything in a good light. Yes, she and Marta do fight over how much time Marta's work takes up, but Vivian is learning to adjust. After all, she was married to a Bay Street operator for years. The children don't seem to mind that the new person in their mother's life is another woman. Paola is, of course, too young to realize the implications. Sasha adores the glamour of Marta's life. The two of them are becoming great pals. Marta has even said she might take Sasha on a shoot.

"Can I tell you something?" Mary asks abruptly. Vivian feels she has been cut off. Mary pours herself a third glass of wine. "This is a great meal. Can I stop being a social worker for a little while?"

"Sure. By all means," Vivian says.

"This guy I've been with—like, living with, I mean—for two years now, he's starting to talk about his kids—like, all the time now, it's all he talks about—I think he's telling me—you know what I mean?—that he wants to go home."

Vivian finds it hard to picture rosy-faced little Mary Ferreira embroiled in a steamy love affair.

"My brothers are after me to leave him. Manuel says he's going to kick the shit out of me. He would, too. He used to do it when we were kids. But Manuel's right. I don't love Ed. I don't know why I'm sticking with him. My whole life's a fucking mess."

"I'll get the scotch," Vivian says.

"I don't like scotch," Mary says.

But Mary discovers that, with an ice cube and a little water, scotch is quite an acceptable drink. The two women lean back on the couch, the whisky bottle and the highball glasses on the table in front of them.

"I hope you don't mind me talking like this," Mary says.

"Oh, no, it's fine," Vivian says. If only that pompous divorce court judge could walk in now and see the two of them with their heads together. Vivian giggles.

"I'm doing social work for the social workers," Vivian says.

"Yeah, that's true," Mary says solemnly. "You know the whole Portuguese thing about family? It's bullshit. It's all about controlling women. Keeping them down. Portuguese men are terrified of women. They get it from the church. The trouble is, I really love my family. My father's a great guy."

"Well, what I think is, you should break your big problem into small problems," Vivian says. "When I was with Trevor, my husband, I used to write him little notes when things were bothering me. So he would know, eh? But I wouldn't be around to have a fight with."

"Yeah, that's a good idea," Mary says. She helps herself to more of Vivian's scotch.

It is two o'clock in the morning when Marta finally gets home. Mary Ferreira has gone. The whisky bottle and a glass, still half filled, remain on the coffee table. Vivian is sprawled on the couch, snoring loudly. Marta sits down beside her and kisses her on the forehead and the cheek and mouth. Vivian stirs but does not waken. Marta goes up to bed alone.

38

GINO EMILIO did not become successful by being overly sensitive with people outside his own family. He knows Trevor Billinghurst must be home because the garage door is open and he can see the big grey Jaguar in there. What's more, Gino can smell juicy, garlicky hamburgers sizzling on an outdoor grill. He keeps pressing the button, sounding the three-tone chime, until Trevor answers the front door.

"Jesus, I hate to bother you on a Sunday night," Gino says. "But I finally got the offer and I don't know how long I can hang onto them."

"No way," Trevor says. "They're trying to jew me down. The hell with them."

"Mr. Billinghurst, if I thought you were going to do any better holding out, I wouldn't bring you this offer. But the market just isn't that strong."

"Oh, yeah?" Trevor says. "Well, I got confidence in you, my friend. That's why I gave you an exclusive on this place."

"Mr. Billinghurst, I think you ought to go to multiple listing," Gino says softly. His narrow shoulders eloquently express his wounded dignity. "This is the best I can do for you, and I'm sorry you don't feel that way."

Trevor quickly calculates the cost: days, maybe weeks of delay. He might well do better with multiple listing, but this kid could be right, too. People always say the real estate market is a roller coaster. What if he is at the beginning of another downslide?

"Give me the papers," Trevor says. Leaning against the door jamb, he signs his name, turning over to strangers the house he struggled so hard to buy and to pay for.

"I honestly think you've done the right thing," Gino Emilio says, accepting the offer and folding it into the inside pocket of his green and gold raw silk sport jacket. "One forty-three is a good price for this house. I tell you honestly, it's better than I thought you'd do."

They shake hands, and Trevor hurries to the backyard, where Sasha is watching the grill and desperately wondering if her father will return before the hamburgers begin to burn.

Gino Emilio slides into his little Mustang and drives off, feeling very pleased. When the commission comes through on this sale, he will be able to show his prospective father-in-law that he has $50,000 in the bank. The old man has demanded that Gino amass that much—enough to buy a small house and equip it properly—before he will surrender his youngest daughter. The old bastard's been a bricklayer all his life and he can't even imagine what fifty grand looks like. Gino knows he just wants to keep his youngest daughter innocent and pure, and at home with her father, for as long as he can. But Gino has put together the required sum in less than two years. That's not bad for a little boy from Naples who was an apprentice barber in Hamburg only seven years ago. Gino starts to sing along with tape he is playing. "Jesus Christ, Superstar…do you believe you're what they say you are?"

Back at the house, Trevor is explaining the transaction to his daughters. They are in the back yard, sitting at the old park picnic table he and Vivian once bought at a small-town auction and had stripped of paint, right down to its natural white pine. The girls are finishing their second hamburgers while Trevor nurses his third bottle of beer.

A hundred and forty-three thousand dollars may sound like a lot of money, but by the time I've paid off all the mortgages, given Vivian her half, and paid off some more debts from Poor Richard's, I'll be lucky if I've got ten cents left for myself.

"Where will you live, Daddy?" Sasha asks.

"I've got a nice little place," Trevor says. "You'll really like it."

But the truth is, Trevor is never going to let the girls see where he is living. He has sublet a basement apartment in Danforth Village, a ring of lofty, rectangular apartment blocks that looks as dark and grim as the monoliths of Stonehenge.

"Why do you want to go away from here?" Sasha asks. Trevor understands: she is not asking about him; she is worried about herself. How can Sasha's father give away the house that Sasha grew up in?

"I get lonely here all by myself," Trevor says. "It's okay on the weekends when you guys can come to visit me, but the rest of the time I'm here all by myself. I won't feel as lonely in a smaller place."

Paola begins to cry.

"It's okay, Daddy. I'll come and live with you."

Trevor sits down beside her. His arms spread out like wings and fold over his two daughters. He is crying and he knows he really shouldn't let the girls see him like this. But so much has happened to him.

"Don't you guys worry. Daddy's a tough old coot. I'll bounce back."

39

VIVIAN KNOWS she has been put on display. She is wearing a tight black mini skirt that barely covers her ass and a red silk blouse and big earrings made of silver hoops and long white feathers that flutter against her neck. It is much too arrogant an outfit for a woman of thirty-five, but Vivian still has thin, strong legs and she doesn't mind showing them off. She has dressed up tonight for Marta. She wants the people at Momma Pippo's to envy Marta. Vivian plunges recklessly into the dancing. Partners shift and change in the darkness. A sweet black girl came to chat with Marta and asked Vivian to dance; now an enormous carrot-topped girl, taller even than Vivian, has moved in on them. Vivian is dancing with both girls but she is hardly aware of them. The new partner smiles encouragingly, but Vivian is concentrating on the music, trying to let the clamour come up through the floor and teach her how to move. The crackling strobe light catches her tumbling hair and powerful legs, shining in the black and silver stockings.

The churning of the electric keyboard and steel guitars suddenly stops; the record is over. The dancers begin to disperse, but Vivian stays where she is, trying to catch her breath. The orange-haired girl touches her arm. "I think you're excellent," she whispers. "My name is Janis." Vivian makes her way back to the table, where Marta is leaning towards an absolutely beautiful young man named Duncan. The two of them hardly look up as Vivian takes her seat. They are talking about somebody called Bobby McGee, but Vivian cannot follow the conversation. She feels damp and overheated. There is a September heat wave in the city, and Momma Pippo's has no air-conditioning. Vivian is wondering how she can get a drink in this place, when Momma Pippo himself arrives, giving them the recognition of personally bringing over a tray of cherry Cokes. He draws Marta to her feet and gives her a big hug and kiss.

"Honey, you just don't know what's been going on around here," Momma says. "You've got to come back!"

Marta introduces Vivian. Momma leans down to deliver a wet kiss to Vivian's cheek. He smells overwhelmingly sweet, a whole bouquet of perfumes. His hand moves rapidly up and down Vivian's back, even pressing her bra straps. The fingers are astonishingly hard for such a pudgy-looking man. Vivian feels she has been thoroughly probed. Momma delivers his judgment to Marta.

"Nice tits," he says, giggling, and sits down at their table. Marta always talks about Nick—whom everybody calls "Momma"—Pippo as somebody dangerous, a person never to be crossed. But Vivian finds him very unthreatening. He looks to Vivian like a human version of the Michelin Tire man. Momma Pippo is hugely, grotesquely fat. But his face saves him. He smiles in a way that makes it seem he is sharing a secret with you. And even though he wears thick, rimless glasses, Momma Pippo's eyes seem as innocent as a baby's.

Momma Pippo's Club is as ordinary as the owner. You have to go up an alley behind Hanover Street and climb a fire escape to get to the door, and that gives the club a faintly demi-monde air. But, once inside, you can see that the famous club for gays is just the apartment above a dress store with the walls between the rooms knocked out. There is a bar at one end, but, since Momma Pippo's stays open after legal drinking hours, he cannot get a liquor licence, and his bar, at least officially, serves only soft drinks. The walls of the club are drywall, covered sloppily with white paint. The only decorations are old movie posters. There are tables for people to sit at, with red and white checked table-cloths. But the table-cloths are made of paper, and all the drinking glasses are plastic. If it were not that men have been dancing with men and women have been dancing with women, it would feel to Vivian like being back at a high-school dance.

"So many people," Duncan says. "On a Thursday night. Amazing."

"Payday," Momma says. "Fucking and fighting time. But you want to know something funny? If people absolutely had to make a choice, I think they'd rather fight than fuck."

"Oh, horseshit!" Marta says.

"And now a couple of golden oldies," the disc jockey announces in a syrupy voice. "Time for a little get-acquainted dancing."

The gentle, insinuating voice of Frank Sinatra flows through the four loudspeakers in the corners of the room: "I give to you and you give to me...true love..."

With a twinge of sadness for herself, Vivian realizes that for the people she is with now, Frank Sinatra and this lovely song are curiosities from another age. Marta takes her hand and leads her onto the crowded dance floor. The couples move even more slowly than the music. Marta's hand presses her back; Vivian feels surrounded and protected. She lets her head drop forward and rest on Marta's shoulder. Beside them two men are dancing together, hardly moving. Vivian is taken aback when the taller one leans down and kisses his partner. But then Marta's lips press against her neck. Vivian shivers with pleasure.

"I love you," Marta calls through the noisy darkness. There is an edge of challenge in her voice. It is not needed.

"Oh, yes, I know," Vivian says. She is seventeen again.

"True Love" is followed without pause by another sweet, sad song. Vivian forgives her lover for all the difficulties they have gone through. Marta is sensitive and highstrung and often at war with herself. Marta's lean, beautiful body presses against her. Vivian is filled with feelings of goodwill for all the world. The music winds down, and the lights surrounding the dance floor come up a little. Vivian gives Marta a quick kiss on the lips.

A messy blonde woman is waiting at their table when they return. Marta introduces her as Peggy. Vivian is angry; the woman ought to know she is intruding. But Marta seems indifferent. Vivian is not fooled; she knows her lover has become tense and fearful.

"I'm really glad to meet Marta's new friend. I shouldn't tell you this, but I just have to...," Peggy says. She has a sharp, nasty voice. "...when I saw you walk in here, I nearly shit my pants. You look just like my vice-principal. Then I saw who you were with. And anyway, you're a lot better looking than my VP; you really are."

"How's Jannie?" Marta asks coldly.

"She's doing great," Peggy says. "She just needs a bit of knocking around once in a while, that's all."

"Yeah, I'll bet," Marta says. She sounds contemptuous.

"Want to dance, Marta? I won't bite," Peggy says.

"Show us your teeth," Momma Pippo says.

Peggy holds out her hand. Marta accepts it reluctantly. Anyone can see she is being dragged onto the dance floor.

"Round two," Momma Pippo says. "Marta used to be with Peggy, you know."

"No, I didn't know," Vivian says. She wishes she could just go home now with Marta. They have been here long enough.

"Then Jannie showed up, the Lucille Ball of Kapuskasing."

In spite of herself, Vivian is intrigued. Who was it the mysterious Jannie seduced? Peggy? Or Vivian's own lover? If it was Marta, then just when did Marta turn to Vivian?

"Uh-oh, here comes trouble," Momma says. The big, orange-haired girl Vivian was dancing with earlier in the evening is now marching towards them.

"You go to Brian Bellamy's painting classes, don't you?" The girl addresses Vivian as though there was no one else at the table. "Is Bellamy any good? I was thinking of going there too. My name is Jannie."

"Brian's okay," Vivian says cautiously. "But you've got to be willing to work hard. Brian is very demanding."

"Would you like to dance?" Janis says. Vivian turns to Momma Pippo. He appears to be studying the people at another table. But his head moves ever so slightly. Vivian catches the warning.

"Thank you, but I'm really tired," Vivian says politely to the red-headed girl. "I just want to rest a bit."

Janis doesn't move. She remains standing, embarrassingly large, in front of Vivian.

"I think you're really a super person," Janis says.

The phoney ingenuousness infuriates Vivian. She'd love to let this girl really have it. But she doesn't want to start anything big, not now, not at the club. There are too many things here she still doesn't understand. The best way to get rid of Janis is to go along with her and then just quietly slip away. There are advantages to being older. Vivian knows more tricks.

"I guess I wouldn't mind dancing after all," Vivian says. Vivian immediately becomes audience, not a partner. Despite her size, Janis takes off with a wild self-absorbed grace. Her long muscular legs beat out a frantic pattern on the floor; her body twists sinuously, this way and that, hands reach up, grasping for the sky. She does have a splendid body. Vivian has to concede that. And it's clear the woman doesn't give a hoot about anybody. They are in the middle of a jam-packed dance floor and the woman is putting on a private performance. Is she trying to fascinate Vivian? Seduce her? What in hell does the girl want? Vivian doesn't care. She is thinking how much she would like to paint Jannie dancing like this. It would make a fantastic addition to her "Woman in Motion" series. Suddenly, it is Marta in front of her. Marta has somehow moved in and cut Janis off.

"Let's go," Marta says. The music is bouncing off the walls, the strobes are flashing like bolts of lighting, and everybody is spinning as fast as they can. But Marta is just standing there, stiff as a post.

"Come on, we're going home," Marta says.

"I'm okay," Vivian says. "I'm having a good time."

"You're making an ass of yourself," Marta says.

This is ridiculous. Marta was the one who said they needed to get out of the house. Marta was the one who said they had to get some fun into their lives.

"We have to leave now," Marta says. And when Vivian doesn't move, she whispers fiercely, desperately, as though Vivian should have known this, "Peggy hates me."

Vivian is overcome by a sense of injustice. Why should she have to pay for anything that happened in Marta's past? She stays on the dance floor.

Marta reaches for her hand. Everybody is grabbing Vivian tonight. She looks around for help, but she and Marta have become invisible people. They are having a fight in the middle of the dance floor and nobody can see them. The table she was sitting at is empty now. Momma Pippo is back behind the bar. He is talking to Peggy. Janis comes up to the bar. She says something to them and they look towards Vivian and they all laugh. Vivian will have to go home. She just cannot stay in this place by herself.

In the cab, Vivian sits rigidly against the door and refuses to talk. At home, she undresses quickly and slides into bed. Her back is to Marta. The anger and humiliation are beginning to subside. But she still needs some time to herself. The privacy of sleep will bring the release she needs. She feels Marta pressing against her. She feels Marta's breath in the back of her hair. "Hey, one kiss at least," Marta whispers.

It is a good rule. No matter how bitter the fight has been, never go to bed still angry. But rules were meant to be broken.

"Hey, sweets, don't be mean," Marta says in her dearest little-girl voice. "I'm sorry. I just couldn't stand them playing games with you."

She pulls at Vivian's shoulder. Vivian stays where she is. Marta pulls harder, really tugging at Vivian now, insisting that Vivian turn to her and be kissed. Vivian has had enough. She does turn, quickly, her arm lashing out, almost pushing Marta off the bed. Marta regains her balance and jumps on top of Vivian. She sits on Vivian's chest, her knees resting on Vivian's upper arms. All she wants to do is to give her lover a kiss. But, as she bends her face down, Vivian twists and turns, refusing to be touched. Vivian looks fantastic. Her eyes are shot with red; they're boiling. It's like steam is coming out of her. One last frantic arch of Vivian's back and Marta is off her chest, sprawled again in the blankets. Vivian is on top of her. Vivian has her by the wrist and she twists her arm up into her back. It really hurts.

"Ow! Ow, I give up!" Marta calls out. "Pretty please with sugar on it!" But Vivian will not be mollified now. Marta has gone too far. Vivian raises her hand and begins to smack Marta as though her lover were a little girl. But Vivian has never punished her children the way she wants to hurt Marta now. Marta won't leave her alone. She won't give Vivian any space. It's all so stupid! Vivian will break her. And Marta is just lying there, her head bowed meekly into the pillow, silently absorbing all of Vivian's fury. Vivian hits her harder. Marta's skin is turning a horrible, livid crimson. Each blow now demands all of Vivian's strength. She can hardly lift her arm. She is gasping for breath, sobbing. She has no control, no dignity left. Then Marta is sitting up, holding Vivian against her chest, comforting her, letting her cry, kissing her fervently.

40

WHOEVER ARRANGED a shoot out here must have shit for brains. There is no way Marta can save it. She will turn in garbage to the ad agency. This had to happen some day. Word will get around. Marta Persofski has lost it. But she is so stale and wooden this morning; she feels hung over, although all she had to drink last night with Vivian was a couple of cherry Cokes. But loving can do this to you, too. Loving can hit you on the head like a mallet and knock everything out of place. Oh, Vivie, she is thinking. We are making history. This is the price we have to pay for it.

She peers through her range-finder. The light offends her eyes. It is dull grey, burning. The four male models have arranged themselves as she directed on the factory loading platform. The grey-haired one is holding a clipboard and pointing to a tractor-trailer truck that looks as long as a railway car. He is supposed to be a company president exhorting his junior executives.

But these young models all look like choir boys. For God's sake, they are as pretty as the young birds at Momma Pippo's. The stiff business suits only make them look like children dressed up in their father's clothes. The older model is a little better. You can see there is at least something going on inside his head. Indeed, as Marta focuses on the older model, it looks like there is too much going on. The man's face is gaunt; his eyes are red and furtive; the grey hair is much too long, coming almost to his shoulders. He looks like a wino who has been plucked off the street. Marta sighs and waits a second longer, hoping that at least some sign of intelligence will appear before her, and when it doesn't, she trips the shutter anyway. Then she signals the crew to take a break while she changes film.

If these models were not so useless, Marta would feel sorry for them. The poor buggers have to go parading around in a succession of wool business suits and vests and fleece-lined overcoats, even though this a muggy, grey September day. The curse of the advertising business: you always have to work a season ahead. The makeup woman spends all her time trying to keep the sweat from corroding the healthy outdoor tints she has daubed onto the models' faces. Better to send them all home. Better to admit defeat.

Marta begins packing up her equipment. A few feet away from her, the older man is lying on his back, his hands cupped behind his head, looking up at the sky. But his eyes are seeing something else, some part of his own wasted life, Marta is sure. She reaches quietly into her bag for a camera. She approaches the model. He is aware of her, but cannot be bothered protecting himself. She stands over him. She is astride him really, looking down through the camera lens. He is bored at first, then fearful and angry. Beautiful. Marta's got him. One by one, she makes the other models lie down too in the burned brown grass, and she stands astride them photographing them. The dark, spoiled-looking one raises his foot behind her and probes her bum. Marta laughs and catches the look of fear and mischievousness. Her energy is back. The headache bubbles away.

Marta reverses the order. She lies on the ground and has the men walk over her. She gets them to mime sports, throwing and catching baseballs, swinging a bat, kicking a soccer ball. They obviously think she is ridiculous, but they are having fun now too. Marta feels alive again, loose and free. And these objects she is photographing, these tight suits and overcoats that look so uncomfortable because they are supposed to project only wealth and authority, are now being made to look human. These are jock clothes, Marta's pictures will say. These are suits you can live in.

Another nothing shoot has been lifted up, saved, by the skill and the raw nerve ends of Marta Persofski.

41

VIVIAN is on her knees. She is in the kitchen, wiping up milk Paola has spilled. The girls are at the kitchen table, working through their supper of shepherd's pie. They all look up in astonishment. Marta has come into the kitchen vividly sunburned from her outdoor shoot and holding an enormous bouquet of white and yellow roses.

"For you, honey bunny," Marta says.

Awkwardly, and a little painfully, Vivian rises to her feet. She wipes her hands on her apron before accepting the flowers.

"Can I have some more hamburger?" Paola asks.

"It's on the stove," Vivian says, without even turning to look at her. She can feel her lover waiting to be embraced.

"Mommy, it's gone all yucky. I can't get it out of the pot."

Marta steps forward, wraps her arms around Vivian and kisses her. Vivian remains stiff and unyielding; she knows her daughters still feel threatened by any display of affection that is not directed at them.

"I'm going to get cleaned up," Marta says as she lets Vivian go. "You'd better get ready too."

Upstairs, in their bedroom, Marta lays three outfits on the bed so she can decide which she likes best and begins to plot her strategy for the night ahead. She and Vivian must go straight back to Momma Pippo's. They cannot let people think that Peggy has driven them away from the club.

Peggy will be there and she will undoubtedly bring Janis along. Janis had been like a wild bird when she first came down from Kapuskasing and began to be true to her own nature. Now, in Peggy's ungentle hands, Janis is getting gross. Marta must figure out a way to help Jannie—get her away from Peggy and with some people who will really care about her. Tonight, though, she will have to be cold and tough. Then, from a position of strength, she will be able to really do something for Janis.

Vivian is still reading to the girls when Marta has finished getting dressed. Marta sticks her head in the door of the children's bedroom.

"You should hurry along," Marta says.

She is standing in front of the mirror, giving her hair a final brushing, when Vivian comes in.

"What are you doing?" Vivian asks.

"We've got to go to the club. I've already called Momma. I told him we want one of the corner tables. We'll be able to see everything that's going on."

"I've got some supper for you," Vivian says.

"I grabbed something to eat on the way," Marta says. "Come on, get out of your frump's outfit. Do you want me to run a quick bath for you?"

"I was planning to work tonight," Vivian says. She sits down heavily on the bed.

"Vivian, we have to go the club," Marta says. She stands in front of Vivian, looking fresh and eager. But Vivian is thinking of the row of canvasses along the wall, that she must look at them and decide which ones need a final touching up before she takes them to Jeremy Richmond.

"Vivian, you can't pull something like you did last night and then just not come back!"

"I didn't do anything. You're the one who made the big scene."

"Vivie, honey, I don't want everybody talking about us. Especially about you."

"Let them say what they want. I've got work to do."

Marta holds her feelings in. How best to explain to Vivian the importance of going back to Momma Pippo's? She knows what her lover saw last night: a cruddy, cheap discotheque with a lot of people power-tripping on each other. But those women at the club are Marta's friends. Yes, they are a little crazy sometimes, and, yes, they are in and out of each other's beds, but it's not just sex—they are not foolish people; it's love that is happening among Marta's friends at the club—real love, genuine love. Marta cares about them, all of them, even Peggy.

"Just a couple of hours, honey bunny. We don't even have to stay very long. And then we can come right home to bed."

"I just don't get it," Vivian says. "I don't need any of that stuff. If I've got you…my kids…a place to work, that's enough. More than enough. All these people you want to drag me to, I just feel like they're wasting my time."

Marta cannot understand whether Vivian is being deliberately obtuse or, for some unfathomable reason, wants to hurt the person who loves her most. But so many times Marta has gone to Momma Pippo's feeling used up and drained and been renewed by the excitement going on around her. How long would her sensitivity last if she abandoned her friends and their life together? How much longer would Marta Persofski be Canada's hottest young photographer?

"You had it too easy," Marta says quietly. "You came out, and you had me. You fell right into my arms. I caught you and I looked after you. You never had even one day of being lonely. You never had to suffer. You never had to think you were a freak. Not the way I did. Not the way my friends at Momma Pippo's did."

"Try childbirth," Vivian says scornfully. "Seventeen hours of labour. Then come and talk to me about suffering."

Marta stops then. She closes down. Life without children, the cruellest taunt one can throw at a homosexual woman. May God now forgive all the sins of Marta Persofski. She has believed in love. She has given herself freely. And she never dreamed she would ever hear such words from the lips of Vivian Billinghurst. Marta thought she had found the core of her life. Now it is over…so quickly, so unfairly. Marta takes her bag from the dresser, sets the leather strap on her shoulder, and sets out for Momma Pippo's.

42

"DO YOU KNOW somebody called Trevor Billinghurst?"

Harry Margulies swivels around in his chair to see who has entered his office without knocking. It is Philip Cohen, a young man who has just joined Carlton and Boggs. Harry does not like Cohen. Harry thinks he is too aggressive, and at the same time, too eager to say whatever he thinks people want to hear. And, indeed, when Cohen sees the distracted look on Harry's face, he begins to apologize profusely for disturbing a senior colleague.

Harry cuts him short. In fact, he welcomes the distraction, although he doesn't tell Cohen this. He has been sitting there, trying to choose between his son, Gordon, and J. Arthur Quinn.

"I acted for Billinghurst's wife in the divorce," Harry says.

"Do you know much about him?"

"Not really. He's behind in his child support. Very WASPish, looks like an SS recruiting poster. He used to be with Jack Cowlishaw."

"Cowlishaw's not much of a character reference."

"What do you want Billinghurst for?" Harry asks.

"He's gone belly up. We're going to the official receivers tomorrow. My guys think he's hiding a bundle."

"Who's your client?"

"Red and White Supermarkets. They think he's parked a lot of dough with his ex. She's supposed to have gone butch."

"She's a friend of mine," Harry says.

"Really?" Cohen says. "Have you known her a long time?"

"We've been trying to get money out of Billinghurst for months now," Harry says curtly.

"Well, my guys are sure he's got some," Cohen says. "I'll let you know how it comes out."

"Yeah, do that," Harry says. The conversation has been distinctly unpleasant. Harry is not sorry to see Cohen step away from his office door. But now he has to turn again to his own problem. Why doesn't he go to see his son? There are many good reasons why he should stay in the city, but Harry knows that he could brush them aside and go to Israel if he really wanted to. He has to face the fact that he doesn't want to. It's not that he's bitter about Doreen. When she told him the marriage was over, he was actually grateful. She was telling him something he had known for a long time but had been afraid to say out loud. He was even pleased that Doreen had found another man, and that she decided to go to Israel with him. It meant Harry Margulies did not have to feel guilty about having used up so much of her life. About Gordon he was ready to fight, but in the end he saw that it was better for the boy to be with Doreen. If there is one person that Harry Margulies can say he loves completely and without calculation, it is his son. And there is no question that Gordon is better off growing up on an Israeli kibbutz than sitting alone in an apartment night after night, waiting for his father to come home from the office.

Harry had a vision of himself descending on Gordon three or four times a year. He would talk to the boy and form bonds with him that Doreen and her new husband could never have. But, still, Harry has not made the trip to Israel. It has been almost three years. He must go. But Harry Margulies doesn't feel he has accomplished enough yet. How can Gordon return his father's love if he doesn't have respect for him? Harry knows he has to earn Gordon's love the way he has earned everything in his life, by brains and hard work.

On the other hand, if Harry keeps waiting until he is ready to be an important person for his son, the kid's going to forget him. He should go to Israel. He must go. Harry gives up staring out the window of his office, rises from his chair, and strolls down the inner corridor of Carlton and Boggs to the corner office of J. Arthur Quinn.

"Ah, Harry, you're just in time for tea," Quinn says. It is after six, and all the secretaries and most of the other lawyers have left for home. Quinn reaches into the bottom drawer of his enormous desk and takes out the bottle of rare Armagnac.

"I'm not coming in with you on Ontario Square," Harry says. "I'm going to Israel to see my kid."

"Yes, well, I'm sure Gordon will be very pleased," Quinn says, pouring the amber brandy into tumblers for Harry and himself. "Here's to Gordon."

The Armagnac is as thick as syrup and has no bite at all. Quinn pays nearly forty bucks a bottle for this stuff. The old boy still knows how to live.

"Max Himmelfarb is crazy, you know," Harry says. "There's a dozen malls out there already."

"Seven to be exact," Quinn says. "And they'll all be at the board, claiming Ontario Square is going to kill them."

"It will too. Two million square feet. It's a fucking monster."

"My job is to head the little guys off at the pass. I've got half the consultants in town working for me."

"And the other half are working for the little guys."

"I would expect so. It's going to be a zoo, Harry. And the stakes are enormous. Max Himmelfarb has pulled the Englander family into this, and Old Man Englander is screaming. They've got all their dough tied up in Ontario Square, and if they lose, they'll be right up against the wall."

"Yeah, the stakes are big," Harry says. He sighs and savours the Armagnac. "How long is the hearing, Arthur?"

"The board has set aside seven weeks, Harry. High profile. Big stuff."

"You know, Arthur, I'm thinking," Harry says, slowly. "If I went with you on Ontario Square, we'd wind up around March, right?"

"Yes, perhaps even sooner."

"It would be just getting warm in Israel around then. It would be a good time to go, eh?"

"I'd love to have you on board," Quinn says. "But you know I'm not trying to talk you into anything, Harry."

"I know, Arthur. But what the hell? I just can't refuse a challenge."

43

"WHEN I TELL people back home I'm not afraid to walk around this city any hour of the day or night, they look at me like I'm crazy. And clean? I've travelled all over the world, and I can tell you there ain't no place clean as Toronto. I remember last time I was here, I was watching people eat their lunches on the grass beside that big bank, the black one, you know the one I mean..."

"The International Trade Centre?"

"That's the one! On King Street, just over from the hotel. Well, when all those people finished, they gathered up all the paper and junk and took it away with them. I just couldn't believe it. I stood there, watching them, thinking, I'm not just in another city, I'm in another world."

Trevor Billinghurst only nods. He can't take the time to speak because he is concentrating on navigating the cab through the dangerous tangle of roads leading from the airport to the expressway into the city.

"Say, now that we're on our way, do you mind if I ask you a question?"

"No, of course not," Trevor says.

"Do you know where I could find some action tonight?"

Trevor has been expecting this. His amusement is apparent even to the passenger in the back of the cab.

"Hey, listen, I'm not talking about girls," the passenger says. "The hookers are six deep in the bars downtown. They sell more pussy than booze in those joints. Naw, what I'm talkin' about is poker. You know where I could get in on a game?"

"I'd help you if I could," Trevor says. "But I just don't know these things."

"Come on, now. You wouldn't kid an old man, would you? Back home, any cab driver I ask can get me to a game in five minutes."

"I've only been at this a few weeks," Trevor says. "There's a lot of things I don't know yet."

"Yeah? What were you doin' before?" The passenger sounds genuinely interested.

"I had an auto-parts place," Trevor says with quiet dignity. "But it went under."

"Ah, Jesus, I am sorry, buddy. I really am. I know what it feels like to be down. I've been down more times than you'd ever want to hear about. And, I want you to know, I always came back. You keep your chin up, y'hear?"

Trevor pulls to a stop in front of the Lord Simcoe Hotel and gets out of the cab to help the passenger with his suitcases. The man is small and wrinkled, his face, in the shadow of the white fedora, looks like an old walnut. He shakes hands with Trevor and gives him his card.

"If you're ever down Memphis way, you look me up, y'hear?"

Trevor decides to wait in the cab rank in front of the hotel. He looks idly at the card he has been given and starts to laugh. "Errol J. Sloane, vitreous clay products." Toilets! For God's sake, the guy sells toilets! Trevor slides across the front seat, rolls down the window, and sticks his head out. His passenger is still out front, talking to the doorman.

"Hey, Errol!" he shouts. "Next time I take a shit, I'll think of you!"

Trevor guns the cab and shoots around the corner. It's one o'clock in the morning and he decides he has had enough. He has been on the road for sixteen hours, a double shift. Trevor drops the cab at the ramshackle garage on Dupont Street and walks the seventeen blocks east to Danforth Towers, where he lives now. The first snow of winter has begun to fall, but Trevor doesn't mind. The air is still warm and the snow falls softly and gently.

The apartment tower Trevor goes to is not the building he lives in. He is in the basement of the Bermuda, one of the low-rent, sixteen-storey buildings in the complex. Elevators in the Bermuda are scarred with graffiti, most of it smutty, and the hall carpets have been worn down and never replaced. But the twenty-seven-storey Monaco, where Trevor is now, still shows aspirations to elegance, framed prints of French impressionist works on the lobby walls, maroon broadloom on the floor. Trevor presses the buzzer of apartment 1808. When asked to identify himself, he calls into the speaker, "Eddy's old pal, Trevor." If he had said anything else, communication would have ended.

He is going to a blind pig. It made perfect sense to Trevor when he discovered, through the good offices of another cab driver, that Danforth Towers had its own bootlegger. After all, the ring of gloomy concrete apartment blocks does have 6,447 individual apartment units. The people living in there need some place to go when the bars are all closed. Eddy's helps provide that service.

Trevor prefers to drink in the kitchen. At four dollars a shot he cannot really afford to be here, but he is not yet ready to face the grimy beige walls of his own one-room basement apartment and the strange, pungent mixture of cooking smells that drift down from the immigrant families on the floors above him.

Trevor pours as much water as he politely can into his rye and settles down to nurse his drink. At the white enamel table with him is an off-duty fireman. Trevor does not speak to the man, but draws a certain comfort from his presence. That is what Trevor likes so much about Eddy's place. You can be with people, but you don't have to actually talk to them.

Bankruptcy is not something you ever get over, you know. It's something you just go through. You start off with an accountant, the public trustee. You're going to him because you're broke, but you still have to find money to pay him. I thought I could get away with talking about Poor Richard's, but then he made me account for everything I'd been doing for the last ten years, my whole life. Whenever I started to slow down, he threw more questions. He said he was really doing me a favour by being so tough. He was making sure there would be no slip-ups when I had to go through the whole thing again with the official receiver. But all I could think was, "If this guy's on my side, God help me."

Then, after you've gone through all that, and proved you really can't pay your bills, you sign everything you still have over to the trustee. You don't own your life from then on. You're afraid to buy a pair of socks. Somebody's going start screaming, "You're robbing us! That money should go to the people you owe!"

After the session with the trustee, there's the meeting with the creditors. There's no real reason for it. You could tell them everything you have to say in a letter. But they make you go through this meeting anyway. It's like some medieval ritual, a public confession.

Most of the people there were suppliers whose bills I just hadn't been able to meet at the end. The trustee told them they could ask me any questions they wanted. But after he went through what he figured to get from selling all my stocks and my car, and added in my share of the house and my life insurance—I didn't have to cash in my insurance, but I did—and explained to them they would get thirteen cents on the dollar, the creditors didn't push me too hard.

But there was this one little prick who was there for Red and White Supermarkets. It was funny, really. They were the people who got hurt the least. They'd already got somebody to take the store I'd been using for Poor Richard's. So all they were out was three month's rent. But this guy started asking me about Vivian and "her lady friend." I couldn't figure out whether he thought I'd hidden money with Vivian or I was paying her off somehow. But it was awful. It was like he had decided that if he couldn't get any more money for his clients, he'd at least take them my hide. I walked out of there feeling like I was nothing. I wasn't a man. I wasn't part of the human race any more.

But I'm okay now. When I first started driving cab, I wouldn't go downtown. I was afraid somebody I knew from the old days would get in and ask me to take them someplace. Then I thought, fuck this. I didn't steal anything. I'm not in hiding.

Sometimes I look at myself and I say, "I've been a failure at everything I ever did. I was a thick-headed husband and a sloppy father and a fool in business." But you know what? I still get up every morning. I go to work and I get everything done during the day that I have to do.

44

JEREMY RICHMOND runs his hand through his thick white hair. They are all waiting for him to pronounce judgment. But who, from Jeremy Richmond's point of view, is the most important person here? Who should he be trying to please? There is Brian Bellamy, the art teacher, sitting arrogantly astride a turned-around chair with his belly hanging out, the hairy little Buddha of Queen Street. But Jeremy likes Brian. Brian keeps him in touch with what's going on at the outer edge, the bars and after-hours clubs where Jeremy can no longer go himself without being conspicuous. Then there is the artist's husband or boyfriend, Richmond is not sure which, a surly character in a scuffed brown leather jacket with a taxi driver's shield pinned to his peaked, working-man's cap. He leans against the door frame, a cigarette drooping from his lower lip, looking bored and more than a little dangerous. Odd how many sensitive, intelligent women seem to feel the need for these rough-trade lovers. Then there is the artist herself, so sexy, so fearful, so vibrant. Who can tell what is in store for her? Who can know what important connections she might have even now? Jeremy Richmond sighs. He walks again past the paintings that have been lined up against his gallery wall. The model in these paintings is very striking. Some people, a few of Richmond's best customers in fact, like to proclaim that art uplifts their souls. Jeremy Richmond always sighs and says he knows exactly what they mean, but, in truth, he has little patience with such nonsense. Art is about sex. If the piece doesn't get you in the gonads, it's not worth bothering about. Richmond pauses at the end of the row. He closes his eyes and rubs two fingers wearily along the sides of his long nose. He takes out a flat tin and removes a stubby black Danish cigar and lights it.

"Excellent," he says. "This is very…very!… interesting work." They are all relieved. The three of them are smiling at each other. Good…good…

"But the question is…" Richmond goes on, "…the question is…" His voice rises and slows, each word is emphasized… "Would I be doing you more harm than good if I took you, at this point in your career, into the Galerie '71?"

The three of them look at Richmond apprehensively, sensing what is coming. Best to move quickly now.

"Your work has 'artist' written all over it. But not 'established artist.' Some of my people—Corrigan, Jay Larter, Sally Moon Trail—get fifteen and twenty thousand a painting now. There's no way I could ask anywhere near that for a Vivian Billinghurst. You know that as well as I do. If I gave you a show now, an unknown artist who's never appeared anywhere else, we'd have to put your work out at bargain-basement prices. You'd be mad at me because you'd have worked all this time and you'd have almost nothing to show for it. And my other artists would be mad at me because I was offering cut-rate pictures and lowering the price of their work.

"So…what we have to do…"—Richmond is thinking out loud now. His hands twist through the air creatively, shaping fate—"is create a demand for Vivian Billinghursts. We have to get you with some of the smaller, more adventuresome galleries, and get people buying Billinghursts so that when you come into Galerie '71…and I have no doubt at all that you will be here one day…you come in at the proper level.

"So…I am going to make some phone calls and I want you to go and see these people. Will you do that for me, Vivian, dear?"

"Yes, I will," Vivian says slowly. "But can I ask something from you?"

"If it's within my power, of course."

"Tell me the truth."

"What do you mean?" Richmond turns around in the centre of his gallery. He looks a bit like an aged dancer doing a slow pirouette.

"The truth? Ah…yes, the truth," Richmond says. "You want me to be honest with you?"

"Please…"

"Well, then…I don't know everything. I don't even pretend to. You're a good draftsman. But your grammar…your language…the way you use symbolic figures—the grizzly bear, the pine cone, the monkey—they don't mean anything to me."

"They come right out of my life!" Vivian cries.

"Of course they do," Jeremy Richmond says soothingly. "But they don't come out of *my* life, and that's the problem. In me…and in this case, I am using myself as a surrogate everyman…you are not striking resonating chords. You see…"

Richmond detests sounding so pedantic but the woman did ask him to be honest; she has only herself to blame.

"...you are travelling a well-worn path. The abstract expressionists, the surrealists, the minimalists—they were all trying to paint what they found inside their own heads. But when an artist does that, you have to set off echoes in the subconscious minds of other people. It's not that you want them to feel precisely what you are feeling, but you want them to feel at least part of it. When I look at your paintings, I don't feel anything. I respect the workmanship, but they leave me completely flat."

Vivian looks again at the pictures she has lined up against the stark, white wall of Richmond's gallery. More than three years' work is sitting there. And the dealer with the best reputation in the city for discovering new talent is telling her he's not interested in any of it.

The paintings ride home in the back of Trevor's cab. Wrapped up in green plastic garbage bags with the necks tied, making little collars, they look like passengers. Vivian rides in the front, peering out the window at people going about the streets, marvelling at, and envying, the ordinariness of their lives. She feels cut off from humanity. She feels like she has been exiled from all the beauty and loving in the world.

Trevor pulls up in front of the house on Kerr Street. She had asked him, as a favour, to help get her paintings over to Richmond's gallery. But staying around and bringing her home was Trevor's own idea. She is glad now that he took the time.

"If you want to take this stuff somewhere next week, give me a call," Trevor says. "I've got the cab most afternoons."

Vivian shakes her head sadly.

"He's just one dealer, Viv. And a prick at that."

"I know," Vivian says. "But I put everything I had into those paintings, Teddy. There's nothing else I can do. It's not like a bank, you know what I mean? I can't go to another account and draw something else out."

"I know what you mean," Trevor says.

"You want to come in and have some supper, Teddy?"

"I should get on the road. I've got to make some money."

"It won't take long. Marta's not here any more. It's just warmed-up meat loaf."

"Well, okay," Trevor says. "I am pretty hungry, to tell you the truth."

45

MARY FERREIRA's report to County Court Judge Amanda Gill on the welfare of the Billinghurst children—Sasha, aged thirteen, and Paola, aged nine—is a model of sensitivity and conciseness. Ms. Ferreira explains that both children function well academically and have good reality-testing responses. They appear to have adjusted well to the mother's lesbian partner. This relationship does show some signs of strain, but no more than one would expect to find in a heterosexual relationship. There is no evidence that the girls' assimilation of adult female roles will be adversely effected by the mother's current domestic arrangements.

"I am very pleased by this report," Judge Amanda Gill says. "I don't mind telling you, Mrs. Billinghurst, that I approved of your living arrangements with some trepidation. But if we didn't allow for variations in our usual practices, how would we know when it was time to accept changes in our society? Let me just say, Mrs. Billinghurst, that I'm happy things have worked out for you. And for me."

"But we don't want it, my lady," Harry Margulies says. "My client and her husband have decided on a reconciliation."

Other couples waiting their turn to be permanently severed are jolted out of their memories and self-absorption and they are angry at Vivian. This woman should get her soppy sentimentalism out of the courtroom. A couple of the young, smart lawyers look up and snicker. Hang around a divorce court long enough and you'll see everything, even lesbian switch-hitters.

"Have you discussed this with your lawyer, Mr. Billinghurst?"

"I don't need one," Trevor says, standing up beside Vivian. "We don't need legal advice to get together again."

Judge Gill studies the couple in front of her. She cannot remember at all what they looked like a year before. Studying them now, the judge can see that the woman is putting on a bit of weight, but she is still quite attractive and rather sensual. She is wearing a plain blue V-neck sweater and rumpled grey flannel slacks. It is plain she doesn't think this court appearance is an occasion she has to dress for. The man looks beaten up. Perhaps he has not been totally defeated but he's certainly been pummelled a few times. What is the likelihood these two shopworn people will really stay together?

"Let me ask for your assistance, Mrs. Billinghurst. You don't have to answer, but in this court we tend to be a shade less formal than in other jurisdictions. I would like to know, was it the nature of your other relationship that led to your present decision? I'm not phrasing this very well, but I think you know what I mean."

The two young lawyers snicker again, and the court clerk glares at them.

"Oh, no. It wasn't like that at all," Vivian says boldly.

"I see," says Judge Gill. She appears to be on the point of asking another question, and then refrains.

But the judge has made it important to Vivian to explain herself. Vivian does not want this person who reminds her so much of the stern and proper world of her childhood to think Vivian Billinghurst is a fool.

"We've talked a lot and we feel there is more reason to go on together than to split up," she says. "But this is still the biggest gamble we've ever taken. And it may be we'll be back here in a couple of years and you'll be giving us a lecture because we didn't go through with it the first time. But I honestly don't think that is going to happen."

"I certainly hope we don't see you here again," Judge Gill says with a warm, forgiving smile. "I wish you both all the best."

Vivian and Trevor pass through the narrow corridor beside the divorce courts, pushing around lawyers conferring with their anxious clients. There is a crowd in front of the elevator, so they take the silver escalators down for five floors. Policemen in dark uniforms glide by them: criminals, all in their best suits and dresses, pass by too, with lawyers in the swirling black academic gowns and stiff white bibs and white cravats they have to wear in criminal court. Sound bounces off these shining marble walls; voices are too loud, laughter is menacing. Trevor takes Vivian's hand and holds it protectively.

The children cannot get enough of Trevor. After their supper and their bath, Trevor must read, first to Paola, and then to Sasha. Even after it is time to turn off Sasha's light, she insists he lie down on the narrow bed beside her.

Finally, his daughter nods off, and Trevor gingerly removes himself from beside her and goes down to the living-room. He pours a scotch and sits down on the couch. He does not feel comfortable. This is still Vivian's house, the house she shared with Marta Persofski. Trevor will never belong here. Vivian joins him. She is wearing a long white nightgown. She sits down heavily on Trevor's lap and takes a sip of his drink.

"You've taken care of the little girls," she says. "Now it's time to take care of the big girl."

"It's been a long time," Trevor says wryly. "I'm not sure I know how any more."

"I'll show you," Vivian says. "You just lie back and relax."

And, oh, yes, it is so good to impale herself on a man again. Not that she dishonours her time with Marta. Marta was sensitive and beautiful and Vivian loved her. She promises herself she will always treasure the time she spent with Marta. But it's time to close that door. She rides Trevor mercilessly. She feels him exploding inside her. She huddles against Trevor's slippery chest. "Oh, God, I'd almost forgotten…," he whispers in her ear.

"Welcome home, lover," Vivian says.

46

DUPONT STREET tantalizes with possibilities. Dupont runs right across the middle of Toronto, the western half of it anyway. But just one block above Dupont, the Canadian Pacific Railway tracks take advantage of the long, low cliff called "The Escarpment" to also cross the middle of Toronto. So, except for a few major roads that tunnel under The Escarpment, all streets running up from Dupont stop, dead, half a block north, at the railway tracks. So Dupont is home to a motley assortment of somber Victorian factories, auto-body repair shops with blaring neon signs, lumber yards smelling like pine forests, listless concrete-box supermarkets with parking lots so big they look like suburban plazas, wholesale chicken dealers who kill and pack on the premises, government liquor outlets, nervous late-night convenience stores, and even a few blocks of private homes looking shabby and lost in the midst of such a variety of commercial enterprises.

Still, Dupont Street's lack of character can be a distinct advantage to people without much capital. Rents on Dupont are still relatively low. An enterprise like "Green Lantern Books" can get started easily there.

Green Lantern carries new trade paperbacks of the better kind and new high school and university texts. But, like Dupont Street itself, the store is an odd assortment. There are tables of second-hand hardbacks that the proprietors, Trevor and Vivian Billinghurst, pick up at auctions and garage sales. They are getting to know the game and becoming quite adept at canvassing other dealers and coming up with rare and out-of-print books. This is a service their academic customers are beginning to appreciate. At the back, there are cartons of second-hand comic books that Trevor sells for fifteen cents a copy. His teenaged daughter, Sasha, sometimes remonstrates with him. She points out that comics are going up in value and he ought to hang on to ones that could become collectors' items. But Trevor only laughs and says he loved reading comics when he was young and he can't take this new comic-collectors' market seriously. He doesn't complain when kids from the neighbourhood sit around the cardboard boxes at the back of the store, reading through his stock.

It is six o'clock at night, and Vivian is closing up. She takes the bills and a couple of cheques from the tin cashbox. She locks the door and goes into the kitchen in back of the store, where Trevor is serving out a stew he has made to Sasha and Paola. Vivian takes a beer from the fridge and sits down at the table with the girls.

"A lot of my old buddies on Bay Street would be surprised to see me now," Trevor says. "But I'll tell you, we're almost off the nut in this place. I'm thinking that when we're bringing in enough to hire someone, Vivie could take over and I could start doing some other things. Like maybe selling real estate. It's not that I'm trying to start my career again or any of that bullshit. But I'd just like to make a few extra bucks. I've got a couple of daughters to put through school."

"Here we go again," Vivian says. "But I don't really mind. We've got the store and it's solid. And I'm happy taking sculpting classes at Central Tech. It's just for myself though, for my own pleasure."

HISTORICAL INTERLUDE: THE AVENUE

The true story of how Max Himmelfarb got his start in the days when Berryman Avenue was, in the opinion of people here and about, the finest place in the city

THE BOYS WHO hang out in front of Stedman's Restaurant are watching Natie Greene take his first shot at driving a cab, and Max Himmelfarb is offering even money Natie never makes it away from the curb. Now, you must understand that Berryman Avenue is a very wide street indeed, and the cars do not line up Indian file beside the sidewalk, but they park at an angle, nose first, with their keisters pointing into the road, so Natie has to back out into traffic going this way and that. It is well known on the Avenue that Natie Greene is not such a guy as you would want to put in charge of anything that requires two hands to be working together at the same time. And sure enough, Natie no sooner manages to get the cab into reverse and start edging its rear end out when a truck comes down Berryman Avenue and smacks right into Natie's rear fender.

The driver jumps out of the cab and starts carrying on something terrible. I figure he is going to take Natie Greene apart. But, suddenly, Max Himmelfarb steps forward and speaks to the truck driver as follows:

"I am your witness, sir. This silly loon backed out without looking any which way at all."

The driver says that Max is a very public-spirited citizen and Max says his good deed is not finished yet because Hughie Bartleman, the plainclothes dick, is just coming out of Stedman's, where he has been finishing off a large plate of lung and liver with a stack of chala on the side. Bartleman is naturally interested in the altercation taking place on the street, and the truck driver says that Max is his witness and instructs Max to tell the nice policeman what happened.

"You crazy bastard!" Max says, jabbing his finger in the truck driver's chest. "You came around that corner a hundred miles an hour. You are lucky you don't kill somebody."

The trucker makes a grab for Max, but Bartleman jumps in his way. The policeman is having his hands full trying to keep the truck driver from committing mayhem upon Max, and a crowd quickly begins to gather. We find we are standing in the midst of many excited citizens, and Max turns to me and says, "It is time we took a powder."

This seems a sensible suggestion, so Max, Natie Greene, and I slip into the doorway beside Stedman's and climb the stairs to Jake Besser's apartment.

"You boys are welcome in my home," Jake says to us. "Just mind your p's and q's and do not get in anybody's way."

A crap game is in progress in the den, which is what Jake calls his bedroom when the Murphy bed is folded into the wall, and Max decides nothing will do but he must partake, even though he does not have two dimes to clink together. Natie and I head for the living-room where the beautiful Nora Besser is pouring out the Crown Royal, at a deuce for half a tumblerful, and entertaining the guests.

At this time there are citizens who will come from all over the city just to hear Nora Besser play the piano and sing songs from the road shows that stop in at the Royal Alexandra Theatre. For this privilege they will happily pay to drink Jake's whisky, even though it is well known that Jake adds a little water to the scotch and rye as the nights wear on. Nora Besser has a face that is white as snow, and long, shiny red hair. People who are knowledgeable about such matters tell me Nora could have gone to New York and been a big star in the night-club-and-musical-comedy department had she not made up her mind that she was nuts about Jake Besser.

I am leaning against the wall of the living-room, listening to Nora sing "It was just one of those things…just one of those crazy flings" and dreaming of things I would not like to tell my mother about, when all of a sudden there is the sound of a disagreement from the den, and Natie and I look at each other and say together, "Oh, no! Not again!"

Sure enough, when we get into the den, a very big and beefy party who goes by the name of Porkchops has Max Himmelfarb pinned to the wall and he is bringing his fist back so he can drive it into Max's kisser because he says Max should not be making side bets he cannot cover. Personally, I think Porkchops is absolutely right and Max is getting no more than he deserves. But Jake steps up and says as follows:

"Leave the kid go, Porkchops. He is a friend of mine."

"The kid is a putz," Porkchops says.

"You wouldn't get no argument from me," Jake says. "But he is in my place and I cannot have such goings-on here."

Porkchops now has his fist, which looks as big as a sledge-hammer, back all the way to his ear, ready to demolish Max Himmelfarb, but he waits. He is looking at Jake, and Jake is looking back at him, and I can see Porky is figuring the odds and not liking them very much. Jake Besser is at this time no spring chicken. He has white hair and wears glasses and is not very tall and not very wide, and if you passed him on the street, you would not notice anything remarkable except that he always wears a grey fedora, winter and summer, and smokes thin cigars, a habit which he says he picks up in Cleveland when he was over there helping some people in the slot-machine line. But it is known on the Avenue that Jake ran with some hard-rock characters on both sides of the border and spent seven years in Kingston Pen. It is said on the Avenue that if Jake Besser gets mad and goes after you, you will have to kill him, because Jake will not stop until he has killed you.

I can see all these interesting thoughts are running through the mind of Porkchops because his fingers slowly unwind from the collar of Max Himmelfarb's shirt and he lets Max sink back against the wall.

"I am never coming back here again," Porkchops says.

"That is too bad," Jake says. "I am very sorry to hear that."

After Porkchops has departed, Jake takes me and Max and Natie Greene into the kitchen of his apartment and speaks to us like this:

"I am always very fond of you boys, but I cannot have this kind of kerfuffle going on. What is wrong with you?"

"There is nothing wrong with me," Max says. "I am in love, that's all."

"Do not worry, Max," Jake says. "It will pass. In the meantime, try not to get into disagreements with people who are bigger than you."

"No! You are wrong!" Max says. "I am in love with Shelley Englander."

Natie groans, and I groan too. We had no idea how bad Max was.

"I wish to state right now, in public," Max says, "that if I can somehow convince Shelley Englander's father to accept me, I will marry her."

"Well, you have come to the right place," says Jake. "It happens I have just what you need."

He reaches into the cupboard above the sink and takes out a teacup and from this teacup, he removes a ring, which is very handsome indeed. It is made of gold and it has little red chips all around it which Jake says are genuine rubies.

"A Johnny out of Windsor who was down on his luck left that with me," Jake says. "From what I hear he will not be back this way for some time, so I am willing to let you have this ring for a mere C-note."

"It's beautiful," Natie Greene and I both exclaim together.

"Nothing but the best," Jake says. "This guy out of Windsor was with 'Canada Steal' and it is well known they do nothing but the finest houses."

"Impossible!" Max cries. "I do not have a nickel for a cup of coffee! How am I going to come up with a C-note?"

"Ah, me...I would not be young again for all the tea in China," Jake says, putting the ring back into the teacup.

"But I will tell you what, Max," he says. "Some people from the other side of the border have been in touch with me and I will be needing a young fellow who is full of piss and vinegar."

"A job?" Max cries in delight. "You are offering me a job?"

"Do not talk dirty in my house!" Jake says. "Jobs are for guys what put on neckties every morning. You are my partner, Max. If I do good, you will do good."

On our way back to the Club Morgan club rooms, Natie and I insist that Max tell us how he manages to do what no one else ever does, which is get close to Shelley Englander. She is, at this time, a very gorgeous doll with thick black hair and rosy cheeks and a smile many guys on the Avenue say makes them feel they can leap over tall buildings.

But Shelley Englander has a very big problem, namely her father, Samuel Englander. He is a house painter who is so religious in his spare time that people call him "Rebbe Shmuel," or "Reb Shmuel" for short. Shelley's father swears that she is going to marry a rabbi or, at the very least, a doctor who keeps kosher. So Natie Greene and I are overcome with curiosity as to how Max manages not only to have a few minutes alone with

Shelley Englander, but to talk to her about such a scary subject as getting married.

"It is really very simple," Max says. "You know that old Mr. Englander never likes to have men working for him steady because they waste time and steal the bread from the mouths of his children. So he is always looking for guys to work a day or two at a time, and Freddy Englander, who is Shelley's kid brother and plays basketball at the Y, says that if I come with him, I can make some scratch.

"So, this day, I come into the shed in back of the Englander house where the old man keeps the paint and ladders and stuff, and Shelley is unpacking a box of brushes, and I say to her, 'You are beautiful and I love you and I want to marry you.' And she says, 'Yes.'"

"Just like that?" Natie says.

"No, not just like that," Max says. "She tells me she has seen me often coming and going on the Avenue and she is getting for me the same feelings I am having for her and she wishes I will do something about it."

"But how can you be so sure...that she is so sure?" I say to him.

"Because she says I smell good," Max says.

Natie lets out a little whistle between his teeth which causes Max to start getting hot all over again.

"Get your minds out of the gutter!" he says to us. "We do nothing more than kiss a couple of times. We are both very worried her father is going to come back into the shed and commit murder upon us. But when she steps back, Shelley says to me, 'I like the way you smell and now I am absolutely sure.'"

Some weeks after this, I am coming out of the Tip Top Tailors factory where I operate a machine that puts buttonholes in men's trousers, when who should I see but Natie Greene, sitting in his cab.

"I am waiting for you," Natie says. "I know it is payday and I figure you will want to go up to Max's new place."

"Before I go anywhere I am supposed to give my mother ten bucks a week for room and board," I tell him.

"I know," Natie says. "That is why I get you before you go home. I am feeling lucky tonight. Give me the sawbuck and we will go up to Max's and I will make enough that you will be able to pay your rent for a whole year."

I am indeed touched by Natie's interest in my welfare, so we stop at

Stedman's for a little chicken soup with matzoh balls and then go on up to what we have started calling Max's place, but which is actually Jake Besser's place. It is three rooms above a dry-goods store, and Jake has got gold and black letters painted on the door saying, "Summerhill Social Club."

Max is sitting at a long wooden table. He has got a telephone stuck to his ear and he is calling out race results to a kid in a baseball cap who is writing them down on big blackboards behind the table. Guys are sitting on folding chairs in front of Max and as the results go up, they are looking either like millionaires or like they want to blow their brains out. But whichever, they still go up to the table at the side where Nora Besser and her friends are taking down new bets and paying off old ones.

Jake has the wire. For years, guys on the Avenue have been talking about how big they could be if they could just get the phone connection from the States that will bring them the results of every race from all over the country the minute the race ends. Just think of how fast the action could get.

And now Jake has the wire. Some guys say it is because of some gentlemen he got to know when he was up in Kingston as the guest of his majesty, and others say the wire comes from the people out of Cleveland in the slot-machine line that Jake spent some time helping out. But everybody on the Avenue agrees that the Summerhill Social Club is just the beginning. Jake is going to open gambling clubs all over the city. And his vice-president in charge of operations is Max Himmelfarb.

But, this night, Natie Greene is not interested in the horses. Nor is he interested in the poker game which is going on in the middle room. Nothing will do for Natie but he must get in on the crap game in the back room.

And luck is, indeed, smiling on Natie Greene. He has been telling me the absolute truth. He keeps making his numbers and covering side bets and before I know it there is a pile of over five hundred bananas in front of him.

"Natie," I say to him, "you are a genius. Give me my half and let us get out of here."

"I am hotter than a pistol," Natie says. "Do not interrupt me."

He is covering side bets all over the place now, and before you can say Jack Robinson, we are up over a grand. I am yanking on his arm now, begging him to get out of the game and give me my half. I am rich! I can buy a car! But Natie will not pay any attention to me. "Go get something to eat," he says. "I am still on a roll. When you come back, we will go."

So I head out to the kitchen, where some very nice dolls who tell me they are nieces of Nora Besser are serving up salami sandwiches with dill pickle on the side, and bottles of beer. When I get back, Natie is already out of the game. But he is broke. I am not gone ten minutes and he has lost all our money. Two bad calls, he says. He is cleaned out. Skint. But we were up over a grand! I have Natie by the throat. I am going to kill him.

"What are you getting so excited about?" Natie says. "I lost over twelve hundred bananas. All you lost was a ten-spot!"

I am stupefied. He is right. I am going to kill him anyway. But we are interrupted by Max.

"I am very glad you guys come by tonight," Max says. "Please get yourselves up and come to Rabbi Langner's house on Landrigan Street by eleven o'clock. He is going to marry me, and I would like you guys, as my best friends, to be my witnesses and all that sort of stuff."

If ever I am so foolish as to get married myself, I will want to do it the way Max does. When I get to Rabbi Langner's, there is just me and Max. Then Natie drives the cab up and Shelley gets out. She is carrying a little suitcase, which is all she has in the world. No one from her family is with her. In fact, they think she is just going to stay overnight at a girlfriend's.

The whole thing takes only ten minutes, including Rabbi Langner's little talk about being loyal to each other and keeping a kosher home. Max slips onto Shelley's finger the gold ring with the rubies. This is a gift from Jake Besser. Natie and I have gone halvers on a bottle of champagne, and we open it in the cab and we all four drink a toast to true love and good times while we drive them to Union Station so they can catch the train to Niagara Falls.

When Shelley calls her father that night to tell him the good news, the old man gives a geshry. She has married a gangster! He hangs up on her. Reb Shmuel stays at home for the next week. He sits in his front parlour, weeping and cursing. Every morning and evening his buddies from the Minsker shul come to say the Kaddish with him. He is sitting shiva for his daughter, Reb Shmuel says, because he doesn't have a daughter any more. She is a dead person.

None of this particularly bothers Max and Shelley. He is doing very well with Jake, and they rent the top two floors of a house and it is like one big party. But, one night, Natie Greene and I are alone in the Club Morgan club rooms, and Hughie Bartleman, the plain-clothes dick, comes to the door. I tell him we are busy right now, but he insists he is very eager for our company, and the next thing we know, we are down at Cherry Beach, sitting in Bartleman's old DeSoto and watching the winking lights of a grain freighter bob towards the docks. The freighter gives out with a hoot from his fog horn that is the loneliest sound I have ever heard.

"You know, a lot of guys come up here from the States thinking they're going to be Al Capone," Bartleman says. "We bring them down here and let them go for a swim."

He takes a mickey of Appleton Estate out of the glove compartment and offers it to us. The last thing I want at this particular time is a drink, but Natie takes a long gulp.

"Detective Bartleman, that is very interesting information," I say to him. "But it is after midnight and if I do not turn up soon at home, my mother will call the police."

Bartleman pays no attention. He goes on as though he is talking to himself.

"Jake Besser is heading for a fall. And your buddy Max is going down with him. Parties on the other side of the border are fighting over the wire. Guys are getting knocked off—right, left, and centre—and some of them are very big people. We hear Jake's number is coming up too."

"So what do you care?" Natie says. He helps himself to another pull of Bartleman's rum. "It'll just save you the trouble, eh?"

"On another occasion, I would teach you manners," Bartleman says. "But I need you boys to deliver a message. We let Jake Besser operate and we let some other guys you've never even heard of operate, as long as nobody gets too big. We like to keep things neat and orderly and we don't want any smart guys coming up here from Cleveland figuring to take over all the action in Toronto. So...you're going to make Jake Besser understand, he's got to give up the wire."

"Well, I can certainly see the problem," I say to Bartleman. "But I think Jake would be more likely to listen to you than to us."

"Jake don't listen to nobody. He thinks he's a tycoon," Bartleman says, with a laugh that makes my hair stand on end. "But he thinks of your buddy Max like he was his own kid. So you're going to talk to Himmelfarb and he's going to work on Jake, and maybe, with a little luck, we can get things back to normal around here."

Natie and I toss for it and I lose, so I'm the one who talks to Max, and together the two of us go to Jake's and deliver the news to him at his kitchen table. He is making big money by now, but he and Nora are still living in the apartment on top of Stedman's Restaurant.

"Bartleman is a straight guy and I am sure he has my best interests at heart," Jake says. "But I get messages from my friends on the other side of the border. They want me to stay open. Besides which...I will tell you boys something I do not talk about very much...but I am away for seven years. When I come back, guys I started out with are already halfway to easy street. And I am still hustling for nickels and dimes. This is my chance to make it big. I am not going to give it up."

It is only one week to the day after Max and I talk to Jake that the roof falls in. He and Max are coming out from having lunch at Stedman's, and Max's pockets are full because he is going out to make payoffs, when an unknown number of parties step up to them with baseball bats and make like it is the World Series. They are so fast and it is over so quickly that nobody in Stedman's sees a thing. This is what they tell the coppers anyway. But the word on the Avenue is that the job is done in broad daylight not just to take out Jake Besser, but to deliver a message to anyone else who may be listening. We can whack you any time we feel like.

Max has a couple of cracked ribs and other bruises and contusions, but Jake is in much worse shape. They have broke both his legs and he has to get a set of choppers for his lower jaw. Bartleman and a squad of uniform cops take the door off the Summerhill Social Club. They hit Jake with bookmaking, bootlegging, selling stolen goods, and a number of other assorted charges that Bartleman must have been keeping in a drawer for just such an occasion. All they've got on Max, though, is keeping a common gaming house, and when he comes up, his father-in-law hires Artie Quinn, who is beginning to make a name for himself as a hot-shot young mouthpiece. Quinn points out that this is Max's first offence and he is just trying to help out his pregnant wife and widowed mother. Max gets off with a fine, which Reb Shmuel Englander pays on the spot.

I am in the hospital room, going over the form with Nora and Jake, when Max and Old Man Englander come for a visit. Reb Shmuel is wearing a black suit and a black hat with a wide brim that makes his whole face look like it is made out of cast iron. He's got a big schnoz on him, and eyes like a wolf. The old man hangs back and lets Max do all the talking.

"Jake, we don't have to live like this!" Max says. "Mr. Englander is going to take us in. He is going to start building houses. We're going to make big money. And we can be legit."

"What are you talking about?" Jake says. "I already heard from our friends on the other side. The war's over. We're going to be bigger than ever."

"I'm going to be a family man," Max says. He sounds like he is going to start crying. "Please come with me, Jake. We can make more money with Mr. Englander than we ever did in the rackets."

Jake smiles at Max like Max is already somebody he used to know.

"I don't want to live in nobody's pocket," Jake says quietly. "But good luck to you, Max. And give my best to Shelley. She's a good girl."

Max and his father-in-law depart from us then. Jake asks me to peel a cigar for him, and I hold the match while he lights up.

"Well, there goes a great player," Jake says, taking a good puff and sinking back on his pillows.

"Aw, don't worry about Max," I tell him. "He'll be back."

"Who's talking about Max?" Jake says. "I mean Reb Shmuel. He used to lay down three, four bills a week with me, horses and baseball.

"But now," says Jake with a big sigh, "I do not think we will be getting much action from Reb Shmuel."

3

PARTNERS: 1974

Victoria Sommers and the fighting tenants on Cotswold Street go up against Max Himmelfarb, J. Arthur Quinn, Harry Margulies, and the perfect real estate deal

47

NUMBER sixteen is in the middle of Cotswold Street, and Cotswold Street is in the east end of the city, and to the people inside the shabby, narrow, three-storey house, it feels like the whole world must be out there, waiting to grab them. They lean their weight against a barricade of upturned sofas, chairs, and tables. They can hear the sheriff calling through a bullhorn.

"Please leave peacefully. This house is owned by the Premier Developments Company. I have in my hand the writ of vacant possession, issued by county court. If you do not leave of your own accord, we will be forced to remove you. Please don't make us do that."

A woman named Winnie Barbeau turns to the man on her right, a social worker named Steve Bukowski.

"That guy sounds like he means business," she whispers. "You better go talk to him."

Bukowski shakes his head sadly.

"I can't," he says. "It's not my place."

Well, who the hell's place is it? Winnie would like to know. Steve was the one who came around, saying he was an outreach worker from the church and they didn't have to pay attention to the eviction notices. He was the one who told people they could fight back.

Winnie looks down to the end of the barricade. There's about a dozen people here, the last weary remnants of the scores of tenants who once occupied rooming-houses on a whole city block. Winnie is searching for a leader, but they're all keeping their backs to her, pressing hard against the pile of furniture—as though that's going to do them any damned good.

Winnie turns to the men on her left, her husband, Billy Barbeau, and her son, Buster. "You'd better go out there," she says to Billy. "Talk to them."

Billy snorts in derision.

"I'm no good at that," he says. "If I was, we wouldn't be in this fix."

"Well, somebody better do something," Winnie says.

She starts to climb up the barricade. Steve Bukowksi is thrilled. This is the way it is supposed to happen, the people throwing up their own leaders. Winnie's husband is horrified. He grabs for the end of her coat, but he's too late. Winnie Barbeau is gone.

In front of number 16 Cotswold Street

Winnie Barbeau stands blinking into a circle of brilliant white lights. Her breath turns to fog in the chilly November air. The mob of reporters scribbling notes and shoving microphones at her almost cuts Winnie off from the cameramen. She's tiny! The beat-up old cloth coat comes almost to her ankles. She's got a pony tail. She looks like a kid with her clenched fist waving in the air. "We got rights!" Winnie is crying. "We're people too! You go away! You leave us alone!"

Ontario Square shopping plaza, suburban North York,
two miles north of Cotswold Street.

Fred Englander, vice-president in charge of marketing for Premier Developments, is just about to open the heavy glass door of an office building. He is a well-fed, balding, worried-looking man; it's hard to believe he'd ever want to hurt anybody. And that is exactly what he's saying.

"Our company is very sorry this happened. We gave those people six months. But we just couldn't wait any longer. It's too bad, that's all.

Englander enters the building, flanked by the two company lawyers, Harry Margulies and J. Arthur Quinn. They are on their way to Premier's offices.

Number 16 Cotswold Street

The remains of the barricade—broken chairs, a sofa with springs coming through the bottom—have been scattered over the lawn. The tenants are coming out quietly now, each one escorted by a uniformed policeman. It seems that once the screaming woman was hustled away in a police car, the fight went out of the people still in the house.

Crowds on the other side of Cotswold Street cheer as the tenants are brought out, and tell them to keep fighting. More fists are seen waving in the air.

But the surly demonstrators are kept back by grey sawhorses and police in black uniforms. The tenants meekly allow themselves to be led into yellow police vans and driven away. They look dazed and hungry.

City Hall Square, thirteen blocks west of Cotswold Street

Alderman Victoria Sommers, whose ward includes Cotswold Street, is holding an impromptu press conference. She still dresses in cashmere skirt-and-sweater sets and looks like an upper-class lady on her way to tea and a shopping afternoon in The Windsor Room of Dagenham's department store. However, since winning a second term, Sommers has been surprising people with her tough talk.

"This is a travesty of justice. This is block busting. It's not over yet. This fight is just beginning. I can tell you this: Premier Developments is never going to build anything on Cotswold Street."

Number 16 Cotswold Street

Workmen are nailing planks across all the doors and windows. Number 16 is beginning to look like the other derelict houses on the block. The crowds are dispersing. Bobby Mulloy, city columnist for *The Daily News*, watches them, composing his lead:

"If the tiny heroine had appeared earlier in this fight, things might have been different. But it was a case of too little, too late. It seems the Cotswold Street houses are doomed. This once-bustling working-class neighbourhood will give way to luxury apartment blocks. Some call this progress. I call it...I call it..."

Mulloy searches for just the right word as he looks for a cab to take him back to the office.

48

MELISSA SANDS pauses before number 33 Talcott Street. She has been going out with Harry Margulies for seven weeks, and this is the first time he has invited her to have supper at his home. She had expected the hard-driving young lawyer to be in something stark and uncluttered. Instead, Harry's home turns out to be a charming little turn-of-the-century row house with bricks sandblasted down to their original earthy red and dark green shutters beside the windows. It looks to Melissa like something painted on the top of an English biscuit tin.

The tidiness makes Melissa feel grimy and out of place. Why, in God's name, was she so coy with herself in the morning? She brought a black skirt and green silk blouse to change into, but she balked at also bringing delicate, fresh underwear. It would have been too calculating. But now, after a full day of teaching and then two hours of directing students in a hectic rehearsal of *West Side Story*, Melissa is grimly aware of stains and clamminess, the badges of hard work.

Well, the hell with it. If Harry Margulies wants her, he will have to take her the way she is. Melissa smiles wryly at her own bravado. If she and Harry do get down to it tonight, it will not likely be a languorous seduction. From what Melissa has seen so far of Harry, she expects he will be very urgent and demanding. The scuffling between the sheets should be quite enjoyable. But however it turns out, what really matters is to allow Harry Margulies to have his way with her. Once Melissa has received Harry into her body, they can settle down to getting to know each other.

Melissa has grown past the stage in life when she must have some poor fellow heaving and groaning on top of her, striving with all his might to push her into the ecstasy that is supposed to be her lawful due as a woman. Melissa is prepared to put her constitutional rights aside in return for other considerations.

Harry busies himself in the kitchen while Melissa relaxes at the dining-room table with a syrupy glass of kir. The table sits in front of newly attached glass doors that open onto the tiny back yard. Discreet spotlights pick out three anorexic young white birch trees standing in the crisp early-winter snow, and against the back fence, a wily old Manitoba maple with a skin like a python. Melissa, who knows trees from her childhood, is amused that this old weed tree, with its grey, misshapen branches grabbing out in all directions, has somehow managed to survive in the newly fashionable frontier of the Grove.

Talented young caterers from Karen's Kitchen came to the house in the afternoon and did all the essential work. This allowed Harry to stop by the Oxford Club to take a little steam and get cleaned up before dinner. Now he pours a soy sauce and raspberry vinaigrette over the snow-pea and kiwi salad, and throws diced shiitake mushrooms into the ragoût de veau au vin blanc Dijonnais. For Harry, these small tasks are a blessed excuse to keep hiding from the woman he has invited. This whole evening, he realized the instant he opened his door and saw the beautiful Melissa standing before him, is a horrible mistake.

Harry wanted a private setting in which to tell Melissa the wretched truth about himself. He was afraid that if he did it in a restaurant or a bar she might turn violent. If Melissa staged a real humdinger—and, remember, this woman used to be an actress!—it might even become an item in a newspaper gossip column.

But he can see now that bringing her to his own house was just setting himself up for a different kind of disaster. Harry should have inveigled Melissa into making dinner at her place. Then, if she began to throw crockery around, Harry could have walked out. But now she is in his house, and what if, when he breaks the news, she goes crazy? How is he ever going to get her out of here?

"Hi, there! Can I help?"

Melissa has finished her aperitif and grown bored with appreciating the cleverness of Harry's landscape architect.

"You're just in time," Harry says. "Grab that plate of noodles."

The ragoût de veau au vin blanc Dijonnais is a fine blending of poignant white Sancerre, mellow Dijon mustard, butter-soft veal, and sprightly young onions. The only problem is that Harry has allowed it to get a little overcooked and dry. Not to worry, as the English say. Melissa is not one of those women who expect men to have acquired all the civilizing skills overnight. She didn't really come here to eat, anyway. But the delicacy of the food, and the fine wine that goes with it, demands, in return, an honesty from the two people facing each other across the blue linen table-cloth.

"I wanted to be an actress from the time I was four years old," Melissa says. "I just wish there was something else I could believe in so strongly."

"This is the year I'm going to see my son. I'm going to take a whole month off and go to Israel. I owe it to myself," Harry says.

The high, stiff collar of the blouse, dark green with a gold paisley pattern stitched into it, rises dramatically to Melissa's bright orange hair. But the face is small and perky, with brown freckles across the small nose and firm cheeks. Harry can imagine her as a tomboy, playing baseball with the boys and going skinny-dipping with them after the game.

"I wish I could believe in myself the way you do," Melissa says wistfully.

"I'm sure you've had lots of people who believed in you," Harry says.

"Well, I've had a great love, if that's what you mean," Melissa says. Her sad little smile is devastating.

"Why did you break it up, then? Or let him break it up?"

"Oh, this wasn't my husband," Melissa says quickly. "This was long after my husband."

"I see," Harry says. The time has come. But where should he begin? Harry does not use the word *impotent* to describe himself. The doctor has assured him he has no diabetes or other emasculating diseases. He is just passing through a stage, a kind of valley of the shadow that all successful men come to know at some time in their lives. The stress of work...the delayed reaction to a broken marriage: it cannot be a surprise to anyone that Harry's energy, abundant though it is, gets distracted before it can descend to his most important parts. But how do you explain all that to a woman you hardly know?

They are in the living-room now. Melissa is on the couch and Harry sits on the floor beside her. Her hand rests idly on his shoulder. Her other hand cradles a bulbous after-dinner snifter of Armagnac. Melissa is staring at the birch log burning in Harry's fireplace and thinking about rainy summer nights in her family's cottage, lying on the floor, playing chess with her father. Her fingers reach and wind through Harry's curls.

"Melissa…" Harry summons up his best lawyer-at-a-meeting voice.

"Marian," she says. She sounds angry at him although Harry cannot think of anything he has done up until now that might have offended her.

"Melissa, there's something I feel I should discuss with you…"

"Marian. My name is Marian McNab." She continues to gaze moodily into the fire. Her fingers tighten on him; she is actually pulling his hair now and causing considerable pain, but Harry is afraid to move.

"Melissa Sands was an acting name, something I dreamed up when I was in England. Like my first husband. I dreamed Nigel up, too. He was real, but I dreamed him up. The truth is, I'm just plain Marian McNab, daughter of the Carleyville town clerk. Sometime actress. Longtime waitress. Presently teaching theatre arts. Not involved with any man at the moment. Or any woman either, in case you were wondering. Reasonably good health, but need a little dental work. Sometimes snore at night. But it's been a long time since anybody complained."

Melissa stops herself. Gawd, she's done it again! She can't help being honest; it's always her downfall.

"Melissa, there's something I've got to tell you," Harry says desperately.

"Have you got a bathrobe?" Melissa asks abruptly.

Harry pretends not to understand.

"If you want to take a bath now, it'll cost you double. The rates change after six o'clock."

"I could use a bath, believe me. But I just want something to keep warm in. If we were at my place, I could put on a sexy nightgown for you."

Harry is horror-stricken. Damn! What's wrong with Harry Margulies? Why can he never keep his mind on the job that has to be done?

"Melissa, I've got tell you…," he whispers desperately, but her hand draws his head to her. Harry cannot stop it happening. He stretches out fully, half lying on the couch, half lying on Melissa. He is overwhelmed by the soft, yielding female power. His mind detaches, hovers above them, listening anxiously to the tidal stirring of his body. Something is definitely happening down there. But does he dare trust it?

"Get me that bathrobe," Melissa demands.

Harry unwinds himself from the couch and climbs obediently to the second floor. Quickly he pulls up the blankets and throws a bedspread across them. He was going to change the sheets before he left this morning, but he told himself, why bother? Nothing was going to happen there tonight. The only bathrobe he has is a black and red striped smoking jacket that his ex-wife, Doreen, gave him for their first anniversary. It will barely come down to Melissa's hips but it will have to do. Harry becomes aware that a phone is ringing. Let it ring. For God's sake, let it go. But Harry can't. For a junior partner in Carlton and Boggs, a ringing telephone is a demand from on high.

"Mr. Margulies? This is Sergeant Hewitt, fourteen division."

A cop? Harry's not a criminal lawyer. Has the night operator at Carlton and Boggs mistakenly given his number to some idiot who got himself busted?

"Mr. Margulies, those people we took out of sixteen Cotswold Street today; they've moved back in. There's six or seven, as near as we can figure. We only had one officer on the scene, and he was in the front. They snuck around the back, I'm afraid. I'm really sorry about this. Do you want us to go in and just take them out again?"

Harry starts to say, "Yes, damn it! Get them out of there!"

But the bastards will have called the media by now. Cameramen will be lying in wait. Premier Developments throws people onto the street in the middle of the night! And where was Harry Margulies when all this was going on?

"No!" Harry shouts into the phone. "Don't do anything. Please! I'll be right there."

Downstairs, Harry tells Melissa he must rush away. He doesn't go into the details but apologizes movingly and explains that being a lawyer is as bad as being an obstetrician. You're always on call.

Melissa looks at the smoking jacket he is carrying. Harry had forgotten all about it.

"I'll wait for you," Melissa says. She plucks the black and red jacket off his arm. "I don't have to be in school tomorrow. It's a professional development day."

49

THE SCRAGGLY little strip plaza brings a mixture of memories to Max Himmelfarb. He had to push his father-in-law, Old Man Englander, into gambling on even these small, nondescript blocks of stores. "Houses, we build houses!" Old Man Englander had screamed at him. "We don't know from stores. What do you think we are, Dagenhams?" If it had not been for Max, Premier Developments would have gone on building shitbox bungalows forever. But Max pushed the Englanders into strip shopping plazas and then into Ontario Square, two million square feet of indoor shopping mall surrounded by acres of parking lots. Max Himmelfarb made Premier Developments into a big and powerful company. So how did that wonderful, religious man, Reb Shmuel Englander, reward him? He pushed him out and put his own son, Fred, in charge. But Max has only himself to blame; he had seen it coming for years. He'd always known he was smarter than Freddy.

The apartment above the constant whine of the dry-cleaning plant is dark and stale. Nora Besser waits at the top of the stairs. Rising into the light, Max composes his face into a hearty smile. The years have not been kind to Nora Besser. The famous red hair is black now, and brittle with dye and age. She thrusts forward a dry cheek for Max Himmelfarb to kiss.

"What do you want, Max?"

"I just heard about Jake."

Nora nods in acknowledgement, but her head comes back up slowly, as though recovering from a blow. She leads Max into the bedroom. A wheelchair rests against the wall. The old brass bed, the only memento Nora brought with them from the apartment on Berryman Avenue, has been replaced by a narrow hospital cot with bars on the side. But even this looks too big for Jake.

He lies gasping in his sleep, his useless legs tangled in the starched white hospital sheets. Who would have ever believed Jake Besser could be so thin? "You get my cheques?" Max asks Nora.

"Yes, they're a big help, Max. They wanted to send Jake to a nursing home after the stroke, but I said, 'No, he'll die in there. You send Jake home to me. I'll take care of him.'"

"You and Jake," Max says. "Two of a kind."

Nora goes off to the kitchen to make coffee, and Max settles down in an easy chair, waiting for Jake to wake up. There is something of the old Jake left after all, and it is reassuring to see. The hands clutching the sheets are as big as ever. Remember the time they were sitting together in Jake's old Chrysler convertible on Queen Street, and Hughie Bartleman, the detective, came up and told them to move along? Jake refused to go. It was his parking spot and he had a right to be there. Max would have gone quietly because Bartleman knew they were booking and he could make trouble for them. But Jake lived by principles; what's mine is mine, so you leave me alone and I'll leave you alone. Jake asked, he damned near begged, Bartleman to leave him in peace. But Bartleman just had to be the big shot. He told Jake to move the car. "I don't want to see your ugly kisser around here again today," Bartleman said. So Jake got out of the car and laid him out. He walked up to Bartleman and threw a punch that Max never even saw and, the next thing anybody knew, Bartleman was lying on the sidewalk, stiff as a board. There was never another like Jake Besser.

Nora comes back with the coffee, and Jake begins to stir on the bed. The panting breath becomes louder, more desperate, as though something is breaking inside Jake's chest. He raises himself on one elbow. Slowly, as though his hands have to force themselves through the empty air, Jake lifts his glasses from the night table, puts them on, and turns to focus his milky eyes on Max.

"Another country heard from," Jake says. "You're on easy street now, eh?"

"But he don't forget his friends," Nora says quickly.

Jake's bitterness is like a balm to Max's soul. Max has lost so much—Shelley's gone, his kids don't talk to him any more, he's out of the company. But they have not destroyed him; he still has his old loyalties. He is still what he has always been, Max Himmelfarb.

"Jake, tell me something. What the hell was wrong with Hughie Bartleman?"

"Bartleman? The cop? He was my partner."

"Jesus Christ! Why the hell didn't you tell me?"

Jake starts to laugh, but it comes out with a sound like tearing paper and he has to stop.

"There's a whole lot of things I never told you," Jake says. "You was a nervous kid, you know that?"

Max takes a couple of cigars from the inside pocket of his suit and begins to peel away the cellophane. Nora starts to say that Jake is not allowed to smoke any more, but, seeing the look on his face, she comes instead and sits beside Jake, holding him up while Max lights the cigar for him. The thick, earthy smoke reminds her of the characters on Berryman Avenue, the boozers and the crap shooters who came to their old apartment, the parties that went on until the sun was up and blazing on Sunday morning. So many good times they had back then.

"This ain't bad," Jake says. A cloud of smoke tumbles out of his thin mouth.

"Dollar cigars," Max says. Jake nods and smiles appreciatively.

Actually, the cigars cost Max almost five dollars apiece, but in the old days, whenever Jake wanted to impress them with how important somebody was, he would say the guy smoked dollar cigars.

"Jake, there's something I want to tell you," Max says. "You were the best friend I ever had."

Jake laughs again.

"You shoulda stuck with me," he says. His voice has faded to a faint croak. "We coulda been kings."

"I know, Jake. You were right, Jake."

Max reaches into his inside suit pocket again and places an envelope on the night table beside Jake.

"Jake, go to Florida this winter. Nora, there's twenty Gs in that envelope. All cash. Take Jake to Florida."

Nora shakes her head sadly.

"We couldn't, Max. He's too weak. I couldn't handle him myself."

"Get nurses, Nora. Get doctors. If you need more money, call me. Anything you want. Take Jake to Florida. Get him into the sun."

Nora wraps her arms around Jake and squeezes his frail chest.

"Oh, Jakey," she whispers in his ear. "We'll have fun, Jakey."

Jake ignores her. He leans stolidly against her shoulder, tilts the cigar up to his lips and blows smoke at Max Himmelfarb. He studies Max's face.

"You going crazy in your old age?" he says.

50

THE TORAH tells us that when Moses finally got the Israelites out of Egypt and across the Red Sea, his father-in-law, Jethro, came to visit. Jethro found Moses sitting all day under a tree, judging the people, and Jethro realized he could not go on this way. The Jews were eating him up alive. So Jethro said to Moses, "Appoint people who are honest and God-fearing to be judges over the people." The Torah says that Moses appointed people who were God-fearing to be judges. This was because he could not find people who were *both* honest *and* God-fearing.

From this, the rabbis concluded that there has never been a man, not even Moses himself, who combines all the qualities of a truly righteous man. The president of Premier Developments, Samuel Englander, Reb Shmuel, is thinking about the lessons of the Torah as he sits at the head of the table, watching his son, Fred, explain the unbelievable happenings on Cotswold Street. There are some things Freddy is very good at and his father would be the first to tell him so. But there are other things...well...

Father and son are in the company's boardroom with their lawyers and half a dozen company executives whose names the old man can never quite remember.

"We only made one mistake," Fred is saying. "When we had the bastards out of there we should have flattened the whole goddamned block."

"That would certainly have saved us a lot of trouble," Arthur Quinn says mildly.

Old Man Englander looks again through the newspapers that have been laid out before him. He peers at pictures of the tenants pulling nailed-up boards off the windows. A dignified, elderly man who looks like a minister is bringing in a load of groceries, as though the people who invaded the house were refugees instead of Communists and thieves. Then there is the woman who everybody says is the ring-leader, standing with her arm protectively around her son. The woman looks crazy, and the poor boy looks scared out of his wits.

But the worst are the pictures of policemen taking the people out. They look like Germans. The police, no matter where they are, always look like Germans.

"How much we got in there?" Mr. Englander asks abruptly. The harsh voice startles Harry. The old man looks so kindly, with his black skullcap and his sad, worn face.

"Three and half," one of the company executives replies promptly. "One hundred thousand of our own, four hundred thousand from our partners on this deal, Silverstein and the Solways. Three million from the bank. We're carrying ninety-four thirteen a month."

"Unload it," the old man says. "Let the partners take it. Or put it up for sale. This is not our kind of business."

The Torah instructs us to leave the corners of the field unharvested so widows and orphans can come and have a little food too. The Englanders will let somebody else have the Cotswold Street project.

"Pa, that would be a dumb thing to do. That would be terrible!" Fred Englander says. Harry turns away in embarrassment. Fred Englander must be over forty years old, yet he is carrying on like a little kid who can't get his own way.

"Pa, we're the first people to ever even think of building condos downtown. We're only a block away from a goddamned subway station. We're going to make history."

"I thought this Eton Towers was Maxie's idea," Englander says, with a teasing little smile.

"Max never had anything to do with this. It was me! I thought this up." Fred is almost shouting. And now that he's really desperate, the man has actually acquired a little dignity.

"I'm telling you—I swear to you, Pa!—I can make this thing work!"

Mr. Englander studies his only son as though he has not seen him for several months. Freddy's putting on weight, there is no doubt about it. He's getting puffy again, and look! he's losing his hair. Freddy is pale and sickly, just the way his mother, may she rest in peace, used to be.

"It's a bad neighbourhood," the old man says quietly. "Who's going to pay good money to live in a bad neighbourhood?"

"Pa, they don't live in it, they live on top of it. They don't even know the poor people are down there."

The old man wrinkles up his lower lip. Why do people always want to fight with him? God struck down the sons of Aaron, and the rabbis say it was because they had been drinking when they approached the holy of holies. But Reb Shmuel has always leaned to the theory that God struck down Aaron's sons because they were disrespectful to their father.

"What does our lawyer say?"

Everyone at the table now turns to J. Arthur Quinn.

"I think Fred is right," Quinn tells Mr. Englander. "But it's a question of timing. Harry and I could get demolition permits this afternoon. Then the sheriff sends in the police; we get those squatters out, and you level the block.

"The only trouble is that every parasite from the media will be there. That kind of publicity can get very expensive when we're talking to lenders—as you know.

"So…what I would suggest is that you offer those tenants alternative accommodation in other buildings you own. Give them three months' free rent, six months if you have to. It'll be expensive, but it's still cheaper than an extra half-point on a mortgage.

"You won't get all the people out, but you'll get most of them. Then that woman can scream her head off, but if she's only got a couple of people left in the house, she'll just look silly."

A large, happy smile begins to light up the mournful face of Mr. Englander. Arthur Quinn is always a pleasure. Reb Shmuel was right to go to him years ago and to keep him on as the lawyer for Premier Developments, even though many other important lawyers who claimed they had better connections have tried to get the company's business. When he is joking with Arthur Quinn, Mr. Englander likes to tell the great lawyer that he has a "Yiddisher kopf."

"Meanwhile," Quinn says, "Harry and I will go ahead with the official plan amendment. We've already been in to see the planners and they like what we've shown them. Give us another six weeks, two months at the most, and we should have it through city council. And I don't think our friends could afford to push this to the OMB.

"So as soon as we've got council approval, Mr. Englander, you could clean out whoever's still left in there, level all the houses, and put it up as a site rezoned for development. I think you could do pretty well with it."

"N-o-o!" The long, painful cry startles the room. It sounds as if it is coming from somewhere deep inside Fred Englander's soul.

Fred jumps to his feet. He rushes to the window and pulls back the heavy drapery.

"Look!" Fred Englander cries. "Look out there!"

The sudden rush of light startles and half blinds the ten people sitting at the boardroom table. The far wall of the boardroom is made up completely of floor-to-ceiling glass panels. Harry was not even aware that the glass was there. But now he finds himself staring out at North York and he is wondering why on earth Fred Englander wants to show them suburbia.

"When we first came out here, there wasn't nothing but tomatoes and cow shit," Fred says, posing dramatically at the side of the huge window, like a master of ceremonies at the side of a stage. "We built all that—us and people like us. Look at it! Just look at it!"

Far below them, endless swarming cars and convoys of boxy trucks pour along the twelve lanes of Highway 401. Motor-exhaust fumes mingle with the morning mist to make a grey, slowly rising industrial cloud that the mid-morning sun is just beginning to burn away. North of the highway, as far as the eye can see, there are hills and fields filled with houses. Running beside the houses, following the geometric lines of the subdivision streets, are the great burgeoning rows of maple and poplar trees. Shmuel Englander remembers when they were tiny saplings, not much more than sticks, that suburban councils insisted every subdivision developer must stick in the ground in front of every bungalow they put up. The old man used to think of the trees as dishonest government interference, another attempt by politicians to rob him of his profit. Now those little nothing trees are a mature forest spreading out beside the houses. Here and there, rising up like sentinels, are clusters of apartment blocks, and shining, glass-walled office towers.

Freddy has a point. Mr. Englander has to admit it. His company built more stuff out there than anyone else ever did.

"How did we do all that? Tell me, Pa. By running away every time somebody gave us a hard time? We got big by taking chances. How many times we were so close to the wall they were sitting shiva for us. But we always came through, didn't we? We made money for ourselves and we made houses for people to live in.

"I'll tell you something else, Pa, maybe you don't know because you never go out any more. But everybody is watching this play, and they're going to see a bunch of nothing people come out of nowhere and grab our property, and they're going to see the Englanders turn and run. They're going to say it's time to go for the Englanders. Where does it end, Pa? When we've got nothing left? When we're poor again?"

"Freddy, you look tired," the old man says softly. "You need a little holiday. Relax and get some sun. Take Estelle and the children and go to the place in Florida for a couple of weeks."

"Pa! No!" Fred Englander cries. "What about Cotswold Street? We can't just leave it."

The old man smiles sweetly. He seems so innocent of guile that Harry has a sudden flash of understanding of the old saying: butter wouldn't melt in his mouth.

"All you young people want to push me into the Moshav Zikeinum," the old man says. "Let me wind this business up for you, Freddy. Let me have some fun, too. I still know a few tricks, eh?"

Fred Englander looks around the room for help but he doesn't see any. He will remember this day.

"Pa, this thing is tricky," Fred says, making one last plea. "I've been on this from the first. I'm the only one around here understands it."

"Freddy, if I get into trouble, I'll call you. First thing," the old man says. "I promise."

Fred can go no farther. He knows what a terrible price men can be made to pay for the sin of pride. He has seen his father push his brother-in-law, Max Himmelfarb, out of the company.

"Pa, I'll keep in touch," Fred says.

"For sure," his father says. "We'll talk every day, Freddy...Now, is there any other business?"

There is no other business. The bosses at Premier Developments have met only to consider the problem of the Cotswold Street houses. Now they begin to tuck their papers into cardboard file folders and return to their offices.

Reb Shmuel Englander deliberately waits until only he and the two lawyers are left.

"Arthur, you and me'll talk," he says. "I got some ideas."

"Sammy, I am at your service. As always," Quinn says.

Quinn snaps the lock on his big attaché case and leaves the Premier boardroom, followed closely by Harry Margulies.

51

DANE HARRISON, planner for the East Midtown district, studies his reflection in the walls of the elevator. He has important things to say to his friend Alderman Victoria Sommers, and he is travelling downwards from the twenty-second floor of City Hall to the curved row of offices on the second floor known as "Alderman's Alley." The three walls of the elevator are mirrored. A lurid, silvery image of himself bounces back and forth on all sides, getting fainter and smaller as it recedes, until it becomes an indistinguishable blur. It strikes Dane that this is a perfect metaphor for City Hall. Everything is out in the open, yet the picture keeps receding from view and you can never see what is really happening.

Victoria's executive assistant, a white-faced, starkly beautiful young woman, treats him as an intruder, even though Dane has phoned ahead to arrange this meeting. It doesn't matter to this girl, Dane reflects wryly, that Victoria would not even be here now if it were not for Dane Harrison. Dane was Victoria's first campaign manager, and without him, she would never have got elected. On the other hand, Dane owes Victoria, too. If she hadn't pushed him and arranged interviews for him, he might still be a short-order cook somewhere. The planning department has been screwing people for years, she said to him. The reform movement needs our own people in there. Dane felt uneasy at first and almost quit half a dozen times. He had studied sociology at university and had to learn the secrets of urban planning on the job. But, for the first time in his life, he was getting paid just to think, and Dane discovered that he really enjoyed that. Now he has something to justify Victoria's faith in him And to justify his accepting a bank deposit of $1,362.37 every two weeks.

"Premier Developments is trying to fuck us around," Dane says. "They've got 3.2 acres. That works out to a lot size of 139,392 square feet. The building they want to put up is 592,446 square feet. There is no goddamned way they can do that."

"Why not?" Victoria says coldly. She is putting on a little show, Dane realizes. Steve Bukowski, the social worker who has been holed up with the Cotswold tenants, is there too, slouched arrogantly in an easy chair.

"Because...because you see," Dane says, and he knows that he is beginning to sound like a teacher giving a math lesson, but there is just no other way to get this across.

"Because...the floor-space index under the official plan is 3.5. That means you can put up a building 3.5 times the size of your lot, okay? So they can get the land rezoned up to...at most!... 487,000 square feet. But that's not enough for Freddy Englander. Premier Developments wants more. So, they're claiming a bonus for landscaped open space.

"If he can keep his buildings down to only twenty-five per cent of the lot, he can claim a three-quarter-per-cent bonus for that extra landscaped open space.

"What that is supposed to mean is that our friends can build on only 35,000 square feet and they have to leave 104,000 square feet vacant. Now you look at these drawings and you tell me where those 104,000 square feet of open space are."

Dane unrolls on Victoria's desk one of the large presentation drawings Premier's architect brought to the planning department. Bukowski pulls himself out of the chair, and even Victoria's slavish executive assistant feels she too must see what is going on.

They are looking down on three large, rectangular buildings rising out of a three-storey parking garage. The drawing is a side perspective. The apartment blocks look like giant grey tombstones with iron balconies stuck on them. There is no open space, anywhere.

"What the hell are they talking about?" Bukowksi says.

"The lobbies!" Dane says. "And the top of the parking garage." He cannot help but laugh. What the guys from Premier have been trying to sell him is so brazen, it is really funny.

"They want us to count the lobbies inside the buildings as 'landscaped open space.'"

"The bastards!" Bukowski says, and he sounds like he is ready to punch Dane, as though Dane is responsible. "That is just fucking unbelievable!"

"You are not going to recommend that, surely to God!" Victoria says.

"Of course not," Dane says. "But I can't recommend against it either. The commissioner, Redmond, has to sign the report. So all I can do is lay out the alternatives."

"It could get through council," Victoria says slowly and thoughtfully. "Stranger things than that have happened around here."

"I know," Dane says. "That's why I came down here. If you want to stop this thing, you can't just rely on the tenants squatting in that house. You've got to get people right across the city moving on this one. It's going to be the Berryman Expressway fight all over again, Victoria."

"Well...well...well." Victoria smiles happily. "It looks like we've got our work cut out for us."

"I don't like it. The people could still get screwed," Bukowski says. "We put all our energy into stopping this thing, and then what? They tear down the houses anyway and do something else."

"Maybe." Dane faces Bukowski squarely. It is like looking at himself, the angry, suspicious person he was only a few years ago. "That could happen, Steve. No question. But what if..." Dane pauses for effect. "What if...we could buy those houses off the Englanders, the whole block of them?"

Dane savours the silence that follows his punch-line.

"You're wondering where we get money to buy downtown houses, right?" Dane says. "The feds! We get it from Ottawa—from whence all blessings flow. I've been reading the new National Housing Act. It looks like the feds want to get out of big public-housing projects and put their money in smaller co-ops and non-profit housing. They want to build new stuff, but there's nothing I've read that says they won't pay for buying existing housing. In fact, they'll probably love the idea. Their per-unit costs will be a hell of a lot lower."

"I'm beginning to get the picture," Bukowski says. "I think my people are going to like this."

"Okay then, this is how you do it," Dane snaps. He can still teach this guy a thing or two.

"You start building support all over the city. You build up enough pressure on City Council to stop Premier Developments in their tracks. So, now they're looking around and they want to unload. But who's going to buy? The tenants are still holding number sixteen Cotswold Street, right? Nobody can do anything until the people are carried out, kicking and screaming. So, who's going to pay good money to do a dirty job the Englanders don't want to do themselves? The Englanders are stuck. They're desperate.

"Then we come up. We're nice guys now. We've got federal bucks. We offer to take the property off their hands. We even offer them a decent profit on the land."

"That's a lot of ifs," Victoria says warily.

"I am well aware of that," Dane says. "It's pie in the sky, right now. But you folks could make it happen."

"I think it's great!" Steve Bukowksi says. He pays Dane the highest compliment he can think of. "You know, you don't sound like a planner at all."

"He's not a planner," Victoria says proudly. "He's one of us."

52

"WHAT THE HELL happened to Natie?" Max Himmelfarb demands. It is ten o'clock in the morning and he is standing naked in the dim, carpeted locker room of the Commodore Club.

"Natie's in the shvitz," Jack Berk says. "He's giving some poor fucker a rub down."

"Are you crazy! You let him do that?" Max says. "He's gonna kill somebody."

Jack Berk shrugs, an eloquent statement. Strangers should not be coming around the Commodore Club and letting Natie give them a workout. Everybody knows that Natie Greene, the old cab driver who used to train prize fighters, is more than a little punchy himself.

"You gonna get that bottle?" Jack Berk says. "Or are you just gonna stand there with your putz hanging out?"

Max has just come out of the shower. He is standing at the head of the short flight of stairs leading down into the locker-room lounge where Jack is waiting. Max has been putting on weight. The sturdy football-player's chest now carries two sagging pink folds, as heavy as a woman's breasts. Water drips from his round belly onto the carpeted floor.

"Do I look like a bootlegger?" Max says. "You already finished off one bottle."

"What the fuck do you care?" Jack Berk says. "What are you, the score-keeper?"

Max shakes his head incredulously and pads off to his locker to retrieve the bottle of Chivas Regal. The early-morning joggers and the young men who work out in the weight room have come and gone. Until lunch hour, when new squash and racquet-ball players begin to arrive, there will be nobody in the Commodore Club locker room but the regulars, Max Himmelfarb and his old friends from Berryman Avenue.

"You ain't gonna believe this," Max says, when he has wrapped a towel around his middle and settled down in an armchair beside Jack Berk. "They got Jake Besser in a crib. Just like a little kid. Jake Besser, the toughest man in Toronto."

"My brother Danny was the toughest man in Toronto," Jack Berk says as he fills a styrofoam cup with Max's Himmelfarb's whisky.

"Like shit, he was. He never tangled with Jake."

"Danny wasn't afraid of no one," Jack carries on as though he has not even heard Max. "Once Danny comes home from the army and he has on his uniform, see, and he wants to show off to the boys. So he comes down Berryman and these three British officers are standing in front of Stedman's. They see this little guy going by in his uniform—Danny was only five-foot-two, remember—and one says, 'There goes Canada's best hope.' Danny turns around and says to them, 'What did you say?' And they say to him, 'You heard us.' So Danny goes and he beats the living shit out of them. They had to put one of them in the hospital. When it comes up in court, the judge says to the Limeys, 'What happened?' 'This little man attacked us.' The judge turns to my brother: 'Is that true?' Danny says to him, 'Yes, it's true, but they left something out,' and he tells the judge what the Limey says to him. The judge laughs, fit to be tied. 'I guess there's still some hope for Canada yet,' the judge says, and he throws them all out."

"Are you still telling that story? You know how many times you told me that story?" Max says. "Your brother Danny was a pimp."

"That's true," Jack Berk says judiciously. "You wouldn't get no argument from me. But Jake Besser never took him on."

They are interrupted by a cry: "Help! Help!" It is so bizarre that Max and Jack Berk cannot take in what is happening. But there's Natie Greene standing at the top of the stairs, screaming and looking terrified.

"He's having a heart attack! Call an ambulance."

Max rushes out to the steam room. There, under the hot, moist cloud, Max, to his complete, utter astonishment, finds his father-in-law, Reb Shmuel Englander, sitting up on the long marble bench, shaking his head.

"Pa, are you okay?"

"I'm fine." Mr. Englander doesn't sound fine. His voice is a faint croak. "Your friend was hurting my back. Help me out of here."

Max holds out his hand, and his father-in-law clutches it. Max pushes open the heavy glass door of the steam room and helps his father-in-law out to a chair. The old man slumps down, but his breathing quickly returns to normal.

"Pa, what are you doing here?"

The old man returns Max's concern with a wintry smile.

"We've got to talk, Maxie."

Max has been expecting something like this ever since he heard about the mess Fred Englander made on Cotswold Street. But he never dreamed the old man would be so desperate he'd come to the Commodore Club.

"Pa, you don't look so good. Maybe I should call a doctor."

"Don't celebrate yet, Maxie. I already had two heart attacks. If I was having another one, don't you think I'd know it?"

"Okay, Pa. You're the boss." He hands Mr. Englander some towels. His father-in-law's scrawny nakedness is embarrassing.

"Could you get me something to drink, Maxie?"

"Sure, Pa. You want a shot of whisky?"

"Like your gangster friends? Nice place you hang around in, Max. Don't they have any tea in here?"

"I'll get you some."

Natie Greene is hanging on to Jack Berk when Max comes back through the locker room.

"Is he okay?"

Max cannot resist. This is turning out to be such a beautiful day, so many delightful things are happening.

"He's dying," Max says angrily. "You killed him, you crazy prick."

"No-o-oh!" Natie throws up his hands. His cry of despair fills the locker room. "No-o-oh!"

Jack Berk studies Max's face and catches on to the joke. He struggles to stifle his laughter.

"What am I gonna do?" Natie moans. Huge tears are running down his face.

"Get outa here," Max says harshly. "I'll take care of it."

"But he's dying!"

"You want to take care of him yourself? I told you I'll look after everything. Get out of here."

"Max is right," Jack Berk says gently. "We better scram, Natie." He takes the trembling Natie by the arm and leads him to the lockers.

Max gets a cup of tea from the snack bar at the front of the club. He finds the old man seated comfortably, towels draped across his middle. Withered and naked though he is, Old Man Englander has taken possession of the Commodore Club. He looks composed and commanding, as though he were in the offices of Premier Developments.

"You're getting fat, Maxie. This kind of life is not for you."

"Forget it, Pa. I'm not coming back."

"Did I ask you anything? I just brought you regards. From David. Him and Marilyn was over for supper on Sunday. Nice girl, Max. You should go see them."

Max stiffens. There are so many things he would like to say to his father-in-law, now that he's got the old man where he's wanted to have him for so long. But the old bastard is so wrapped up in himself, he'd never understand. It was because of Mr. Englander, because of his crazy bullying people and playing everybody against each other, that Max's marriage wore out and his own son lost respect for him.

"Pa, I like the way I live. And there is no way on God's green earth that I am ever coming back to work for you. Life is too short."

The old man nods, letting Max's words sink in. Then he says, "How about the company, Max?"

Reb Shmuel says it again, very slowly and carefully. "How would you like the whole company, Max?"

"What the hell are you talking about?" Max can feel his heart begin to beat faster. This, he has to admit, he did not expect.

"You make Cotswold Street work, and I sign the place over to you. You pay me out, a fair price—and we bring in an outsider if you and me can't agree on the price—but you still got the company—lock, stock, and barrel."

"What are you trying to pull?" Max says. His words are belligerent, but his delivery is not.

"Max, when I pushed you out, I made a big mistake. I was trying to protect Freddy. But I was stupid. Nobody can protect Freddy. He's my son, but I can't live his life for him. So why am I killing myself? Better to sell out, enjoy what little time I have left, and when I'm gone, Freddy can still be a rich man."

"Sell to me now," Max says. "What are we waiting for?"

"You don't trust me, Maxie?"

"Aw, come on, Pa."

"Maxie, if you don't trust me, then nothing Artie Quinn puts down on paper is going to make any difference. I'll still beat the pants off you. But I'll tell you the truth, Max, if I sell out now, I'm giving you too good a deal. The company's only worth half what it should be—maybe not even that. This Cotswold thing is killing us. Half the banks in town want to call my loans. But you get Cotswold Street moving again and they'll back off. It's clear sailing then, Maxie. You pay a fair price and I walk away. The joint's yours."

"Yeah, sure," Max says. "What about Freddy?"

"I'll handle Freddy."

"Yeah, I'll bet you will," Max says bitterly. All the old memories—the angers, the fights, the fears, the yelling and screaming—come back to him in a rush.

"Max, you always thought I was Laban and maybe you were right. But you worked your time with me and you got Leah. Just do a little more for me now, Max, one last job, you get Rachel."

The stakes are too high. The old man is so smart. Max sticks out his hand. Mr. Englander reaches up and clutches it. The deal is made.

Max helps his father-in-law to dress and they leave the Commodore Club together.

Max is thinking he has won something that few people ever get, a second chance in life. This time he will do everything right. He will put together the perfect real estate deal. He will pay all his debts and settle all outstanding accounts in his life.

Reb Shmuel is thinking about a story the Rabbi of Yivunsk once told. A wealthy man had died and left everything to his slave. His son, who lived in a distant city, was allowed to come and pick only one thing from all his father's possessions. The slave took good care of everything, warding off thieves and vandals until the son arrived, because, of course, everything belonged to him now. When the son learned of his father's will, he rushed to the rabbi and wept that his father had ruined him. The rabbi laughed and said his father had been a wise man.

"Your father made sure everything would be looked after until you got here," the rabbi told the son. "Tomorrow, when you come to the house of study and they ask you what you want, you put your hand on the slave and you say, 'I pick him.' Then, according to the law, you get the slave—and all his possessions too."

53

VICTORIA SOMMERS sits at the back of the stage in the basement of the Landrigan Street United Church, listening to Winnie Barbeau. This meeting of the Grove ratepayers has been called especially for Winnie. Since that thrilling afternoon three weeks earlier when she burst out of the barricaded house to face the police and the television cameras, Winnie has become the saviour of Cotswold Street. Victoria ought to be ecstatic. Winnie is building exactly the kind of constituency Dane Harrison said they needed. But now Victoria finds herself worried and even a little frightened.

"Elda Harwood's baby is doing all right, but we need some oranges, fresh stuff, you know?" Winnie is saying. "It's godawful cold in that place. There's no insulation, and we couldn't find no storm windows. The bathroom feels like an igloo. Elda spends most of her time down in the kitchen.

It's the only room in the house where you don't see your breath. We take turns looking after the baby when Elda has to go out to see her social worker."

Winnie speaks into a bouquet of microphones that have been clipped to a stand in front of her. Roving television cameramen turn from the upturned, curious faces crowded into the church basement to scrutinize Winnie. Winnie hardly seems aware of them. The brilliant lights illuminate a tense, small, clear-eyed woman who seems much younger than thirty-one, which is what the press has been reporting her age to be. Winnie is wearing blue jeans and a ragged brown turtleneck sweater. Her hair has been pulled into a ponytail. Her hands are jammed tightly into the pockets of the shabby, cast-off man's tweed overcoat that hangs on her shoulders and drags almost to the floor. The oversized coat has become Winnie's trademark. She wears it everywhere.

"I want to tell you about Mr. Birdsell too. He wasn't really living in those houses before, you know. He was just kind of an old rubby-dub who was hanging around the street. But when we went back in to number sixteen, he came with us. Some people said Mr. Birdsell was bad news and we should get rid of him..."

Victoria knows that Winnie is referring to her and to her assistant, Marlene. Winnie is not telling the audience that—at least so far, she isn't. But, Victoria understands, the threat is there.

"...so we said, like, Mr. Birdsell, where's he gonna go, eh? So he's with us, and you'd be surprised, he does a lot of things around the place and the kids really love him.

"Y'know, something that strike me as really funny? People like these guys who want to tear down our homes, they got so much and they don't want to give away any of it. But people like us, who don't have nothing, we're willing to share everything we got."

Steve Bukowski, standing at the back of the room, is experiencing the guilt and the emotional turbulence Winnie creates around her and he is feeling jealous. It is ignoble of him, he knows, but Steve can't help himself. If only he were up in front of those microphones, there is so much that he could articulate. But who would ever listen to him? Fate has cheated Steve Bukowski. He has a working-class soul, but he was born into the ignorant, self-indulgent middle class. The best Steve can do is turn his back on the middle class and help people like Winnie move into positions of power.

"...so we're askin' you to join us. It's not charity. We don't want handouts from no one. We can look after ourselves. But if they kick us out of there, they'll be after you next. They'll come and throw you out of your houses too. They want everything, the whole world. The only way we're ever gonna beat 'em is if we all join up together."

That is so true! Don McPartland, former vice-chairman of Citizens Against the Berryman Expressway, is thinking he would like to run up there and give Winnie a big hug. He'd like to take her home and give her a good meal. He'd like to give her a good bath too, but that's another problem. The point is that Winnie is saying something the urban reformers should have figured out for themselves, but they were too cocky. They thought when they stopped the Berryman Expressway they'd saved the city. But there are always greedy developers and God only knows who else out there ready to tear up the old neighbourhoods. The only protection is for people in all neighbourhoods to join hands—just the way Winnie Barbeau, the passionate little waif from Cotswold Street, is telling them to.

"So I'm sayin' to ya, come down and join us on Cotswold Street. And when they try to take your houses—and they will, you know they will!—we'll be standing right up there beside you, shoulder to shoulder. And we'll win! 'Cause we're together"—Winnie raises her right arm, the oversized sleeve falls down, the tiny fist waves in the air—"We're together! Together! Together!"

The crowd claps and cheers. But Winnie is rudely cut off from them. Reporters and TV cameramen crowd around the front of the stage. This is great stuff.

"How long can you hold out, Mrs. Barbeau?"

"Forever!"

"Will you talk to the developer?"

"Yeah, I'll talk to him. I'll tell him this is my home and you get the hell out of here!"

"What if they send in the police again?"

"Let 'em come. We're ready. This lady ain't gonna die in bed."

Just look at her, both fists raised in the air now. The reporters race away to their stations and newspaper city rooms. They are replaced by people who have been at the meeting, pressing Winnie with still more questions, some of them pushing money on her. By the time Steve Bukowski and Victoria can get to her, Winnie seems dazed. Steve thinks of her as being like a prize fighter who doesn't know the round is over. Winnie is still looking around for more microphones and cameras.

Winnie refuses Victoria's offer of a ride back to Cotswold Street. She will walk back with Steve. She needs to unwind a little.

"Was I okay?" she asks shyly, as they scuff along through the cold January slush. She holds fast to his arm. "I can't tell. I get so scared up there."

"You were great, Winnie. You were fantastic."

It seems to Winnie they are surrounded by flashing lights, cars splashing by them, neon signs bouncing off the pools of water, huge office buildings downtown with their thousands of glowing windows. In the northern Ontario mining town of Cromwell, where Winnie and Billy Barbeau come from, there was nothing going on at night, just a few drunks wandering around. Down in Toronto, everything keeps going all the time. Anything is possible down here in the city.

"I feel so grown up right now," Winnic says.

The description puzzles Steve Bukowksi, but to Winnie, it is very important. When you are small, everybody treats you like a little kid, no matter how old you are. Winnie thought she'd finally shown them she was a full-grown woman when she had a child of her own. She looked down at the breasts she had always thought of as useless knobs because they didn't mean anything to the boys and she saw herself giving life to another human being, and she thought she had achieved a new depth of adulthood. Nobody would ever be able to take it away from her.

But they did. Billy Jr. grew up. Winnie went from Mother, to Mommy, to Mom, and now to Maw. The very name her son calls her now sounds to Winnie like a surly command. Her own son is ordering her around.

But Winnie Barbeau is not just sitting there, taking it. Winnie is beginning to do things that nobody will ever be able to take away from her.

Winnie kicks at a puddle and laughs at the black spray. Steve feels her hand clutching his arm like a vice and he is happy, too. Power to the people, they used to chant back in the sixties. And now it's really happening.

"Let's go by the hotel where Billy works," Winnie says, suddenly. "He ought to be getting off shift by now. We've earned our beer tonight, Stevie my boy."

54

FIRST COMES the small talk, the personal stuff. Then Harry can get down to business. He has taken his old friend Dane Harrison to Spencer's, the ornate restaurant around the corner from the stock exchange, where brokers, lawyers, and Bay Street deal makers come to have lunch. Harry wants Dane to know that his clients at Premier Developments belong to the élite of the city.

"Harry, the time you don't put in with Gordon now, you'll never get back. You're going to lose your kid, Harry. Just the way Annabel's husband lost Paul. I don't think Paul can even remember what he looks like."

"You're right, Dane. I know it. But I keep thinking: I go over there and what does the kid see? A pasty-faced Bay Street lawyer. What does he see around him every day? All these tough kibbutzniks walking around with submachine guns. He's going to take me around and what's he going to say? Meet my dad, he's a really important man back in Toronto?"

"Harry, the longer you put it off, the harder it's going to be."

"You're my conscience, Dane. I'll make a reservation. As soon as we get clear of this mess on Cotswold Street. You want a shot of brandy?"

"Why not? I don't have to do much this afternoon. Do you eat like this every day?"

"Just when I'm corrupting an honest civil servant...Bring us some more coffee and a couple of Courvoisiers...Dane, tell me, honestly, what do you think? Can you imagine a better deal than this?"

"I don't think anything. I'm just a planner—grade C."

"Bullshit! Sommers listens to you. And there's no way you can tell me this isn't a good deal for her people—three hundred and eighty-seven units of low-income, non-profit housing. We're offering to take care of the whole gang on Cotswold Street, and a lot more people besides."

"It's a long way from downtown, Harry. For these people, Scarborough is like the end of the world."

"Dane, I grew up in suburbia; there's nothing wrong with it. I mean, I like your idea, but there is no way you can have non-profit housing in the centre of the city. The land is just too damned valuable."

"Harry, what if your client couldn't build what he wanted to on Cotswold Street? What if all he could see ahead of him was years of getting hassled? And what if somebody came to him then and said, we'll take this site off your hands, and give you a decent profit? What then, Harry?"

"We'd tell you to stick it in your ear, Dane. My guys spent seven years buying up those properties. They've got a dream, Dane. And they're going to see it through. And I'll tell you something else. Those squatters are going. The only reason we haven't sent the cops in already is that it pays us to leave them there. It's winter; let your people keep the pipes from freezing. Let them pay for the gas and electricity. But comes the first robin of spring, they're out on the street—I guarantee you. And this time, the minute the door closes, the bulldozers go in."

"There is another way, you know, Harry. You don't have to play the shit-head. You could compromise, eh? Let just a couple of the houses on Cotswold go for non-profits. You'd still have plenty of room—more than three bloody acres—to do what you want with. What's wrong with that?"

"Dane, my guys are going for luxury condominiums. Who's going to pay two hundred grand to live next door to a woman on welfare with six kids?"

"Harry, what the hell do you want from me?"

"Nothing, Dane. Absolutely nothing. All I want to do is be able to talk to Victoria Sommers by myself."

"I work for the city, Harry, not Victoria Sommers."

"Dane, there's thousands of people out there who would believe you. But I'm not one of them. Victoria's been talking too smart lately. And so's that woman she's trotting around to the ratepayers. You're on her team, Dane. And I'm not telling you not to be. And I'm not asking you to go to Victoria and tell her Harry Margulies is selling the greatest thing since sliced bread. I'm only asking one thing: just don't talk against me before I get to her. Let me go in to see her on my own. Let me have a level playing-field, Dane. That's all I want."

"You're trying to use me to get to Victoria? I think that's pretty crummy, Harry."

"Dane, you know me better than that. That is the last thing in the world I would do. I'll make you a promise: If I can't sell Sommers on the deal in

Scarborough, I'll set things up so you can see the guys from Premier and try to sell them your scheme for Cotswold Street. And I won't say a word about it one way or another. I'll let them make up their own minds."

"Harry, I can't get involved in anything like that!"

"Nobody will ever know. This will be a strictly private meeting. You've got my word on it. You give me my inning with Sommers. If I can't get anywhere, you get your inning with the guys from Premier. Is that fair?"

"Well, I guess it's not unreasonable, Harry."

"Thank you, Dane. Waiter, a couple more of these Courvoisiers, please."

55

MAX HIMMELFARB has come to the apartment of Angela Porter, whom he refers to in public as "the woman I've been seeing lately," to do serious and painful business. But Angela has greeted him at the door with a glass of ice-cold champagne. She is wearing a long white silk dress Max bought for her one day when he was walking down Bloor Street and it jumped out at him from the window of Creed's. The dress rises to a thin and very revealing halter top. Her soft, honey brown hair comes down straight as a board to her naked, bony shoulders, and her wrists are circled with wide golden bracelets, both of them also presents from Max. Before he can even say hello, she tells him she has prepared his favourite meal—shrimp cocktail and a thick T-bone steak, seared and then just barely cooked.

"We're celebrating," she says, lifting her own glass in a toast. "This is the first day I had every girl on my list, all twenty-nine of them, out-placed and working. I think it's a 'Go,' Max. This is the first day I honestly believed Angela's Angels could be a real business."

"That's great, Angie. I'm really happy for you. Here's to good times. Mazel tov."

Max didn't even realize he was hungry until Angela set the feast in front of him. Then he dug into it gratefully. It's almost eight o'clock. He has been so pleased to be back at work in his old office that he hasn't even noticed how quickly the days go by. It really is amazing how much people can change in a short time.

Take Angela, for instance. When she was Max's secretary at Premier Developments, she was a rangy, bitter woman with a permanent scowl on her face. Max cannot even remember how he got started with her. Probably he just felt sorry for her. But when the Englanders pushed him out and then his own wife told him she couldn't stand the way he was drinking and carrying on, he wound up at Angela's apartment at eleven o'clock at night and she let him in.

He was there for weeks. She let him stay in her bed and she slept on the couch. She gave him massages and listened to his tirades and his horrendous whining. She looked after Max quite efficiently and still managed to get into the office ever day, wearing her dark, stiff suits and the white blouses with the big, prissy bows under the chin. When the Englanders asked if she knew anything about Max, she told them only that he had called her once from Florida and she hadn't heard from him since.

Every day when she came home, she changed into blue jeans and a T-shirt and took money from Max's wallet to buy steaks and alcohol—white wine for herself, scotch for Max. He kept apologizing for all the trouble he was causing and promising to make it up to her when he was on his feet again.

"It's not such a big deal," she said to him. "After three husbands, I'm kind of used to this sort of thing, if you want to know the truth. But I'm making myself a promise, right now. The next person who has a breakdown in my living-room is going to be me."

It wasn't until he'd got a place of his own and was really on his feet again that Max understood how much trouble he had caused her. Without Max Himmelfarb at the office to protect her, the Englanders had treated Angela like dirt. But she never once complained. In his whole life, Max has never met a woman with more class than Angela Porter.

Max told her, virtually ordered her, to quit Premier. Then he gave her the money to start her own business providing temporary help for overworked offices.

"It's the least I can do," Max said. "You brought me back to life again."

"You saved yourself," Angela said. "The life instinct was always there, deep inside you, Max. You just lost touch with it, that's all."

Now the time has come for Max to settle his bill with Angela Porter. He pushes an envelope at her over the pink tablecloth. The hard block letters in the corner say "Carlton and Boggs."

How beautiful she looks with the candle light sliding off those sharp cheekbones.

"What is this, Max?" Angela does not even pick up the envelope. She is staring at it as though it contained something that was going to hurt her.

"It's a deed," Max says gently. "Three lots in Richmond Hill, almost two acres. You sell them tomorrow, you'll get close to two hundred and fifty. You hang in for a couple of years, you'll walk away with half a million—or better."

Still Angela does not touch the envelope.

"Did I do something wrong? I don't get it, Max."

"What's to get? You're a rich woman, Angie."

"Why are you doing this to me? Are you going back to Shelley?"

Max hesitates. It already seems indecent to be discussing his private life with Angela.

"Maybe," he says. "I don't know. I don't think she'd take me back anyway."

"It's not fair. You won't even tell me what I did wrong," Angela says bitterly, but she reaches for the envelope and draws it to her.

Max reaches across the table, covers Angela's hand with his own, and squeezes it warmly.

"You've done the right thing, Angie."

"I'm not a young woman," Angela Porter says. "I'd like to have some money in my life. But this doesn't pay for anything, Max. Don't ever think it does."

56

IN THE FREEZING DARKNESS, cars prowl the streets like wolf packs. Their lights flash through the windows of number sixteen Cotswold Street.

A sudden glare hits the wall, furry shadows race across the peeling red and white striped paper and then the rooms fall into darkness again. At the end of the front hallway there is a watery glow that seems to be coming from the depths of a cavern. The tenants and their friends and supporters have gathered in the kitchen. An open case of beer sits in the middle of the floor. Marlene, Victoria Sommers's secretary, is trickling leafy flakes of marijuana into a cigarette paper.

"I was going to the Loblaws yesterday," Elda Harwood is saying, "and this car, this big Cadillac, came right around the corner at me. If I hadn't jumped back on the sidewalk, he'd of got me for sure."

Billy Barbeau takes another bottle of beer and sinks back to where he has been sitting under the kitchen table. He watches Marlene lick the end of the paper and seal the shreds of leaf and twig up in a limp cigarette. She looks like a vampire, that one.

"There was two guys following me around all day yesterday," Mr. Birdsell says. "They was sitting in the hotel all afternoon, and when I come out, they come out too. They stayed with me all down Walton Street. There was a big, tall guy, blond like some kind of German, and the other was an Indian, I think. When we got to the corner of here, I turned 'round and I really give them the eye. 'You guys lookin' for somebody?' I says, but they didn't say nothing. They just turned and walked away. But they'll be back, I can tell you. They'll be back."

Marlene takes a drag on the cigarette and passes it to the person beside her. She holds the smoke in until Billy Barbeau is certain she is going to suffocate. Her cheeks go rigid and her eyes begin to stare. Then the smoke begins to leak out her nose. Horrible, disgusting, and she's just a kid.

"Listen, folks, I think we're winning," Steve Bukowksi says. "They got rid of the guy we were dealing with before and they brought in this new guy, Himmelfarb. You ought to see him. He looks like he lives on raw meat."

"Himmelshit!" one of the university students says, and everybody laughs.

The merriment irritates Steve. These "students," as people in the house have taken to calling them, are actually members of the Red Sun Commune. They are followers of Leon Trotsky, true believers in a permanent world revolution. Steve thinks of them as parasites who can never get anything going on their own but just attach themselves to whatever others are doing and try to take it over. Unfortunately, though, Steve Bukowksi doesn't have the authority to order the Trots out of number sixteen Cotswold Street.

"This Himmelfarb says he's working on a new plan," Steve says. "He tells us he's going to look after everybody who was living in the houses. So Victoria says to him, 'Well, what about Mr. Birdsell, he came in after but he's part of the group now. So this Himmelfarb——"

"Himmelshit!" The Trotskyite students call out again, interrupting Steve. But the joke is getting stale, and there is hardly any laughter at all. Pleased, Steve Bukowksi goes on.

"So this Himmelfarb looks stunned. You'd've thought Victoria'd slugged him. He scratches his head and says he'll have to think about that one."

"I ain't afraid of him!" Mr. Birdsell cries. He waves his beer bottle belligerently in the air. "I was in the North Atlantic four fucking years."

Elda Harwood steps forward and puts her arm around him, calming Mr. Birdsell down.

"Don't you worry," she says. "There's nobody around here going to split us up."

They make a touching picture, old Mr. Birdsell and young Elda Harwood. He is small and skeletal, startled after all these years to feel a woman's arm around him. She is thick and sturdy, with a wide, brave face that seems to be always struggling against pain and sadness. To Steve Bukowski they are the living alliance of working class and underclass. Elda Harwood and Mr. Birdsell are the reason he went into social work.

Why should good people like this have to grub around just for a place to live? The Himmelfarbs of this world say they should get out in the streets and fight just like he has, and make lots of money too. But not everybody is built to be a fighter. Some people just want to be left alone. It used to be, in ancient times, that people were divided into hunters and gatherers, and everybody got along. But, somehow, the hunters took over and now everybody is supposed to be ready to go out there and kill. To Steve Bukowksi, this way of life is so wrong it drives him into a fury. It is a denial of love, compassion, joy—all of the qualities that make human beings human.

Steve quietly, almost surreptitiously, slips his arm around Marlene's waist and draws her to him. She can feel emotion seething inside him but she has no idea what has got him going. Still, Marlene complies willingly, pressing her thigh against his, letting her head fall back meekly on his shoulder. She doesn't care whether the tenants, these people Victoria depends on so much, are offended. Let them know that even if Marlene is "a big shot," or whatever other names they have for her, she is not ashamed to be seen, in public, looking after her man.

"You know what I say?" Clara Pugh says. "I say we shouldn't all be hiding in here like rats in a trap. We should go up where this guy Himmelfarb lives."

"All the Jews live in Forest Hill."

"Yeah," Mrs. Pugh says. She is a chunky, sweet-faced, grey-haired woman with enormous, beefy wrinkles around her eyes. "We should go march around this Himmelshit's house. Talk to his neighbours. See how he likes it."

"That's beautiful!" Marlene says. "That is really beautiful. I'll talk to Victoria about it."

The droopy marijuana joint reaches Winnie. She takes a quick, final gulp from her bottle of beer and accepts it. Billy watches her take a deep drag. It's embarrassingly obvious that Winnie doesn't know anything at all about this stuff. She's sucking on the marijuana cigarette as though her life depended on it.

"The way I see it," Winnie says slowly, thinking out loud, "the way I see it is...Clara's right. We're just sitting here, fucking the dog."

"That's not true, Winnie. You're out every night, talking to people," Steve says.

"Yeah, yeah, that's good," Winnie says. She is having trouble forming her words. "They give us food and money and all. But you don't see no reporters coming around any more. You don't see no TV cameras. People are forgetting us. We gotta do something!"

Winnie tilts her head back. She has forgotten to pass on the dark brown cigarette. It hangs on her lip now, a sharp, little burning coal, but Winnie doesn't even seem to feel it. Watching her, Billy Barbeau is thinking that Winnie is going to get people hurt. What Winnie needs is a good licking to bring her down to earth. Billy realizes, with bitter resignation, that this is his responsibility, he is Winnie's husband. Billy Barbeau feels the ghost of his own father sneering at him, laughing at him. You thought I was such a bastard, Billy's father is saying. Now you know what it's like to be a family man.

"What do you want to do, Winnie?" Steve asks.

"We should do like when they were fighting that expressway thing," Winnie says. She goes slowly, forming the idea even as she speaks. "We should go out into the middle of Bay Street. We should sit there and we should say, 'We ain't moving!' We should say, 'We got a right to live. We ain't moving 'til you give us those houses!'"

"That's pretty heavy stuff, Winnie," Steve says mildly.

Winnie turns on him.

"You heard me say it. This lady ain't gonna die in bed. I wasn't kidding. I'm not ascared of them."

The little clenched fist goes up, waving in the air, Winnie Barbeau's salute.

Billy Barbeau scrambles out from under the kitchen table and grabs his wife's hand. "Come on," he growls. "It's time to go upstairs." Before Winnie can respond, Billy yanks her after him.

Steve starts to follow them, to rescue Winnie. But Clara Pugh steps in his way.

"Family stuff," Clara whispers to Steve. "Leave them alone. They'll be okay."

Dragging Winnie behind him up the stairs, Billy feels very calm and in control. He is not like his father. The old man just used to sit in a corner of the kitchen, guzzling beer and getting more and more surly, while his wife and children tiptoed around him, hoping just to get through the night. But, inevitably, something one of them did would penetrate the old man's gloom and he would erupt on them, pouring out hatred and abuse, until the children fled the house and Billy's mother cowered in a corner, sobbing. Billy Barbeau's father was mean and rotten, and in the end, everybody left him. But that's not going to happen to Billy. He is going to beat his wife scientifically, lovingly, just enough to bring her to her senses and no more. In the end, she'll thank him for it.

Once inside their room, Billy pushes Winnie down on the bed and begins to tug his belt out of its loops. Winnie covers his hand with kisses. This is the old Billy. The boy she loved has come back to her, full of fire and passion again.

Billy shoves her away from him and on to her stomach. Damn the woman. Why can't she just lie there and take her medicine. As God is his witness, Winnie has this coming. He presses one hand into the small of her back and starts pulling at her blue jeans. They come down with a rush. Winnie rolls over and covers Billy's hand with more kisses. Never has Billy wanted her so urgently. She kicks the jeans off and stands up in the bed. She bends down and kisses her husband on the lips and presses his face to her chest. The belt drops from his hand. Winnie has not even seen it. She sings into his ear, "My man. Oh, my Billy man." She pulls her husband into the bed with her. His last thought is that he shouldn't be letting her do this. But it's too late. Billy Barbeau is lost, lost.

57

TIME... TIME... why is there never enough time? Why are people who want only to help others driven frantic, ridden on rails right over the edge, to total exhaustion? Alderman Victoria Sommers is on the phone, listening to her husband tell her about the boring, stupid PhD oral exam he has spent all afternoon presiding over. Why is Terry Sommers safe at home, making dinner for their daughter, getting to spend so much precious growing-up time with her, while Victoria is alone in her office, waiting for Marlene to bring a cold snack from the City Hall cafeteria? Those cynics who smugly assert that all politicians are thieves, or fools, should spend a day in the life of a city alderman. They should follow Victoria Sommers around for twenty-four hours. They'd learn what principles and dedication really are.

"You really must try to save the Cotswold houses," Terry is saying. "You realize that the one on the corner, the big stone-and-brick one, was designed by Gustav Baird, who did the art nouveau farm-machinery building at the Canadian National Exhibition? It would be vandalism, a war crime as vicious as the bombing of Dresden, if that house were to be torn down."

Victoria asks him to put Ashley on.

"Hi honey-pie, did you like the trip to the zoo? Did the snow tiger come out of his little house? You can tell me all about it in the morning. We'll have breakfast together. Goodbye, lovey. Sleep tight. Don't let the bedbugs bite."

Why does doing the right thing have to get so goddamned complicated? First thing in the morning she had to face Harry Margulies. There isn't a trace left of the brilliant young man who helped stop the Berryman Expressway. Margulies has become a complete sleaze. He unrolled drawings of the Scarborough project on her office floor, like he was some kind of travelling rug salesman.

"You win, Alderman Sommers! You've got the best deal a politician ever knee-capped a developer for."

Victoria tried to pretend she was not impressed. Margulies was not fooled and Victoria knew it. The drawings showed neat, two-storey, red-brick row houses arranged around a little park. It looked to Victoria like a reasonable attempt to duplicate the charming squares she had seen once on a trip to London.

It was ridiculous, really, a fat, greedy slob like Max Himmelfarb trying to reproduce the sophistication of Kensington and Belgravia out in the miserable, weedy patches of northern Scarborough. Talk about culture shock! Who would believe an alderman has to handle so much before she even has time to get a cup of coffee?

"Whatever you do is all right with us," Margulies said. "The last thing in the world we want to do is put pressure on you, Alderman Sommers. But what I'm offering here is...I hope...something that will satisfy you and also give my clients a chance to get moving. Because every day that you and I are sitting here talking, Alderman Sommers, it's costing them money. So they've got these two parcels out on Dennison Road and they're willing to turn one of them over to non-profit housing and make sure your people get first pick. But that makes sense only if they can get Eton Towers under way."

"Yeah, sure, Margulies," Victoria said. "Eton Towers goes up and the tenants are out on the street. Where do they go then? It could be a couple of years until this Scarborough thing gets built. Where do the people live in the meantime?"

"Alderman Sommers, Premier Developments owns a lot of houses they're holding for future developments. And I don't have to tell you, Premier owns a lot of apartment buildings too. We can look after your people until Scarborough's ready for them."

"They can't afford fancy rents!"

"Who asked them to pay fancy rents? I said we'll take care of them, and we will. We understand their situation...but I don't want you to feel that I'm coming in here first thing in the morning, trying to put heat on you. That's the last thing I want to do. I'm just laying out the choices. You take your time. Let me know if there's anything else I can help you with. I'm at your disposal. You call if you need me..."

There is a shiny, bulbous little aluminum coffee urn in committee room number four. It rests on a shelf behind the T-shaped table occupied by the aldermen, civil servants, and record-keeping clerks of City Council's Parks and Recreation Committee. Thank God they had the machine going when Victoria came in. She was able to grab a coffee before scuttling to her seat. That bastard Margulies made her late. Public deputations had already started. A middle-aged woman with a torch singer's whisky voice was explaining why her ratepayers' association doesn't want swings or playground equipment in the little park at the end of her street. She wore a tartan pin and a string of pearls as big as marbles, and she said this was a quiet community where everybody knew everybody else and they all tried to help each other.

Where do such women come from? Did she think she was settling a small domestic problem with family retainers when she addressed elected politicians?

It's not the little children that she and her friends object to, the woman explained with a throaty little chuckle; after all, they have families themselves. It's the teenagers. They've already started hanging around the park at night, holding parties and making the most unbelievable noises. The police try to control the teenagers, but just as soon as the police drive away, the kids come back. They use drugs. She has sat in her living-room window and watched them making drug deals.

The front rows of the committee room were packed with moms. They were minding toddlers in strollers and holding babies on their laps. Victoria's heart went out to them and she voted for the swings, but the ward alderman, Walter Winczinksi, was against the playground extension and, as a courtesy, the other committee members supported him. Winczinski thinks that anything government does, even collecting taxes, is a Communist plot.

The mothers gathered up their children and their strollers and baby bottles and stomped out of the committee room. They created so much confusion in their leaving that the chairman held the next item until they had cleared out of the committee room. They looked tired and angry, and a couple of the women snarled at the politicians and said they'd see them at election time. Victoria longed to be able to do something for them. Victoria serves the working class because the poor need her help more than anyone else does, but those women were her people too, young middle-class mothers trying to make a decent life for their children in a city devoted only to getting and spending.

Just for once, Victoria would like to win something. But who could believe it would be Mayor Sid Dewhurst—of all people!—the old fart himself—who would bring her the opportunity.

The mayor came around just before the lunch sandwiches were brought to the committee and asked Victoria to step out into the hall in back of the committee room, away from nosy reporters. Dewhurst promised to put the vote together for her if she went for Himmelfarb's Scarborough deal. But, even better, the mayor had figured out they could get more units out of Himmelfarb. Dewhurst would insist on 450 units of non-profit housing, instead of 387, as the price for approving Eton Towers. That is, if Victoria herself liked what the mayor was proposing.

The mayor's breath smelled rancid and mouldy; Victoria hoped Dewhurst didn't notice how much she turned her face away when he bent close to talk confidentially. The mayor was once a flaming socialist. It's hard to imagine this overly tailored man, with his buck teeth and receding, chipmunk jaw, leading marches of rent strikers, but it did happen. Dewhurst is part of the living history of the city. Victoria has to give him respect, even if everybody says Dewhurst is now in bed with the developers.

Dewhurst tells Victoria he's ready to go to the wall for her. Together, Summers and Dewhurst will stick it to the high and mighty Max Himmelfarb. If that bastard wants Cotswold Street, he'll have to cough up 450 units of low-income housing out in Scarborough. That's 63 more units than Himmelfarb has been talking about but Dewhurst has been studying the plans and he's figured out that the site can take that much density. So, it's 450 or no deal. Will Victoria stand up with the mayor?

She says she'll get back to him. Right now, she's got to get to the Parks Committee.

A big fight is going on. Should the city spend $768.93 on buying heavy-duty work gloves for the men who go around with spiked sticks, picking up papers in the parks? Victoria is furious. These politicians, her colleagues, God help her, can and often do, with no more than half an hour's perfunctory debate, vote in favour of multimillion-dollar apartment blocks that chew into fine old neighbourhoods. Then they spend endless hours arguing over meaningless small details, like whether to buy work gloves.

Someone walking into this committee room would consider these people idiots, Victoria is thinking. She is certain they carry on this way only because they feel guilty. Everybody knows they take payoffs from developers. Victoria can't actually prove that, but she has no doubt at all it's happening all the time. And then these politicians who are on the take get to thinking they are, after all, supposed to be representing the people. So they get involved in these dreadful, endless fights over spending small amounts of money so they can convince themselves they are still protecting the taxpayers' dollars.

Victoria swallowed her anger—she is always having to swallow her anger in City Hall—and tried to present a reasonable argument why the city should buy new gloves for the parks workers. But she didn't stay around for the vote. She saw she was going to lose anyway. She slipped back to her office and went to work on the phone. Marlene had a whole stack of pink messages for her to respond to. Victoria put her feet up on the desk and started dialing. She congratulated herself on resisting the craving for tobacco until three in the afternoon and lit up a cigarette. Hello, this is Alderman Victoria Sommers, what can I help you with? Victoria promised to be at the Board of Health meeting that night. School nurses are fighting for overtime pay.

Molly Scanlon, from the M. J. Coldwell Non-profit Co-op, told Victoria she could put together a group of non-profit resource groups and they could probably build the whole 450 units in Scarborough.

"Hey, wait a minute! How did you find out about four hundred and fifty units? I just heard it myself."

"It's all over town," Molly said.

Victoria continues working her way through the pile of messages. Yes, she will find out what happened to a parking permit. Yes, she knows there are no garages downtown, and not having a place to park is like a death sentence.

No, sorry, but a city alderman just cannot do anything about a hospital charging for anaesthetic when they didn't tell the person before her operation that the anaesthetist wasn't covered by health insurance.

There is no message from Dane Harrison, but Victoria puts a call through to him anyway. He tells her he honestly doesn't know what to think. He's seen the plans for the Scarborough co-op and they're pretty impressive. Himmelfarb went to Grossman for the design and he does good stuff, very people oriented. But, on the other hand, there is no question that if Victoria holds out, she'll get Cotswold Street. It's just a matter of time.

When Marlene comes back into the office she finds Victoria tilted back in her chair with her feet up on the desk and her eyes closed. Victoria's skirt has fallen back over her white legs and her slip is hanging down. Victoria is sleeping heavily. If the people who always attack Victoria Sommers could see her now—so worn out, so vulnerable—what would they say?

Marlene gives Victoria a gentle tap. Victoria blinks. She is instantly awake. Her feet come down with a thump and her skirt falls back into place. She sits up and starts in avidly on the little supper her secretary has brought. Marlene delivers the latest bulletins. Steve Bukowski, the social worker, will take Winnie Barbeau to the ForWard 9 meeting. Marlene will drive Victoria. They've arranged for Victoria to speak first so she can get away to the Board of Health. Victoria should figure on being there for half an hour, no longer. The Moore Park Ratepayers are meeting at Whitney Public School. They've got Eton Towers on their agenda and Winnie is going to talk to them after the ForWard 9 meeting. But they want to hear from Victoria too, before they vote on any resolutions of support.

"Marlene, you've heard all the shit. What do you think about the Scarborough deal?" Victoria draws the last of the sickly sweet apple juice through the straw and pulls the plastic lid off a styrofoam cup. The coffee is already cold.

"I don't know," Marlene says carefully. She is not going to be guilty of adding to the pressure on Victoria. Marlene takes pride in having rid herself of superstitious Catholicism before she reached the age of thirteen, but the symbols of the church still remain with her. Marlene often thinks of Victoria as the Host. She sees the tribune of the people as being consumed every day by the very people she seeks to help.

"I think we've got to go for it," Victoria says decisively. "A non-profit housing project in the hand has got to be worth two in the bush, eh, Marlene?"

"Yes, I think you're right," Marlene says.

Victoria picks up the phone and spins through her Rolodex file for the number of Carlton and Boggs.

"Hello, this is Alderman Sommers. Is Mr. Margulies there?"

She unwraps a chocolate bar while waiting for Harry to get on the line. It may start showing up on her waistline, probably sooner rather than later, but it's still great energy food.

"Hello, Victoria. Is there anything I can help you with?"

"Yes, there is. We'll go for the Scarborough deal, Mr. Margulies—with one condition. You go from three hundred and eighty-seven units up to four fifty."

"Whe-ooo!" Harry's long whistle of exclamation grates on Victoria's ear.

"That's a big jump, Alderman Sommers—almost twenty-five per cent. It means my client has to put up even more land in Scarborough. I'll talk to him though. I'll see what I can do for you. But let me ask this: if I can get my client to go for the four hundred and fifty units, can we count on your support for Eton Towers?"

"Yes," Victoria says. "You can count on my support for Eton Towers, Mr. Margulies."

58

SHELLEY HIMMELFARB is in room 113 of Cawthra Avenue School. Max peers at her through the tiny window in the door. Shelley is talking to somebody who must be the teacher. Shelley has lost some weight. And she has got the thick, coal-black hair that used to drive Max wild cut short and twisted into tight little curls that cover her head, like a Persian lamb helmet. Why the hell would she do that to herself? Could Shelley be seeing somebody? Max enters the room. Shelley gasps, her hand flies to her mouth. Max smiles broadly trying to reassure her. Shelley always bites her finger like that when she's afraid. Their kids do it too.

"Max, it's not Pa!"

Wouldn't you know it? Her first thought's about her father, not about her husband. Nothing changes.

"The old man's all right. He'll outlive us all. I told you that a million times."

The grade two teacher clears her throat.

"Uh...umm...Shelley?"

"Oh, I'm sorry. Heather, this is my husband."

The teacher extends her hand. It is so small and thin it feels to Max like a chicken claw.

"I'm so pleased to meet you, Mr. Himmelfarb. Shelley's the best teacher's aide we have."

The woman is cheerful and sweet and seems to be dressed from head to foot in strawberry-coloured cardigan sweaters. She looks to Max younger than even his own daughter. But he can see that Shelley is watching the teacher nervously. In here, this kid is the boss.

"I came to take my wife to lunch," Max says. "If that's okay, I mean."

"Oh sure, no problem," the teacher says, sounding a little flustered. "I'll start the valentines myself, Shelley. Take your time. It's been really nice meeting you, Mr. Himmelfarb."

She slips quickly away. Max and Shelley are alone in the classroom.

"What do you want, Max?"

"I want to take my wife to lunch. What's wrong with that?"

Max has a reservation downtown, at Spencer's, because important business should be done in a comfortable setting, with good food and a bottle of wine. But Shelley says she has only fifty minutes for lunch and she insists on going to a little place around the corner from the school. It appears to be run by blond young men in blue and white striped butcher-boy aprons. One of them kisses Shelley on the cheek and leads them to "her table." It is surrounded by potted trees with thick green leaves. Max feels like he is in a corner of the jungle.

"You look good, Max."

Shelley is being honest. There is life in his face again. In the bad years, when Max was drinking so much and fighting with everyone, his face was becoming rigid. It was as though his skin was hardening, like concrete, right in front of her. But now his face is soft and clear again; Max Himmelfarb radiates energy. He is again like the dangerous boy from Berryman Avenue whom Shelley Englander allowed to undress her and make love to her in the back room of Club Morgan so long ago…two children and half a lifetime ago.

"We'll have the mushroom and watercress salad, Derek. You'll love it, Max. It's the house specialty. What would you like to drink?"

"Soda water," Max says sharply.

"We'll have Perrier," Shelley tells the waiter, and when he is gone, she says to her husband, "It doesn't have a much of a kick, Max."

"I'm off the booze. Work is enough of a kick for me now," Max says.

He reaches into the inner pocket of his suit jacket and lays an envelope from Carlton and Boggs on the table.

"What's this, Max? Divorce papers? You're finally going to marry that little girl?"

Shelley laughs gaily. She raises her glass of sparkling mineral water to him.

"Congratulations, Max. I wish you all the luck in the world, I really do."

Max shakes his head grimly.

"It's not what you think, Shelley. Open the envelope."

"I'll leave it for the lawyers. Isn't that what you always used to say?"

"Shelley, please. That's not why I'm here."

"I've lost twenty pounds, Max. And you haven't even said anything."

"You were never overweight. You just talked yourself into it."

"And I don't cry myself to sleep at night any more, Max. I don't cry at all. I feel so sorry for these teachers I work with. They come to work in the mornings and their eyes are all red and I want to tell them, 'Hey, listen, don't do this to yourself. Nothing is worth breaking your heart over.' But I hold my tongue. Who would listen to an old woman?"

"I listen to you," Max says.

"Ah, but that doesn't count," Shelley says.

Max tears open the envelope and pushes a thick document across the table. Shelley keeps her eyes on his and ignores the papers in front of her.

"What is this, Max?"

"A little something I asked Artie Quinn to do. You sign that and you got three-quarters of everything I own. If you're not happy, you can sell me out."

Shelley's hands remain locked together. They do not go anywhere near the thick contract lying in front of her.

"I don't get it, Max. You're going too fast for me."

"I'm taking over Premier," Max says. "That's the deal I got with Pa. I wrap up Cotswold Street and he retires. I'm going to control the company, and you'll control me. Any time you think I'm going off the rails again, you can stop me. You're the boss."

"You are crazy," Shelley says.

"Not any more, I'm not," Max says. "I want you back, honey. And I want you to feel a hundred per cent secure."

Shelley's fingers slide towards the contract. They lift it up. Shelley makes an effort to study the opening paragraphs. But then the weight of the paper seems to become to much for her. The contract slides to the table again.

"You remember you used to talk about a'win-win situation?'" Shelley says slowly. "Everybody walks away from the table happy? For me, Max, this is a 'lose-lose situation.' If anything goes wrong with Cotswold Street, you'll start drinking again. If you do pull it off, you'll go back with the company, and no matter what Pa says about giving up and retiring, he'll still be coming to the office every day. He'll start in on you again, like he always does. And you'll start drinking again—just to get away from him. So no matter what happens, we'd just be going back to the way things used to be."

"You are so wrong!" Max says angrily. "You don't understand anything."

"I understand you," Shelley says. "And I understand myself, Max. I like the way I live now. It took me a long time to get here and I'm not giving this up—not for anyone, and especially not for a crazy deal like this."

59

"HMMNN...well, I think...I must say...I have never seen anything quite like this," Howard Redmond is saying. "Not even when I was with the Greater

London Council and we were doing the South Bank in London and the National Theatre. I think you chaps have come up with something quite unique."

"We think so too," J. Arthur Quinn says with becoming modesty.

Harry Margulies pushes himself down into a corner of the couch, watching Quinn shuffle architect's drawings and explain Max Himmelfarb's "new concept" for Eton Towers to Mayor Sid Dewhurst and Redmond, the city's planning commissioner. They are all in the mayor's second-storey office, overlooking the people struggling across City Hall square through a livid March storm. Lightning is flashing across the square and rain is pouring down, but Harry Margulies still longs to be out there. He'll take any place...any thing...rather than be in this cheerful little room, listening to the appalling dishonesty of his senior partner.

"I'm glad you feel this way, Howard," the mayor says. "I didn't want to put in my two cents' worth until you'd had a chance to look at this stuff yourself. But Max Himmelfarb showed me the concept last week and I think what we've got here is a real 'people place.'"

"We believe there is something here for everybody," Quinn says.

The three looming oblong blocks that looked like tombstones crawling out of a concrete box have been replaced by two tall, slender, circular towers soaring out of a five-storey glass box that Quinn calls "The Gallery." The towers are going to be thirty-seven and thirty-nine storeys high, whereas the tallest of the earlier oblong blocks was only twenty-eight storeys. But, people will hardly be aware of the additional height, Quinn points out, because the Eton Towers Gallery will have stores right at the street level and the three floors of the Gallery above that will be taken up by professional offices—doctors and dentists and that sort of thing.

Where is Dane? Harry longs for his old friend to be in the room and stand up to the mayor and Redmond. But it's obvious they've pushed Dane out of the way.

"And your open space will be on top of this Gallery, I take it?" Redmond says.

Quinn pulls another drawing out of his pack. "This is a good view of the Gallery swimming pool. And I think you should be aware that the health club is going to be open to all members of the public. It won't be limited just to people in the building—as you find in so many other places."

The drawing shows grass, flower beds, trees in concrete pots, a rubber-cushioned running track, and a glass-walled swimming pool, all on the roof of the Gallery, five storeys above the street.

"If you add the solarium on the top of tower A," Quinn says, "I think you'll find we exceed the maximum open-space requirement by thirteen thousand square feet."

Harry has heard many stories about shmeering, but this is the first time he has ever seen it happening right in front of him. He feels—the analogy is crude, Harry knows, but apt—like the time when he was a little boy and a friend finally explained to him the step-by-step mechanics of how babies are made. You mean Harry's mother does that? The Queen does that?

"Hmmnnn...," Redmond says, stroking his elegant little goatee. "And you also want a bonus for good planning, Mr. Quinn?"

"We are providing the land that will be needed for the widening of Cotswold Street," Quinn says. "We are also providing commercial and office space in the Gallery. We have had two consultants' studies—and I'll be happy to make them available to you, Howard—which show there is a demand for enterprise space in this neighbourhood."

Suddenly the mayor jerks his large chair around and turns his wary chipmunk face to Harry.

"What do you say?" the mayor demands. "Is this kosher?"

Harry draws in his breath slowly. He feels Quinn's anxiety and avoids looking at him.

"There are precedents for what Mr. Quinn is proposing," Harry says to the mayor. "The planning act does allow a municipality to award a density bonus for good planning."

"If there was ever a project that deserved a 'good planning' bonus, it is Eton Towers," Quinn says quickly. The mayor ignores Quinn. He keeps his nervous little eyes fixed on Harry.

"What about this new concept?" The mayor asks Harry. "Mr. Quinn's been doing all the talking this afternoon...What does Mr. Margulies have to say?"

Harry's reply is smooth and reassuring.

"I've been up to my hips with this non-profit housing project out in

Scarborough," Harry says. "I'm afraid I've had to leave everything else to Mr. Quinn."

Quinn shoots Harry a murderous look, but it's unnecessary.

"So how's things going with your end?" the mayor asks Harry.

"Very well, sir," Harry says. "The people seem very pleased with it."

"Good...I'm real glad to hear that," the mayor says, dismissing Harry. He turns now to his chief planner.

"Well, Howard," he says with a long, patient exhaling of breath. "What do you think?"

"Hmnn...," Redmond says. "There are some things we are going to have to talk about, Mr. Quinn—especially setbacks from the street line and about the size of the swimming pool. But, by and large, yes, I think if we can clear up the details...we can give this project our full support."

"I think so too," the mayor says happily.

The mayor accompanies Quinn and Harry past the cubicle offices assigned to his aides, and out to the reception area at the front. He thanks the lawyers for coming by and says he is sorry he cannot give them more time. But he does have to get off to another event, the Estonian Cultural Society's annual dinner.

"They tell me it's not official unless Mayor Dewhurst's there," the mayor says, laughing, sharing a confidence with the lawyers about the funny ways of foreigners.

Harry and Quinn ride the elevator down to the first floor in silence. The heaviness continues as they set out across City Hall square. They have almost reached the skating rink when, finally, Harry cannot stand it any longer.

"Arthur, what the fuck was going on in there?"

"Harry, please, what on earth are you talking about?" Quinn replies mildly.

"Those two bastards were pieced off," Harry says. "And you and me are part of it."

"Don't make foolish statements, Harry. You haven't seen anything happening. And neither have I."

"Don't try the bullshit on me, Arthur. Landscaped open space five storeys off the ground! A bonus for good planning for widening the fucking street! I nearly puked in there. Those guys are on the take, Arthur. You know it, and I know it."

"Harry, let's discuss this back in the office."

"The shit is going to stick to us! Can't you see that, Arthur!"

Quinn sits down on one of the benches facing the skating rink. A spring storm has wiped out the last of the ice. Quinn is going to have to find some form of exercise to replace skating. Swimming might do.

"Sit down, Harry."

Harry is still furious, but he does sit down beside Quinn.

"Harry, you have no hard evidence—no matter what you may think. But, let us suppose, just for a moment, that you are right. Let us suppose Max Himmelfarb is, indeed, paying off. What is he getting for his money? Something he's not entitled to? I don't think so. All Max wants is to get the politicians and bureaucrats to open the gate to the marketplace. If Max is wrong, if people won't pay fancy prices for condos downtown and if nobody wants to rent an office that far away from King and Bay, then the market will cut Max down to size—and very fast."

"Arthur...with all due respect, you are trying to close your eyes to something you should not be closing your eyes to."

Quinn sighs wearily. Even though the rain squall has passed, the air is still bitter and damp.

"Think of it this way, Harry: Charlie McConnachie never has our problem." There is a sourness in his voice that Harry has not heard before. "Charlie's clients all went to Upper Canada College with him. They were all Kappa Sig at university. Everybody's pals; they look after each other. Our guys didn't go to the right schools, Harry. Half of them never got past grade eight. It's not very proper of me, I know, but there are times, Harry, when I think paying off is the only way a poor man can get an even break. Sometimes I think bribery is the outsider's justice."

Harry stares down at his shoes, nervously flicking them back and forth like scissor blades.

"You know where I draw the line, Arthur?" Harry says slowly and thoughtfully. "I just do not think I can get up and say things I know are totally stupid and preposterous."

"We stopped an expressway, Harry. You didn't mind saying some pretty strange things on that occasion, as I recall."

"That was different, Arthur. We were working for the public interest."

"Really? I thought we were working for a bunch of pansies."

"Arthur, it's not funny."

Yes, it is, Arthur Quinn is thinking. It is bloody hilarious. No matter how smart you are, you can never predict what is going to happen. Sometimes a client comes in with something that looks like a dog's breakfast, but the pieces start falling into place and everything goes off, clickety-click. Other times, they come in with something that looks neat and rational, and before you know it, you've got far too many players out on the ice and people are getting shoved into the boards.

"Well, Harry, you've done a grand job on the Scarborough end," Quinn says. "I think I can handle things myself from here on in."

Harry does not believe what J. Arthur Quinn has just said to him. He ignores it.

"I'm seeing Victoria first thing in the morning," Harry says. "There's still a couple of things to go over with her before she goes to her people."

"It's all right, Harry. I can talk to her."

This is going too far. Harry tries to laugh it off. This is not at all what he expected.

"People will wonder what happened to me, Arthur. You can't just fire me."

"Yes, I can, Harry. I'm still senior."

"Hey, take it easy, Arthur. I'm just trying to get a few things off my chest, that's all."

"You'll get your full fees, Harry. Everything you've done up to today—and then some."

Harry is suddenly furious. He cannot remember being so insulted.

"Fuck you, Arthur! What the hell do you think I am?"

It is after five now, and Arthur Quinn really must be on his way. People are streaming across City Hall square to get to the hooded entrances to the parking garage which runs down three levels under the skating rink and the public square. Quinn has been invited to dinner at the home of Richard Millichamp, chairman of the Ontario Securities Commission. He still has to shower and dress.

"What you are, Harry, is none of my business," Quinn says gently. "All I know is I've got less than two weeks to stick-handle this thing through City Council and it's going to be a squeaker. I don't have time for a suffering Jesus."

He stands up and hefts his attaché case; it looks like a small steamer trunk.

"Don't feel bad, Harry. We'll work together again."

He is gone. Harry stays on the bench, watching Quinn hurry down to Queen Street.

60

MELISSA SANDS fixes a drink just the way her father taught her to. Put the ice in first, then cover the cubes with scotch. She hands the stubby crystal old-fashioned glass to Harry Margulies. She brushes his fingers, slowly, invitingly, but Harry hardly seems aware of her. He simply goes on doing what he has been doing for what seems like hours now, stomping furiously and compulsively up and down his living-room. Melissa returns to the couch and folds her long, beautiful legs under her. She feels like she is seventeen years old again; she is picking her way through one of the dangerous parties that always followed the Friday afternoon high-school football games in Carleyville, Ontario.

"I'm out. Fuck him. This isn't law. Up your ass, Carlton and Boggs. I'm a lawyer, not a fucking errand boy. Up your ass, Max Himmelfarb. Up your ass, J. Arthur Quinn!"

The girls back in Carleyville all said you were crazy if you went to the football parties. Unless you were madly in love...or unless you were tired of being a virgin...you just didn't go anywhere near the boys after they'd spent all afternoon watching the football players hit and smash each other. Even the nicest guys thought they were bush pilots the night after a football game.

"Can you believe Quinn did this to me? That sanctimonious, hypocritical old cocksucker! This thing's going to blow up, Melly. Why the hell should I be the fall guy for the great J. Arthur Quinn? Tell me that! I didn't do anything! Why the hell am I out of booze? Get me another drink, Melly."

"I've got a better idea," Melissa says, and unwinds herself from the couch.

Harry is shocked at being denied a drink, but he does not object when Melissa takes him by the hand and leads him upstairs.

The night ends for Melissa the way so many nights after the football games in Carleyville did. She is in bed with a man. Harry's outrage, or whatever it is he is feeling, has made him hard and strong. Melissa rejoices for him, sharing with Harry the recovery of his power. It feels so good to have a man inside her again.

But it is not exactly like being back in Carleyville. Melissa does not have the sense that she has flung herself wilfully over the edge of a cliff. Melissa tightens her muscles around Harry. Harry begins to move, to ride her. Melissa lies back, closes her eyes, and begins to sing to herself. Then, suddenly, Harry rears up and it is over for him. Melissa wraps her arms around him and holds him tightly. Harry, she knows, is far too smart to ask her any questions. She kisses him on the cheek; she bites the lobe of his ear and whispers, "I love you."

In the morning, Harry is still sprawled across the bed when Melissa has to rise and dress for work. She showers, breakfasts alone—a bowl of granola at the counter in Harry's stark white kitchen—and joins the tributary streams of people making their way through the murky streets to the subway station. Melissa stands on the platform, wondering what dramas of their own these stiff, sleepy-looking people crowding around her have lived through during the night.

The train pulls in, and Melissa just barely manages to fight her way onto it. The closing doors catch the hem of her quilted overcoat and she has to tug it free. Melissa leans back against the door, flustered and embarrassed. She begins to laugh at herself. How could she ever have dreamed her life would come to this? She is Melissa Sands, the drama teacher and still aspiring actress who comes out of Marian McNab, former pitcher for the Carleyville Lionettes. But now it seems that her future happiness depends on the ups and downs of a real estate deal. It's really funny, when she thinks about it.

61

"MA-A-AX? What is this, Max?" Reb Shmuel Englander stands in the doorway of Max Himmelfarb's office. Max feels his energy being drained. "What kind of business is this, Max? Why are we giving away land, Max?"

"Pa, we're not giving away anything," Max says wearily. The old man is holding the letter from Canada Mortgage in his hand. It is the official notice that the government's housing agency has accepted terms for the Scarborough non-profit housing project.

"Max…how do we stay in business if we don't make a profit, Max?"

"We'll make, Pa. Believe me, we'll make. I got to go now. Davis from the bank."

Mr. Englander nods his head sadly as though dealing with a child who cannot understand the seriousness of the questions he has been asked. When the ark finally stopped moving, Noah sent out the raven first. The raven lives on carrion. Only when the raven didn't come back did Noah decide to send out the gentle dove, to seek out the freshly blooming fruits of the earth.

"Freddy called me last night. He's got a location down in Florida. Right on the highway."

"That Freddy!" Max says with extravagant admiration, the satirical quality of which is not lost on Fred Englander's father. "You can never get him to take a holiday."

"Freddy put three hundred on it. His own money, even!" Mr. Englander says. "Freddy says if we don't want to go in with him, he'll do it by himself. It's that good."

"Maybe you should go have a look, Pa."

"If only I could, Max. But I'm getting all fahrblungit. I don't sleep at night. Now you tell me we're going to build houses for these crazy people. We're not a company any more, Max; we're a public charity. We can't go on like this, Maxie. My heart can't take it."

Max is going to be late for his lunch with a vice-president of the National Commercial Bank. Why does the old man always pull this stuff just when Max is rushing to get away from the office?

"Pa, non-profit means for the people who do the deal, not for us, okay? We're going to do fine. First, we sell them the land, right? At market prices; there's nothing says we have to give anything away. We're going to make six, maybe seven hundred, right off the top. Then we build the joint. They're the developers; they go fight with the government for the money. But they got to hire builders, and nobody can give them a better price than us. We already talked to them about that. Then we manage the place. They couldn't tie their own shoe laces, never mind collect rent from four hundred and fifty units. So they're going to sign a contract with Premier Management. Every time we turn around we're making money on this non-profit project. And because we're doing this little job out in Scarborough—because Reb Shmuel Englander is such a public-spirited citizen!—Eton Towers goes ahead, and we get those Cotswold Street people out of our hair. We make money coming and going, Pa. You want me to add it all up for you?"

Mr. Englander does not respond. He does not even seem to have heard his son-in-law.

"You know the trouble with you, Max? You got an answer for everything. But I'll tell you something I learned very early in this business. Don't count a deal done 'til the cheque clears the bank."

Mr. Englander retreats to his own office and lets Max rush off to his luncheon appointment.

Murray Davis called and said he had important things to talk about. He sounded cold and nervous, not at all like the old friend Max has known since he was a teller in the branch on Berryman Avenue.

"Hey, Murray, you're looking terrific," Max says, sliding into the big, horseshoe-shaped leather banquette at Spencer's, where Davis has already installed himself. "They must be treating you good downtown."

"Playing squash again, Max. Three times a week."

Davis orders a double vodka on the rocks; Max, some plain soda water.

"It's doing wonders for you. You look like you dropped ten pounds at least."

"I got to do something to keep myself together. Remember, you told me I was crazy to go downtown? You were right, Max. I should have listened to you. Out in the sticks I was running my own show. As long as I stayed a few bucks ahead of the game, they let me alone. Downtown, I'm afraid to go take a piss. I come back and some sonofabitch'll be in my office, banging my secretary."

"Who're you trying to kid?" Max says. "You know you love it. You're going to be the next president."

Davis orders the poached Arctic char with hollandaise, the radicchio salad, and another double vodka. Max orders a grilled entrecôte with frites and more soda water. He wonders when Davis is going to get down to business. Light bounces off the banker's thick glasses. The man's eyes are so pale, so without expression, they disappear completely behind the shiny surface of the lenses.

Can Max believe the way that asshole Trudeau is screwing up the country? It's just an act of God if Trudeau doesn't push the country into another depression.

Max couldn't agree more. The trouble with politicians, he adds enthusiastically, is that they don't understand business and they won't listen to businessmen. They've got all these stupid university professors who couldn't run a corner cigar store telling them how to run the country. Max takes out a cigar and begins to peel away the cellophane wrapper.

"This Eton Towers business has got them worried downtown," Davis says at last.

Max sinks back against the side of the banquette and lights up slowly, being careful to roll the blunt end of the cigar slowly over the tall flame of his lighter so that the entire tip becomes a glowing coal. He watches the grey pungent smoke rise up towards the ceiling of the restaurant.

"So what else is new?" Max says. "They're always worried downtown."

"They want a little comfort, Max. An extra point."

"You've got to be kidding!" The cigar drops from Max's jaw. He has to scramble to grab it off his lap before it burns a hole in his trousers.

"It's not so bad, Max."

"Why don't you just take over the company? And take my left testicle while you're at it. You've got everything else."

"Don't do a number on me, Max. This is just business."

"Like hell it is," Max says. "Y'know, Murray, my people always get it in the neck. In Europe, they killed us. They made soap out of us. You think it's different in this country? Here they talk nice, but they don't let us live."

"Oh, for Christ's sake, Max, cut it out," Davis says angrily.

But they both know the bank is making a harsh demand. Condos are a terrific deal because you can usually get all your money out. But it can still take three to five years to get the place up, sell all the suites, and then jump through all the legal hoops to get the titles for each individual apartment properly registered with the government. And until you go through registration, you can't tell the buyers they've got to come up with the full purchase price. All you've got from them is a small down payment.

Max has been figuring on a cost of $80,000, land and construction, for each suite. That comes to $88 million and when you add in the public spaces he has to include—the swimming pool and the health club and meeting rooms—Max is figuring on a cost of $100 million. He has been expecting to raise all of that with a mortgage that would be partially secured by Premier's older rental buildings that have almost paid off their original mortgages.

Max didn't expect National Commercial to carry the full $100 million. They'd lay off some of that, but National Commercial was going to be the principal lender. Now Davis is telling him his rate is going to jump from eleven per cent to twelve per cent.

That extra percentage point means Premier's carrying costs are going to go from $11 million to $12 million—presuming that nothing more goes wrong and the company can get those condos built, sold, and registered within five years.

Max has been figuring to put the condos on the market at around $180,000 each, which should give the company, at the end of the day, better than $198 million.

But now Max's carrying costs have just risen by $1 million a year. If it takes him the full five years to build and register the condos, his profit will be only $38 million. And if there is any further delay, it will be even less than that.

To somebody outside the business, $38 million sounds terrific. But if you took $100 million and put it into treasury bills and reinvested the interest over five years, you'd do a lot better than $38 million—and have none of the aggravation.

But who in the world ever has a $100 million cash to invest?

That's how the banks get you by the throat.

Those squatters on Cotswold Street think Max Himmelfarb is such a mean sonofabitch. They ought to see the people Max has to deal with.

"Y'know," Max says slowly, measuring out his words. "When the old man started, the first place he went to was National Commercial. Even when he could hardly speak a word of English, he went to your branch on Berryman Avenue because he said they were good people."

"Don't I know it, Max! I'd hate to tell you how many times I put my own ass on the line just because I liked old Mr. Englander."

He orders another double vodka on the rocks from the waiter.

"I can't imagine us being anywhere but National Commercial," Max says.

"We'd hate to lose you," Davis says. "It's not just Cotswold Street, Max. It's this Scarborough co-op. We're handling that one too."

"I see," Max says. He waves the waiter to his table and orders a double vodka on the rocks for himself.

"Hey, Max, I thought you were off the sauce?" Davis says. He sounds genuinely concerned.

"I am," Max says curtly.

He can see the squeeze play very clearly now. Canada Mortgage doesn't actually pay for building non-profit co-ops. The co-op gets a regular mortgage from a private lender, and then Canada Mortgage guarantees the loan and gives them a subsidy so they are only paying two or three per cent interest, instead of the prime rate. This "write down" of the mortgage, as the bureaucrats call it, is what allows the co-op to offer units for less than market rents.

The group doing the Scarborough co-op has gone to National Commercial because it is Premier's bank. It's simpler to have all the money flow from one source. But now, if Premier leaves National Commercial, the co-op will have to go too. It could take weeks for Premier to set up another mortgage loan. And then the lender might not want to deal with the co-op. They'd have to start shopping around. It could take months to get all the pieces of his deal in place again.

But Max doesn't have even one month to spare. The promises that he and J. Arthur Quinn have secured are a delicately balanced pyramid. If the politicians have too much time to think about that "bonus for good planning," they'll lose their nerve. A real estate deal depends on momentum. If Max refuses the extra percentage point of interest to National Commercial, he will be slowed down, probably fatally. They know that and that's why the bank is sticking it to him.

"Y'know, when I was a kid," Max says, "I worked for a bookmaker. Half our customers were thieves. But they would never have done to me what you're doing to me now."

"Max, I just want you know one thing," Davis says. "This wasn't my idea." He stares into his glass and shakes his head.

"It's a funny thing, you know. Whenever anybody sticks a knife in you, it never has any fingerprints," Max says. "You want another drink, Murray?"

"Yes, I would, Max. Tell me, how's Shelley?"

"She's okay. She's doing great, Murray."

Max orders the vodka bottle brought to their table. "Can I tell you something, Max? As an old friend, I mean?"

"You already told me more than enough."

"You can hit me in the mouth if you want to, Max. But Shelley was one classy lady. She used to come into the bank, every guy there would have died to get into her pants. But the only person Shelley ever looked at was you. When you two split up, I thought to myself, that was the saddest thing I ever heard."

Max holds up his heavy-bottomed glass to Davis in a toast.

"To better times, Murray," he says sadly.

The streetlights have come on by the time Max emerges from Spencer's, each one surrounded by a faint rainbow in the moist, cold, early-evening darkness. Max shakes hands with Davis in the doorway of the restaurant and makes his way a little unsteadily through the crowds pouring out of the office buildings. The men and women still wrapped in winter overcoats and scarves and wool toques rush past him. For Max the sharp air is a blessing. He has to walk three blocks north to get his car out of the City Hall parking garage. The cleansing wind sobers him up a little.

Still, he sits in the Cadillac a long time, trying to figure out where to go next. He would like to see Shelley. She'd get a kick out of hearing that funny old Murray Davis still has a hard-on for her. But he dare not let his wife see him in this condition. And he certainly can't go back to Angela Porter's, not after he kissed her off so unceremoniously.

Max ought to go home. But there is nothing to eat in his little apartment. Anyway, he doesn't want to be alone, staring at the four walls. On the other hand, if he goes to the House of Chan or any of the restaurants where he is known and feels comfortable, word about him is bound to get back to the Englanders. All he needs right now is for them to hear that Max Himmelfarb is boozing again. Max sits in the Cadillac with the motor running and ponders the crazy, unfair way in which life works out. Who would believe a man could be forty-nine years old and not have anywhere to go at night?

62

"YOU MEAN we've won?" Elda Harwood says. "I don't believe it."

The other people at number sixteen Cotswold Street are having the same difficulty. The drawings Steve Bukowski has laid out on the kitchen table show red-brick houses with steeply sloping, old-fashioned gable roofs and rectangular apartment buildings that go up only four or five stories, all arranged around a park and surrounded by small hills with lots of big trees and a couple of playgrounds for children. Who wouldn't want to live in a place like that? It looks like a dream come true. But the idea of the place is still confusing. What does non-profit mean? Who is the landlord?

Molly Scanlon explains it again. Victoria Sommers has brought the president of the M. J. Coldwell Non-profit Co-op to the Cotswold Street house to answer any questions the Cotswold Street tenants might have. Scanlon, a red-haired, stocky pugnacious woman, looks like she doesn't take any nonsense from anybody.

"What you get is the right to live there for as long as you want—your whole life, if you want," Scanlon says. "And you control everything that happens in the project. You decide what kind of repair work should be done, for instance. You decide when—and if—there should be any new additions to the building. You even decide who comes to live there with you. So, for all practical purposes, you own the whole project."

Billy Barbeau leans against a wall of the kitchen, his eyes drooping wearily.

"Why should we trust old Himmelshit?" Billy says. "If it wasn't for him, we wouldn't be in this trouble."

"All I can tell you, Billy, is that they've already started work out in Scarborough," Victoria says. "I told them they were crazy, they were rushing things, they should wait until they get Eton Towers approved first. But they said they weren't worried. They said they wanted to get the first houses in Scarborough built this summer. Some of you people could actually be living out there by Labour Day."

"Yeah, and where are we supposed to be living until then?" Billy Barbeau demands.

"Some people could stay here if they really wanted to, I suppose," Victoria says. "But it won't be much fun once they start construction on Eton Towers. Himmelfarb says his company owns a lot of rooming houses around here. He says he could find places for all the people in number sixteen until Scarborough is ready."

"Yeah, sure, and how much would old Himmelshit charge?" Billy demands.

Victoria says slowly, "Himmelfarb says…he'll let you stay in his buildings for nothing until he's got Scarborough ready for you to move in."

"Yeah! Sure!" Billy says mockingly. "You got all that in writing?"

"I will have," Victoria says triumphantly. "The lawyer, Quinn, is supposed to bring it to my office tomorrow. I told him if it's not iron-clad that you people live for free until this place in Scarborough is ready, Eton Towers goes down the tubes. I told them you people were ready to stay here on Cotswold Street 'til hell freezes over."

Roberta Millward, the Indian girl from Kenora who is expecting a baby, leans over the drawing and puts her finger on one of the free-standing town houses.

"I want that one," Roberta says.

Some people laugh but other people begin to crowd around the drawings too, picking houses for themselves.

"I think you people are incredible," Molly Scanlon says. She is practically bursting with satisfaction. "You start off trying to hold on to one crummy old house downtown and you wind up making four hundred and fifty new places for people to live in. You people are just fantastic!"

Steve Bukowksi pulls an enormous bottle, a jeroboam they told him it is called, of Bright's President from the canvas bookbag at his feet.

"I didn't want to take this out 'til you people had a chance to make a decision," Steve says. "But I guess it's pretty clear now which way we're going."

Never mind that this is cheap, sickly sweet Canadian champagne. Glass tumblers and old cups are pulled out of the cupboards. Steve works the plastic cap out of the top of the bottle. It bounces off the ceiling and everybody laughs. The champagne makes a delightfully fizzy sound as it tumbles into the crockery.

"I want to make a toast," Victoria says. She lifts her cracked tea cup. "To the Cotswold Street tenants, you showed the world how to fight—and win!"

Nobody notices at first that Winnie Barbeau is not joining the celebration. She has been sitting in her favourite place, an old wooden chair in the tight nook between the fridge and the wall, and she has not been saying anything. Now she pulls herself up.

Winnie comes to the table, takes the giant bottle of champagne, and holds it upside down. The golden wine flows down, soaking the beautiful drawings.

"You people can do what the hell you want," Winnie says. "This lady ain't for sale."

"Ah, I see," Victoria says. Victoria has known this fight was coming and she would have preferred to have it in the privacy of her City Hall office. The last thing in the world Victoria would ever want to do is humiliate Winnie Barbeau. But if Winnie insists on having it out in public, Victoria Sommers is ready for her.

"I can understand what's bothering you, Winnie. If we win this fight now, you won't be on television every night. If you go out to Scarborough, you'll be an ordinary person again, just like the rest of us."

"That's part of it, for sure," Winnie says evenly. She is looking straight up at Victoria. "But it ain't everything. We got as much right to be here as old Himmelshit does. Don't you people see what they're doing? They're trying to sweep us out of the way, like we were garbage."

"You tell them, Winnie!" Billy Barbeau says gleefully. "That place is all to hell and gone. How am I supposed to get down to work, eh? If I could afford to buy a car I wouldn't be living down in this shit hole in the first place. Winnie's right. They're trying to stick us way out in Scarberia. And once we're out in that place, they'll let us rot out there. They'll forget they ever heard of us. You watch!"

Winnie smiles gratefully across the room to her husband. One thing has to be said for Billy Barbeau, he's always there when you need him. But now Elda Harwood steps into the centre of the kitchen.

"Winnie, I've got a little baby and I was three years on the waiting list for Ontario housing," Elda says. "This is the best chance I ever had for a good place to live."

But Winnie doesn't back down from Elda either.

"I'm not telling you what to do, Elda," Winnie says. "I'm just telling you what I'm going to do. When old Himmelshit came here with his sheriff and his cops, I went out that door to face them. I didn't know what was going to happen to me. I thought maybe I was going to die. But people listened to me then. And they're listening now. I have been up and down this city, Elda, and I can tell you people are watching us and sayin' to us, 'You lead the way!' And I am not going out there and tell those people, 'Hey, don't worry, it was all a mistake. They're giving me a house out in Scarborough. So when old Himmelshit comes barging into your neighbourhood, don't come bothering me. Himmelshit's looking after me.'"

"Winnie, it's going to be a beautiful place," Victoria says.

"Then you go live there," Winnie says. "This woman ain't going anywhere."

Victoria decides she had better end this now.

"Winnie, do you want to stand in the way of four hundred and fifty families getting decent places to live?" Victoria says. "Because I don't. I told Himmelfarb we'd accept his offer."

"You what?" Winnie cries. "You fucking did what?"

Everybody can tell Winnie is carrying on too much. But Winnie is also making an important point.

"You had no right, Victoria. Who told you to speak for us?"

Why do people always do this to Winnie Barbeau? It's like that awful time she can still remember when she was a little kid and they told her they were going to give her a candy and then the nurse pulled her pants down and stuck her behind full of needles while her father clasped her hands together. It's like her mother telling her, 'Oh, sure, you can go out Saturday night, Winnie,' and then leaving her to feed the little ones and get them into bed every other night of the week so poor old mom can go out drinking beer and playing bingo. It's like Billy, her own husband, giving her a bottle of Chanel No. 5 the day they got on the bus to come down from Cromwell and telling her how great life was going to be when they got to Toronto.

"I have a whole ward to think of," Victoria says. "I have responsibilities for the whole city—not just the people in this house."

"You...made...a...deal...with...Himmelshit," Winnie says slowly, emphasizing every word, making sure everyone in the room is taking it all in. "Who are you working for, Mrs. Sommers? Himmelshit or us?"

This is so unfair. Victoria is in City Hall only to keep the city from ramming things down people's throats.

"I think we should put this to a vote," Victoria says. "I want to know what other people here think."

"They can think what they like," Winnie says. "I'm stayin' right here."

Victoria turns away from her.

"Would all those who want to accept the offer and get a house out in Scarborough please put up their hands," Victoria says.

Slowly one at a time, four hands go up. Victoria waits, but four votes is all she gets. She shakes her head sadly, not really believing this can be happening to her. She looks over to Steve Bukowksi. His eyes are rolled up to the ceiling, avoiding her.

"Well let's be absolutely clear about this," Victoria says. "Let's see how many of the people who don't want to go out to Scarborough also want to stay here and fight."

"...to the bitter end," Winnie adds.

Nine hands go up. Winnie looks scornfully around the room. And then, so decisive for Victoria, the four people who had first voted with her now change their minds and vote with Winnie. It is unanimous.

"Well then, Mrs. Sommers, I think you've got your marching orders," Billy Barbeau says.

It is time to make peace. Victoria accepts their decision with a gracious smile.

"I guess I do, Billy," she says. "We stay. And we fight." Victoria feels no bitterness. She is already counting this a healthy, learning experience. Victoria almost let that bastard Harry Margulies lead her astray. But Victoria can see now that Winnie is right and always has been. Why should the poor be driven out of the neighbourhoods where they have always lived just so a fat slob like Max Himmelfarb can make a bigger profit?

"All the way," Winnie adds.

"All the way!" Victoria says.

Bottles of rye and vodka now appear. People are breaking into their private stock. But everybody needs a drink tonight. Victoria accepts a glass of Wiser's Old. She stands alone beside the tableful of soggy architect's drawings, trying to think of how she will explain this to J. Arthur Quinn in the morning.

"Mr. Quinn," she will say, "I have a job to do just like you do. You represent your people and I represent mine. It's nothing personal."

63

THERE ARE twenty-two wards in Toronto and each ward has one alderman. That makes twenty-three votes, counting the mayor's, and J. Arthur Quinn has less than two weeks left in which to convince a majority of these politicians they must vote in favour of Eton Towers. He sits now in his office with a yellow legal pad on his knees, doing the human arithmetic and feeling decidedly gloomy.

When Victoria Sommers first told him about the turn-around by the Cotswold Street tenants, Quinn was furious, but not worried. He felt he still had enough votes to overwhelm them. But when he began making his rounds on Alderman's Alley, he discovered that Victoria's change of heart had completely altered the chemistry of City Council.

The five people who, along with Victoria, call themselves "reformers" listened to her explain her change of heart and, as they like to say in City Hall, "had no trouble with it." The reformers' wards run through the web of reborn, tree-lined midtown streets spreading east and west from the Grove. This is the heartland for the homeowners who still boast that they stopped the Berryman Expressway. Victoria told them Eton Towers is another case of people trying to stop City Hall from destroying their neighbourhood.

The six members of the New Democratic Party caucus were unwilling at first to back the tenants because it meant giving up the Scarborough project, and how could they be against so much good housing for needy people? But when Victoria marched Winnie Barbeau, the little heroine of Cotswold Street, into their offices, the socialists began to cringe. Wasn't Barbeau one of the people and wasn't she standing there, telling them the deal they want to make on behalf of the people stinks?

According to Quinn's calculations, Victoria may already be within one vote of getting her way. His own support, on the other hand, is beginning to crumble. When Quinn adds the work Max Himmelfarb has done to what he has accomplished himself, he should have eight solid votes. But some of Quinn's people have found that ratepayers' organizations in their own wards are getting agitated about Eton Towers. Victoria's been out to their meetings too, bringing the fiery Winnie Barbeau along with her.

Time is running out. Quinn writes down the names of the vacillating politicians and tries to think of new buttons he can push with them. His scheming is interrupted by a polite knocking at his office door.

"Go away," Quinn growls. "There's nobody here."

The door opens. Harry Margulies stands in the sudden and unwelcome rectangle of light.

"Oh, hello. How are things going, Harry?" Quinn asks mildly.

"Great," Harry says. "I just picked up a nice little rezoning in East York. It's an official plan amendment, but it should be a piece of cake."

Harry does not wait for an invitation. He comes into Quinn's office, shuts the door and sinks down into the leather chair in front of Quinn's ornate and massive desk.

"I heard about our friend, Victoria," he says. "What are you going to do?"

"What can I do, Harry? It's too late to change anything now."

"What a first-class bitch that woman turned out to be!" Harry says.

"She's just doing what she's paid to do, Harry—represent her constituents. If they change their minds, she's got to change her mind too. They call it democracy, I think."

"You remember when we went up to four hundred and fifty units in

Scarborough?" Harry says bitterly. "I can still hear her saying to me"—his voice goes into a cruel falsetto—"'You can count on my support for Eton Towers, Mr. Margulies.'"

Quinn only shrugs. Four new bottles of different-coloured pills are lined up on his desk. Harry watches in silence as Quinn opens two bottles, takes a pill from each, and downs them with a glass of water poured from a chromium carafe.

"Tell me something, Arthur. Has Max Himmelfarb ever given his word, like Victoria did to me, and then taken a walk?"

"Not in my experience," Quinn says. "And the same holds true for the whole Englander family, for that matter—even Freddy. If they tell you something, it's like money in the bank."

"That's what I thought," Harry says.

"Don't romanticize them, Harry. They cut corners and they drive hard bargains. They'd take you to the cleaners without thinking twice about it."

"But they do keep their word," Harry says thoughtfully.

"That is true."

"I think," Harry says, "that I prefer people who keep their word to people who keep their principles."

"It does bring a certain simplicity to life," Quinn says.

They remain for a moment just looking awkwardly at each other.

"Well, I guess I'd better go now; lots of work to do in East York," Harry says. "But, you know, I was thinking about your problem. Winczinksi out in the west end, he's one of the guys you've got to lock up, right? What if some of his fellow Polacks out there started sending him letters?"

Quinn looks up cautiously.

"How could I do that, Harry?"

"Andy Dubowski, the real estate agent. He does a lot of business with Premier doesn't he? You start with Andy and work your way around to the businessmen in the neighbourhood. Maybe you can even get to the priests. After all, what's a nice, upstanding Catholic boy like Walter Winczinski doing getting in bed with a Commie bitch like Victoria Sommers?"

Quinn claps his hands gleefully. The sound is like a pistol shot.

"Harry, we have to talk."

"I'd love to, Arthur. But I've got this little thing going in East York. I'd better get back to work."

"Harry, it's supper time. I'll take you up to the Sai Woo. Tai dop voy. Garfield's double martinis. Shrimp with lobster sauce. My treat."

"You're on," Harry says happily. "Now you're talking my language, Arthur."

64

VICTORIA SOMMERS marched into Alderman Jack Painter's office as soon as he arrived at City Hall, and forty minutes later she is still talking at him. Painter slumps behind his desk and studies his colleague over the rim of the blue Wedgwood coffee mug his wife gave him when he won his first election. Victoria has certainly got herself up for this lobbying campaign. She is wearing a long grey skirt, fetchingly tight over the behind, and a softly pleated pink blouse which is shaped enough to show that Victoria has a respectable bosom. And Jack Painter knows enough about women to see that Victoria has had her famous chestnut mane permed and highlighted and she is wearing enough makeup at nine in the morning to give her face an unnaturally healthy hue. It's a bit bizarre to see the sanctimonious Victoria Sommers making herself attractive in order to try to score a political point. She can certainly be a damned sexy-looking woman when she takes some time with herself. Still, it is hard to imagine Victoria writhing on a bed with her knees up, moaning, "Yes…Oh, yes…" Victoria Sommers never says "yes" to anything!

It is this eternal negativity that is beginning to disturb Jack Painter. Does saving the city mean an alderman can never say anything but "No"? Painter got into politics, as Victoria herself did, because of the fight to stop the Berryman Expressway. Does that mean he has to stop anything else from ever happening in the city? What if, others have asked Jack Painter, there are no more apartments? Where will his children go when they leave home? Where will the old folks go when they are empty-nesters and they don't need big houses any more? These arguments are coming from the other side, obviously, but an honest politician—at least a politician like Jack

Painter, who is striving mightily to be honest—has to keep his door open.

"Jack, what we really need is a new official plan," Victoria says. She has finally stopped pacing in front of his desk and now she stands facing him in such a forthright, heedless manner that it is not difficult at all to begin speculating on what Alderman Sommers would look like without any clothes on.

"It's obvious the old official plan isn't working. Every developer who comes in here wants to get it amended. So we say to them, 'Okay, you're right! We'll look at the plan and see where it needs to be rewritten and expanded so you guys can go on building and we don't go on forever having terrible fights in every neighbourhood every time you guys want to do something. But meanwhile—while we are working on this new official plan for the city—you guys give us a little breathing space. No applications until we get the new plan in place.' Doesn't that sound reasonable to you, Jack?"

So this is what the whole tirade has been leading up to. Jack Painter has certainly misjudged Victoria. She does know how to think creatively. She is showing him how he can be both for and against something at the same time. He can tell the people in his ward he is absolutely opposed to putting high-rise apartment blocks in family neighbourhoods and he can tell the people downtown—the lawyers and the corporation executives at the Kiwanis Club who keep making suggestive little remarks to him about campaign contributions—that he is all in favour of new developments. That's why he's fighting to get a new official plan, so developers can get to work without a lot of interference from City Hall. What Victoria is saying to him is beautiful. But Jack Painter had still better make sure his ass is covered.

"Let me get back to you on this, Victoria," he says. "I just want to touch base with some of the people in my ward."

"Absolutely!" Victoria says. "Take all the time you need, Jack. I'll get back to you tomorrow morning."

A sign has been erected in front of number sixteen Cotswold Street. It is so big it almost hides the house. In the drawing, the awful concrete tombstones have been replaced by the two slender, glassy towers. They seem to blend unobtrusively into a sparkling night. A long black Cadillac has pulled into the curved driveway. A doorman is holding open the car door. A young, blonde woman in a beaded white evening dress is emerging. Her head is thrown back and she is obviously laughing at something the driver has just said. The message at the top of the sign says Premier Developments will erect Eton Towers, "A Prestige Condominium Building," on this site. At the bottom are two phone numbers for people interested in making early purchases.

And just to keep up the sense of eager anticipation, Premier installs beside the sign a searchlight, just like the kind one sees outside the theatre on Academy Awards night. Its powerful beam will cut circles in the night sky proclaiming that, here, glamour and sophistication will one day live.

Steve Bukowksi calls a press conference. Standing right in front of the searchlight, Winnie Barbeau tells the reporters and TV cameramen that its beam is shining in the windows of number sixteen and keeping everybody awake at night. It's especially bad for old Mr. Birdsell, who has emphysema, and for Mrs. Harwood's little baby. Winnie says she wants to go shine a flashlight in old Himmelshit's window and see how he likes it. The TV people ask her to go through it again, and this time, not to play games with Max Himmelfarb's name. They can't use dirty words on air.

A statement sent by cab from the public relations firm Premier has hired gives the addresses of nine downtown rooming-houses where the company has offered to let the Cotswold tenants live—free of charge! An editorial in *The Daily News* argues that since the tenants have insisted on staying at number sixteen Cotswold Street and are not paying rent, they can't really complain if Premier Developments makes use of its own property. The editorial goes on to say that the Cotswold Street tenants are beginning to wear out public patience.

Victoria Sommers stands outside the door of her City Hall office, thinking that whatever else may be said about Harry Margulies, he certainly does have a cute little ass. He is bent over the drinking fountain in Alderman's Alley, typically, arrogantly, unaware of anything going on around him. How delightful it would be to grab hold of those taut buns and dig her fingernails in until the sleazebag lawyer howled for mercy.

Harry straightens up and turns around. He finds Victoria gaping at him.

"Well, well, the honourable member from Red Square," Harry says. "How's it going, Victoria?"

"If you think you are going to get any of my people, you are out of your tree," Victoria says.

"Oh, really?" Harry says. "I've just had a very interesting talk with Alderman Dalgleish. It seems the Council of Building Trades is coming out for Eton Towers. New Democrats do have to worry about jobs, you know…"

"Aw, come on, you're not hauling O'Brien down here, are you?" Victoria says.

"Jobs…jobs…," Harry says airily. "Connie's chairman of the council. I've never seen a union man worry about the rank and file the way Connie O'Brien does."

Victoria wrinkles up her face as though the very name "Connie O'Brien" gave off a bad smell.

"Everybody knows your guys have got O'Brien in their pocket. He'd come out for building concentration camps if you told him to."

"Hey, I've got an idea," Harry says brightly. "Why don't we compare lists? I'll take you out to lunch and I'll tell you every one I've got. And you'll tell me who you've got. We could save each other a hell of a lot of time."

He is probably kidding…with Margulies you can never be really sure…but what he is saying would actually make a lot of sense. They have been bumping into each other coming in and out of aldermen's offices all week. If she knew who Margulies was counting on, she would not waste time trying to work on them herself. But, then again, Victoria can just imagine what Winnie Barbeau and the other people over on Cotswold Street would say if she told them she'd made a deal with Harry Margulies.

"Go piss up a rope," she snarls at him.

Harry turns away and strolls down Alderman's Alley to his next call. Victoria's response is further proof that not only is she a dishonest person, she has no sense of humour at all.

The Reverend Arvo Timmusk sits in his rectory office, his fingertips touching each other in a prayerful steeple, silently contemplating the interesting tidings which have just reached him. Reverend Timmusk is a member of

City Council too, but he is certainly not a politician. He is there only because somebody has to speak for the city's elderly.

His political career began when the good ladies of his Finnish Lutheran Church organized the neighbourhood's first meals-on-wheels program. Reverend Timmusk went with them when they brought the first foil-wrapped trays to the frail and grey-haired shut-ins. The word quickly got about that the minister was a bit of a saint. One revelation led to another, and Reverend Timmusk quickly discovered there were thirteen nursing homes and senior-citizen apartment buildings in the neighbourhood. They are sanctuaries for last survivors of the days when the east end was like a branch of the Orange Lodge, filled with tough Scottish Presbyterians and Ulster Irishmen. The young people have long since migrated out to the suburbs, leaving their parents behind. Reverend Timmusk wishes everybody in the city could see the way those old folks light up when he comes to play the piano and lead them in a sing-song.

The storekeepers on Bailey Avenue liked Reverend Timmusk too. They were impressed by his dignified white hair and his hearty public manner. It was the storekeepers, through their Bailey Avenue Businessmen's Association, who convinced Reverend Timmusk that he had a calling for politics. And it is one of these businessmen, Saunderson, the plumbing contractor, who has now brought him such interesting tidings.

The message is from Max Himmelfarb, of course.

Himmelfarb is too intelligent to come to the Reverend directly. He knows that Arvo Timmusk is not for sale. But Saunderson is an old friend of Himmelfarb because he does work for Premier Developments, and Saunderson has told him how highly Himmelfarb thinks of the good work Timmusk is doing among the old and infirm.

In fact, Himmelfarb wants to help the Reverend in a manner that will really be appreciated. In the next election, Premier Developments will send over half a dozen people from the office to help in Timmusk's campaign. They'll still be getting paid by the company, of course, but they'll be working full time to help the Reverend get re-elected.

Such assistance would be a godsend to Timmusk's campaign. The elderly support him happily, but you can't expect them to go out every night, handing out leaflets and knocking on doors. With six full-time campaign workers he can really count on, Reverend Timmusk would have no trouble at all getting back to City Hall.

The beauty of Himmelfarb's proposal is that it there is nothing improper about it. Reverend Timmusk is not benefiting in any way personally. He is only making sure he returns to City Council again to speak for those who are too far gone to speak for themselves.

Of course, Reverend Timmusk will have to vote for Eton Towers. But he was probably going to do that anyway. It's a nice-looking apartment building and it will help to pull up a neighbourhood that is, let's face it, getting pretty seedy. So Reverend Timmusk is not doing anything for Himmelfarb that he would not have done in any case.

Some day, Reverend Timmusk is thinking, he should write a book, or least do a series of sermons, about how, when you choose to work for a good cause the way he has done, you find the world unfolding before you.

There is considerable speculation and even a few bets are down about what Winnie Barbeau is going to wear today. Newspaper reporters and TV crews have gathered in the enormous white and gold ballroom of the Royal York Hotel to report on Winnie giving a speech to a luncheon meeting of the Commonwealth Club. Some say Winnie's going to come in her old jeans and ratty overcoat. Others say Victoria is going to put Winnie into an old housedress and put her up as "frump of the month." No one is prepared for the entrance of the real Winnie Barbeau.

Winnie is wearing a strawberry-coloured pant suit with a black and white polka-dot blouse and high-heeled black shoes. She certainly doesn't look like a lost waif now. Her hair has been washed, and the ponytail has been wound into a tight, lush coil around her head. The boys had come to think of Winnie as having dirty brown hair, but it turns out now to be much lighter—a delicate, pale, ash blonde. Standing at the microphone, Winnie is a petite, composed, and glamorous young woman. The cameras can't get enough of her.

Winnie gives what reporters have come to recognize as her standard speech to potential middle-class supporters: Help us or you'll be next. If the big bad developers tear down our street this week, they'll go after your street next week.

But then Winnie works in a variation. Maybe Sommers put her up to it, but it's more likely Winnie thought it up herself. The woman is uncanny when it comes to sensing what will move a particular audience.

She calls her son up to join her at the microphone. He came in with her and he's been at the head table with Sommers and the executive of the Commonwealth Club. It's probably the first good meal the kid has had in weeks.

"This is my son, Buster—Billy Junior," Winnie says. She puts her arm protectively around his shoulders, but if she wasn't in heels, the kid would probably be taller than she is. "Billy is what it's all about. We just want the same things you people want—a chance for our children to grow up decent. Are we asking too much? You people tell me, am I asking for too much?"

The applause starts slowly and a little uncertainly, but then builds and surges across the room. The Commonwealth Club is the crème de la crème of the city, corporate presidents and vice-presidents, senior partners in law and accounting firms. There are more than five hundred members of the club at this meeting, and they are all cheering for Winnie Barbeau. Looking around, the reporters see that some of the old guys are even standing up. This is unbelievable. They are giving Winnie Barbeau a standing ovation.

It is nine o'clock at night, and J. Arthur Quinn is sitting disconsolately in the office of Charlie McConnachie. He is listening to his old enemy wind up a telephone conversation.

"Well, that would be most appreciated, Keith," McConnachie is saying. "I'll see you at the riding association dinner. Give my best to Judy and tell her I saw young Doug playing squash at the club. She's going to have her hands full with that one...Goodbye now, Keith, God bless."

He hangs up the phone and turns his freckled, belligerent face to Quinn.

"You've got nothing to worry about, Arthur," he says. "Young Mr. Vito Alcamo will be told tomorrow that if he ever wants to do anything with the federal Liberals, he'd better learn to love Eton Towers."

"Thank you, Charlie," Quinn says. "I owe you one."

"Don't be silly," McConnachie says. "What else are partners for?"

Quinn again promises help when it is needed and, leaving McConnachie, begins the long, lonely trek across the thirty-seventh floor to his own corner office. The last thing in the world he ever wanted to do, he reflects bitterly, was put himself in debt to Charlie McConnachie. But Quinn has obligations to his own clients. They have to come first. But, oh, it hurts sometimes. His first mentor at Carlton and Boggs—old "Windy" Boggs himself—used to say, when he got into trouble, "Arthur, it's a long and dusty road."

65

WINNIE BARBEAU broadcasts a welcoming smile to Billy Barbeau as he weaves his way through the crowded, clattering beverage room of the Ascot Hotel, deftly carrying a tray with six tulip-shaped glasses of beer. Her husband will have no reason to complain tonight, she is thinking. She has come to meet Billy after he finishes his shift and she is all alone. It's been a long, grinding day, and what Winnie would really like is just to crawl into bed and try to make her mind stop racing. But Billy says he has something very important to tell her and he doesn't want anybody from the house listening in on their private business.

"You look like the cat that swallowed the canary," Billy says, sliding in across from her and setting the beer glasses down in front of them.

She tells him she has done well today. She and Steve went after Cliff Dalgleish, the old alderman from the NDP, again, telling him the bricklayers and plumbers and electricians from the Building Trades Council will get just as many jobs building a non-profit co-op on Cotswold Street for poor people as they will building luxury condos that old Himmelshit can sell to the rich. Steve says that if he and Winnie go at the little bastard again on Monday, they might, finally, get the old-time New Democrats away from the construction unions.

"That's great," Billy says. "I've got some big news too. I got a call this morning, my cousin Henry."

"Oh? Yeah?" Winnie says warily. She has never liked Henry Barbeau.

He's over fifty, a bustling, egg-faced man who never has time for anything in life but his three "Johnny Canuck Hamburger Heaven" franchises. Once, when Billy was down on his luck, Winnie went to him in secret to ask for help, but Billy's cousin said to her that he already had more people working for him than he knew what to do with.

Now, it turns out, Billy's cousin is desperate to get Billy back to Cromwell. He's opening a fourth Johnny Canuck place and he wants Billy to come up and get it going. Henry's son, Peter, was supposed to do the job, but Peter's just got a big promotion with the chain, managing everything from Sudbury out to Winnipeg. Henry's got a bad heart and just can't do everything by himself.

"He says he'll start me off at five hundred dollars a week," Billy says. "Then, when the place opens, I'll be getting a percentage too. Henry says I could be making fifty grand a year in my first year."

"Yeah, I'll bet he does," Winnie says. "And when are you supposed to get up to Cromwell?"

"He tells me I should have been there yesterday, but I'd better be there by Saturday. He says he can't wait. If I'm not there by the end of the week, he'll have to go outside the family and get someone else."

Winnie looks at her husband scornfully.

"You know what this is, don't you!" she says.

"Sure, I do," Billy says. "Henry's saying the words, but it's old Himmelshit doing the talking. They're trying to get you out of here. Old Himmelshit probably owns the company."

This is not true. Max doesn't even have shares in Johnny Canuck Inc., which is really the Canadian branch of the gigantic American Flag hamburger chain. However, the general manager of the Canadian operation is Paul Holtzman, whose oldest brother, Sid Holtzman, was, with Max himself, one of the seven original members of Club Morgan on Berryman Avenue.

"I hope you told Henry to go fuck himself," Winnie says.

"I told him I'd be there on Friday morning," Billy says.

Winnie stares at him. She feels like a crack is beginning to open in the earth, separating her from her husband.

"Listen...what's so wrong with it?" Billy says earnestly. "Everybody else is getting something out of this. Half the politicians down there are getting paid off. You told me that yourself. Old Himmelshit's going to make millions. Victoria's going to be a big hero...probably run for mayor. The people on Cotswold Street are all going to get good houses to live in. So what's wrong with you and me getting something too?"

"How long do you think it would last?" Winnie says with a sneer. "Once they have what they want, they'll drop you like a hot potato."

"Maybe," Billy says patiently. "But Henry's there, and him and me have been friends all our lives, besides being cousins. And maybe I'll be such a good manager they'll want to keep me on, no matter what happens down here in Toronto. Maybe they'll want to make me president of the company, eh?"

How can the husband of Winnie Barbeau come out with such awful nonsense? Billy sounds like one of those crooked politicians Victoria and Steve are always going on about. Winnie feels ashamed.

"Can't you just hear the people in the house? They'll be saying you and me ran out on them, Billy."

"They'll be mad, that's for sure," Billy says. "But then they'll say how smart we were."

Winnie shakes her head. No! No! No! Nobody is going to blacken the name of Winnie Barbeau.

"I made promises," she says firmly. "And I keep my promises."

Billy grips her hand so hard Winnie feels as though he is cracking her bones.

"Winnie, if we stay here, what am I goin' to be? A beer waiter all my life?"

"If I go back there," Winnie says looking straight back at him, not paying any attention to the sharp pain he is making her feel in her hand, "what will I be, eh?"

"What you've always been, Goddamn it! Winnie Barbeau! What's wrong with that? Only now you'll have some money in your purse."

"I ain't going nowhere," Winnie says. "You can do what you like."

Winnie feels like she wants to cry, but what good would that do? Billy's right. This is a chance for him, and she should not be trying to keep him from it. But what else can she do? Other people besides Billy are depending on her. How can she abandon them?

"You know, I'm thinking, maybe they're not so smart as they think they are," Billy says slowly, with the manner of a man playing a card nobody ever thought Billy Barbeau would be smart enough to hold.

"Henry didn't say nothing about you coming up. He just figures I'll bring you with me. I'll bet they never even told Henry why they're so all-fired eager to get the two of us up there. But what if I come alone, eh? What if I tell Henry you got the flu, eh? Or you're in hospital with pneumonia? Henry can't very well tell me to turn around and go back just because you're not with me, can he? Not after him making such a big fuss to get me there. So I go to work and you're free to do what you have to do here. When you're done, you come home."

Winnie watches him carefully. He tricked her into coming to the city, telling her how good life down here was going to be. Is he trying to get her back home now with the same kind of stories?

"What if it's nothing up in Cromwell?" she says gently. "It most likely is nothing. You'll be back home and you won't have any job at all. You'll have to go on pogie."

"If I have to, I will," Billy says. "But I started out working underground in the Deodar. I figure they'll take me back. They're always looking for good miners."

"You hated the mine," Winnie says. "You swore you'd never go underground again."

"I'm older now," Billy says, with a sad smile. "I'm not so particular any more."

She has never heard this from him before, that's for sure. It's not fair. He has raised the stakes too high. Billy is putting his whole life on the table in front of her. How can Winnie say no to him?

But, damn Billy! Damn him! What he wants to do is going to hurt her so much. Because, even if nobody else ever knows the Barbeaus got taken care of, Winnie herself will know. People listen to her now because they can feel that everything Winnie says comes bursting out of her, honest and straight, right from the heart. Billy, and Himmelshit, and who ever else is in this with them—all of them, damn them!—they are snatching her secret strength away from her. Even if she still says the things she has always said, her voice will not sound the same. Winnie knows...she just knows it.

Roughly, urgently, she lifts Billy's hand, and right in that gross, smelly beverage room of the Ascot Hotel, she kisses the tips of her husband's fingers.

"I love you," Billy says. "You never heard nothing different from me, did you, woman?"

"No, Billy, I never heard nothing different from you."

The details are settled quickly. Billy will leave in the morning. He will take Billy Jr. with him. The boy will have a bit of trouble with school, but he's still better off up there than running loose in the city.

They walk the three blocks back to Cotswold Street, hand in hand. Winnie knows what's coming and she's not unhappy about it. In thirteen years, Billy Barbeau has never been longer than three days away from her bed. But tomorrow night she'll be all alone in the city and no one can tell her for sure when she and Billy will be together again.

Winnie is overcome with a sudden, insane desire to murder Max Himmelfarb. Strangle him, stick a knife in him! All Winnie ever asked for was a decent place to live. Look what they have done to her life!

But, then again, didn't her own mother, on the very morning she went to church with Billy, say to her something that sounded more like a funeral hymn than a joyful blessing for a daughter going off to her own house: From this day on, Winnie dear, you'll be a married woman and you must always put your husband first.

I shouldn't have let him get away with it! That is what Winnie is thinking when they are finally in bed and she wraps her skinny legs around Billy Barbeau and locks her ankles together. I should have said more!

66

IT IS TUESDAY, APRIL 9, three months to the day since Melissa Sands's quiet dinner with Harry Margulies was interrupted by a phone call from the police. Melissa is on the phone with Harry right now. Tomorrow, City Council will decide the fate of Cotswold Street. Harry is still at the office, but he is finally convinced that he has done all he can do. It is in the lap of the gods now, he tells Melissa. He will pick her up at her school. They will go out for a good dinner. Harry needs to relax.

Melissa says she would love to go for dinner. But she just can't. It's a tech rehearsal for *West Side Story*. So how about tomorrow night? Could she come down to City Hall? They've got Cotswold Street up for a special meeting, starting at 7:30, but everything should be wrapped up by 9:30—10:00 at the latest. Harry and Melissa could go out afterwards and have a few drinks to celebrate. Melissa says she will try to come, but she can't promise. Her show opens in just ten days and the kids are really under-rehearsed. Well, okay, Harry says. At least they'll be able to get together on the weekend. He sounds grumpy and offended now, but Melissa does not change her mind. Yes, the weekend should be all right, she says coolly.

She returns to the auditorium where her Maria, a grade-eleven student who is very young and a little dumpy but who can sing gloriously, is holding hands with Tony, who doesn't sing nearly as well but who looks marvellous on stage. The two of them are working together on, "Make of our hearts one heart...make of our hands one hand..."

Their mingled voices sound fresh and ardent; they reinforce for Melissa the decision she has made. She is not going to move in with Harry Margulies. In fact, she is going the other way. As soon as Harry is safely finished with the business of Eton Towers, Melissa Sands is going to wind down this love affair.

In these past weeks, Melissa has discovered something quite interesting about herself. She can live without passion, quite comfortably, if she has to. But she cannot live without, at least, the memory of passion. She could put up with Harry, his obsessive interest in his work, his nervous wisecracks, even his sporadic ability to be sexual, if only she could look back on a period of her life when she had loved Harry Margulies madly. But there has never been a time when her whole being seemed to depend on whether Harry Margulies smiled at her. So Melissa cannot imagine growing old with him. She is not going to grab a man just because she is afraid of going on alone.

Melissa longs to be with those poor, doomed young lovers singing their hearts out up on the stage: "one heart...one life...only death can part us now..." Thank goodness the school auditorium is dark. None of her students can see the tears running down Miss Sands's face.

67

DONNY BOSSIN is astonished to see Max come crashing into the Commodore Health Club. Mr. Himmelfarb hasn't been here since he went back to work for his old company.

"You got any scotch, Donny?"

Mr. Himmelfarb looks as though he has already had too much of the stuff, but it's not Donny's place to tell him so.

"I think we could find some, if you'd like," he says cautiously.

"I'd like!" Max says bitterly. "Hey, you weren't closing up, were you, kid?"

The electric clock over the counter where Donny has been folding towels reads just a few minutes short of ten o'clock, which is the formal closing hour of the Commodore Club, and Donny's wife, Gloria, is waiting for him at home with a late supper. But there is no way Donny Bossin is ever going to burden Max Himmelfarb with any of his own troubles.

"I'll bring the drink to your locker," Donny says. "You go ahead, Mr. Himmelfarb."

Max has already stripped down and is sitting on the padded bench in front of his locker when Donny arrives with two plastic tumblers, one with whisky, the other with ice.

Max takes a long gulp of the whisky and then stops himself. He holds the plastic tumbler at arm's length and stares at it.

"I'm a schmuck," Max says at last. "Kid, I am schmuck like you wouldn't believe."

Max flings the plastic tumbler of whisky away from him. Donny does not react. He does not even look to see where the tumbler has landed.

"Is there anything else I can get you, Mr. Himmelfarb?"

"Donny, I wish there were," Max says, with a long sigh. "I'm going to take a little steam. Is the massage guy still here?"

"He's gone home," Donny Bossin says. "But I'll look after you, Mr. Himmelfarb."

"You?" Max says. Phil Bossin, Donny's father, was a bull but this kid doesn't look like he weighs more than a hundred pounds. "You know how to do that stuff, Donny?"

"You bet, Mr. Himmelfarb. When you run a health club, you learn to do everything the help does. Or they'll eat you up alive."

Max goes back and forth from the steam room to the shower three times. The final time, Donny brings him a glass of freshly squeezed orange juice with an ice cube to take into the steam. The coldness helps him stay there longer. By the time Max stretches out on the massage table the numbness from the alcohol has finally been driven off—never to be experienced again, Max vows!—and he is beginning to laugh to himself.

Max can see it all so clearly now. The goyim like to tell people it is more blessed to give than to receive. Tomorrow night, when Eton Towers comes to City Council, Max Himmelfarb will find out if the goyim know what the hell they are talking about. If this were a show, the lights on the marquee would say, "The Last Big Gamble of Maxie Himmelfarb!"

"You feeling better, Mr. Himmelfarb?" Donny says.

His fingers work slowly, competently, up the muscles of the spine. It's surprising how strong the kid is.

"I'm getting there, Donny. How's your father?"

"He's fine, Mr. Himmelfarb. I'm going down to see him next week."

"You give him my best, y'hear?" Max says.

Phil Bossin spends the winters in a seven-room apartment overlooking the boardwalk in Hallandale, Florida. He would not be there if it were not for his old friend from Berryman Avenue, Max Himmelfarb. Nor would Donny have had his own health club. If it were not for Max, Phil Bossin would have gone to jail.

Phil was working for a couple of stockies who were using a phoney assay report to hype a silver claim and then washboarding the shares, selling them to each other, to drive the price up still farther. Phil swore a solemn oath he never knew what they were up to; he was just on the phone, talking to his own customers.

The Ontario Securities Commission would not believe him. When the two partners took off for Brazil, the commission sent the mounties after Phil. The boys said Phil Bossin was a lost cause.

But Max Himmelfarb refused to give up. Max got a young lawyer named J. Arthur Quinn to take Phil Bossin's case and handled all the bills himself.

And after Quinn got Phil Bossin off, Max helped Phil start the dry-cleaning plant that eventually became a seven-store chain.

Phil Bossin paid off every nickel he owed Max Himmelfarb, of course. But where some people turn on those who help them, unable to bear the weight of a lifetime of gratitude, Philip Bossin never flinched. The name "Max Himmelfarb" was always spoken with reverence in the Bossin household. And now, working over the massive shoulder muscles of Max Himmelfarb, Donny Bossin thinks of himself as being his father's son, part of a chain of obligations and good deeds extending across generations. He feels safe.

68

IT IS FOUR in the morning, and the first, faint, pink rays of the rising sun can be seen fanning out over the city. But on Cotswold Street, the searchlight beams on as though this were still the darkest hour of the night.

Steve Bukowski squints down his sights at the searchlight. This is awkward to do because he is trying to balance a pillow over the air rifle in order to muffle the sound. An air rifle does not have a great deal of power, so the problem confronting Steve is how to hit the searchlight at just the right angle so that the pellet does not ricochet but penetrates the surface of the lens and reaches the crackling, sausage-shaped glass tube where the beam is generated. Several times Steve was sure he was ready, but the light swung on before he could pull back the trigger. Now he really must get the job done. It will soon be day. The searchlight is coming around. The trick, Steve has figured out, is to start squeezing the trigger just as the light turns towards him so that by the time he has actually fired the gun, the light will be facing him and the pellet will strike at the perfect angle. Gently…gently…

Tap. Tap. Someone is at his door. Steve pauses, holding his breath, waiting for them to go away.

"Steve, have you got any cigarettes? I saw your light on…"

Damn, it's Winnie. Steve looks into the room behind him. He has forgotten to turn off his little reading lamp.

"I'm sorry to bother you," Winnie whispers hoarsely though the door. "I'm all out."

Steve has a small stash of marijuana, but he is certainly not going to give Winnie any of that. He doesn't want to be responsible for getting Winnie stoned on the morning of the big day.

"I'm all out too," Steve whispers back.

"Can I come in anyway? I can't sleep."

Steve rolls his eyes upward, even though there is no one else in the room to see his appeal for heavenly justice. This shot at the searchlight is a treat he has been promising himself for days, a celebration of his farewell to Cotswold Street. He really ought to refuse to open the door. His whole purpose since he came here has been to train people to take charge of their own lives. But what if Winnie really needs him? Steve slides the air rifle under a blanket and opens the door.

"I'm really sorry," Winnie says. "I guess I'm more nervous than I think."

Her appearance is alarming. There is a clammy whiteness to her face, and Steve begins to worry that she might be coming down with flu. She is wearing only a thin nightgown and a blue terrycloth beach robe that barely comes to her knees.

"You want to hear something crazy?" Winnie says. "I'm going to miss this place."

"I know what you mean," Steve says. He makes a mental note to get Marlene to come over from Victoria's office and help Winnie get dressed up before the council meeting in the evening.

"I mean, things were rough in here, eh?" Winnie says. "But we had some good times. I'm really going to miss the people."

"It's not forever. You can come down for visits," Steve says. The Barbeaus have not talked at all about Billy's job in Cromwell. The people in the house know only that Billy has gone home to be with an ailing father and Winnie will join him as soon as things are settled in the city.

"What about you?" Winnie says. "Where are you going?"

Steve shrugs diffidently. It is difficult to explain.

"Something will turn up," he says. Some friends want him to help organize a food co-op, Molly Scanlon wants him to come work with her group, and the University Settlement House has been after him to organize their outreach program. But Steve doesn't want to tell Winnie about his prospects for fear that she will think he has been using Cotswold Street and the people in the house to advance his own career. And that just isn't true; Steve didn't seek any of these offers.

"Can I ask you a personal question?" Winnie says.

"Sure. Go ahead."

"Are you a Communist?"

Steve laughs out loud. So that's what they have been saying about him!

"Christ, no!" Steve says. "My people are from the Ukraine. The Communists tried to starve them to death. I hate the bastards."

"You talk like a Communist sometimes."

"How would you know, Winnie?"

"I know," Winnie says firmly. "We had them in Cromwell. They were in the miners' union."

"Well, I'm no damned Communist. If I'm anything, I'm a social democrat. But most of the time, I'm nothing."

"Well, don't get hot about it," Winnie says. "I was just curious, that's all…I hate that bloody, fucking thing, you know."

She is standing by Steve's window now, looking down at the creaking searchlight.

"I haven't had a decent night's sleep since old Himmelshit put that light there. It comes right in my window."

Steve takes the air rifle out of the blanket and shows it to Winnie.

Her haggard face breaks into a broad, appreciative smile.

"Oh, ho ho, so this is what you've been doing up here!" she says. "Naughty little boy."

"A little present to myself," Steve says. "I was just trying to figure the right angle when you knocked."

"Here, let me do it," Winnie says brusquely. "I grew up with these things."

Before Steve can stop her, Winnie has taken the gun from his hands and put it to her shoulder. Winnie needs no time at all to aim. Kapow! The air rifle resounds in the small room…followed immediately by the sound of shattering glass, and the white beam of the searchlight is gone forever.

Steve grabs Winnie and pulls her out of view. His weight presses her into the floor.

"Steve," she says gently. "I'm not goin' anywhere."

He stands up. He steps away from her.

"I'd better get back," Winnie says. "Lots to do today."

But she doesn't move. The excitement of shooting out the searchlight has gone. She will be alone in her room again. Her mind will start racing again. Winnie is sure that she really did try her best. But there are so many other things that she might have done… and should have done.

Steve has taken hold of her. He has her awkwardly, partly by the wrist and partly by the hand. He leads her to the mattress. He sits down first and draws her down beside him. Winnie does not resist. She has no fear of Steve Bukowski. He draws up the blankets around them and puts his arms carefully around her.

"I'm not worried about what's going to happen, you know," Winnie says.

"Me, neither," Steve says. "We're going to win tonight."

"That's for sure," Winnie says. Her eyes slide closed. She did not realize how tired she was.

Steve lies motionless, looking at her worn, little child's face. He is afraid to move. Finally, Steve's eyes close too.

69

BOBBY MULLOY composes a lead for his page-one story in *The Daily News*: "Victoria Sommers lost a squeaker last night." But he doesn't know that, damn it. That's the betting in the press gallery, the bank of seats up behind the last row of spectators' benches in the Council Chamber, but you can never be absolutely sure until the vote is taken. And when the bloody hell is that ever going to happen? They waived the eleven o'clock closure rule, and now it is after midnight and they should be getting close to the moment of truth. But the mayor has just announced he still has seven names on his list of alderman who insist they still have to make a speech about Eton Towers.

Bobby Mulloy is growing frantic. He's only got until one in the morning, at the very latest. Mulloy has sent most of his story, the buildup to this climactic meeting, downtown, and it's already in type, but they are still holding space on the front page for him. They want the results on Cotswold Street. But if those asshole aldermen down there don't get to the vote fast, Bobby Mulloy is going to have to come up with a lead that doesn't have the final outcome but still grabs people. How about, "There was blood on the floor of the Council Chamber last night as the politicians fought into the wee small hours over the fate of Cotswold Street." The chamber does, indeed, look a bit like a cylindrical Spanish bull-fight stadium cut in half, with the horseshoe table where the politicians sit down at the bottom and the curved, padded benches for the spectators rising steeply behind them. Mulloy could go on to compare Sommers to a wounded bull, and Mayor Sid Dewhurst, who has been fronting for Eton Towers all night, to a matador skilfully turning Sommers's charges aside.

But, no, that's too featurish for the black-line story on the front page. How about, "Police were called to the Council Chamber last night, for the first time in the history of the city?" Dewhurst did, indeed, walk in and see the packed seats and the ranks of people standing at the back and the stupid bastard panicked. Sommers had all her troops from the ratepayers and the non-profit housing projects out, but a lot of people had turned up to cheer for Eton Towers too. The word in the press gallery was that most of them were secretaries and junior executives from Premier Developments and some of the subcontractors Premier does business with. There was some jostling for seats and a lot of booing when aldermen from one side or the other scored a point, and old Dewhurst threatened to have the Council Chamber cleared and actually had a couple of uniformed cops sent in to stand beside the steep staircases.

But the spectators cooled down as the politicians droned on. The crowds on the benches began to thin out as it became apparent that it was going to take a long, long time for the big decision to come. Still, the calling of the cops will have to do for a lead, unless...unless...Vito Alcamo is up on his feet now. He's a swing vote. If he declares himself one way or another, that could do it. Mulloy leans forward so he can get a good look over the padded railing at the handsome young alderman, and begins making notes.

"So you are telling us that Cotswold Street has to be widened because of the size of Eton Towers?" Alcamo is saying.

"Yes, sir," Howard Redmond replies. He has risen courteously to his feet to answer questions from the council. "By one lane, about eleven feet."

Alcamo has been going at the planning commissioner for almost ten minutes now. Dane Harrison is seated beside him, and although the word around the hall is that Harrison has been pushed aside on this one, it's obvious they still need him to do the number crunching. Redmond leans over now and confers with his junior planner. Then he straightens up and faces Alcamo again.

"I think I should add, Alderman, that all the land for this widening is being provided by the developers from their site. So there will be no cost to the city. That's one of the reasons we are recommending the bonus for good planning."

"But we still have to pay for actual work on making Cotswold Street wider, don't we?" Alcamo says.

"Yes, sir—as the city does for all road widenings."

"Now, let me see if I understand what you've been telling us," Alcamo says. There is a threatening note in his voice. He is closing in for the kill. Bobby Mulloy is scribbling furiously now, leaning so far out over the padded press-gallery railing he is in danger of toppling forward into the spectators seated below him.

"You are telling us that we are giving Premier Developments additional density over and above the city's official plan—about four hundred thousand square feet of residential and commercial, as near as I can figure—because one of the things they are doing for us is giving us land to widen the roadway. But if they didn't want to put up such a big building, we wouldn't have to widen Cotswold Street, would we? So why don't we just say to them, 'Hey, put up something smaller, and we won't have to do anything to the street?'"

A wave of titters runs through the spectators' benches. The bonus for good planning really does sound silly when Alcamo puts it that way.

"It is certainly within the power of council to turn back this proposal," Redmond says. Mulloy thinks of comparing Redmond to the unctuous English butler in a bad movie, but his editors would never let him get away with it. What a pity the truth is so often libellous.

"But I should point out again, Alderman Alcamo, that the street widening is only a part, a small part I should add, of the general good-planning bonus. We still believe that Eton Towers is a unique, mixed-use building and deserves City Council support because of the rejuvenating impact it will have on this neighbourhood."

Alcamo shakes his head melodramatically. The man must have been a great performer in his other life, teaching school.

"Thank you, Mr. Redmond, you've been very helpful," Alcamo says. "I'd like to speak now, Mr. Mayor."

The mayor asks hopefully if anyone else wants to question the planning commissioner. No one does. It's clear the politicians have had enough of Redmond's patronizing manner. He sits down beside Dane in the little half-circle beside the council table reserved for top civil servants. The mayor then nervously, and somewhat reluctantly, asks Alcamo to continue.

"I am going vote against Eton Towers," Alcamo announces. "People from my ward have been calling me all week, telling me it's too big and it doesn't belong in a family neighbourhood. And Mr. Redmond has just confirmed what my people have suspected: the bonus for good planning is a travesty. People will laugh at us for years if we approve Eton Towers tonight."

Bobby Mulloy is delighted. He is going to make his deadline after all. Bless you, Vito Alcamo. Bobby Mulloy will now canonize the alderman if he will just come up with a good quote. And what do you know? Here it comes! Alcamo is pointing up to the far-right corner of the spectators' gallery, the seats closest to the wall, where the group from Premier Developments is sitting.

"Not too long ago, Mr. Quinn up there said to us that if we wanted to build a city for people, the Berryman Expressway was good place to stop. Well, I say that if we want to build a city for people, Eton Towers is an even better place to stop!"

The tiered ranks of spectators break into applause. There is whistling and cheering. Victoria's supporters have outlasted the Premier employees who came out to support the project. The mayor has to bang his gavel and threaten again to clear the chamber.

"I thought you said we had Alcamo," Harry Margulies whispers to Arthur Quinn.

"That's what our esteemed partner told me," Quinn whispers back.

"I think we're in trouble," Harry says.

Vito Alcamo does not turn to acknowledge the applause. But he does not want to look straight ahead either. He might not be able to restrain himself from glancing over at Dane Harrison, and that could give away the connection between them. It was Dane, over a casual cup of coffee in the City Hall cafeteria, who first put Alcamo onto the absurdity of the bonus for good planning.

But just as he feels he cannot look behind him or in front of him, Alcamo cannot look up either. He can feel J. Arthur Quinn and the people from Premier Developments up in the stands, cursing his name. What they should be doing is saying that Vito Alcamo is a politician with balls. He has made a difficult choice and he has made it in public, where everybody can see him.

The people Alcamo respects back in his ward have told him they think this whole Eton Towers business is a big mess. They wanted him to be against it. So what was Alcamo supposed to do? Turn his back on the old timers who made him an alderman just because he got the word that if he voted for Eton Towers, people in the federal Liberal party would owe him? What do they have to give that Vito Alcamo really wants? Alcamo's wife has already told him she cannot spend half her time in Ottawa just because Vito wants to be a member of Parliament. Gillian Alcamo has her own career as a consultant in early-childhood education to think about. So tonight Vito Alcamo has told the world he is going to be a city politician. This is the only career he desires. Let the chips fall where they may.

Up in the press gallery, Bobby Mulloy decides to wait for Jack Painter, who is up next—just to be certain. And sure enough, Painter sings the same hymn. He even turns to the stands and publicly acknowledges the inspirational leadership of the "little heroine of Cotswold Street." Winnie Barbeau waves her clenched fist in the air. The mayor bangs his gavel furiously, but he is unable to quell the boisterous applause.

Bobby Mulloy is going to make his deadline. Victoria's got it for sure now. She had five midtown reformers and the six NDP members; now she's picked up two votes—one more than she really needed—from the mushy middle. Bobby's got his lead composed before he even sits down at his desk: "Victoria Sommers won the victory of a lifetime last night..."

Mayor Dewhurst recognizes Victoria. She's not the next person down to speak, but what the hell...the game is over. He might as well be a gentleman and let Victoria have her moment of glory.

"I feel very proud of this council tonight," Victoria says. She looks stunning; she is wearing a simple black suit with a wide gold link chain around her neck. The chestnut hair falls grandly to her shoulders.

"We are not just saving a neighbourhood tonight," Victoria says. "We ought to put up a plaque on number sixteen Cotswold Street. This is where the people took power. We are telling developers that they are not running this city any more. People on this council used to look at the developers"—she pauses to look up at Max Himmelfarb and the row of Premier executives and lawyers—"like they were father figures. They were afraid to do anything unless the developers told them to. Developers ran this city. But no more. The people run the city now. The days when Max Himmelfarb could walk in here and get whatever he wanted are gone forever."

Up in the gallery, Max whispers to Quinn, "What's she saying?"

"I think," Quinn says, "that she is calling you a crook."

"Yeah, I think so too," Max says happily. "Go down there and tell them I want to say a few words."

"You can't, Max. This is a council meeting. Only the politicians get to speak."

"They call me names and I don't get to answer back?" Max says. He sounds deeply offended. "Go down there and tell them I want my inning."

Quinn hesitates. Letting people come down from the stands—no matter who they are—to speak at a council meeting is against all the rules of procedure.

"Do it, Arthur," Max says.

Quinn turns to study his client. It comes to him that this is the opening Max has been waiting for all night.

Quinn rises, pushes past Max and Mr. Englander and Freddy, who has just got back from Florida, and begins to descend the stairs, thinking quickly about how he can carry out the instructions of his client.

"Yes, Mr. Quinn?" the mayor says.

Quinn explains that he is well aware that what he is asking is most irregular. But Alderman Sommers has made personal allegations about his client. Mr. Himmelfarb has no real desire to begin legal proceedings, but he asks the indulgence of council to be able to respond to Mrs. Sommers.

The mayor asks for the will of council. Even Victoria votes to let Max speak. Fair is fair. And besides, she doesn't want her victory tonight marred by any lawsuits. Members of a municipal council do not have the same protections from libel and slander actions that members of Parliament enjoy.

Everyone turns now to the upper row where the developers are sitting. Max is whispering something to Mr. Englander. The spectators see a gaunt old man in a black suit who looks like he's having a heart attack on the spot. He is clutching the arm of the fellow beside him, a stocky, balding character with a rich, strawberry tan.

Victoria's supporters have heard about old Himmelshit—that's why they're here tonight—but this is the first time they've actually had the devil right in front of them. They have to concede that the fellow down on the floor facing City Council now looks pretty impressive—a big, ruddy man who seems to be swaggering even when he is standing still.

"Our company, Premier Developments, has been in business in this city for thirty-seven years," Max tells the City Council with grave dignity. "We are proud of our company and we are proud of the housing we have built for people."

"And your big fat profits!" someone calls from the stands behind him. Max turns around, but he cannot tell from those rows of angry little faces which person spoke. He smiles gently, forgiving all of them; he is an old Chassidic rabbi now, delivering a homily to his followers.

"We are not ashamed to make a profit," Max says. "Look around you! Everything in this room—the walls, the windows, the benches you're sitting on, the clothes you're wearing—everything in this room was made by somebody for a profit. That's the way the world works. We didn't invent the system, but I can tell you we are very proud to be part of it."

The Premier employees still left in the stands applaud enthusiastically. Even some of the midtown ratepayers who have come out to support Victoria clap for Max Himmelfarb. Just because they are trying to protect their neighbourhoods, it doesn't mean they have turned into socialists.

"Thank you very much, Mr. Himmelfarb," the mayor says.

"I'm not finished yet," Max says. "We have offered to build four hundred and fifty units of non-profit housing in Scarborough if you approve Eton Towers tonight. But we have another lot right beside the one we have offered you and we are prepared to put that into non-profit housing too.

"We are prepared to build eight hundred and ninety-five units of non-profit housing in Scarborough."

The astonished, confused faces of the politicians and the audible gasps in the audience behind him thrill and delight Max. He is thinking that he missed his calling; he really should have gone into show business.

"I have got to warn you, though, that we can't hold this open forever. But if you approve Eton Towers tonight, I give you my word that Premier Developments will put up eight hundred and ninety-five units of affordable, non-profit, family housing on our property in Scarborough."

Up at the top of the stands the ancient cry of distress rushes uncontrollably to the lips of Reb Shmuel Englander: "Oy vay iz mir!" His gnarled, workman's fingers dig like talons into the arm of his son, Fred, the only person left in the world the old man can still trust. What evil spirit ever possessed Mr. Englander to offer control of the company to Max? "My heart," he moans. "My heart..."

"It's all right, Sammy," Quinn whispers. "Max knows what he's doing."

Victoria looks up to where Molly Scanlon is sitting. The president of the M. J. Coldwell Co-op Builders Foundation looks like she is going to spring out of her seat and land screaming right in the middle of the Council Chamber. Scanlon could live, however bitterly, with Victoria's decision to stick with the tenants and turn down the 450 units. But is Victoria going to turn down nearly 900 units! That project alone could keep the co-op builders busy for a couple of years at least. And, of course, it is good, decent, affordable housing for more than 2,000 people!

The New Democratic caucus cracks and then crumbles. One by one they ask to be recognized and then announce they are changing their votes. They all have great respect for Mrs. Barbeau, they say, but they cannot put the interests of a dozen people in one old house against the interests of more than 2,000 people who will get new places to live.

When the vote is called and the hands begin to go up around City Council's horseshoe table, Victoria sees that she can have it both ways. Eton Towers and the Scarborough housing project are going to be approved, so Molly Scanlon will be happy. That leaves Victoria free to vote against Eton Towers, the way Winnie Barbeau and the tenants still must want her to. But Victoria Sommers decides she will not play the games that other politicians play. Victoria puts up her hand for Eton Towers.

As soon as her vote has been counted, Victoria turns to look for Winnie and Steve. But the row where the Cotswold Street tenants were sitting all night is now empty.

It is 1:47 in the morning. The clerk calls out the names for the recorded vote. The final tally is eighteen to four in favour of Eton Towers and the 895 units of non-profit housing in Scarborough. The only people to stay opposed to the project were four midtown reformers who listened to Winnie Barbeau and who still believe she was right. Eton Towers, they say, is just the beginning. Giant apartment towers are going to spread like cancer all across the city.

The spectators have almost all left, but Max Himmelfarb still has to push through a throng of Premier employees and well-wishers to reach Mr. Englander.

"Maxie, what have you done to me?" the old man cries.

"Relax, Pa," he says. "You're going to make lots of money. You just got a new partner that's all: the government."

"Max is right, Mr. Englander," Quinn says.

"We'll talk about it in the morning," the old man says.

"Talk about it with Freddy," Max says. "I quit."

The old man looks up at him warily. What kind of trick is this?

"Ma-a-ax? What are you doing, Max?"

"Half of Eton Towers is mine, that's enough for me," Max says. "More than enough. I'm getting out, Pa."

This is happening just the way Max planned. It's beautiful. Revenge is so sweet. A man could get drunk on it. Reb Shmuel Englander is stunned, like he has been hit on the he head with a two-by-four.

"Maxie, don't talk stupid."

"Goodbye, Pa," Max says. "You got a great company. You can't even give it away."

And then Max Himmelfarb turns around and walks out of the Council Chamber. Reb Shmuel Englander is left alone with his lawyers, his company executives, and his son, Fred.

Up in the press gallery, Bobby Mulloy is desperately calling his lead into the city desk: "Premier Developments won such an overhwelming victory last night that even the company's arch enemy, Victoria Sommers, turned against her own supporters and voted for Eton Towers..."

70

THE DAY is a tussle between spring and winter, and spring is winning. The children have unzipped their parkas and they careen about the schoolyard, crashing joyfully into each other, looking like little Eskimos gone mad. Their whooping and screams of delight fill the air around Shelley Himmelfarb. She loves it. The teachers may complain about having to do yard duty, but Shelley thinks she is privileged to be out here, standing in the midst of so much fresh, young, animal energy.

Max Himmelfarb has no trouble at all spotting his wife. Who else but Shelley would wear a fur coat at recess? The sight of her trying to untangle two little boys stirs sweet memories. Shelley has always been like that, loving the good things in life, but careless about them too. He tosses away his cigar, still only half smoked, and enters the schoolyard.

"I've been expecting you," Shelley says. She is still holding on to one desperate little boy.

"I walked out," Max says.

"I know," Shelley says. "Pa called. He says I should work on you."

"You want to do that?"

The little boy escapes from Shelley's grasp. He charges off to find another little girl to jump on.

"I told my father I don't run errands for him any more. I told him to go to hell."

Max throws back his head and laughs.

"I wish I'd seen his face when he heard that!"

"What are you going to do, Max?"

"I don't know. I'm not going back to the Commodore Club, that's for sure. I'm going to take a little vacation. Then see what turns up."

"Well, good luck, Max." Shelley extends her hand. "I'm glad things worked out so well for you."

The bell is ringing to end recess. The children are filing back into the school. Shelley must join them. But Max won't relinquish her hand.

"I got a reservation," he says. "The Royal Island Hotel, right on the beach in Bermuda. It's a double room."

"Oh? Yeah? I'm supposed to go with you, just like that, eh? The last time you were here, you talked about giving me three-quarters of everything you own."

"Not on your life," Max says. "You had your chance; you blew it."

This is going to be something to talk about for days. Little Mrs. Himmelfarb is kissing the strange man right in the middle of the schoolyard. He's got his arms around her and he's hugging her so hard he's lifting her right off the ground.

"I can't do this, Max!" Shelley cries. "I have to work!"

"Says who? If I can walk out on Premier Developments, you can walk out of this place."

"You will never change," Shelley says. She clasps his arm and starts heading towards the gate with him. "The only person you ever think about is yourself!"

"What are you talking about?" Max says. "Didn't I just pull off the perfect real estate deal? Everybody got what they wanted."

71

THE EXPRESS BUS to Edmonton has pulled up to the windy loading platform and opened its front door. Steve Bukowski moves up the line towards it, carrying Winnie Barbeau's worldly possessions, one canvas suitcase. He has been with her through the night, listening to Winnie rage against Victoria's betrayal and curse people back in Cromwell that Steve has never heard of before. Many times Winnie burst into tears. But now her eyes are like two small blue stones. By the time the day had begun, Winnie had made her choices. Her face is pale, but set and hard. She is not going back to her home town a failure. She cannot face Billy Barbeau telling her he knew all along that Victoria would sell them out.

Winnie's sister told her over the phone this very morning that there are jobs out in Alberta. Winnie will have no trouble finding work. The only time she feels anything now is when she thinks about Buster. Through the night, she cried whenever she talked about her son. But now she's starting to be all right about that too. There's no question Buster is better off, for the time being, with his father. But Winnie will not let herself be forgotten. She has promised herself she will write to her son every day. She will come back to Billy and Billy Jr. just as soon as she has got herself together.

"You don't have to do this, you know," Steve says.

They are getting close to the bays where the driver will store Winnie's suitcase underneath the bus. Steve has been allowed to accompany her to the bus station only because he has promised not to carry on. But Steve cannot let her go without making one last plea.

"You could get a job here," he says again. "You could get your own place."

"I know," Winnie says. "It's a good idea. Maybe I'll come back, sometime."

They are at the door. Winnie turns her cheek up to be kissed.

"I'll write," she says. "Don't you worry. You take care of yourself."

She enters the bus and is lucky to find, halfway down, an empty seat beside a window. Winnie takes this as a good omen. She sees Steve waving to her as the bus pulls out of the station. He looks like he is crying, but the bus window is dirty and Winnie is too far away to be able to say for certain. Huge office towers zoom past the window as the bus turns down University Avenue and pulls on to the highway. Winnie's time in Toronto is over. But she cannot say, she cannot even imagine, what is going to happen next. Being free, Winnie is thinking, is only this—not knowing where the hell you are going and not giving a flying fuck either.

4

STREET PEOPLE: 1976

The ballad of Willy McNiven, Gracie Calder, and Dolly Oliver, in which Peter Dagenham, J. Arthur Quinn, Harry Margulies, and our friends from Landrigan Street have parts to play and choruses to sing

Dane Harrison, July 1: I will tell you the truth. What you are seeing here is not just a summertime experiment. The outdoor mall is permanent. When people get used to this, they will never give it up.

Nothing like this has ever been done before. Some American cities have outdoor malls, yes, but just for a couple of blocks, on streets off to one side of downtown, where no one cares very much. We have completely closed off the main thoroughfare, half a mile of Hanover Street.

No private cars, no buses, no cabs, not even delivery trucks can come onto the street after ten in the morning. We have turned the heart of Toronto into a public park. We have given the street back to the people. If somebody tries to take it away from them now, there will be a riot.

Peter Dagenham, Chairman, Dagenham's Department Store, July 5: My father used to say Hanover Street was a sewer. I used to say to him, a lot of our customers come in off that street, and our customers are not sewer rats. But since they started this summer mall, I know exactly what my father meant. I wouldn't walk out there for love nor money.

That outdoor mall is a hell hole.

You will say I have a hidden agenda. I want to get rid of the mall so I can tear the old stores down and put up a shopping plaza. I say to you, I am not hiding anything. My partners and I have acquired almost all the properties we need to build Dagenham Square. When we get the last ones, we will raze the old Hanover Street and put up a fine, modern, indoor shopping mall, one point six million square feet, all enclosed, all climate-controlled, all gorgeous.

People in retailing say I'm crazy. A regional mall, they say, has to be out in the boondocks, with miles of parking all around. I say to you that I'm sitting on top of a goddamned subway station. Once people come down here, they'll keep coming back. You will hear that myself and my partner, Fred Englander, are heading for trouble, but I am telling you that Dagenham Square is going to be the biggest business success you ever saw.

The store my grandfather started is dying. If he were here now, he'd slap me on the back and say, "Go to it, lad!" Dagenham Square is going to have a swimming pool, and not one but two of those movie houses where they have a dozen screens. We'll have pubs and restaurants and cafés, and a zoo and a playground for the children, and two hotels, and I've been talking to the minister of my church and I think we're even going to have a chapel, a non-denominational place, where people can take a load off their feet and talk to their maker.

Now, you go and look at the misery that's out on Hanover Street, and can you honestly tell me you'd rather have that than Dagenham Square?

Michael Pappas, Proprietor, Skyline Open Kitchen, July 6: It's like the old country when I was a kid. I look out my front window and it's wall-to-wall people. I love the mall.

Louise Hacker, Secretary, Confederated Life Assurance, July 6: A group of us went up to Fran's for supper after work. They have tables out on the street now, and I liked being able to be outside after being in an office all day. But you sure do see a lot of weird people on Hanover Street.

Vivian Billinghurst, Bookseller, July 6: A little kid came right up to my husband and stuck a leaflet in his hand. It said "Screwy Looey's Massage Parlour." I didn't get it at first, but Trevor explained that massage parlours are a kind of prostitution. This was happening in the main street of Toronto; I couldn't believe it.

Annabel Harrison, Housewife, July 6: Dane was in charge of getting out all the benches and potted trees and flower beds. They did it all in one night, and that morning, I came downstairs and found him sound asleep at the kitchen table. I took him up to the bedroom and undressed him. Then I got undressed myself and got in with him. I usually wear long nightgowns, a sign of middle-aged insecurity, but this time I didn't wear anything at all.

I don't think I can, Dane said. I've been up all night.

You just lie back, I said. Leave everything to Annabel.

What does the thermometer say? Dane asked me.

It didn't say anything, I told him. This is a freebie. A little gift to celebrate the opening of the mall.

Dane wrapped his arms around me.

I love you, he said.

Walt Bowen, Folk Singer, July 6: The mall's like a slalom course. But all those benches and concrete pots with trees and flowers in them are good places for artists. They're like rocks in the stream. The flow of people divides to get around the obstacle and this creates a bit of empty space where you can set up. My first night on the mall I took in seventy-five dollars. People love me because I give them plain, honest folk music that grows out of the land. One guy and his girlfriend stayed for over an hour, listening to me, and finally I asked them if there was something special they wanted to hear, and he asked for the old Pete Seeger song, "Where Have All the Flowers Gone?" As soon as I started, they wrapped their arms around each other and started this heavy kiss. They were still at it when I got to the end so I did a couple of extra choruses for them. But nobody minded. And this was the main street of Toronto. It shows you how much the mall has liberated people.

Grace Calder, July 7: A lot of people think a body rub is the same as being out on the street. But that just shows how ignorant they are. I've been on the street and, I can tell you, this is like paradise. I don't have to come here until two in the afternoon. And then the guys come to me. I have my own place, a little cubicle, sort of, where I work. It's like going to the office. The best part is I don't have to do anything I don't feel like doing. They pay at the front and then they go down to the end of the corridor and take a shower—there's these sort of metal stall places—and then they come in to me or to one of the other girls. Six of us are here on a regular day; they can take their pick from the photographs out front. The shower is supposed to relax them because they are supposed to be getting a real massage, but I think Looey, the owner, makes them do it so they'll be like clean for us. I think that shows Looey's a decent guy, although a lot of people really hate him.

The customers pay thirty-five dollars for a half-hour, from which we're supposed to get seven at the end of the month, and then anything we make on our own we get to keep. Except we have to give Looey two hundred a week for towels and for the hard-rock guys he keeps out in front. Some girls say they used to make more on their own, but they're not thinking about the hassles and people ripping them off.

Mostly I just do hand jobs in here, but if I really like the looks of a guy and he's clean, I'll ball him. Like yesterday, I was jerking this guy off and nothing was happening. I'd figured he'd come quick because his cock was so small and he was so excited, but he was an Indian or something, I think maybe he must have been some kind of yogi, because then he started deep breathing and it was like his cock just stopped. It was up all right, and good and hard, but it was ice cold. I reached over for a cigarette. Then I looked down and he was looking up at me and he was so sad, these big brown eyes watching me light up while I was pulling his wire at the same time, I thought he was going to cry. So I balled him, even though he'd only paid for a hand job.

I've got seven hundred and thirty-six dollars in the bank; when I hit one thousand I'm on my way. I'm going home first and then out to Vancouver to see my girlfriend, Linda. I'm going to look my father right in the eye and I'm going to say to him, I paid for Graeme, Daddy. I paid more than you ever did. You can go on hating me if you want. But I don't hate myself anymore. So, goodbye. This is the last time you'll ever see me, Daddy. Maybe I'll even kiss my father goodbye.

Yesterday, I came downstairs, and the Nazi was there. Willy gets out tomorrow, he says. We'll go pick him up. Without even thinking, I said to him, I can't, I have to work. He just looked at me, the death ray, like he was going to turn me to stone on the spot.

Clem, I said—I was pleading with him—I'm clean. I haven't done anything in four months. Not even a glass of beer. Leave me alone, Clem, please.

Willy told me to find you, he says. You didn't know it, but I been watching you. Oh yeah, I can really believe that, a two-hundred-and-fifty-pound biker with a beard down to his belly button. I'm just one of the crowd, folks. Pretend you don't see me. Be here at ten o'clock, he says. I'll pick you up. I can't, I said. I'm going away, Clem. He gave me the evil eye again, and this time I couldn't take it any more and I started to cry.

I ran back up to my room, and I just sat there staring at the fucking wall. Tee John and the Indian—the guys at the front desk—came down to see what was wrong. Tee John offered me some shit—he's a good guy really—but I said, no, don't worry, I'm all right. But oh, Jesus God, I wanted to take it. They wouldn't go away. The two of them just stood there watching me and I could tell what was going through their minds, if they have minds.

I was having that dream again: out on the ice, all by myself, but the frozen river wasn't frozen any more. I'd waited too long. It was cold and that fooled you, the way it always does in Alcorn because the sun is out, even if you don't feel it, and underneath the snow, where you can't see anything, the ice is going rotten, so when you step on it, it's just like quicksand, and I was going down into the freezing water and I was going to die.

Then the little voice inside said to me, Where's Graeme? And I knew I was going to be okay. For the first time I could remember, for the first time ever since that day, I wasn't thinking about my brother when I was in trouble. That used to be my secret weapon. Whenever things came down on me, even when I tried to kill myself and I opened my eyes and I thought, oh no, how the fuck am I going to get out of this, I started thinking about my brother. Like, as bad as people think I am, they don't know anything. They don't know how bad I was to Graeme. And he was the first person I ever loved. So nothing else I do really matters because it can never be as bad as what I did to my brother.

One of the reasons I could never get away from Willy McNiven, even when people told me he was killing me, was that Willy was so much like Graeme. Not that Willy looked like my brother, because Graeme was always thin and sharp and Willy is built like a brick shit-house. But because both of them were so complete inside themselves. Graeme could make you think you didn't need anybody else in the world but him. And Willy was the same way.

So why am I running away from Willy? Why don't I go with the Nazi and be there, standing at the prison door, when my man gets out? But it hasn't been easy for me either. Willy's been gone three years, and I had some bad times, some really bad times. I kept trying to off myself and every time I did, Silvester, the guy I was living with at the time, would beat the shit out of me. But I never cared. I only stopped because, one day, a light went on in my head and I said to myself, Okay, you've been here long enough, it's time to move on.

I dried myself out. I didn't go to any of the clinics and I wouldn't even tell my old social worker, even though I really liked her, because I was afraid she would get me sent away somewhere. It's really hard doing it all by yourself. You can't even imagine how sick it makes you feel.

But anyway, I did it. I dried myself out And I got this job and I'm putting money away and I'm going out to Linda. I spoke to her on the phone just last week. She sounded great. She said they have courses in this community college where she's going, for social workers. I've always wanted to be a social worker, help people who are down, the way I've been down.

But, yes, I still love Willy McNiven, and if you love someone, you don't run away from them just when they're going to need you most, right?

Yes, you do. Sometimes you do.

Lewis Gough, July 8: I opened the first body rub on Hanover Street and Screwy Looey's is still the best. I'm a revolutionary. I'm like the guys who were out in the street, getting civil rights for the niggers and stopping the war in Vietnam. I'm liberating people. In Screwy Looey's they have a good time, anything they want.

The cops come around and tell me to clean up my act, and I tell them to kiss my royal Canadian ass. We're strictly legal. The only crime in this fucking country is soliciting. As long as my girls don't ask first, they're okay. They can sell pussy, but they can't advertise it. It's crazy, but, hey, don't look at me! I don't make the laws.

Willy McNiven, July 8: They opened the door this morning and I said, You fuckn dickheads, you were waiting for this. And they said to me, Well, why don't you just stay here, Willy? Save us all a lot of time. Rain was coming down so hard you couldn't see the other side of the street. Ten o'clock in the fuckn morning and it looked like the fuckn middle of the night. I would have stayed, I honest-to-shit would have slammed shut the fuckn door. But the Nazi was standing out there, waiting for me. God knows how he got two hawgs up there, but he did. He even had my running-suit. We took a couple of long pulls from the jar he had, Wiser's Old. I hadn't tasted good rye in three fuckn years. Right there in the street I stripped off the crap they gave me to come out in and put on the stuff the Nazi'd brought up. It was leather pants and my old Devil's Own jacket. Clem must have been keeping it all this time. I took another long pull of rye, and we got the fuck away from there.

It felt so good to have the wind in my face again. You ask me what I missed most inside and it was just that, the wind. Everything else I could get: booze—loving, if you didn't mind putting your dick up some guy's asshole and it never particularly bothered me—and every kind of dope you ever heard of. But you could never get the wind in your face.

The Nazi started bombing cars, showing off like he always does—nothing changes in three years—but this time I kept right up there beside him, laughing like crazy. Cars were jumping to the sides of the road to get away from us and people were screaming when we went charging past. I knew what Clem was doing, testing me to see if I could still handle a 1200 Harley shovelhead after three years in the can. He almost fuckn won. The road was wet and greasy, and a couple of times I was sure I could feel the wheels sliding out from under me. I thought, this is it, one hour out of the can and it's bye-bye Willy McNiven. Tell them to cremate me, Clem; I always did want to go out in a ball of fire. But then I started to get the feel of it, all that power roaring between my legs. Everything came back to me. I was flying.

We stopped once, and the Nazi wanted to get out of the rain, but I said I'd been out of the rain for three years, so we sat on a hill, chewing keilbasa that the Nazi had brought with him. We going straight to the club? I asked him. There's some people I got to see. Clem shook his head and turned away, like he was afraid to look me in the eye. No club, he said. The Devil's Own is done for, down the fuckn tubes. We're a chapter of The Warriors. I mean they are a chapter of The Warriors. Vince is the president now.

I let that one sink in. I'd kind of known it was happening from letters I'd been getting in the joint. I didn't think about it too much in there, but now I was out, and here was my best friend telling me the club I started and gave half my life to had turned to rat shit. Welcome home, Willy McNiven.

Where's Gracie?

She said she had to work today.

Work? Where the fuck does Gracie work?

Hanover Street. In a cathouse. She's going out to her girlfriend; they're going to start hustling in Vancouver.

He said all that flat, like he was giving me the weather. But he knew what it was doing to me inside.

Fuckn shit! I said. I finished the rye and threw the bottle in the air. It came down and smashed on the highway.

What do you want to do, Willy?

Do? What the fuck do you think I want to do? The Devil's Own is our club. We started it. We're taking it back.

He goes, Just the two of us, Willy?

I'll do it myself, I said. You can sit on your ass.

Willy, he says, you don't know how I missed you. The fucker gives me this big bear hug, like he almost broke my ribs.

We came in by the lake and I looked up at the big office buildings. It seemed like there were a hell of a lot more of them than from the time I left, and an old line from when I was a kid came back to me: I will lift up my eyes to the hills. I hadn't thought about any of that shit in a thousand years. I think it was coming to me now because getting out of the can was in a lot of ways like being a kid again.

Vince Logan, President, The Warriors, July 10: This is the story of Willy McNiven. Poor, old Willy McNiven.

He comes into the clubhouse and he says, Who's all these fuckn Warriors? We're The Devil's Own. Rip that shit off your backs. We're the band of brothers, the Malvern musketeers. Yeah, yeah, and all those fuckn dickheads are cheerin'...Yeah, yeah. Listen to Willy, first leader of The Devil's Own. Here's to Willy McNiven. They're slappin' his back and pourin' beer over his head, and all the time he's watching me. What's Vincie gonna do, eh? What's ol' Vincie gonna do?

I take off the silver cross and chain Willy hung on me the night before he went into the can. He told me his mother gave it to him when she was dying, but I hear he stole it from a crippled nun. I hang the cross around Willy's neck, and everybody's yelling and smashing beer bottles against the walls. I lean forward and I kiss Willy on the cheek, and I'm holdin' his face in my hands and he's trying to pull back, but he can't. He keeps watching me with those little snake eyes, and I start talkin' real quiet, and everybody cools down because they want to hear, eh? And I say to him: Willy, my good, old buddy, with The Warriors we're connected—world wide. We got shit comin' in from all over and we're makin' big bucks—really big bucks! You hearing me good, Willy, my old leader, my old blood brother? Because you're dead meat, you dumb cunt!

He moves, but I move faster. I'm still holdin' his face in one hand and I've got the pipe out of my pocket and I nail him right between the eyes. Willy drops to his knees. The Nazi jumps in. It takes six guys to bring him down—fuckn fat tub of shit. They've got their guys all over the room, but they never even get their hands out of their pockets. My guys've got pipes and chains. We learned that from the fuckn Warriors. Don't waste time. Even Cathy's in on it. I seen her take halfa nigger's face off with her fingernails. So what? He'll be back. Where the fuck else is he gonna go? It's over so fast some of my guys are madder'n shit. They didn't get no kicks in, they're saying. Out in the yard, I tell them. A dozen Warriors are standing around, putting the boots to Willy McNiven. He don't even turn to get out of the way no more. He looks like he's been run over by a train. But he gets to his hands and knees and starts crawlin' towards me. The guys move aside to let him come. Lisa Bee's beside me, pouring tequila down my throat. Be my guest, I say to her. She gets him right in the eye. She's got steel toes in those pretty little boots of hers. Willy gurgles and blood starts coming out of the place where his eye used to be. But he rolls over and starts crawling towards me again. I bring up the old highway specials and get him right in the mouth. And he's still coming at me! The guys wanted to tear him apart then. I'm not sure they didn't after I left. It's none of my business. I don't mind somebody being born a pussy. But if you were a rider once and then you turn yourself into a pussy, you're worse than shit.

Clement Caldecott, July 11: People think I'm the Nazi because I got this big swastika on the back of my jacket. They don't know I got a swastika tattooed on my chest too. This isn't just a costume I put on when I want to scare people and take off when I go to bed at night. I am what I am. I'll be the Nazi 'til the day I die.

When we started The Devil's Own, when there was just the seven of us, we pricked our thumbs and we squeezed our blood into an old skull, and we all drank from it, and we swore our oath to the brotherhood of blood and iron.

Only me and Willy are left. But listen, eh? When Hitler was in jail, when they tried to take over Munich in twenty-three, there was just him and Rudolf Hess. Ten years later, they took over the whole fuckn country.

We spend a lot of time on the mall now. Willy's getting himself together and we're watching the action, getting to know who the real players are and who's just pissing around. Willy's getting better. We're going to make a big score, and I've been talking about knocking over Screwy Looey's. It's a perfect set up for us—especially with Gracie in there. Willy says, okay now, he likes it too, but he's got to be able to see straight first.

I took him that night to Betty, an old customer of ours who works as a nurse, and she wanted to whip Willy right into a hospital. But Willy said, No, he was out on a ticket and they'd send him back inside again. So Betty fixed him up, and she's going to check him out every day. Betty is from the old school.

So am I. The person I think a lot about right now is Joseph Goebbels, even though I probably look more like Hermann Goering. Goebbels never flinched. He said right at the start that Hitler was his leader and he stuck with his leader right to the very end. Goebbels killed his own wife and his own kids, then he waited until Hitler'd offed himself and then he made sure his leader's body was destroyed. Only then, when he'd done this last job for Hitler, did Goebbels take himself out. I'm not saying I could do any of that, but I understand Goebbels. I understand the soldiers of the Wehrmacht who marched backward from Stalingrad and El Alamein, fighting every step of the way. They never quit. That's why I love them so much and why I try to honour their memory with my own life.

Paul Olivier, July 12: The last person I ever expected to see on Hanover Street was Gracie Calder. I thought she was dead. But there we were, staring at each other, Gracie in her underpants and me with my hands knotted in this dink's hair, smashing his face into the wall.

Hi, Gracie, I said, catching my breath. It's me, Paul Olivier. I could see I was not getting through, so I said, Hey, it's Dolly Oliver. That did it. Her hand flew up to her mouth. She was in shock. I could understand. I would not have known what to say to me either. My clothes were filthy and I had a three-day growth of beard. I definitely did not look like anybody's idea of a good time. Besides, I was still smashing this dink's face into the wall. He was finally starting to be a good boy, so I kicked his feet out from under him and put my knee in his back while I got the cuffs on him.

Yes, Gracie, I said, standing up. You can see I have done well in life, I have become a cop. Gracie giggled. And it was like nothing had happened in the last ten years. We were still back at Alcorn Regional Secondary School. I was still her brother Graeme's best friend. And Grace Calder was still the most beautiful girl in McCrae Township.

There were a million things I wanted to ask her, but my first thought was to get the dink out of there before my brother officers came charging up the stairs to rescue me. It's been nice seeing you, Gracie, I said. I'll come back when things are a little cooler.

Down in the street, broken glass from Scobey's Jewellery Store was everywhere. It crackled under your feet. The sergeants kept telling people to go home, the show was over but they hardly moved. They were still hoping to see one of us get kicked to death.

Coppers from other divisions had been brought in to stand guard in front of the jewellery store. We may let the occasional good citizen get raped and beaten to a pulp, but you will never find us derelict in our duty when it comes to protecting private property.

The hassle started just after one in the morning. There are eight bars on Hanover Street, and at one o'clock they have to stop serving and turn the drunks loose. Some of them don't want to go. This particular dink picked up an iron table outside the Zanzibar and hurled it into the middle of the street. The uniform guys cornered him in front of Scobey's, but he turned out to be a tough little bastard and he wouldn't stay down. The sight of cops having trouble was just what the Hanover Street crowd was waiting for. They closed in.

By the time I got there, it was every man for himself. I'd been down the alley, watching for a drug deal that, as usual in my line of work, never happened. I came around the corner, and the mob was screaming, Kill the pigs! Kill the pigs! I got out my blackjack and forced my way through, trying to figure out what was going on. The uniform coppers had been driven apart, and every one was surrounded by howling dinks.

One of our people was already down, and they were putting the boots to him. The sight of blood pouring out of his mouth and nose was driving the mob to a frenzy. I swung my sap like a hatchet and managed to clear enough space so he could at least stagger to his feet. But we were all being forced back in, and I heard the window behind us beginning to crack. This is it, I thought. I am going to be driven onto the broken glass. I will bleed to death in Scobey's window with a ten-thousand-dollar Rolex watch hanging from my nose.

Then we heard the cavalry, the sweet sound of the sirens coming from Fifty-three and Fifty-five. The mob heard it too, and the mighty heroes who had been howling for blood began to run for their rat holes. I had this one little cocksucker by the collar, but his pal was clawing at me and spitting into my face. I remembered that rabies doesn't qualify you for workmen's compensation, so I took out the guy in front and turned to the spitter. He ran into Screwy Looey's. He was probably thinking about making it through to the alley in back. But I got to him first. And that's when I met Gracie Calder again.

I got the dink down to Fifty-one and made a reasonable start at the paperwork before my shift ended. It was four o'clock in the morning by the time I got home, but I was too wound up to sleep. I went out back to my pool. My house is on a hill near the Don Valley, and I stood for a long time on the diving board, just looking down on the lights of the city. My wife, Tina, used to hate that view. She said it made her think about how many crazy people there are out there. I used to tell her that my going downtown every day was just like my father going into the bush for Calder's Lumber Company. My father cut down trees; I collar whores, pimps, and dope fiends. We are both harvesting a natural resource. Tina didn't think that was very funny, which is, I guess, one of the reasons why she isn't here any more.

I am not a religious person, but I do believe in ghosts. When my mother was dying and I went up to Alcorn to see her, I could feel my dead father going into the hospital room with me, using me. And now I could feel the presence of Graeme Calder, just the same way. I had the sense that Graeme had lost track of Gracie too, and now, through me, he had found her again. But I had no sense of whether Graeme was pleased or sad that she had wound up in Screwy Looey's.

The sun was starting to come up, and it occurred to me I had better get into the water. I like to swim without a suit and I had begun thinking many thoughts about Gracie. Some of the good wives in my neighbourhood might look at me out their back windows and think I was advertising for work.

Alexander Scobey, July 13: First thing in the morning they sent their shyster lawyer around. I had just got here and managed to find an old piece of plywood I could use to cover the front until I could get a new window. I turned around and this goddamned ghoul was standing there. He had another offer in his hand. I told him, Listen, Margulies, no more deals, no talk, no nothing, not 'til you get rid of that son of a bitch.

They think that goddamned whorehouse they've got going over my store will drive me out. They're going to find out that Sandy Scobey doesn't drive so easily. My grandfather fought with the Forty-eighth Highlanders at Vimy Ridge.

They used to say that you haven't made your mark in the world until you can do your Christmas shopping at Scobey's Jewellery Store. We are unique. We look old and think new. We've still got my grandfather's Persian rugs and the walnut showcases he had built, but I travel all over the world, buying the latest designs and the finest quality.

My lawyer tells me my old customers'll find me no matter where I am. She says she can get me this fantastic deal in Dagenham Square and, meanwhile, we can make a bundle, selling them this old place. For all I know, she's right. She's a smart cookie. But I still don't like being pushed around. Hanover Street may be rough sometimes, but I've been here all my life. Peter Dagenham can go to hell.

Harry Margulies, July 14: I was sitting in my office, minding my own business, contemplating the wreckage of my life, and Arthur Quinn came in. He told me that Lewis Gough has not paid any rent in three months and I should go have a talk with him.

Jee-zuss, I said. Isn't it enough the charming clientele of Screwy Looey's tried to smash up Scobey's store? Freddy Englander wants rent from Looey too?

The rich are different from you and me, Quinn says. That's why they're rich.

So I haul myself off to Screwy Looey's, and the rest of it, I must tell you, is not to be believed.

She was naked and bent over a massage table and tied to it with these thick yellow ropes. Her toes could barely touch the ground. They'd told me at the front that Looey wasn't there and I told them I wanted to look around, thinking maybe I could get my hands on him before he disappeared into a crack in the wall. And in the back room, I came across Grace—that's her name, I found out. She was absolutely breathtaking. If I am anything at all, I am a tit man, not an ass man. But I stood there looking at her, at her long thin legs and her tight, childish little behind, tied up so helplessly and, I must say, delightfully, to the table, and it seemed to me she was like a perfect flower. I thought to myself, I am in love. Which is probably the stupidest thing I have ever said in my whole life. But that was how I felt.

She must have been aware of me standing there, staring at her, because she spoke to me.

John, get me out of this shit, she said. I want to go for supper.

I told her I wasn't John, and she wriggled around then to look at me. Her face was all sweaty and her hair was slick and plastered down. But she was stunning. Her features were perfect. She was like a little English school girl.

I'm busy, she said. One of the other girls will take care of you.

I told her I wasn't a customer. I'm a lawyer, I explained very politely, and I was there to discuss business with Mr. Gough. I took out my card and went around to the front of the table and held it out so she could see.

Do you do this sort of thing very often? I asked her. She laughed and it sounded completely natural, as though we were old pals.

I don't tie myself up, she said. A customer likes to do this. Then he jerks himself off. Crazy, eh?

No, I said slowly and thoughtfully. No...I don't think your friend is so crazy.

She began to get nervous then.

Listen, untie me, she said quickly. I haven't eaten all day and I'm starving.

I didn't do anything. I could not have made myself move if my life depended on it.

If you touch me, she said coolly, I'll yell and Tee John, that big guy out front, will come down here and kick the living shit out of you.

I told her I didn't want to hurt her.

Then what the hell do you want? she said. She was really getting angry. You just get the fuck out of here!

I thought about it for a moment and then I told her I wanted to make love to her. I said it in an easy, conversational way, but I was deadly serious. I told her: I have never seen anybody in my whole life that I wanted to make love to more than I want to make love to you right now.

It'll cost you a lot of money, she said. She made me count out one hundred dollars in front of her, and stick it under her chin.

Don't make a lot of noise, she said.

It was glorious. All my old troubles were forgotten. I was as hard as an iron pipe. I felt like a king.

I didn't go back to the office. That was the last place I wanted to be. I just joined the thick, aimless crowds out on the mall. I listened to a folk singer, quite a good one really, doing Pete Seeger and Joan Baez songs. I went down Archer Street, where the street merchants are all set up, and spent a long time looking at the candles and the silver jewellery. I bought myself a good, hand-tooled belt. By the time it was starting to get dark I was in front of the Black Rooster with a pitcher of beer. Then I noticed Victoria Sommers was a couple of tables away. She's the alderman in charge of the mall, which means she's opposed to the interests of our clients, and she favoured me with one of her patented sanctimonious glares. I smiled back, all sweetness and light. I thought of going over to her and saying, Hey, Victoria, you want to hear a funny story? I just found this beautiful kid tied to a table, so I gave her my business card and then I shtupped her. But you want to hear the really good part? I was so happy afterwards I walked off and left her there, still tied up.

Vernon Kobulczak, Kiev, Ontario, July 15: It says right in the Bible, "Let us make a joyful noise...," Psalm 95, and I can tell you what God meant by that is there is so much grief in the world, people are drowning in it, and the man who can make people sing and dance is doing the Lord's work more than any kiss-the-ass-of-Jesus-and-be-saved preacher ever could.

So when they came to me, Cheryl, my ever-charming wife, and my son, Roman, and his friend James Reilly, who never says a word, and even Lara, the light of my existence, my darling daughter, Lara, and they all said to me, The end, Dear Father, has come—I was not dismayed.

When they said to me, the Kobie Family Band has played every Legion hall, Ukie wedding, high school dance, and every cheap, crummy hotel beverage room in the county at least twice, and some of them three times, and much and all as we still do love you dearly, Poppa, we cannot go on this way any longer, I was not dismayed. I merely turned my eyes upward to heaven and I said, Hanover Street!

They looked at me in amazement, and I said, The Mall. I have read in the papers and seen on the television that they have started an outdoor mall on Hanover Street. Great musicians are coming there from all over the country. We will go too. Club owners and agents will see us performing out under the stars. We will go to Toronto, and before you can say Jack Robinson, we will be on our way to the best rooms in Las Vegas.

Lara came and kissed me. Tears were running down her cheeks. Oh, Lara, for you! Never will I forget that day we took you from that butcher. You looked like you had been turned to ice. Lara, darling, I said. Trust me. Just one more time.

Roman came up then and pumped my hand and said, Okay, Pops, one last gig, but if this don't go, I'm off to Alberta and the oil fields. I said to him, Son, if we don't make it this time, I'll sell the old squeezebox and go with you. Finally, Reilly came, and his face was all knotted up and he couldn't get the words out, but I said to him, It's all right, Reilly, I know. Wherever Lara goes, Reilly goes too. Her people are his people.

Andrew Anderson, July 17: I was in my "Andy Dandy" outfit out on the mall, so Vernon didn't know who I was at first, and I just stood to one side trying to figure out what I could do to help the poor bastard. He had set up his band in front of Scobey's Jewellery Store and they were pathetic.

Vernon and me were in the Air Force together, and we had some wild times over in England, I can tell you. Now here was my old pal again, a bald-headed little guy, trying to entertain the crowds with a squeezebox that sounds like a dying moose. His little band was so out of it, people were laughing at them.

I will come back to Vernon when I have finished work, I said to myself. I was still somewhat short of the C-note I try to go home with every night. So I went looking for some more happy little children. Picture this: you're a mother and you're dragging a couple of kids down Hanover Street and all of a sudden, standing right in front of you, is this six-foot-two clown, with a baggy white silk suit and big red polka dots. Hi, there, folks. I'm Andy Dandy. You're thinking you want to get the hell out of there, but the clown is already working the kids. He is blowing up balloons and, suddenly, right in front of their eyes, he twists them into the shape of a dog, or a giraffe, or a Bambi. The kids love the little animal, and the clown gives it to them. Then he looks up at Mommy and asks you for two dollars. You say, No, you're sorry, you can't afford it, and the clown says, Aw, gee whiz. I wish I could let you have it... The clown starts to take the balloon animal away from the kid. The kid starts to bawl. Now the mother's got two sad faces in front of her, her own kid and the six-foot-two clown. She coughs up the deuce, and everybody's happy again.

I give people real value for their money—a little entertainment and a little something they can put on the knick-knack shelf at home. And even if I gave my little balloon critters away for free, I wouldn't be helping anybody. They'd just go on down the mall and get gaffed by somebody else.

The first time I came down here, I looked around and I said to myself, Andrew, you have died and gone to heaven. You are back on the road again with Royal Canadian Shows. Every carny and midway road agent I ever knew was down on the mall. So I kissed my night-watchman's job goodbye and got out my old clown suit and went by Dominion Smallwares and picked up a gross of the big balloons, the kind that look like elephant-safes. Then I came down to the mall, and I've been here ever since.

So after things had begun to slow down, because you don't see so many little kids in the night-time crowds, I went over and introduced myself to Vernon. He greeted me like a long-lost brother, and I told him I was going to save his bacon.

Vernon, I said to him, why are you trying to play all this rock-and-roll shit?

It's what the kids want to hear today, he says.

Vernon, I said to him, can you do dance music? Like, going back, the kind of stuff we used to chase girls to? You betcha! Vernon says. We got the sweetest music this side of Guy Lombardo.

I mean, it was sad, really. The Kobie Family Band couldn't hold a tip longer than half a minute. But Vernon was telling me he had trained this little outfit—himself on the accordion, his daughter singing, his wife on keyboard, his son on lead guitar, with this pimply little guy doing clarinet and doubling on sax and cornet, a one-man wind and brass section—and he was going to take them right to the big time.

I didn't crack wise. I just told Vernon to come back the next night ready to do some good solid ballroom stuff and I would be there, in my civvies. I told him I was going to be his MC.

Buddy Berringer, President, Berringer Productions, July 18: It was like coming across a diamond in the middle of a garbage dump. There, right in the middle of the sleaze and sweat and stink of the Hanover Street Mall, was the greatest voice I'd heard in years.

I don't mean she was a good musician, not by any means. But she had that special purity you see only in the very best. I've handled talent who could barely sing on key, but you'd come back to see them night after night because they were acting out their whole lives in front of you. That was what Lara Kobulczak had.

I was just about ready to pack it in. All the hotels on the circuit want from me now is strippers. I tell them I've got some great bands for them, they won't even listen. I was thinking, I can't take any more of this. I'm a talent agent, not a pimp. Then I went to hear the Kobies.

They were doing golden oldies, stuff from the forties and even earlier. They had this white-haired character who looked like a crane in a white grandfather suit fronting for them, and he was getting the girls to dance with him and then introducing them to the boys and getting a whole little dance scene going. It was kind of sweet, like an old-fashioned summer resort right on Hanover Street. Then Lara stepped up and started singing "My Funny Valentine."

She's no great beauty. Her face is dead flat and looks like it's been rolled in flour, and she's got big purple shadows, like somebody slugged her, under the eyes. You watch her and you know it's taking every ounce of guts she has just to be out there, singing. She sounds so frail you worry she's not even going to finish the number. Then, all of a sudden, her real power cuts in, and you can feel your hair standing on end.

I introduced myself and gave her my card. You're not ready for Vegas yet, I told her, but if you're willing to work, and to work hard, I think I can do something for you.

James Reilly, July 18: Mister, 'K' should do something. The...the...the last time the guy almost ki-ki-ki-killed her. I'm going...I'm going...to...kik-kih-quit! I am!... I am...But...but...I love Lara. Oh Mary, Mother of God, help me. I love Lara.

Victoria Sommers, July 19: People like me are not supposed to break down. Not only is it bad manners, it is bad politics. If my enemies had seen the great tribune of the people in Joe Scalisi's back office, weeping like a baby and belting back glasses of vodka, they'd have whooped and hollered.

Well, like little Winnie Barbeau used to say, I don't give a flying fuck. Not any more.

I always used to think of Joe Scalisi as a sleaze because he's the power in the Downtown Businessmen, even if he doesn't have any official title in the association, and those guys fought the mall every step of the way. Now they're making money, hand over fist. That's how come I happened to be in Joe's office; I was checking on how the merchants were doing, and they all told me they are up and the restaurants are doing two and three times their normal business. I was telling this back to Joe because he was always the biggest mouth against me when I was organizing the mall and, out of nowhere, the tears just started to come. I couldn't make them stop. I was bawling like a baby.

Joe went out and closed the door behind him, and after a while he came back and put a glass in front of me. I thought it was water and I nearly choked. Vodka, Joe said. Best thing if you got to go out with people. I wanted to tell him why I was making such a fool of myself but I couldn't make myself do it. If you've been a well-behaved little girl all your life, you don't let go of that so easily. And Joe was too much of a gentleman to ask me outright, so he just tapped his heart with his finger and I nodded. He filled up my glass again.

It's not fair! I said to him. I don't deserve this!

He said to me, I don't know too much about these things, Vickie, I'm just a tailor. Which is a lie, because he is smart as a whip and knows everything that is going on in the whole city. But I can tell you something somebody once said to me, Joe said. She was a woman too, and she was going through a bad time, I guess, and she said to me, Joe, everything that happens to other people sooner or later happens to us.

That is so true! I said. I started to cry again and then I started to worry about what I was doing to poor Joe and I started getting up to leave, and he said not to worry, his son was out front and his son could look after business better than he could himself. And anyway, I couldn't go out there looking like that. So he sat with me all morning and listened to me, and out of this whole mess, I know at least one thing: I have some friends I didn't know I had before.

Sandra Hunnicut, 126 Appleford Street, July 19: I did not go to university to fall in love with Professor Terry Sommers. I have spent half my life training to be an athlete and preparing to be a physiotherapist, and that is still exactly what I am going to be. I only took English because we have to take two minor courses, and it was a choice between that and religious knowledge. I picked English because I've always read a lot, especially science fiction. And the first class I went to, Terry was just there, if you know what I mean, standing in front of the blackboard, with the sunlight coming through the Venetian blind and lighting up his beautiful long blond hair, like he was a Viking warrior.

My mother is going to be really pissed when I tell her. But she always taught us we were free to make our own choices.

It's not my fault Terry has a wife and a kid. I really feel sorry for them, if you want to know the truth. I'd be suicidal if I was in the same position as Victoria Sommers. And I easily could be. I have been around enough to know that being young is no protection. But just because I feel sorry for Victoria and her little girl, that doesn't mean I am going to give up my life for them. Why should I? Would they give up their happiness for me?

Terry Sommers, 126 Appleford Street, July 19: What I am experiencing now is something I suppose I should have anticipated, but which, frankly, never occurred to me as a cause for concern—the contempt of my colleagues. They can understand, and even condone, having an affair with a student. But the cardinal rule is that one must not embarrass the people in one's department. They expect one to be discreet, so that their own wives can remain unaware of what is going on and still feel secure. I have not met this requirement.

And so, in the overheated and somewhat bitchy style of the university, my colleagues in the English department have begun to despise me.

I thought I would get some credit, win points, as my students say, for the fact that I have taken full responsibility for Ashley. When I apprised Victoria of my situation, I offered to move out of the house that very night. But Victoria was then in the midst of organizing the co-op housing project left over from the big Eton Towers mess and she had also foolishly taken upon herself responsibility for the Hanover Street Mall. So, since I was in the midst of my summer hiatus anyway, I volunteered to stay at home with Ashley—at least until the fall, when we will have to make more permanent arrangements.

However, the respect that would normally have been due to me for acting selflessly was dissipated by the fact that Sandra moved in three days after Victoria moved out. This should not have surprised anyone, least of all Victoria, but there was, apparently, a feeling that I should have suffered a longer period of deprivation before installing my chosen companion.

Well, I have never believed that suffering is a valuable learning experience.

In the eyes of the world, I appear to be a classic academic buffoon, the aging professor trying to recapture his fading youth by having a sexual relationship with a young woman who, in her own good time, will no doubt abandon me.

The truth is that my physical relationship with Sandra is qualitatively no better than my relationship with Victoria was. Indeed, Sandra perceives lovemaking in very simple and unimaginative terms.

Why, then, did I break up a perfectly good, or at least serviceable, marriage and put my whole future in the hands of an ignorant and wilful child?

The best answer I can give is that my mind has been turning relentlessly to Yeats's poem about the Irish airman foreseeing his own death. Like that solitary killer in the sky, those that I have abandoned, I do not hate, and those that I guard now, I do not really love. But I am trading all—the respect that is due me for past accomplishments and the comforts that might have come in the future if I had stayed with Victoria—for the excitement and vividness of the moment, the doomed Irish airman's "tumult in the skies."

Ashley Sommers, 126 Appleford Street, July 19: I'm never going to have children. All parents do is hurt children.

Harry Margulies, July 19: I was in the boardroom of Fulford, Blaught and Smith, listening to this other lawyer explain why the new, vastly improved offer my clients had made to buy out the lease for Scobey's Jewellery Store was not acceptable for the following seven reasons, and all I could think of was, what kind of underwear was this other lawyer wearing?

Probably a stainless-steel bra with conical cups and virginal white cotton panties. They would go logically with the high-necked pleated blouse and the three-pound gold watch and the tight black skirt and jacket and all that stiff-shoulder body language telling me that she is a long-haired thoroughbred and an experienced lawyer and she is not going to take any shit from me or Fred Englander or pompous Peter Dagenham—no matter how much clout the Dagenhams still have in this town.

So I'd better understand I am going to have to show her something a lot better than a seven-year lease with annual increases at one per cent below—get that, below!—inflation and no contribution to public space before she was going to bother taking my proposition back to Scobey.

So take that, you big prick, Harry Margulies.

On the other hand, maybe she is a free spirit and she likes to show off her nipples. Maybe she has no brassiere at all under that high-powered suit, which probably cost twice as much as the suit I've got on. Maybe she just goes for the skimpiest little itsy-bitsy, teeny-weeny bikini panties. Striped bikinis, big, wide yellow, or better still, red stripes, one coming right up the middle and protecting what I knew instinctively was a smelly, oily, man-eating cunt.

The words were half out of my mouth, I swear it. I thought it was a perfectly fair exchange: you lift up your skirt and show me your panties, I will go back to my client and get him to sweeten the offer. But, just then, Old Man Blaught himself knocks at the door and says we are already fifteen minutes past the hour and he has six clients waiting to use the boardroom. So she says to me she is sorry she wasted my time this afternoon but if she had known how little I had to offer, she would never have agreed to this meeting.

I tell her not to worry, the pleasure has been all mine.

But now it's too late to go back to the office, right? I mean there is nothing waiting for me there except a whole lot of telephone messages from people I don't want to talk to. So I take myself over to Screwy Looey's in the hopes of encouraging the good Mr. Gough to justify our faith in him and finally drive old Scobey out of there.

Looey isn't around but, fortunately, Grace is and she is not otherwise engaged, so we get to play our little game.

First, I tie her to the table. I'd like her to be face up, but she says she's more comfortable on her stomach, so that's how we do it. She's got a bunch of old neckties now, and I tie her hands together behind her back and then I wrap some more ties around her to hold her to the table, with her legs hanging down. She's held pretty snug against the table, but I leave the knots loose so circulation's not being cut off or anything like that. Then I go around behind her and pull her pants down and do my thing. Which is anything I feel like doing.

I am well aware that all this is a game that is being played for me only because I can afford it, at a bill and a half a round. Nothing is real in Screwy Looey's. But I don't care. In those times in Looey's back room, I am in total control. I don't have to worry about Grace or what she's feeling. I don't have to think about anything but myself. I feel like a complete man again.

Victoria Sommers, July 19: I started off at the Black Rooster just wanting to see what the strippers were like. They're just kids. And they have fantastically beautiful bodies. It makes you want to cry. All those horrible men just staring up at them. Nobody even smiles. I don't think they dream about screwing the girls. I think they want to kill them. Nice place, eh? If there was some way the city could do it, I'd close the Rooster down. But, for now, it's my best hideout. Nobody would ever expect to find Victoria Sommers sitting every night in a girlie bar.

It stinks of frying onions in here, no matter what time you come in. But the food's not bad, really. I ate worse meals when I was a student. The other day, Harry Margulies came over and sat down, without me even inviting him, and tried to tell me his clients have the whole block now, except Scobey's. You got nothing, I told him. You got nothing cubed, you fucking bastard. Even if Scobey did sell out to you, which he won't, I was talking to him and he hates you even more than I do, but even if you did manage somehow to get to him, we'd never let you build an indoor shopping plaza in the heart of the city. The outdoor mall is a big success. So your client is fucked, Mr. Margulies. So why don't you just fuck off and leave me in peace?

He said to me, Are you okay, Victoria? like he was an old friend. I told him I was fine and it was no concern of his. He said he'd take me home. I told him again to fuck off and he finally went away. After, I was sorry that I didn't take him up on it. Or at least invite him to sit down for a drink. It gets lonely sometimes just watching people you don't know. And, anyway, I don't feel so superior to Harry Margulies as I used to.

Gordon Margulies, Kfar Galil, Israel, July 19: Dear Dad, Mommy had the baby and she's fine. They're going to call the baby Edith. I wanted to give her one of the really good Hebrew names, but Morry said Edith was his grandmother's name.

Morry's going down to Jerusalem next week, and I'm probably going with him. His kids are coming to stay with us for August. I wish that you could come too. You'd really like it here. There's lots of things to do.

A man came last week from the air force and he said that the air force pilots are the real warriors, protecting the country. But I still think I'm going to go into the border police when my time comes.

Mommy says the baby is my sister, but I don't think so. She only has half the chromosomes that I do. So she's not really a blood relation.

I have to go now. Some soldiers are here and they're going to take us for a hike down in the valley.

Please come. I miss you.

Your loving son, Gordon.

Reb Shmuel Englander, Mt. Sinai Hospital, July 23: Sovereign of the universe! Behold, I freely forgive everyone who hath aggrieved me or vexed me, or who hath sinned against me...I forgive, and I pray that no human being whatsoever may be punished on account of me...

I would like to live until Yom Kippur. Is that so much to ask? Seven more weeks. I would like to stand in shul one last time with my fellow Jews and listen to Kol Nidre and beg the Lord's forgiveness for the sins I have committed.

Freddy comes to the hospital, and all he talks about is the big project he is doing on Hanover Street. He tells me it will be the biggest indoor shopping plaza in the whole world. He wants to show me how smart he can be in business. As though I am lying here on my deathbed and that is all I am worrying about.

What I want to say to Freddy is that he should say Kaddish for me. Max too. But I have to be careful how I talk to them. I want to make them understand that it is not for me, but for themselves, they should say Kaddish.

The world judges people sometimes even harder than the Lord judges them. No matter how bad your father, and even your mother, might be, if you turn against them, the world will condemn you. The world will say you are a bad son because, no matter what your father and mother did to you, they are still your parents.

So, when you say Kaddish for a whole year, you are saying to the world: I loved my father and I remember him and I am a good son.

Fred Englander, July 23: One thing my father always taught me in business is that you have to be a realist. Don't make commitments you can't keep. Don't offer more money than you can afford and then think you're going to run around town, borrowing the difference. They'll eat you up alive. When Pa is gone, the whole weight of Premier Developments is going to fall on my shoulders. I'd be kidding myself, and kidding my father too, if I said I was going to take time off from business to go to a synagogue every morning and every night to say Kaddish.

But what is the necessity to tell my father that? It'll just give him more to worry about in his last days.

There are always old men hanging around the shul, looking for something to do. Hiring one of them to say Kaddish for you is a mitzvah. They make a little money, and you're giving them something important to do. Kaddish is going to be said for my father, and it'll be said faithfully every day by a religious person. That's what really matters.

James Reilly, July 25: I w-w-went to her and I said Lara...Lara...Lara...le-le-lets get away from here. I love you, Lara. And she said...she said to me...don't leave me. Jimmy, please don't leave me. And I said...I said...I said, I have to go home. And she said, Jimmy, I love you. Jimmy, stay with me. And I started to cry. And we held onto each other. Lara cried too. Stay with me, Jimmy, she said. Stay with me.

Buddy Berringer, July 30: When the kid left, I went to the old man and I said, Listen, Pops, I have this friend in New York; he used to work the bars himself and now he's got this club of his own. I want him to hear Lara.

I didn't have to spell it out. The old guy may not have too much going for him upstairs, but his heart's in the right place. He knows Lara's not going any place if she has to drag the whole pack of them behind her. Besides, without the kid there on the sax, the Kobie Family Band is pretty well out of business anyway.

The old lady was a tougher nut. She said there was no way she was going to let her daughter go to New York alone with me. For which I can't really blame her. So I said, we'll wait 'til the mall is over—it's just another couple of weeks—and then I want you to come with us. The old lady lit up like a Christmas tree. But it's good for me, too, because there's a lot better chance to keep Lara out of trouble if Momma's down there with her, making sure she keeps her knees together.

So I figure I am in for five grand, anyway, just to get a few people in New York to listen to Lara, and before this is over, before she's properly on her way to the top, I mean, I figure I'll have shelled out twenty-five big ones, at least.

You want to hear something really crazy? I don't even have a contract with Lara. Now, if I was really smart, I'd have her tied up six ways to Sunday, right? Well, I didn't do it. I'm just in this to help her get started. The big push will have to come from people who are a lot more plugged in than I've ever been.

I'll be lucky if I get back my original investment. She'll use me up just the way she used the kid. Talent is like that. They make their own rules.

So what's in it for me, eh? Have I suddenly gone stupid? Maybe. But, just for once, I want to handle somebody who's going to be a star. And then I'm getting out of this crummy business.

Lara Kobulczak, July 30: Buddy tells everyone I have this great voice. I wonder sometimes, does he know my singing comes from crying so much? I love Buddy the same way Reilly loved me. That's funny, isn't it? But the people I really feel sorry for are the people who don't have any love at all, the lost and the lonely. I sing my music for them.

Goodbye, my beautiful Reilly. I loved you then and I love you now.

These days on the mall are so beautiful, the final performances of the Kobie Family Band.

Grace Calder, July 30: I came downstairs just to get a little air, and Willy was on Hanover Street, watching the little band that plays all the time in front of our place. I had been feeling him out there for days, waiting for me. Run, Gracie, run!

The Nazi was there too, and I stood in the doorway of Looey's, puffing on a cigarette and staring at them over the heads of the crowd, and the two of them were staring back at me, and there was no expression at all in their faces, like they didn't even see me, but I knew they did.

I wasn't really worried. I thought, if they knew where I live they'd have already been there. I can still get away. I can turn and go upstairs and out the back fire escape. I can get my money out of the bank and take a bus to Vancouver.

I was starting to back into the doorway, and this guy grabbed my hand and asked me to dance. He's a skinny old geek who gets himself up in a white suit and works the crowd for the Kobies. I tried to pull away, but he held onto me and kneeled down in front of me, like he was begging me. I could feel people laughing and staring at me because all I had on was my old bathrobe. But I let him take me out to the street where the people were dancing, and I began to dance too. He was hardly touching me at all, letting me go any which way I pleased. You're a dancer, he said. You've had training, I can tell. I leaned way back, letting him support me, and turned my head up to the sky.

The girl who sings with the Kobies, the girl with the really sad voice, was singing this old song like she had picked it special for me: Yesterday, all my troubles seemed so far away, now it looks like they are here to stay…Oh, I believe in yesterday.

The old man stopped in front of Willy, and he gave Willy my hand. I thought, How in Jesus' name does he know to do that?

You look really good, Gracie, Willy said, and I said, I'm going away, Willy.

Yeah, I know, Willy said. I could hardly hear him over the music. It's okay, Gracie. Don't worry about it.

I felt myself starting to cry. What did they do to him in there? Willy McNiven with grey hair. And he had this awful black patch over his right eye. Bye-bye love, bye-bye sweet caress, hello loneliness: she was doing it really slow. That used to be Willy's favourite song. I let Willy hold me and I felt like I wasn't touching the ground any more and I could see way up high over the street and the neon signs, a big orange moon, a harvest moon, like they used to have back in Alcorn. Graeme, my sainted, holy brother, Graeme, where are you, Graeme? Why don't you save me, Graeme? Bye-bye sweet caress, hello loneliness, I think I'm going to die...Do you love me? I said to Willy. Do you still love me, Willy? Then the Kobies stopped playing, and Willy said, Let's go, Gracie. They were parked around the corner, and I hung onto Willy and we took off on his bike, with the bathrobe flying out from my bare legs. And the Nazi came roaring up behind us, protecting Willy and me, like he always does.

Dane Harrison, August 2: The early morning is one of my favourite times. The cleaners haven't come through yet, and you get old newspapers and coffee cups and all kind of brightly coloured wrappings from the fast-food joints blowing around the benches and flower pots. Hanover Street feels like the morning after a big party.

At noon hour, the street fills up quickly. All the bars, and even some of the restaurants that don't have liquor licences, have put tables out on the sidewalk. Every one of them is supposed to get permission from the City, which means permission from me, but I'm not bothering anyone.

This isn't Paris, and no matter how many outdoor cafés pop up, Hanover Street will never, by any stretch of the imagination, even remotely remind anyone of the Champs-Elysées. The tables are too crowded together and at noon hour, the people are too frantic. The sun is beating right down on them, and they gulp down draft beer and gobble sandwiches, then rush back to their offices. So the interesting question is: why do they bother with the mall at all?

They could find quieter, cooler places closer to where they work, and get better service. Most of the big office buildings have underground malls now, with lots of places to eat.

But Hanover Street is still where people want to be.

If you're cooped up in an office all day where everything, even the air you breathe, is artificial, you are mad to get out into the sunshine. It's a natural instinct.

The clothing stores and the shoe stores live off the outdoor restaurants. The secretaries and the clerks from the big offices are not just out to have a beer and bit of a chinwag with each other. They're looking all around to see what's being worn. The action on Hanover Street is an all-day fashion show.

In the early afternoon, there is a lull, like rest hour in a summer camp, then the serious shoppers and the entertainers start coming down. People think of Hanover Street as being bars and restaurants and cheap boutiques, but there are a lot of high-class stores here too—Royal Alaska Furs, Scalisi Custom Tailors, Scobey's Jewellery, Illingsworth China. Some of the carriage-trade places complain that their regular customers won't walk through the crowds and crumminess of the mall. But I have noticed that a lot of the old stores have big signs in the windows, advertising fancy sales. So I don't take their complaints too seriously. They may have lost some of their old customers, but they are more than making up for it with the tourists.

The entertainers like to set up early so they can hold on to their places for the evening rush. Most of them come down with a guitar and maybe a small set of amps, and they do folk or country or a bit of rock. But you get other interesting people too. One night we had two girls come down with a flute and a violin and play classical music. I thought they'd die on the mall, but people stopped and listened. The girls had a violin case stuffed with money when they went home.

Then there was the jazz clarinettist. He was from the States I think, a black man about six feet tall, very skinny, with a knitted cap, like a Jewish yarmulkah, and a curly grey beard. He started off just playing by himself. He'd come down and stand in front of Elias Radio and just go to it.

He must have been somebody pretty important because other musicians started bringing saxophones and trumpets and bass guitars down to the mall and playing with him. It was the kind of brittle, sophisticated jazz I imagine you used to hear late at night at Birdland or some of the famous old New York clubs, but it was happening at three in the afternoon in the bright sunshine out on Hanover Street.

At night the crowds start to build up, and when it gets so thick with people down here you can hardly move, even I have to admit a person can feel threatened. The kids from the body rubs are out in force, pushing leaflets from places like Delilah's Den, The Sultan's Harem, Screwy Looey's. There are eleven body rubs over the stores on Hanover Street, and a lot of people are very offended by them.

I think people are overlooking the fact that, even though the kids handing out the leaflets can get pretty aggressive, and some of the spiels you hear over loudspeakers on the mall are pretty raunchy, the real business of the body rubs is done in private and they are not physically bothering anybody.

By ten o'clock all the stores are closed up, and people are on the mall for just one purpose: they are looking for a good time. That's when you get the feeling of critical mass. There are so many people bumping up against each other that the slightest incident could turn them into a mob. There is no question that can happen. We had a pretty bad scene not too long ago in front of Scobey's, when his front window got busted.

But most people don't come down here late at night. And I don't think Hanover Street is any more dangerous with the mall than without it.

Marta Persofski, August 2: We were coming out of the Black Rooster and we saw this big commotion on the corner in front of Scobey's Jewellery Store and we thought we were in real trouble. I was with Peggy, who I went back to after Vivian turned against me. People were jumping up and down, and I heard a police whistle, and I said to Peggy, We've got to get out of here. I mean, Peggy's a teacher. What happens if she gets busted? But Peggy said she wanted to see what was going on and she grabbed my hand and pulled me along.

When we got up to the crowd, I found I was in the middle of joyfulness and peacefulness like I have never experienced in my life before. The people weren't hitting each other, they were dancing. The roaring sound wasn't fighting, it was music. It was drums, pounding drums, a crowd of young guys were playing on drums that they carried slung around their shoulders.

They were Brazilians, I think, from the way they were talking and they must have come from some club, because a couple still had on rainbow-coloured shirts with silly ruffles. But most of them had thrown on old T-shirts and they had obviously come down to the mall just to be themselves and play for the people.

Some of the drums were tiny and flat, smaller than pie plates, and others were conical and egg-shaped and as tall as a man. All around the drummers, everybody was dancing. Peggy and I started dancing too. Peggy can't keep time to save her life, but she didn't care, she just wanted to be part of it. There were women with women and men with men and heteros with each other. Everybody dancing, just dancing to those crazy Brazilian drums that had so many up-and-down tones they were like a whole symphony orchestra. It was so beautiful.

The whistle I'd thought was a police whistle actually belonged to the leader of the group. When they came to the end of a number he'd call something out in Portuguese, wait a moment 'til all his buddies were quiet and watching, then he'd blow the whistle and away they'd all go, at it again. All the leader had on was a torn old pair of jeans, not even shoes or sandals, just torn old blue jeans, and he had hair down to his shoulders. He looked like a painting of Jesus. I couldn't believe it was happening. I kept wishing I had my cameras with me. In this city, which is so uptight and mean, there we were, right out on the main street, dancing with Jesus on Saturday night.

Paul Olivier, August 3: You'd have thought we were going to church. Gracie turned up, wearing a long white dress and a pink straw hat with a ribbon and a wide brim, which made her face seem even smaller and sweeter. She put her hand on my arm, very dignified like, and we walked slowly away from the front of Screwy Looey's, which is where Gracie had said she would meet me. It was ten o'clock Sunday morning, and except for a few Indians and other assorted original Canadians sleeping on benches, the mall was deserted. Gracie and I didn't talk much at first. We walked over a block and then down Bay Street because all the newspapers and garbage from Saturday night were still left over on Hanover Street, and it was smelly as well as dirty. But Bay Street, which is where the money comes from, was neat and clean, and the streaks of sun coming between the big office towers reminded me a little of the way light used to come through the stained-glass windows at home. Do you remember Metcalfe Street United? I asked Gracie. She laughed a little. Oh yes, I sure do, she said. You were the best-looking boy in the choir. I laughed too. Well, Gracie, I said, we are doomed. No matter how far we go, we will always be carrying that stupid little town around with us.

We took the ferry over to the islands, and we were walking along the south side, the Lake Ontario side, where hardly anybody goes. I spread out my windbreaker for Gracie to sit on. I've learned to live with the past, Gracie told me. But I still have dreams about my brother. He comes to me when I'm asleep and he says terrible things to me.

Nobody blames you, I said. You know that.

She had pulled the white dress tightly over her knees and she was resting her cheek against them. She turned and smiled at me as though I was a child instead of a seven-year cop.

You don't know my father, she said.

Gracie, I said, your father hasn't drawn a sober breath in twenty years.

Gracie pulled herself up, and I followed her down the beach towards Centre Island. The wind blew the long white dress against her legs and out in back of her. I talked a little about Tina. I figured Gracie was one of the few people in the world who could understand what it felt like to come from Alcorn down to Toronto and then, before you knew which end was up, to find yourself married to a Greek girl who had been sat on all her life. Gracie was very sympathetic. She said she had known a lot of girls who went crazy the way Tina did.

With Tina, I told her, the trouble was that she didn't stay crazy. We'd no sooner scraped together the down payment for a house of our own than Tina started running back to the restaurant every day to see her mummy and her daddy, and then going off at night to see her sisters and her cousins and her aunts. They had a whole world going, and I didn't seem to fit into it. After a while, I didn't even bother trying.

Did you love her? Gracie said.

I think so, I said. When Tina finally went home for good, I came apart. That must mean I loved her, eh?

There is a little amusement park in the middle of Centre Island. It is got up like an old-fashioned country village, with wooden storefronts and women with flowery dresses and bonnets behind the counter. It doesn't look like any pictures I ever saw of Alcorn in the early days, nor like any other small town I ever heard of, for that matter. This was more like a TV cartoon but I guess it lets people in the city think they are keeping in touch with their country roots. I bought a bag of fudge that was supposed to be homemade and Gracie and I walked over a hill to the giant merry-go-round. Gracie and I stood there for a long time, just listening to the corny merry-go-round music. I said it reminded me of the August fair that used to come to Alcorn every year. Gracie said she always loved the fair. I went up and bought us tickets.

Gracie got onto a pink and blue horse, sitting sidesaddle; I got onto this big black horse beside her. The saddle and the harness had been carved into the wood and painted gold. The music started, and the horses went up and down as well as around. When they were at the top, you could look out and see the great huge waves on scummy old Lake Ontario. When you came around the other side, you could see the skyline of Toronto, the big black and gold and silver office buildings. Well this really is us, I thought, Gracie and me, caught between the city and the deep blue sea.

The ride didn't last more than a couple of minutes, and when it was over, Gracie just sat there, not moving. The kid came by and I gave him ten bucks. The merry-go-round started again. Gracie had to hold on to the pink straw hat because it was so wide that if the wind caught it, it would have blown right off. I reached out for her hand and she gave it to me, and I held on to it. We spent most of the afternoon like that, holding hands and going around and around on the painted horses.

Finally, Gracie said she had to get to work. I took her to the ferry and walked her back up Hanover Street to Screwy Looey's.

I'll come by tomorrow, I told her. But Gracie shook her head.

It was nice seeing someone from the old town, she said. Thank you very much, Paul. But I'm going out to Vancouver, just as soon as I get a little more money together.

Then don't mess with Willy McNiven, I told her. The boys have got him marked. They'll take him down the first move he makes.

I have a girlfriend in Vancouver, she said, as though she hadn't heard what I had just told her. I'm going to stay with her when I get out there.

I can't just say goodbye to you, Gracie, I said. Not after all this time.

She was standing in the doorway of Screwy Looey's and I leaned forward and I saw her stiffen, so I kissed her on the cheek instead of the lips, as though she was my sister too and I was standing in for Graeme. But I could feel her being afraid and I knew she did not think of me like a brother, nor even like an old friend. But I didn't want to press my luck, not yet, so I turned quickly and walked away. I walked all the way home, to my empty little house in the suburbs.

Harry Margulies, August 4: Victoria Sommers was absolutely smashed. It was unbelievable. She was leaning against Scobey's window, listening to the band, but she wasn't hearing anything. Her eyes were totally glassy. My first thought was: call the media guys. What a beautiful picture for the public—

Saint Victoria, out there on Hanover Street, drunk as a skunk.

I went up to her and said, Hello, Victoria, I'll buy you a cup of coffee. She didn't acknowledge me, didn't say anything at all in fact, but when I gave up and started down Hanover Street, she came behind me, following me like a puppy. I got her around the corner and into the Concerto Café, figuring a couple of shots of good black espresso would have more impact than ordinary coffee. And it did work to some extent. She came around enough to ask me to take her home.

But as soon as we got into my car, she passed out. I started up the ignition and said, Well, where are we going, Victoria? and, clunk, her head came down and she was dead to the world. I haven't seen anybody go out like that since parties back in high school.

I couldn't think of anywhere else to take her, so I brought her back to my place. Getting her up the stairs was a nightmare. She was a dead weight. I had her arm pulled over my shoulder, but I am hardly in good condition and a couple of times I was teetering on the edge of a stair and thinking we were going to go over and having visions of Victoria breaking her back and suing me from her wheelchair.

I dumped her on the bed, thinking I'd go off to the couch in my den. Then I looked down at her and I thought, She's really a mess and she's got this beautiful yellow suit on that looks damned expensive and she's going to wake up in the morning looking like the wrath of God. So I figured the least I could do was get the skirt and jacket off for her, not that she'd thank me for it. I got started, and the next thing I knew, she had her arms around my neck. She was wide awake. And she just wanted to screw. To be perfectly honest, she probably would have done it with anyone who was there at that particular moment. But I didn't mind at all. I figure I had just hit it lucky. Victoria Sommers was fantastic.

Victoria Sommers, August 5: When I woke up, the morning sun was pouring in through the window. I lay back on the deep pillow, thinking you never know when you start out in the morning where you're going to wind up at night. I was admiring the intertwined pink and white roses on the dark green wallpaper. Who would ever have imagined that Harry Margulies would have the kind of cheerful, cosy, little bedroom I had when I was a little girl?

My clothes were on a chair beside the bed, all neatly folded as though a maid had done the job. Harry was dressed and sitting at the kitchen table when I came downstairs. Do you want some orange juice? How about a cup of coffee? It was very fresh and good. I didn't have any hangover at all. I'd better call a cab, I said. I'll get you one, he said. Are you okay, Victoria?

I'm fine, I said to him. I'm just fine. He put his arms around me and kissed me on the lips and held me and I kissed him back and then he went to the phone.

I was thinking that if this is bottom—and it would be hard to imagine doing anything stupider than this—I don't mind at all. So stick that in your pipe and smoke it, Terry Sommers. You don't break me so easily. I'm the one going home this morning with my underwear in my purse.

If Terry wasn't such a humourless twit, I'd call him up and share the joke: Hey, Terry, guess what? I'm a politician with a strange bedfellow.

Inspector Johnny Johnston, August 5: The only way I could control what is happening out there would be to fill Hanover Street with uniformed officers. But then it would look like Nazi Germany. How do you think the public would go for that?

Nobody ever consulted the police about this mall. They just set it up and left it to us to keep order down here.

What's happening is exactly what you'd expect. The rest of the city is dead quiet because every thief, dope peddler, second-storey man, hippie, yippie, and prostitute is flocking to Hanover Street. Why shouldn't they? We created a huge market-place for them.

It's not just tourists we're getting from the States, you know. The whores are coming in from the border cities too. I'll tell you something I haven't told the papers yet: There's a gang of them comes in from Buffalo every night in a school bus.

I've got eighteen men in uniform out here and twelve working plain clothes. And that's still not enough. Last night, one of my lads tried to take in a woman who was causing a ruckus at Illingworth's China Store and the mob jumped him at the door. He was down, and the dinks damned near got his gun away from him before the other officers could get there and break it up.

And you ask me why I'm against making a permanent mall?

Trevor Billinghurst, August 5: I had to apply for a permit to be here, but the guy in charge, Dane Harrison, is an old friend of Vivian's, so there was no trouble. A lot of the jewellery you see around here is from South America. The people selling it say they made it themselves, but the truth is they bring it in by the suitcase full from Guatemala and Mexico. The stuff I'm selling is at least halfway genuine. These belts are made right in Toronto. I've got a partner up on Dupont Street who does the work. He uses a metal die and stamps the pattern into the belts, so they are not really hand-tooled the way some people think they are. But this is high-quality leather, and they're getting good value for their money.

You know, Hanover Street and Bay Street are really the same. It's pure capitalism out here. If I was a storekeeper, I'd be screaming. They pay rent, taxes, heat, light, God-knows-what. Then the blanket people—that's what I call my colleagues down here, because most of us just lay out our stuff on a blanket—come along and set up in front of their doors. We're killing them. It's dog eat dog. But this time, at least, I'm with the right dogs. I took in three hundred dollars last night alone.

J. Arthur Quinn, August 6: I have been trying to decide if I should cross to the other side of this overly large, and much too expensive office and walk in on McConnachie and say to him, Charlie, I have had a vision.

It happened Sunday morning. Harry had been telling me how busy he is and giving me ye olde run-around whenever I try to find out what he is up to, and meanwhile, Dagenham is blowing his stack, and our client, Freddy Englander, is having a nervous breakdown. So I finally got a commitment from Harry to meet me at the office Sunday morning.

I had my usual Sunday breakfast at the Simcoe Club, kippers and toasted bagel, and when I stepped out the front door of the club onto Bay Street I heard the bells ringing. It was the natural hour for churches to be calling in the sheep but these bells seemed to go on too long, and they were coming from every corner of the city.

I was utterly alone, and when I looked north, the outside of the old City Hall had become the inside of a cathedral. Those massive stone blocks, over a hundred years old now, black with the grime of God only knows how many successful but long-forgotten souls and how many wasted human lives, were suddenly clean and glowing with light. They had become a place to worship. There was even a cross, the square, tapering cenotaph, put up so many years ago to remind people of all the poor fellows who died in the war.

The bells faded out and I began to pick up the whispering of a thousand elevators. People began to pour out of the office buildings. There were accountants and stock salesmen and other assorted crooks in their bow-ties and bright red suspenders; and the bankers in their thick blue suits and all the corporation presidents and vice-presidents, with their grey hair and their sickly faces, followed by all their various fawning business consultants and their suck-hole lawyers; and assorted, various other pimps and parasites. And beginning to push through them to get there first, the women of Bay Street, the ones in glasses and business suits, and the hordes of secretaries, the tough, thick-lipped divorcée secretaries with their cashmere sweaters and gold bangles, and the grey-haired, motherly ones, and the long-legged girls in their thin skirts. The young ones looked bewildered and they were beginning to cry, but the older women took them by the hand and led them up Bay Street, joining the crowds going towards the old City Hall.

When the people got to the old City Hall, they spread out on the broad stone steps and dropped to their knees and bowed their heads. A priest came down in front of them and placed a twenty-dollar bill between their teeth. This is my body which is given for you, the priest said. Then another priest came behind him with a bottle and poured a little good Canadian rye into the open mouths. This is my blood, which is shed for you, he said.

Now some might call such a vision blasphemous. But I was thinking it showed God's mercy. We all have to believe in something, and God was letting the people who make the money on Bay Street worship Him in the only way they could understand.

But I think if I went down to Charlie's office and told him all this, he would get me sent off to the funny farm. Not because I think I am having visions, but because I am stupid enough to tell my old enemy about them.

And Harry, when he finally arrived at the office, told me that Scobey has dug in his heels, and nothing short of dynamite is going to get him out of that goddamned costume-jewellery store. So, back to work.

Paul Olivier, August 7: How many people ever get something they have dreamed about and which they thought was impossibly beyond their reach? When I was growing up, Grace Calder was the most incredibly beautiful girl in the history of Alcorn, Ontario, and I was her brother Graeme's funny little friend from "Frog town" that everybody called Dolly Oliver because they claimed they couldn't pronounce my name.

And now, as they say in the Bible, I have known Grace Calder.

I was coming off shift, another useless stakeout in the lane behind Hanover Street, and Gracie was out on the mall, sitting by herself on a bench. The sun was starting to come up, and Hanover Street was completely deserted, except for the street cleaners who were trying to get rid of at least some of the mess before the people started coming back again. I sat down beside Gracie and we didn't talk for a long time, and finally she said she was back with Willy as though I didn't know that, and I could tell from the way she was talking, like her tongue was too big for her mouth, that she was on something again.

We're all cheering for Willy, I said. The only question is, who gets the points for bringing him down.

I love Willy, she said in that same, awful, slurry voice. Willy's my old man.

I asked her if she wanted to go for a drive and she said, yes, that would be nice, and she even sat quietly in the car while I went through roll-call at the division, and then we went bombing up and down the expressway, enjoying the hot wind in our faces. Then, when the roads started to fill up with the morning rush hour, I took Gracie to my house.

She went crazy for the pool. She couldn't believe it was mine, a heart-shaped pool. I told her it was Tina's fantasy. I didn't add that I am still paying for it. Gracie said she had to go for a swim. And before I could say anything more, she'd peeled off all her clothes and she was in the water. I just sat there, in a chair, watching her, thinking how strange it was, how unaroused I was. When the two of us were younger, I would have killed, gladly, just to be able to look at Grace Calder without her clothes on. But now we were two people down in Toronto, and Gracie's body was just another woman's body.

I held out a robe for her and I made us some coffee and, as you'd expect, we started talking about her brother again, and about Alcorn. She was starting to crash. I guess swimming in the cold water had helped her come down. Her father wasn't a bad person, she told me, Mr. Calder just found it so awful having to work for the lumber company his family had owned once.

I told her my father hated going into the bush for Calder's too, and he never owned anything.

But what really wrecked her father, she said, was thinking that Graeme was going to get rich and bring back the family again and then having that snatched away from him.

Your brother was a mean son of a bitch, I said. I can say that, I told her, because I was Graeme's friend and he never did anything to me, but I saw him do things to lots of other people. I told her how people all over Alcorn had hated Graeme. People put up with him, I said, because he was a good athlete and captain of the Junior B team. But there was no way Graeme was ever going to make it to the NHL. He was too small. And there was nothing else besides hockey that Graeme was any good at.

She looked at me, with her eyes all squinting and hard, her street-girl look, trying to figure out what my game was. But I didn't have any game. I was just talking to Gracie like I hadn't talked to anyone in years.

I know all about you and Graeme, I said.

That really jolted her.

Teenage boys brag a lot, I said. And Graeme was no better than the rest of us.

She shrugged her shoulders and said it didn't matter, she'd met a lot of people who'd done the same things when they were kids that she and Graeme had done. That was one of the good things she'd found out when she left home and came to the city.

I used to think Graeme and I were really evil, and God was going to punish us, she said.

It was on the tip of my tongue to say, Well, God punished Graeme, didn't he? But I didn't think that would help her any.

I'd better get back, she said. Willy'll be going crazy.

Gracie, I said to her, would you think I was a complete yo-yo if I said this has been a really great morning for me and I will never forget it?

She laughed and said, Yes, because I always was a complete yo-yo. But then tears started to come up into her eyes and then I was holding her, trying to comfort her, and then I was kissing her, and then...well, we were in the sack. I guess we had both known all along that was going to happen.

Somewhere in the back of my mind the cop part of me was saying, She's so good at this because she's had on-the-job training. But another part of me was crying, just the way Gracie was crying.

She wouldn't let me drive her back downtown. She said I could just take her to the subway. So I did that, and then I came back here and got out the rye. God only knows how I'm going to get through work tonight.

Lewis Gough, August 7: This here is Gorgeous Gracie, folks. Ouch, Gracie! Don't bite. I just want to show the folks those beautiful legs. Tell the truth! You ever see muscles like those before? Gracie used to have a job polishing mufflers with those legs. Now she's going upstairs to wait for you. Hey, hey, hey, it's Screwy Looey's. Girls, girls, girls. We got Juicy Lucy. We got Sister Susie. We got Maggie the Maniac. We got Annie the Animal. It's Screwy Looey's, good people. Girls! Girls! Girls!

Clement Caldecott, August 10: I haven't said nothing to Willy about taking out Screwy Looey. I don't want him getting all nervous on me. As far as Willy's concerned, we're just going to knock over this little body rub and get the hell out of there. It's a perfect setup for us. Gracie told us on Saturday nights they get so much action they don't have time to clear out the money until they close up. So as far as Willy knows, all we are doing is going in and helping ourselves and then taking off to Windsor, where some of the old Devils' Own are running stuff across the border. Maybe we'll even go across ourselves a few times, and build up our stake. When we come back to Toronto, we'll have enough cash to start dealing like real people. Willy is even starting to talk about getting some of our old pals to leave The Warriors and come in with us again.

I have started taking our hawgs to the lane back of Hanover Street, and I chain them up there so anybody hanging around will get used to seeing them and think we are part of the local scene. We will make our hit just after one o'clock. I will go around to the back and undo the bikes and go up the fire escape. Gracie unlocks the back for me, and Willy comes in the front. We'll have them sandwiched. We take the cash and then go out the back, hop on our bikes, and get the fuck out of there.

With the dough we had and even with what Gracie could throw in, all I could get for us was a couple of old sawed-off shotguns. But I figure the sight of us waving those things around will be enough to scare the shit out of the pansies Screw Looey has working for him. And a shotgun will do just fine to blow the head off Screwy Looey. I hate that little fucker, not just because of the way he's treated Gracie but because of what he is—filth. Making a score may be enough for Willy, but not for me. I want to do something for other people.

Grace Calder, August 12: It was dark that day and so cold, little spider webs of ice were forming on the top of the water. The bullrushes had faded to a rusty brown. In the summer they were so thick you couldn't even get a canoe into the old Beaver Meadow, which is where we were, but now the rushes were dry and thin and they snapped in your fingers. The trees had lost their leaves and they looked like stick figures we used to make when we played Hangman in school, which we did all the time. I sat in the back of the boat, holding Grandpa's big, old shotgun across my knees. I had a blanket wrapped around my shoulders and I was freezing and I just wanted to go home. Father gave me some coffee from his silver thermos. I remember thinking how crazy he was to think that killing birds was somehow going to pull us together and make us all love each other. He had poured so much rum into the coffee, that was all you could taste. Graeme was standing up in the front of the boat with his hand shielding his eyes because the sun was starting to come up. I was furious at him because I knew he was just trying to impress Father. We got to the blind, and Father turned off the motor, and we started to get out. But the big old shotgun was too heavy and too clumsy for me and it fell into the boat. I tried to grab for it, but I was too late. The first sound was dull, like an axe splitting wood, but then, I remember, it seemed to bounce off the hills and rocks and it got so loud, it was like an atomic bomb. I saw the cherry-coloured blood burst out all over Graeme's face. All I could think of was, No! No! This is all wrong. I don't hate my brother. I don't want this to happen. Please, please God, No!

Clement Caldecott, August 12: Gracie scored some shit and I got a couple of jars of wine, which just about cleaned Willy and me out, although I think Gracie still has something stashed in a bank or somewhere. Anyway, we all got to feeling no pain, and I was going to go off and leave them the bed. Willy and me have been in the basement of my sister's place for the last couple of days, and Gracie's been with us. But they both said, no, no, they wanted me to stay with them.

So pretty soon we were all lying in the bed together without any clothes and smoking up the last of the hash that Willy and me had been trying to deal, and all of a sudden I felt Willy's mouth on me and I thought, oh, Jesus! I fucking should have known! I tried to push him away, but he wouldn't stop. I gave him a shot like I was going to take out his other eye. But at least it put him away for a while. Then my hands were all over Gracie. And I was crying out to her, Gracie, I love you. That's funny, eh? Me, the last lieutenant of the brotherhood of blood and iron, carrying on like a dickhead.

But it was true. I just never had the guts to say it before.

Paul Olivier, August 13: Cops are really slow, especially me. I was on my roof again, keeping watch on the lane behind Hanover Street and, as usual, falling asleep, and I saw this big fat guy going up the stairs in back of Screwy Looey's. I was going to call out to him, Hey, asshole, go around the front. They keep that door closed, and then I saw it was the Nazi and the door was open and he was going through it.

I did my Tarzan of the Fire Escapes number, and I was coming up right behind him. But before I got to the door, I heard the bang.

I had my own gun in my hand before I even knew I'd reached for it—score one for emergency training—and when I got inside, the girls were screaming and running all around and I couldn't see anything. Then I saw Willy McNiven coming down the hallway, bearing down on me, waving this big gun in his hand, and I yelled at him to stop. I was in the crouch, both hands on my own gun aiming right at him, and I called out to him, Willy, stop! Please, stop! But he just kept coming like he didn't even see me. Then there wasn't any more time. I moved my finger half a millimetre, and I blew the bastard away.

Vernon Kobulczak, August 13: We heard it out on the street, but we didn't think anything about it at first because Lara was just getting into a new song Buddy has been working on with her, and the good people on the mall were just enchanted with Lara, like they always are: You just call out my name and you know wherever I am, I'll come running to you, 'cause you got a friend…

Then, all of a sudden, just as though Lara'd given him a cue, this huge biker came bursting out of the door of Screwy Looey's and banged right into her, knocking her over. The policemen, bless their hearts, were right onto him. But I tell you, I have never seen such a fellow; he was like a grizzly bear. There must have been six policemen hanging onto him, I swear it, hitting him with everything they'd got, but he still kept getting to his feet, blood running all down his face. Buddy cried out to me to get away and then he picked up Lara, carrying her in his arms like a baby, and ran down the street with her. The crowds were ganging up on the policemen and trying to help the big fellow, and I heard glass cracking all around us and I grabbed Cheryl's hand. She wanted to stop and fold up her keyboard, but I pulled her away. It's time to run for our lives, I said.

Inspector Johnny Johnston, August 14: They're already calling this "The Hanover Street Riot." We've got charges on a hundred and thirty-seven people. Nine of my men had to go to Emergency, and two of them are still in hospital.

Andrew Anderson, August 14: I got a ring out of Scobey's window. A good one too, "18 carat" it says on it. Why not? It was shopping night on the mall, only you didn't have to bring any money.

Walt Bowen, August 15: They were using tear gas. I was up at the other end of the mall and I kept playing my guitar and singing, thinking this was what I could do to help keep things cool, and all of a sudden this little tin landed beside me. It was like a soup can, except it was all brown and it was spinning around, spewing off white spirals of gas. Half the cops didn't even have masks themselves. They must've got it as bad as we did. I just barely got out of there.

Peter Dagenham, August 15: I told them. I warned them this would happen.

Grace Calder, August 15: The tear gas was burning my throat even worse than it was hurting my eyes, and I didn't have anything on because I'd just run out after they killed Looey and I was so scared. I thought I was going to die too. Then I just bumped into Harry, the guy who used to tie me up, and all I could say to him was, Graeme! Graeme! I was crazy and I was screaming, but he got me out of there. He took me to his place and got me cleaned up, and I told him what had happened, how I was in Looey's and I saw it all, and he said we'd better go to the cops. Then I started to bawl and I told him what really happened, that I was part of it. He just looked at me, and I hated him for that look, like he was telling me I was a lying piece of shit. But I thought, No, you can't throw me out. I've got nowhere else to go. So I reached out and undid him. I kneeled down in front of him and I took out his dick and I put it in my mouth.

That was the worst thing I have ever done.

Because all the other times I was balling men it was just for money and I never cared anything about money. But this time it was to save my life, and for the first time, ever, I felt like I was a real whore.

Alexander Scobey, August 15: The shyster lawyer was there first thing in the morning. I was still trying to sweep the glass off my floor and fires were still burning in the trash baskets outside. Okay, Mr. Margulies, I said, but I want the last deal Peter Dagenham offered me—any location I choose and three years rent free. He looked at me like I was crazy. Mr. Dagenham didn't say anything to me about that, he says.

Well, what have you got then? I asked him. He opens up his fancy briefcase and shows me. A standard lease, thirteen hundred square feet, not a bad location, right by the front door, but no other comforts. I pay the same rent as everybody else, for the public space as well as my own space, and I have to hand over to them the same share of the gross as the other tenants.

Give it to me, Mr. Margulies, I said. And I signed then and there. The hell with Hanover Street. This isn't my city any more.

Harry Margulies, August 17: If you are a lawyer with a major firm and most of your clients are developers, you can get into some pretty strange situations. But negotiating with a character who likes to be called "The Nazi" and who has, so I am told, a big swastika tattooed on his chest, has got to be something nobody could have anticipated back in law school. But I was doing it for Grace, and for the cop who says he is going to take her away, so it was all for good cause.

They brought him into the lawyers' room and left us alone, and I was thinking, I'm glad the police are just outside that door because this guy is really dangerous.

But I stayed cool and laid it out for him. He was going away, have no doubts about that, my friend, but because of all the confusion that night, there is still some question about who actually did in one Lewis Gough. A good criminal lawyer, which I was prepared to get him through Carlton and Boggs, could probably get him off the murder-first-degree charge and leave him with a reasonable chance of getting out of the can before he is too old for it to make any difference.

In return, he would keep Grace Calder out of it.

Why should I trust a Jew? he said.

For the same reason I'm willing to trust a member of the National Socialist Party, I said.

Then he really surprised me. He laughed, like we'd just shared a good joke.

Say hello to Gracie for me, he said. Tell her to take care of herself.

He held out his hand and we shook on the deal. Odd as it may sound, I have no doubt at all he will keep his word.

So why didn't I hang onto Grace for myself, eh? I could have, you know. I could have had her as a permanent slave. And I will admit I was tempted. But then I thought about women, and I guess especially about Victoria Sommers, and I thought, that's what I want, a woman. I don't need a slave. I'm not a little boy any more.

Fred Englander, August 15: Why is it we never do what we should do when we should do it? All the time my father was dying he was trying to get me to promise I would say Kaddish for him myself, and I kept putting him off. I felt like he was still treating me like a little kid. Now he's gone and it seems like the most natural thing in the world; all I want to do is say Kaddish.

I am going to put up a plaque to my father in Dagenham Square. Peter Dagenham thinks it's all his doing, but the truth is, he couldn't build an outdoor shithouse by himself. He's too scared. We've got everything we need now and I'm going to see this project through and it'll be named after Dagenham. But just inside the door, there's going to be a gold plaque, in Hebrew, saying, "This building is dedicated to the memory of Shmuel Englander." Because, without my father, none of this would have been possible.

Grace Calder, August 18: I always thought Clem hated me and he'd hate me even more because of what happened that last night. But Harry says I shouldn't worry, everything's going to be all right, he's looking after everything, and Paul and me can leave the city.

I said to Paul, I really did love Willy, you know. And he said that was okay, he could understand, he'd been in love once himself.

Then I said to him, Well, Paul, I don't love you, you know. And he said that was okay too, he didn't ask me to.

We're just going home, Paul said. We're going to have a little talk with your father and walk around Alcorn a bit, and then we'll see which way the wind is blowing.

But I think that Paul and me will really stay together. Because when you've done all the things we have, growing up in Alcorn, and then going down to the city and all, it makes you very close—like family.

Victoria Sommers, August 18: I found Dane sitting on the sidewalk. The guys from Public Works were still trying to get up the last of the broken glass and they were hauling away the concrete pots with their trees and flower beds. There were uniformed policemen everywhere. I told Dane what had happened at council. I didn't try to sugar-coat it for him. The Hanover Street Mall was cancelled, as of right now. But I did manage to get in a small amendment. We're going to have a study and consider possible other sites for the future.

I should have been there, Dane said. I'm sorry. I should have been there.

Why? I said to him. What would you have done? I'm the elected politician. This is what they pay me for.

I sat down on the curb beside Dane and put my arm around him. I don't understand it, he said. Some nights it was so good out here.

We tried, I said to him. But the people just weren't ready for it.

Walt Bowen, The Purple Onion, Halifax, Nova Scotia, November 18: And now I'd like to do for you a little song I wrote when I was up in Toronto last summer…

Oh, they could not stand the music,
They could not stand the joy,
They could not stand the laughter,

Of the dancing girls and boys.
So the police they came with tear gas,
With guns and blackjacks too,
And they beat the people back...
From Hanover Street
...from Hanover Street.

5

TAKING POWER: 1979

In which our friends get what they want,
but not always what they expected

72

THE HEAVY spring rain may be replenishing other parts of Toronto, but going east, out along the suburb of Scarborough's portion of Eglinton Avenue, the nourishing quality is lost. Out here, it is just tons of dirty water bouncing off the fierce neon signs and concrete blocks of the strip plazas that run on and on. Out here, the rain is an unnatural act, keeping people away from what they should be doing: spending money.

Victoria Sommers looks out the car window now at the dripping supermarket windows plastered with signs proclaiming last week's bargains, the dirt-splashed muffler and transmission-replacement shops, the cheerless fast-food restaurants, and the seedy stereo and appliance stores. She catches herself replaying painful memories of the fight with Winnie Barbeau.

Victoria cursed Winnie for being pig-headed when Winnie refused to move out to Scarborough. Winnie said the poor were being swept out of downtown as though they were so much garbage. Victoria is certain Winnie has never forgiven her for surrendering the houses on Cotswold Street in order to get nearly nine hundred units of co-op housing Molly Scanlon's group built out here. Well...there's not much chance Victoria will meet Winnie Barbeau again, but if their paths ever do cross, Victoria will say, "Winnie, you were dead right."

I am burned out, Victoria is thinking. Molly Scanlon called and insisted that Victoria must come with her all the way out to the housing co-op to see a boy named Lonny. But Molly refused to explain why the kid was so important. It was something Victoria would understand when she met him. Victoria hated Molly's manipulative games. But she didn't have the strength to say no.

Molly is hunched over the steering-wheel, peering nearsightedly into the sheets of rain. Wisps of grey can be seen now in Molly's vivid, carrot-coloured mop. Victoria knows that Molly is too proud to do anything about her hair or about the heaviness beginning to drag down that angry street-urchin's face. Molly will go on forever, fighting on in the name of good causes. But Victoria Sommers will no longer be there for Molly to draw on. Victoria has built up a new life. She is going to tell Molly about it this morning—if she gets the chance.

When they reach the co-op, Molly parks in the lot and, holding a plastic raincoat over her head, leads Victoria over the sodden grass walkways to a basement apartment. Lonny is waiting for them in the tiny kitchen. He turns out to be a chubby boy with arms hanging limply in front of him. Victoria's first thought, which she instantly orders out of her mind, is that with his broad, pumpkin face, the kid looks just like a little gnome.

Considering him more closely, Victoria can see Lonny is a friendly youngster, neatly dressed in a red and black checked shirt and brown corduroy trousers. Molly has said the boy is seventeen, but Lonny looks so weak and soft to Victoria she would have said he wasn't much more than half that age. Lonny offers sugar doughnuts from a brown paper bag. "These are good," he says busily. "I'm Lonny. I'm not going to school today. I've got a cold. Do you want some more? These are good."

His father, James Dixon, sits with hands squarely, aggressively, planted on his knees, leaning forward, back erect and proudly free from the support of the plastic back of the old dinette-suite kitchen chair. His long blond hair has been gathered into a ponytail and bound with an elastic band. Dixon's shirtsleeves are rolled up, and his wiry forearms show off winding tattoos of tigers and flowers and the motto "Death Before Dishonour."

"Lon's a good boy," he says slowly. "He's been a good brother for Lynette. People think, y'know, that because he's Down's syndrome he doesn't have feelings like other people. But I tell you, I don't think you have to have a lot of brains to know what's happening. I think Lon feels things just as much as I do—maybe even more."

"Can I go to my room, Daddy?" Lonny says. It strikes Victoria that the kid is unconsciously right on cue, offering proof of what his father just claimed for him. He is sensitive enough to feel embarrassed when people are talking about him.

"Can I go to my room, please?"

"Yes, son, you may go to your room," Dixon says ponderously. "Keep the television low."

Victoria feels respect, almost awe, for James Dixon. She knows she could never give up her life to a retarded child the way this man and his wife have obviously done. But their sacrifice does not now give them the right to make demands on Victoria. I gave at the office, Victoria says grimly to herself.

"My wife and I are going to miss Lon something terrible," Dixon says. "But I realize it's not right to keep a kid at home forever, eh? Even a kid like Lon."

"There are places that look after people like Lonny," Victoria says gently.

"Not any more there aren't!" Molly says loudly. Victoria winces and then mentally braces herself. This must be why they have got her out here.

"The province is closing down all the mental hospitals. They've got a great name for it: 'deinstitutionalization.' All it means is that people like Lonny have to get out and make it on their own. Or stay home forever."

"I wouldn't send Lon to those places, even if they were still going," Dixon says. "I went out to the Lakeshore once. It looked like the Kingston Pen."

"The choice is a group home—if we can get it going," Molly says.

"Yes, I would consent to send my son to one of those places," James Dixon says. "I approve of group homes."

"Well, so do I!" Victoria says enthusiastically.

If a vote is all they want from her, they are welcome to it. She looks over at Molly. Molly seems very pleased.

"I can assure you, Mr. Dixon, that I'll be supporting group homes at City Council," Victoria says. "Thank you for having me today. And thank Lonny too. This has been very helpful."

She shakes hands warmly with Dixon. If a vote from Victoria Sommers for a group home somewhere is all James Dixon wants, he is welcome to it. She can hardly believe Molly has dragged her all the way out here just to reassure this fellow, but Victoria is happy to oblige. Her vote is all that Victoria has left as a politician. And right now, she is so weary she'll give it to anybody who asks, just to keep people from yelling at her.

The rain has stopped when Molly and Victoria leave the Dixons' apartment. The sun is overhead and beginning to feel warm. Victoria helps herself to one of Molly Scanlon's cigarettes and begins to talk about Harry Margulies. This chance to share a confidence is her reward for letting Molly use up so much of her time. She is feeling happy, Victoria explains, for the first time since she and Terry Sommers broke up. She's finally going ahead with her divorce. She can't tell Molly what her plans are because she doesn't have any plans. She feels free, for the first time in her life. But Victoria confesses that she has been living in a little apartment just around the corner from Harry Margulies's house.

"That's wonderful, Victoria. I'm really happy for you. There are some people, you know, who still say Margulies is a shyster. But people like me, who've been around a while, we know lawyers are just hired guns. And I've got to say, Margulies is a very good-looking guy. He's supposed to be rich too. I think you're really lucky."

Now Molly feels free to work on the public Victoria Sommers again. What Lonny calls school is actually a sheltered workshop, and him and a whole gang—it's really something Victoria should see; Molly will be happy to take her there!—put together the parts for taxi meters. It's funny, really, people who can't even add two and two and Victoria should see them putting together high-tech machinery.

What these people really need most is a decent place to go home to at night, Molly explains. That's where the Home Care Alliance, the group Molly is working for now, comes in. They buy the houses and set them up, so that people coming out of institutions, people recovering from mental illness, convicts out on parole, and the mentally retarded, like Lonny, can be part of a community again.

The place she's got in mind for Lonny will be run by the Greenstone Foundation, and it'll have mentally retarded adults and some kids like Lonny, who are almost adults. They're supervised, of course. There are social workers with them all the time. But the people in the homes become just like a real family.

"Well, you know I'm with you," Victoria says.

They have reached City Hall. It's time for Victoria to get out of the car and return to her office.

"I knew you would be," Molly says. "The house is on Landrigan Street, number four sixteen, right across from the park."

The door is half-opened. Victoria does not leave the car.

"The Grove? You want to put a group home in the heart of the Grove?"

"Why not? It's the best place. The houses are big, and the sheltered workshop where Lonny and the gang work is right around the corner, on Dupont."

Cars are beginning to honk at them. Molly is holding up a whole lane of traffic on Queen Street.

"Molly, for God's sake!"

"Hey, come on, Victoria! You don't think I took you all the way out to Scarborough just so you could tell me you're in favour of motherhood, do you? We want to go into the Grove. And we'll never make it if you're not on side."

"Listen, Molly, I haven't made any formal announcements yet," Victoria says quickly. "But I've decided not to run again. I'm getting out."

"Yeah, sure, everybody says you've come to the end of your string," Molly says. "That's just one more good reason to line up with us. If you were going for another term, I wouldn't bother you. You'd get creamed. But this way you've got absolutely nothing to lose. We're giving you a chance to go out of City Hall the way you came in—fighting like hell."

73

FOR ALDERMAN Vito Alcamo, the time is now. He sits in his City Hall office with the door locked and a pad of yellow legal-sized paper resting on his desk and when he looks at all his calculations, there can be no doubts. Vito Alcamo can become the next mayor of the city.

For the first time in almost a decade, there will be no incumbent to battle against. The present mayor, "Smiling Sid" Dewhurst, is retiring to claim a city politician's reward—summers on the Board of Trade's lush golf course, winters at an oceanside condominium in North Miami.

The public will probably expect one of the nine members of City Council's "Old Guard" to replace Dewhurst. But those guys are just part-time politicians. They all have something else going for them—an insurance agency, a bakery, a law practice. They sometimes talk as though they'd like the prestige of being mayor, but they don't want to give up their outside work. Being mayor would mean a cut in income.

On the left, Victoria Sommers would be a natural, but she blew her brains out on the Hanover Street Mall, and the word on Alderman's Alley is that she's getting out.

The other people in the loose coalition of reformers and New Democrats are too busy knifing each other to put together a mayoral campaign. They have a primitive village mentality. Vito understands the Left better than they understand themselves. It comes from studying history and from being an Italian who didn't leave his crumbling little village south of Rome until he was almost nine years old. In a village, it is more important to keep your neighbour from getting ahead of you than it is to get ahead yourself.

So with the people on the Left holding each other back and the Old Guard too preoccupied to try for the mayor's job, the opening is there. Who better to go charging up from the pack at centre ice than Vito Alcamo?

He is young, thirty-six years old, and good-looking, which, distasteful though the thought is, must be added to his calculations. And Vito knows how to appeal to every group in the city. He has a resonance with people.

However...in spite of all the pressure being put on him to run for mayor, Vito left the final decision to his wife, Gillian. They have two children now—Janice, aged seven, and Linda, the delight of Vito's life, aged two and a half. If Vito loses, all of them will have to live on what Gillian earns as a consultant in early-childhood education until Vito can land another job. Vito explained to Gillian, very carefully, that not only would they lose his salary for an unforeseeable length of time, weeks, maybe even months—but they would very likely be stuck with campaign debts that could take years to pay off. Defeated mayoral candidates do not get to hold fund-raising parties. Vito told Gillian that if she said no, that would be the end of it, he would forget about running for mayor.

Gillian said, "Yes, go for it. The city needs a good mayor. I love you, Vito."

Vito has always been proud to be married to a modern, liberated woman. He was thrilled to discover that his wife also possessed old-fashioned values.

Once the decision to run had been taken, Vito began calculating where his support would come from.

The Italians he can pretty well count on from his years of work for St. Cuthbert's Liberal riding association, his prominence as an alderman, and, of course, the spelling of his name.

The Portuguese, who came later, are still working their way through the downtown neighbourhoods the Italians once occupied, and they are worried because middle-class white-painters are beginning to invade their streets and push property values up—which means property taxes will also go up.

Vito has the same fears. He and Gillian bought their brick semi-detached house three years ago, and if the city brought in this market-value tax system the newspapers have been talking about, Vito's own property taxes would shoot up.

It's true, Vito knows, that the property-tax system is an unholy mess. But this is not the time to change it. As mayor, Vito will be in a position to see that homeowners like himself and the people in the Portuguese wards don't get screwed by tax reform.

The Poles and Ukrainians out in the west end are getting frantic because they are close to the old mental hospitals. Now that the province is closing these institutions down, the people who used to live in them want to stay in the west end so they can be close to the clinics that still dole out therapy and tranquillizers. So the former inmates are moving into boarding-houses and group homes all over the old Polish and Ukrainian neighbourhoods.

Vito understands how people in the west end feel. He has two young daughters. He doesn't want lunatics roaming his neighbourhood. Vito believes the city has got to stop letting these group homes open up anywhere they want.

The Chinese and the Japanese are the easiest people to satisfy. They want high-status positions to show they have overcome prejudice and achieved membership in the ruling élite. It always amuses Vito, the student of history, that people who come from countries obsessed with racial purity complain bitterly about racial discrimination when they become immigrants to other countries.

But Vito Alcamo is a politician, not a sociologist. As mayor of Toronto, Vito will control many appointments to the boards of hospitals, libraries, and the Art Gallery of Ontario. He will be pleased to appoint Japanese and Chinese citizens to them.

Then there are the blacks, with whom Vito lumps together, for political consideration, immigrants from India and Pakistan and East Indians making their way here from the Caribbean and Africa. What the blacks want is somebody to jump up and down and scream at the police, or the housing authority, or anybody else they think is giving them a hard time. Vito will perform that service for them.

This could get him into trouble with those who like to refer to the police force as "the finest," and to wear buttons saying, "Our Cops Are Tops." But Vito believes he will be able to make the police and their admirers understand that he is not a radical. He wants only to make people happy.

What the cops really want is to be left alone to run their own show. They want to be self-governing, like lawyers and doctors. They will appreciate a mayor who talks to people who attack the police but who does not go so far himself as to insist on changes in the way the police do things. He will convey to the police the criticism of other people, then leave them to solve their problems in their traditional, fraternal way.

When Vito adds up the people who will be part of his coalition, he realizes with great satisfaction that there is one group he is going to be able to do without, the white Anglo-Saxon Protestants, who once absolutely controlled the City of Toronto. What a delightful prospect that is.

Peter Dagenham from the department store came to Vito to support the new municipal concert hall he and his friends want to build. He didn't even know how insulting he was being. Peter Dagenham just assumed that Vito must be an opera fan. Dagenham talked like he really believed all Italian women weigh two hundred pounds and sing out "Mamma Mia!" and arias from Puccini while they cook up mountains of spaghetti.

Vito was greatly tempted to tell Dagenham to stick it up his ass. But a man running for mayor might need the Bay Street money that Dagenham represents. So Vito did not give a flat, outright "No" to Peter Dagenham. He just said the concert hall was something he would have to think about.

But if the coalition of interests Alcamo wants to put together is strong enough, he will be able to thumb his nose at the city's oldest power bloc.

This might just be the election when power in the city shifts and a man of the people, Vito Alcamo, winds up on top.

74

FIRST CANADIAN PLACE did not even exist when Devorah Ishmaeli left for Israel. Now it stands in front of her, intimidating her, an eighty-storey white marble rectangle rising out of a three-storey white marble square that covers a whole downtown block. To Devorah, just two days away from her little chicken-farming community near the Syrian border, walking into First Canadian Place feels as strange as entering an alien city.

She has flown all the way from Jerusalem to talk to her former husband, Harry Margulies, in his new offices at First Canadian Place. She should perhaps have written in advance, or at least called Harry when she arrived. But Harry would certainly have wanted to know why she was making such an arduous trip, and if she told him the truth right off, he might well have refused even to see her. So Devorah is just going to walk in on him. She has become an Israeli in more than just name. Devorah is proud of how tough and blunt she can be. She is going to tell Harry that the time has come formally to give up his son. Gordon is only a year away from military service. He has spent all his formative years with Devorah's second husband, Moshe Ishmaeli. Now Moshe wants to adopt the boy. Devorah is going to tell Harry that, for Gordon's own good, Harry should sign the legal papers she is carrying in her big leather purse.

But before she can do anything, she has to find her first husband. She is standing inside the front door of First Canadian Place and all she can see are stores selling beautiful things. They offer her fine clothes, delicate underwear, fur coats, bracelets of gold and diamonds, luggage and shoes fashioned of leather dyed in many different, unnatural, shades. Devorah feels as if the wealth in First Canadian Place is surrounding and suffocating her.

At last she finds a pale, wispy man in a commissionaire's military-style uniform. He is sitting at a white marble desk. Everything in here seems to be made of white marble. It is as though Devorah has stepped into a mausoleum for the human spirit. Carlton and Boggs can be found on the sixty-fifth floor, the commissionaire tells her. Devorah is on the elevator already zooming upward before she realizes that this elevator, goes only to evenly numbered floors. She has reached the thirty-second floor before she can get out and go back down to the first underground level again, where the elevators start.

Devorah has not caught anyone gaping at her, but still she is beginning to feel conspicuous. Her face is sunburned and her thick black hair is gathered into a white kerchief tied tightly around her head, peasant style. She wears a full blue denim skirt and a white shirt open at the neck, and a simple denim jacket. She thought it would be best to be honest with Harry and present herself to him as she is now, an observant Jew joining the struggle to reclaim the earth of ancient Judea and Samaria. Seeing what Devorah has become might help Harry to understand better why he no longer has anything in common with the son they made, back when Devorah was Doreen Margulies. But now, with all these men rushing around her with their razor-edged business suits and their polished, ivory-coloured faces, Devorah is beginning to feel like a country bumpkin.

She is alone in the elevator. The numbers are flashing in front of her. The doors open and she is on the sixty-fifth floor. The simple, dignified gold letters carved into the dark oak-veneer wall say "Carlton and Boggs," and nothing else. The person bending over the receptionist's shoulder, conferring with her, looks familiar.

Baruch HaShem, blessed be the name of the Lord, it's J. Arthur Quinn. Devorah is shocked by how bloated and unhealthy he looks. Dear, gentle Mr. Quinn. Devorah pulls the kerchief from her head. She advances on him, smiling warmly, hands outstretched. Quinn looks up from the receptionist and sees her. He bends down to say a final word to the girl and then turns and disappears through a door in the wall behind her chair. Devorah didn't even see that the door was there. Now it has opened and closed and swallowed Mr. Quinn.

"Hello," the receptionist says. "Can I help you? Is there someone you'd like to see?"

Mr. Quinn was looking right at her. He didn't even remember her.

"No, thank you, it's all right."

Devorah retreats quickly to the elevator. But this doesn't mean she is giving up. Devorah Ishmaeli has come here to do something important for her husband and her son, and she is not leaving Toronto until she has accomplished it.

75

"YOU'VE GOT TO admire Vickie Sommers. To stand against those who cry out, with such anger,'Not in My Back Yard' requires a special kind of political courage..." In her early days at City Hall, Victoria would have been delighted to read such praise. But now, Bobby Mulloy's column in *The Daily News* just means trouble.

Victoria has, indeed, decided to support Molly Scanlon's group home. But she had been hoping no one would notice—at least, not until it was too late. The City's zoning bylaw says that no more than three "unrelated adults" can live together in a single-family house. Victoria is supporting a site-specific rezoning that would allow twelve adults to live together in the Home Care Alliance house on Landrigan Street. But Victoria had planned to ease it through City Council before any opposition could get organized.

If, later, people in the Grove started howling, Victoria planned to say blandly that she thought the group-home rezoning was just a routine bit of business. If they charge her with betraying the voters, Victoria will tell them how hurt and grieved she is and remind them that, if they really feel that strongly, they can go to the Ontario Municipal Board. Victoria suspects that they will not have the energy and money needed for a serious OMB fight.

Victoria does not think her group-home strategy is deceitful. She is simply being a professional politician. Victoria is using the knowledge she has acquired over the years to help some deserving people—before she leaves City Hall for good. There is nothing wrong with that.

But after Mulloy's column appears, Victoria's telephone starts ringing off the wall.

Victoria is appalled by the callers. If one of the people in that house runs amok and attacks a little kid, what will Victoria do then?

Victoria tries to respond to what she believes is their real fear. She quotes thick studies Molly Scanlon has given her, showing that in other cities there is no evidence group homes in any way lower the value of the houses around them.

But if it doesn't hold true in the Grove, what will Alderman Sommers do? If I have to sell my house and I can't get even as much as I paid for it, will Alderman Sommers reach into her pocket and help me?

Victoria reminds them that she has spent her whole career defending neighbourhoods. They tell Alderman Sommers that is all the more reason why she should be against the group home. We don't want that goddamned thing in our neighbourhood, Alderman Sommers, and you ought to be out there fighting for us.

J. Arthur Quinn professes to be very amused. He tells Harry Margulies, "All these years I've been listening to Sommers preach to me about protecting neighbourhoods. Now her own people are taking Victoria's own words and sticking them up her ass. I almost feel sorry for her."

At night, in the peacefulness of his own bedroom, Harry holds Victoria against his chest and tells her that these people who are getting so hysterical are all newcomers to the Grove. They have no sense of history or they wouldn't talk that way. Victoria should not waste her time worrying about them.

But then Victoria gets a call from Don McPartland from Citizens Against the Berryman Expressway. Could Victoria just come up and have a beer with Don and Peter Strassner?

"I promise we'll be on our best behaviour," McPartland says brightly. "I'll even buy you a bag of potato chips."

McPartland and Strassner marched with Victoria into the middle of Berryman Avenue. They all sat together blocking the traffic until the police came and arrested the demonstrators from CABE. Victoria Sommers cannot refuse to have a beer with those two—not now, not ever.

But then Victoria is immediately sorry she let sentimental memories overcome her good sense. McPartland insists Victoria come first to his house. There is something he wants to show her, he says. Victoria understands she is in for trouble.

McPartland is waiting on his porch when the cab pulls up. He comes down to the sidewalk to greet her and he looks a little plumper than in his CABE days, but still bedevilled by a host of unspoken worries. McPartland is still too much the western Ontario farm-boy to give Victoria the casual, big-city cocktail-party kiss on the cheek. Instead, he takes both her hands in his own and squeezes them warmly.

"You're looking really well, Victoria," he says. "This is what I wanted you to see."

Oh, dear Lord. Victoria should have known. Molly gave her the house number, but there were so many other things going on at the time, Victoria didn't even think about it. The house the Home Care Alliance has optioned is right beside Don McPartland's home.

Well, Victoria can see why Molly Scanlon is so eager to get the place. The house is big and square, three storeys, with steeply slanting gables over the upper windows, making it look a bit like a small French château. The house must have fifteen rooms at least.

"Just imagine that place filled up with retarded people," McPartland says. "And all their social workers and doctors and everybody else coming and going. I'll be right next door to a government institution, Victoria."

"Those people have to live too," Victoria says resolutely.

McPartland says he doesn't want to talk about the group home right now. Peter Strassner is waiting for them. He leads Victoria down Landrigan Street. She is surprised and saddened by how much the Grove has changed. The air is beginning to feel warm, and green buds are beginning to pop out on the thick old trees. But many more of the old lawns have been paved over to make way for cars. What would old Clair Lipsett, the roads commissioner, say if he ever saw this? The people who stopped an expressway so cars from the suburbs would not swamp their neighbourhood are now paving over the lovely front lawns of the Grove so they have a convenient place to park their own cars.

And even where the lawns have been allowed to remain, the wide, gracious old front porches have been sheared away. It seems that people no longer want to sit in front of their houses, watching what is going on in the street and chatting with neighbours. The new residents of the Grove live inside their houses and go out only into their fenced-off backyards. Life in the Grove is becoming private and fearful. Victoria tells McPartland she had no idea of how much things have changed.

"You notice it most at Hallowe'en," McPartland says. "The kids used to get dressed up and start knocking on your front door around six. We used to buy half a dozen huge bags of candy and apples, and we'd be lucky if they lasted the night. Last year, we bought one bag of Smarties and we had half a bag left over. There are no little kids left in the Grove."

"Well, I wouldn't cry too much, Don," Victoria says. "After all, the value of your house keeps going up."

"I hate that kind of talk, Victoria," McPartland says with a sudden flash of anger. "Yeah, sure, I paid thirty-nine thousand for my house back in sixty-seven and I could probably get six or seven times that for it today. But what do you think I should do with the money? Where do you want me to live, Victoria? Forest Hill? Florida? The Grove is our home. Why do we have to be driven out of here?"

76

IN THE OLD DAYS, they would have gone to the drafty old Brunswick House and they would have felt they were back in the beverage room of a small-town Ontario hotel. Victoria used to think of the Brunswick as being close to the spiritual roots of people who wanted to save the city from being gobbled up by expressways. But McPartland says only students go the Brunswick now. He leads her, instead, west on Bloor Street to a converted corner bank. It still has grooved concrete pillars with sculpted tops, like the sides of a Greek temple, and narrow windows that go up two storeys. The painted wooden sign hanging out from the front announces "The Shepherd's Rest."

Inside, Peter Strassner has taken over a table. The years have been kind to Peter. He looks gentler and less pedantic than he used to. Peter has ordered Bass ale for all of them. Victoria is shocked to find that the heavy glass mugs cost $2.75 each. The slender, shapely glasses they used to get in the Brunswick didn't hold as much but the Brunswick back then charged only twenty cents for a draft beer.

"Where's your friend?" Strassner says. "You didn't bring him?"

"What friend?" Victoria says.

"You know...the lawyer guy."

"Is that what's going around the Grove these days?"

She can just imagine the dinner-party nattering. Remember the terrible names Victoria Sommers used to call Harry Margulies? Now she's sleeping with him. Fucking him, is what they're probably saying.

"Hey, Victoria, if Harry Margulies is good enough for you, then he's fine with us," McPartland says quickly.

"That is for sure," Strassner says emphatically. "So if Elinor calls and says we are giving a little dinner party, you'll bring Mr. Margulies, no?"

Victoria wonders what her high-tension Bay Street lover would find to talk about with Peter Strassner, the Catholic professor of moral philosophy and chairman of the City Ratepayers' Confederation that has opposed Harry's clients so many times. Peter Strassner must wonder that too, even if Harry did help stop the Berryman Expressway. But for Victoria's sake, Strassner is prepared to welcome Harry into his home. Victoria feels touched and chastened.

"Peter, we'd love to come," she says.

They drift only gradually towards the subject of the group home. Victoria is certainly in no hurry. Both men want to talk to her about Vito Alcamo running for mayor. Victoria tells them Alcamo has calmed down since the days when he wanted to build the Berryman Expressway. Victoria sits next to Alcamo at City Council, and she has come to respect him. She thinks the ratepayers will have no trouble dealing with Alcamo. He is certainly light years ahead of old Mayor Dewhurst.

Finally, after a second round of beer, they get down to the group home.

"Why would it be so terrible? I honest-to-God don't understand," Victoria says. "It's just a dozen people living in a house. Sure, they're a little slow, but the way people talk, you'd think they're all going to be drooling sex maniacs."

"It's the principle of the thing," Strassner says. "The government should not come to us and tell us who we have to live beside. That's not right."

"You know better than I do what happens if you push that too far, Peter. You start off saying you don't want a group home on your street. Who do you keep out next? Black people? Jews?"

"That is being ridiculous, Victoria, and you know it. All I am saying to you is that you should not be sitting up in City Hall, telling me that, because you want to do something nice for some people who can't look after themselves, Don has got to live next door to them."

Victoria is saved by the waitress. Do they all want the same again? They have to stop and think. Yes, the afternoon is pretty well gone anyway, they might as well have another round. McPartland says he is getting this one. He would also like some barbecued potato chips, because he promised to buy them for Victoria.

"I am sorry I talk so much," Strassner says when the waitress has gone. "This isn't why we wanted get you up here, Victoria. Listen, how do we know Landrigan Street is the best place for these people? How many other neighbourhoods did they look at?"

"I'm sure they did a thorough search," Victoria says.

"That's what they told you, yes, but you don't really know, do you?" Strassner says. He sounds quite jolly.

"Nobody knows. So what we say is this: the City should hire a consultant. Let him look around, if he comes back and says this is the only place, that they absolutely have to be in this house on Landrigan Street, we'll deal with it then."

"I'll be gone by then," Victoria says.

"Not necessarily," McPartland says. "He might finish before the election."

"So maybe you are gone by then. So what?" Strassner says. "So maybe this alderman who comes after you wants this group home even more than you do. But now we got facts to deal with, not just everybody shooting their mouths off."

Victoria knows what they are thinking. They figure that Molly Scanlon's option on the Landrigan Street house will run out before the consultant finishes and City Council deals with his report. But they could be wrong too. Molly might be able to hang in and fight for the rezoning she needs.

McPartland and Strassner are telling her the ratepayers are willing to take that risk. They have put together something that offers Victoria an honourable way out. Molly Scanlon will never be able to say Victoria has backed out of her commitment to the group home. The people in the Grove will never be able to say Victoria is ramming the group home down their throats.

"You guys!" Victoria says, shaking her head and laughing. "You're way ahead of me."

"So? You think you're the only one's been around a long time?" Strassner says. He is laughing too. The deal has been made.

"We know how to make the system work too, Victoria. We're not so stupid."

There is to be a big public meeting at Huron Street Public School. They decide they will let the crazies sound off, and then Peter will ask everybody to vote for getting the City to hire a consultant. Victoria will say it's absolutely impossible, but gradually, with great reluctance, she will concede that hiring a consultant is a good idea.

It's not a perfect compromise. But at least Victoria will be able to leave office without spending her last months involved in a bitter quarrel with people who have always supported her. She would like to call Harry right away and tell him the good news. But instead, she stays and orders another round for her old friends.

"Do you remember *The Entertainer*?" Victoria asks.

"Oh, sure," McPartland says. "John Osborne's play. I used to love the Angry Young Men."

"Well, remember, Archie Rice was always saying he wouldn't come to Canada because he couldn't get draft Bass? I was just thinking: now he couldn't say that any more."

77

THE TROUBLE with Fred Englander is that life has brought him so many good things he doesn't know what to do next. Now that his father is gone and Max Himmelfarb has pulled out, Fred has Premier Developments all to himself. He is a rich man, and probably a powerful one. But he still doesn't know what is important in life. So Louis Seltzer is going to help Fred find out. Mr. Seltzer remembers fondly how awkward Freddy was when he first started saying Kaddish for his father. He stayed in the back row with the little blue velvet bag that held his father's tefillin, and at first he was afraid even to put them on for fear he would make some mistake in the ritual and embarrass himself. Mr. Seltzer went to Freddy and helped him wind the leather thongs so the little, square wooden boxes with the prayer scrolls would sit properly on his forehead and left wrist. Mr. Seltzer stood beside Fred every day, helping Fred to pronounce the ancient Aramaic words of the Kaddish.

Fred came faithfully every day through the year of Kaddish, and when Kaddish was over, he kept coming on Saturday mornings. But then he started to drift away. Mr. Seltzer has seen it happen so many times. People get to feeling very religious when they say Kaddish, but then they lose touch. This is the first time Mr. Seltzer has seen Freddy in three months.

Aleynu l'shabeyah l'adon hakol...it behooves us to praise the Lord of all...Mr. Seltzer has his white linen prayer shawl pulled up over his head to improve his concentration and he sings out softly but fervently...*Anachnu koirim*...for we bend the knee...and make acknowledgement before the supreme King of Kings...Mr. Seltzer bows his head according to tradition.

Fortunately, there is no Bar Mitzvah today, so it is only the two dozen regulars who go downstairs after the service for the Kiddush, the traditional glass of whisky and piece of honey cake, in the catering hall. Mr. Seltzer is able to get Freddy off into a corner.

"Listen, Freddy, religion isn't something that happens to you all at once, like a lightning bolt. Religion happens a little bit at a time. You start coming to shul regularly again, like when you were saying Kaddish, and one day, before you even know anything is happening, you'll be saying to yourself, 'This is where I want to be. This is the life I want to lead.'"

Fred Englander admits there is a lot of wisdom in what Mr. Seltzer is saying. But right now, he's got to rush away. The boys are waiting for him up at the Home Style Restaurant.To ordinary people, the Home Style is an unimpressive little place with a dozen arborite tables and padded chromium chairs in the old suburban dinette style. But insiders know that bookie Joey Bookspan, the owner of the Home Style, was a member of Club Morgan, along with Max Himmelfarb and a lot of other people who became pretty important when they got older. And for the Jewish boys in the development industry, the Home Style is the place to go on Saturdays to shmooze, pick up the gossip, and maybe get a deal going here and there.

In the year after his father died, Fred made a point of dropping into the Home Style on his way home from shul. Being accepted there was one of the rewards Fred felt he was entitled to when he became top man at Premier Developments. And he has certainly established himself. He doesn't even have to order. Bookie shoves a bowl of thick cabbage borscht in front of Fred as soon as he sits down with the other guys, because cabbage borscht is what Fred always has. But today, a surprise! Bookie adds a heavy twisted bagel instead of the stack of chala with unsweetened butter that he knows Fred likes.

"We're pushing bagels today," Bookie snarls. "Bagels killed more Jews than Hitler."

Fred has some good news for the half-dozen men in V-neck sweaters and suede windbreakers who have gathered at the corner table. They are older than Fred by at least six or seven years, but that doesn't seem so important any more. Fred tells them everything is on for a week Thursday night. There are ten people coming, and they are going to the House of Chan because they don't have enough to get a private room some place and it makes sense just to have everybody at a single table. Everybody's going to put in one big one so they will have ten grand to give Natie Greene when he gets out of the hospital.

"Natie will blow that on the horses in one week," Eddy Cooper says. "But at least the old bastard'll have a good time."

Fred doesn't really know Natie Greene; he just remembers him as one of the hard guys who used to hang out in front of Stedman's Restaurant and do jobs for Jake Besser, the famous bookmaker. But Eddy Cooper says Fred should go down to the hospital with him to tell Natie how things are going. After all, Fred is organizing the affair.

They find Natie just finishing a treatment for emphysema. A nurse is taking a clear plastic mask away from his mouth and nose. A second nurse stands beside the bed, watching the dials on the grey oxygen tanks that look to Fred like equipment from a welding shop.

"How you doing, Natie?" Eddy Cooper says when the nurse takes the mask off him. "You look terrific."

Why do some people always insist on being cheerful with someone who is on his last legs? Does Cooper really think Natie Greene doesn't know how terrible he looks?

"Hey, we got this big dinner going and you're the guest of honour!" Cooper says in a loud voice. "What do you want, Natie? I'll bring you some sweet and sour spareribs? You want chow mein? I'll bring you chow mein too."

The man is resting on one elbow, staring at Cooper. Fred wonders if he has understood any of it.

"Hey, the boys took up a little collection for you," Cooper says. "Ten grand. But there's one condition. You hear me? If you got any good tips, you got to call me before you call your bookie."

Fred Englander is overcome by an old sadness. When he was young, all he wanted in the world was to belong to a social club, like Club Morgan, and hang out with the guys on Berryman Avenue. But Fred's father kept him too close to home.

Now he is being accepted as an equal by people he used to look up to. He just wishes he had been able to be one of the boys when they really were still boys and out on the Avenue, having so much fun.

Fred enters his own home without disturbing anyone. The flagstone ranch house overlooking the peaceful fairways of the Elmwood Golf Course has been solidly constructed, an offering of respect from the brick-layers, dry-wallers, and carpenters who do work for Premier Developments, and the floors have been covered with thick broadloom in French château colours—burgundy, claret, and rose. Estelle Englander does not even know her husband has returned until he is outside the door of her bathroom, calling to her.

"The door's not locked, lovey," she calls back.

Estelle is lying in the tub, enjoying a good soak. Fred sits down on one of the low, flowery chairs Estelle has placed around the room. Fred's eyes look a bit woolly to her and his face is getting puffy again. He needs a shave. Estelle takes a long sip from the glass of white wine and soda water that sits among her soaps and creams.

"So how did it go today?" she asks. "Did you see the clothes I laid out for you?"

"Honey, I'm not wearing that shirt," Fred says. "I'm not a faggot looking for work."

"At your age, I don't think you have to worry about getting offers," Estelle says. She takes another sip from her spritzer. "You've got other shirts. I only put that one out because it looks so good on you."

Left to himself, Fred would probably go out tonight in one of the plain business suits he wears to the office. And, left to herself, Estelle would be happy to let him. But they are going to a dinner party for her cousin Betsy's son, Larry, who has just got engaged, and Betsy's insisting it be black tie, even though there are going to be only about twenty couples. But if black tie is what her cousin wants, Estelle is damned well going to come through for her. Because back in the dark days, when Estelle was sipping her way through a bottle of vodka every day, not just weak white-wine spritzers, Betsy gave her a good talking to and helped Estelle get herself straightened out. So today, Estelle had laid out Fred's midnight-blue evening suit with the wide cummerbund and pale pastel-blue shirt that has scalloped edges running down beside the front pleats. The shirt is unusual and it looks good on Fred, and it protects him from having people think that maybe he rented his formal clothes—the way a surprising number of men still do.

"You know what I'm thinking?" Fred says. He is smiling down at her sturdy legs stretched out under the blue water. Dear Fred. As far as Estelle knows, he has never done any running around. But even if he had, and she'd found out about it, Estelle would not have made a fuss. A little running around might have done Fred a world of good.

"I'm thinking we go to your family every week. Tonight, let's just go out by ourselves."

"Hmnn," Estelle says, considering the idea and finishing off her spritzer. "I'm not against it. Where should we go, Fred?"

"Oh, I don't know. Dinner. Dancing."

"What place have you got in mind, Fred?"

She waits for him to come up with a name, confident that he won't be able to. The restaurants they used to go to, nice places where they had a little orchestra you could get up and dance to, don't even exist any more. And Fred, she is sure, is not going to suggest taking her to a discotheque—whatever that is.

"We could go to a show," Fred says.

"That's a good idea. What do you want to see?"

It's been five years at least since Fred lined up in front of a box office. Fred is completely unaware of movies and plays and things like that.

"Go get dressed, Fred," she says gently.

"I know what we could do," he says brightly. "We could stay home and pretend we're not married."

She smiles, pleased that he brings up this intimate joke from their newlywed days.

"I'd love to," Estelle says ruefully. "But I've got the curse."

"Oh," Fred says glumly. "When did that happen?"

"This morning. After you left for shul."

"I knew I should have stayed in bed today."

"Just be thankful I can still have them," Estelle says. "It won't be long now. Go take your shower and get dressed, honey."

Fred hauls himself up and does as his wife directs. But as he is making his way down the hall to his own bathroom, an old advertising slogan comes back to him. Comedians used to make a joke out of it, but it doesn't seem so funny now to Fred Englander: "What do you give to the man who has everything?"

78

THE SHUTTING of the brass locks on his thick lawyer's attaché case has a sharp, military snap to it. Harry Margulies likes that sound at the end of a day. He turns off the light in his office and steps out into the main square of Carlton and Boggs. It is gloomy and pleasantly dishevelled out here, homey almost, now that the frantic busyness of "the girls," as the firm's secretaries are called, is over for the day. But on the outer edge of the floor, in offices a little smaller than his own, lights are still burning. The younger lawyers are still hard at work, and Harry knows that many of them will be going long into the night. They undoubtedly think Harry Margulies is exploiting them because they can see Harry walking out of here so many nights at six o'clock. But Harry has paid his dues. Now it's time for the people coming behind him to pay theirs. The system can sometimes be cruel, but Harry has seen that it does select the best people to rise to the top.

Harry steps next door into the very large office occupied by J. Arthur Quinn. Even in Carlton and Boggs's new quarters, two full floors of First Canadian Place, Quinn has managed to commandeer the best corner, southwest, with a good view of the lake, for himself.

But tonight Quinn keeps the blinds drawn, and he is sitting with a tumbler of scotch, reading over a report. It has orange covers, and Harry can just imagine how upsetting Quinn must be finding this material. He wishes Quinn would go back to keeping the pills for his various heart conditions lined up on his desk. When the bottles started to get empty you could at least be sure he was still taking the stuff. But Quinn has been getting self-conscious lately and he's taken to keeping his medicine in a desk drawer.

"Well...well...Mr. Shit-Shower-Shave-and-a-Shampoo," Quinn says sourly. "You must be going pussy hunting tonight. Sad to see in a man your age."

"Actually, I'm going out to have dinner with Doreen."

"Ah yes," Quinn says. "I'm sorry; I forgot. Would you like a little fortifier?"

"No thanks," Harry says. "Why don't you come down in the elevator with me. This is when you're supposed to be doing your mile walk, isn't it? I'll go a couple of blocks with you."

"I'll go later, maybe," Quinn says. "Have you read this little gem Charlie's been sending around?"

He holds up the report with the orange covers. Harry nods grimly. Yes, he is familiar with it.

"We can't just say 'No,' Arthur. Not this time."

The report says Charlie McConnachie has been approached by a law firm in North York that wants to merge with Carlton and Boggs. Harry suspects that McConnachie has actually hunted these people up, but that's not going to matter to anybody in here. The other firm is too impressive. They've got a head office a block away from the North York municipal building and branch offices in Etobicoke, the city's western suburb, and in Peel, the big regional municipality growing out beyond Etobicoke. The merger would be a perfect fit, McConnachie says. Carlton and Boggs would gain a presence out on the borders, where the city is growing fastest. And these guys would gain entry into Bay Street, where the big corporate clients come.

"I don't believe the names," Quinn says. "I think Charlie's making them up."

"I wish he were," Harry says.

The firm is called Azevedo, Fong and Quemoy. One partner is Portuguese; one is Chinese; and the other is Filipino, and a woman too. The firm is so perfectly, delightfully multicultural it sounds like a TV family show. But the people are real enough. Azevedo, Fong and Quemoy have thirty-eight lawyers, and the biographies McConnachie has so thoughtfully provided are chilling. Half the shop at Azevedo, Fong and Quemoy seem to have taken a Master of Law degree or at least done a Master of Business Administration. Collectively, they seem to be on just as many boards of directors as the partners at Carlton and Boggs, although the firms may be smaller. Even more threatening, it doesn't look like there is a person in that whole firm who is over forty years old.

"We'd be swamped," Quinn says. "We'd be even more of a factory than we are now."

"We'd be the second-largest law firm in the country," Harry says.

"Jee-zuss!"

"Don't panic, Arthur. I got some ideas. We'll talk," Harry says. "I'd better get going now."

"Yes, well, good. Give my best to Doreen," Quinn says. "She was a beautiful girl. Where are you taking her? Scaramouche? Fenton's?"

"United Bakers Dairy Restaurant," Harry says in a flat, deadpan voice. "Doreen keeps kosher now, she tells me."

"Oh, dear. That doesn't sound like your ex, Harry. Well, say hello to Hymie Ladovsky for me. Tell him to give you the baked carp. It's delicious."

"Arthur, do the world a favour: go take a walk," Harry says.

Doreen is waiting for him in front of the restaurant. Harry extends his hand. She pushes forward and kisses him on the cheek. Thank you for coming here, she says.

They settle down in a corner table. Ladovsky's, as it is known because of the family that has owned it for three generations, is a favourite place for the Jews who still work in the garment factories at the bottom of Berryman Avenue and for their children, who have become lawyers and university professors. But the regular people come only for breakfast and lunch. There is almost no evening trade. Harry and Doreen have the little restaurant all to themselves. Their voices bounce off the walls and sound metallic and artificial.

Harry can see that Doreen's face has become harder and a little thicker, although it's certainly not fat. There is hardly a trace of the sensitive, jittery young girl he was once married to. Her skin is rosy; she glows with health. She is wearing a fine white silk blouse with lace across the bodice and a gold necklace and long gold-wire earrings.

She tells Harry about the new life she and Morry have made in Israel. They have gone through a religious conversion. It happened after the Yom Kippur War. Their little settlement was right in the path of the Syrian troops and even though the Syrians never got that far, she and Morry could hear the fighting going on all around them. Morry just about went crazy. First, he was going to send Doreen and the children back to Canada. Then, he tried to get into the army even though he was far too old, and, of course, they sent him home. But Morry was able to get in with some people who were taking truckloads of stuff up to the soldiers and that made him feel he was at least doing something.

When it was over, Morry and Doreen started to ask each other, What is it all about? Morry said that, if they were going to get themselves killed in Israel, surely it would have to be for more than just hanging onto a few square miles of rock and sand. There are lots of other places in the world to live. So Morry and Doreen decided the only way they could stay in Israel, and they do certainly want to stay there, was to become observant Jews.

It was Morry who came up with their new name, "Ishmaeli." They are the true, spiritual descendants of the outcast and wanderer, he said. Devorah and Moshe, as Doreen and Morry decided to be, would reclaim Ishmael from the Arabs, who claim they are the true descendants of Abraham's lost son. Moshe is over on the West Bank now, looking for a new place where they can settle.

"That is quite a story," Harry says. "Your mother must be very pleased."

"So, surely, you can see now, Harry," Devorah says slowly, looking straight at him, holding tight to her coffee cup, "why it makes so much sense for Moshe to adopt Gordon. He's changed his name to Gideon, by the way."

Harry does not respond. It is as though he has lost the power of speech.

"Gideon wants it too, Harry. You can call him in Israel and ask him. I wouldn't be here now if this was not something that Gideon wants as much as Moshe and I do."

"You are crazy," Harry says. The words come slowly. "There is no way. Forget it!"

"Harry, please…you haven't seen him in almost ten years. You don't even know Gideon any more."

"That may be so," Harry says. "But that doesn't mean I'm giving up on my son, Doreen. I have done a lot of stupid things in my life, but there is no way on God's earth I am giving up my connection to Gordon."

"Harry, why are you doing this? You have a new life too. You don't need us."

"If you're talking about Victoria Sommers, that has nothing to do with it. You and your new husband are not taking Gordon away from me. That's all there is to it, Doreen!"

"Harry, I'm here and I'm not going back until you've signed the papers."

"Then, Doreen, you're going to be a very old woman before you get back to Israel."

79

A SPLENDID June night is a bad time to hold a public meeting for people who live in the Grove. They like to be out in their back yards, drinking fizzy gin and tonics, or they like to stroll down to Bloor Street to browse in the bookstores and sit in the outdoor cafés. Nevertheless, Trevor Billinghurst finds the auditorium of Huron Street Public School so crowded he and Vivian have to stand against the back wall. This is the first public meeting they have been to since they moved into their new house. The Billinghursts have done better than might have been expected. Trevor has long since discharged his personal bankruptcy and, in fact, paid off more old debts than his accountant said he was really obliged to. They now have three Limelighter bookstores, and the Billinghursts have been able to buy a spacious old house in an immigrant neighbourhood that real estate agents have begun to call "The Western Grove." People on Trevor's street found leaflets dropped through their mailboxes, urging them to come to a public meeting about the group home on Landrigan Street, where Vivian once lived in a commune.

Trevor had expected opposition to the group home, but nothing like what he is hearing from the floor of the auditorium now.

"Mrs. Scanlon...can you promise me that nobody's going to touch my children, Mrs. Scanlon?"

"Why us? There are dozens of neighbourhoods in the city, why do you have to pick the Grove? Why do you want to hurt us, Mrs. Scanlon?"

"Are you going to live in that house, Mrs. Scanlon? You're just going to dump them on our street and run, aren't you? Tell the truth, Mrs. Scanlon!"

"I'll be honest with you, lady. I don't care what these other people here say to you. I got everything I own tied up in my house. You're not going to turn my street into a garbage dump!"

Vivian is keeping silent, but Trevor knows what she is thinking. Vivian does not like what these hysterical people are saying, but she is still glad they are saying it.

The Billinghursts have two lovely teenaged daughters. How could Vivian support anything that might endanger Sasha and Paola?

"Please! Please, let me speak!" From the stage far away at the front of the room Molly Scanlon strives desperately to defend the home. The residents will be supervised twenty-four hours a day. They could be your own children. All they want is to live in a house on Landrigan Street and go to work in the morning and come home at night, just like everybody else. Please, please, give them a chance.

The tears in Molly's voice intimidate the crowd. But a woman rises in the front row.

"If you think these dummies are so damned wonderful, you go live with them."

Scorn and contempt quickly supplant whatever feelings of sympathy Molly was able to arouse.

"We don't want those people here!" The speaker this time has the aristocratic, angular good looks that go with a couple of generations of inherited wealth. Trevor instantly recognizes one of his own kind—the fields of Upper Canada College, glorious summers and canoe trips at Taylor Statten summer camps, final arrival on Bay Street.

"What do we have to do to get the message across? You call a public meeting and you don't listen to the public. We're telling you in plain, simple language, we don't want those people!"

Victoria steps to the microphone, beside Molly Scanlon. She looks to Trevor more nervous than a politician with all her years of experience should be. "Well, I've certainly heard what you have to say, sir. Thank you, very much. Is there anyone else?"

A stocky fellow, with thick, disorderly hair rises in the middle of the auditorium and turns so everybody in the room can take him in. He has the conceited air of a man who expects to be recognized.

"I don't think we have enough information," the man says. He has a caramel-soft German accent. "I am Peter Strassner, chairman of the City Ratepayers' Confederation. And what I am saying to you, Alderman Sommers, is that we have one person here telling us one thing, and another person telling us another thing. So we should be getting an expert, somebody who is from outside, somebody objective, to tell us what is really going on."

Trevor admires the man's grit. He is the only person tonight who has said anything even mildly conciliatory. He'll be lucky to get out of this auditorium without getting a punch in the nose.

"I agree with that. I don't think we should make any decisions tonight," someone else is saying in a dry, scratchy voice.

"We've heard so much conflicting evidence I don't think any of us knows what is happening. This is the city's idea, so the city should hire a consultant, somebody objective, to look at the whole group-home situation and then report back to us."

Well, thank God for these guys, Trevor is thinking. The bigots haven't taken the world over yet.

"Consultants are expensive," Victoria says. She sounds hesitant, but Trevor can tell even from the back of the room that Victoria is relieved.

"I don't know if what you're suggesting is possible. But if people here want me to, I'll see what can be done about engaging a consultant to look at group homes."

A man at the back wall, where Trevor and Vivian are, steps forward. He has a ragged beard and wears a soiled white T-shirt, but his manner is brusque and patronizing. Trevor takes him to be a university professor.

"Alderman Sommers, have I missed something tonight? The only person I've heard speak in favour of this group home is Mrs. Scanlon, and I think you'll have to admit that Mrs. Scanlon has a vested interest. So what we want to know, Mrs. Sommers...what we have an absolute right to know, Alderman Sommers...is why you want to play this little consultant game with us and keep this issue alive?"

Victoria's answer seems to Trevor haughty and dismissive. She must really be losing her nerve; she's going back to her ethnic roots: the prudish young girl from a private school.

"On the evidence of what I have heard tonight, I agree with the previous speaker; the matter needs further study," Victoria says.

"Alderman Sommers, could you tell me why a dozen mentally retarded people have more rights in this city than people like myself and my neighbours, who have worked hard to pay for their houses and are struggling to keep up the quality of this community? I don't understand why my rights mean nothing and the rights of Mrs. Scanlon and her mental retardates are so important. Could you help me with that question, Alderman Sommers?"

Victoria's face is beginning to glow.

"I have been your alderman for eight years and I do not believe there is a person in this room who can say I have ever treated them unfairly."

It is becoming a duel—the angry Victoria up on the stage, the nagging professor at the back of the hall.

"Alderman Sommers, I think you should record the sense of this meeting."

"This meeting is for public information only. We didn't come here tonight to make any decisions."

"Nevertheless, I see no harm in putting the matter to a vote. All those who say 'No group homes in the Grove', put up your hands."

Trevor and Vivian are looking out on a thick forest of waving hands. They are accompanied by clapping, hooting, and cheering. The sense of the meeting is clear.

"Let's get out of here," Vivian says.

The day's heat has finally dried up from the streets. The air is thin and chilly.

"I hate those people," she says.

"Don't look now, babe," Trevor says. "But 'them' is us."

"Just because I don't want a group home, it doesn't mean I'm paranoid."

"Do you want to know what I think?"

"You know I do."

"I went there feeling cynical in the way I used to be cynical about everything," Trevor says. "I figured I'd hear a lot of highfalutin' talk and it would come down to one thing: people afraid a group home might knock a few bucks off the resale value of their own houses. But it was much worse than that. Those people are afraid of everything."

"But what if they're right, Teddy? What if they put druggies or people right out of jail in the house next door to us? What if those people attacked one of our girls?"

"I'd want to kill him with my bare hands, just like you would," Trevor says. "And if I thought going along with the gang we saw in there tonight would keep my daughters safe, I wouldn't hesitate. But I don't believe it for a minute. So what if they don't put ex-cons in a group home? They get out of jail and they go off and rent rooms by themselves where nobody knows who they are or what they're doing. You can't keep strangers off your streets. The city's always been dangerous and always will be. You can never make neighbourhoods safe, but you can sure as hell make them mean and ugly. That's what we were seeing tonight."

Vivian sighs.

"Teddy," she says. "When did you start getting so smart?"

"When I went broke, babe. It clears the mind wonderfully."

"So I guess we go help Victoria Sommers," Vivian says wearily.

"Victoria's beyond help," Trevor says. "It looks to me like our esteemed alderman just got her head handed to her."

80

FRED ENGLANDER started off the evening worrying about how he could say no to Peter Dagenham, who is sitting beside him, without causing offence. Now Fred is worrying about how he can say yes, without making a mess of his own life.

Dagenham wants Fred to take over from him as chairman of the Concert Hall's board of directors. Fred knows that's just a fancy title for a fund-raiser. Peter says they need somebody from the development industry, a man who's used to making deals and getting things done. Fred suspects they also want someone who is Jewish and can talk to the big players in the Jewish community. Some people might feel they were being patronized, but Fred doesn't mind. He is pleased that a businessman like Peter Dagenham, whose family has been important in the city for almost a hundred years, recognizes that Jews have a role to play too. Fred has no problems about writing a cheque and making a few telephone calls. But taking on the job of getting the whole project under way, that is too much to ask.

When the curtain went up and the dancers began to move around on the stage, it seemed to Fred that his reluctance was more than justified. The men were all in tights that were so stretched in the crotch you could see their natural equipment bulging out. Fred was embarrassed for them. He thought with a smirk that if those guys had not been wearing heavy-duty jockstraps, you could have told which ones were Jewish. The girls were all got up in little pink and white skirts that stuck out stiffly from their hips and flounced up when they were dancing, to show off their panties.

The feeling in the auditorium was definitely lascivious. To Fred it was like being in Las Vegas again, watching the practically naked showgirls go through their paces. But he recognized something else also going on in the darkness around him. It was an activity Fred Englander is very familiar with. Power was being exercised here. These delicate young women had squeezed themselves into revealing, childish outfits and they were cavorting on the stage, showing off just about everything they owned, for the private pleasure of the men out there.

And the women were getting off on it too. Women are a lot harder on other women than men ever are. The women in the audience were sitting in their black evening dresses and their heavy-duty gold jewellery, and they were thinking how superior they were to those little dancing girls up there. The dancers have to display themselves whenever they are commanded to. The women who come to the ballet only as patrons get to pick their times and places.

Then, his analysis complete and his arguments ready, Fred settled back and found, to his surprise, that he was beginning to enjoy the spectacle of muscular young bodies springing into the air and floating through the dusty spotlights. How much can one of those dancers earn? Fred probably pays more for a secretary. Yet, there the dancers are, working their hearts out for the pleasure of others. Fred has to respect them.

At the intermission, Fred promises to write Peter Dagenham a cheque for considerably more than what he had originally intended to give. Peter thanks him warmly and gives Fred a plate loaded with delicious little cakes. A buffet table has been set up in the lobby for patrons of the fund-raising gala. Peter snags a couple of glasses of champagne from a passing waiter.

What Fred should understand, Dagenham says, is why a new concert hall is so important. You can spend a fortune on publicity for the city, but people who make investment decisions are swamped in that kind of bumpf. However, the city puts up a beautiful, new concert hall, that's a message the outside world pays attention to. It says Toronto is wealthy. It tells somebody who's thinking, Where should I put my new head office? that this is a place for successful people to be.

Fred Englander says he appreciates what Peter Dagenham is telling him. But Fred is all alone now at Premier and he doesn't mind telling Peter, because, after all, they are friends as well as partners in Dagenham Square, that the development business is not what it once was. The welfare of literally hundreds of people depends on Fred Englander sticking close to the office.

The second half of the gala performance begins with bits and pieces put together to show off to potential donors the great depth of talent in the company. The curtain had been up only a few moments when Fred Englander begins to feel he has entered a new dimension of being. The program said the first number was called "Brandenburg Number Three" and it had been choreographed by a student at the ballet school. The tinkly sound coming out of the orchestra pit reminds Fred of music boxes. But the movements on the stage enchant him. The women are in long white skirts and black tops, and the men are in black trousers and white undershirts. They all flow back and forth across the stage so that the moving bodies make up continually changing patterns of light and darkness. The dancing here is delicacy and perfection. Fred Englander longs to be part of it.

The grand finale is "Salute to Canada," with the full symphony orchestra pounding out so many different evocative themes it sounds to Fred Englander like a carnival midway. Up on the stage there is everything from Quebec step-dancing to guys pulling in fishing nets to girls prancing around in mountie uniforms. It is totally silly, but Fred can see the people up on stage know that too and yet they are still good-natured and exuberant. Fred feels exuberant too. They are all sharing the joke and happy just to be there together.

Max Himmelfarb would sneer at Fred Englander now, and his father would bawl him out for wasting time. But Max and Reb Shmuel are not around any more. Fred sometimes feels, bitterly, that they have both abandoned him. Well, if Fred Englander has been left alone, he will decide for himself what is right. The city has been good to him; it is time he gave something back. And it's not so some salesman can go on the road, peddling Toronto; Fred would never base a business decision on whether a city had a concert hall, and he doesn't believe anyone else would either. No, Fred is going to do this for those boys and girls up on the stage, so they can have a home, a decent place in which to perform. Fred leans over to Peter Dagenham and whispers, "I know I'm crazy, Peter, but I'll take the job."

Dagenham reaches out and wraps his enormous paw around Fred's hand and gives it a hearty tug.

"I'm delighted," he says. "I knew I could count on you, Freddy."

81

HARRY MARGULIES was a little surprised when he discovered he had a talent for foot massage, but now he is very grateful for this skill. It is one of the few things he can do to help Victoria relax.

"I don't want to leave politics like this," Victoria says bitterly. "Do you really think I'm dead?"

"You are dead," Harry says. "If you run again in your own ward, they'll put up someone who wants to keep out group homes. You'll spend all your time trying to explain why you're ramming the Landrigan Street place down their throats when the people voted against it. You blew your brains out at that public meeting."

"I don't care about it for myself," Victoria says. "I'm a big girl and I can take my lumps. But I hate what they did to Don and Peter."

"Those guys certainly gave it the old college try," Harry says.

"This is a miserable way to go out," Victoria says. "There's got to be something I can do."

"Mhmn," Harry mumbles. "Give me your other foot."

"Can I take off my pantyhose?"

"Be my guest," Harry says.

Victoria wriggles out of them and puts her bare foot in Harry's lap. She settles back and rests her cheek against the cool chintz of Harry's sofa.

"There is one thing I could do," Victoria says.

"Oh?" Harry says, letting the question hang in the air.

"Vito would be furious. He'd say I promised him not to run."

"Did you?"

"I certainly did not. The only thing I ever said to Vito was I had no trouble with him going for mayor."

"Hoo, boy!" Harry says. "You really have become a City Hall pro."

"Can I have another Armagnac?"

"No."

"That's not fair. You've had two."

"I can handle the stuff. You can't."

"Harry, I want to go for mayor!"

"Why doesn't that surprise me?"

"I shouldn't, eh? If I was the old Victoria Sommers I'd say I was just there to represent the people. So bye-bye group homes."

"But you're not saying that now?"

"I'm right and they're wrong."

"So no more listening to the people? From now on you just talk to yourself."

"And my friends. And a few people that I trust. And my conscience."

"That could get a mite lonely."

"I'm not running for dictator, Harry. I'm telling people what I stand for, and if they don't like me, they can hand me my walking papers. What's wrong with that?"

"Nothing that I can see," Harry says, with a small, self-pitying sigh.

"Harry...if you give me another Armagnac, I'll be nice to you."

"How nice?"

"Very nice. Nicer than you could ever imagine."

"That sounds interesting," Harry says.

He splashes more of the rich amber brandy into Victoria's glass.

"What you are saying is only one scenario," Harry says. "There is another one, you know."

Harry does not look at Victoria. He concentrates on pressing delicately on the sensitive spaces between her toes. Victoria studies him suspiciously.

"I was thinking, you know," Harry goes on, "that if you're getting out of politics and going private, you could come here. Like move in, I mean."

"Oh? Really?" Victoria says. She sounds grotesquely coquettish. She was hoping she would come out sounding sophisticated and amused.

"Yeah, well it is a little crazy to be keeping up two places, eh?" Harry says. "You spend most of your time here anyway."

Victoria pauses, sips her Armagnac—such a lovely silky taste. So many good things Harry has introduced her to. The idea of living together, more or less permanently, has occurred to Victoria too, and she has rejected it.

"I'm still an old-fashioned girl, Harry. If I have to go through all the rigmarole of living with a man again, he's going to be my husband."

"Yeah, well, that too," Harry says quickly. "I don't see any reason why not. We could get married. Just bring a note from your mother."

"My mother thinks you're a creep," Victoria says. Harry suddenly stands up. He drops to his knees beside the couch. He presses his fingers together and raises his hands beseechingly towards Victoria.

"Victoria Gwynneth Sommers, wilt thou have me?"

She does not answer. She is thinking that he needs a shave. Harry is one of those strange men who get all bristly before the day is over, but no matter how much Victoria complains, he won't shave in the evening unless he has to go out. And he's moody. The smart remarks hide many griefs and angers. Harry can change in an instant, right in front of you. You can never be sure what is coming next. Victoria takes Harry's face in her hands.

"Oh, yes," she says. She has no power to control what is coming out now. "Oh, yes, Harry, my darling. I would like to marry you."

They are lying stretched out on the couch now, Victoria resting on top of Harry, his arms around her, his hands resting in a proprietary fashion on her bottom. She can feel the rough heat of his fingers right through her clothes. She does not mind. She luxuriates in his possessiveness. She rests her cheek against his chest. The starched cotton broadcloth is stiff against her skin. She can feel his heart thumping.

"I'm thinking," Harry says.

"Don't."

"I can't help it."

"I'll kill you if you don't stop thinking."

"I'm seeing us a couple of years from now." He sounds frightened. Victoria has come to know that voice. When Harry is trying to be absolutely honest, all the disguises drop and he sounds like a squeaky little boy.

"Alcamo or some similar jerk is in there. And you're saying to yourself, 'I could have won that election. But I gave up everything for my husband.'"

Victoria does not answer. What he is saying is true. But why worry about it before she has to?

"You've spent almost ten years as a politician. You should play out the last round. Then you'll be free."

"What if I win?" Victoria says. She raises her head to look at him. She presses her chin into his chest. She wants to make him feel pain.

"I could win, you know. What then, Harry? Will you wait for me?"

"You make it sound like a jail sentence."

Victoria is cold and demanding.

"Will you be there for me?"

"I'll be there for you," Harry says. "I have taken the Queen's shilling and I am the Queen's man."

She pulls herself up to his face and kisses him. She presses her lips against his, making sure he takes in all of her.

"What if I don't want you?" she says. She rests her elbows on his chest and looks into his face. "A million things could happen."

"Don't I know it?" Harry says. "It's a risk I'll have to take."

"Then why, Harry?"

"Because we both have to start off free and clear," Harry says. He is still struggling to be totally honest; he sounds like somebody Victoria hardly knows. "I'm coming to you a free man. No attachments, no regrets—I don't owe anybody anything. You should be coming to me the same way."

Victoria feels she has been given an incredible gift. But there is no gratitude, only amazement. Who would have believed this of Harry Margulies?

"You really are liberated!" Victoria says. She is breathless with admiration.

"Naw, that's just feminist horseshit," Harry says. "I'm still thinking of myself, if you want to know the real truth. If you're happy and contented, you're going to make sure I feel happy and contented too. But if you've got all kinds of hidden regrets about marrying me, you're going to make my life miserable. So I'm still a selfish bastard."

"I'll take it," Victoria says and kisses him again. She has found her man. But then another thought occurs.

"I'm going to have to go like a bat out of hell. Will you help me?"

"What do you want me to do?"

"Everything!"

"I can't," Harry says. "I can't be seen too up-front. I'll do some of the financing. I'll be your bag man. Starting with Freddy Englander. He's a client of ours."

"Yuck!"

"You want to be mayor don't you?"

"Not that bad."

"Freddy's all right. You'll get to like him."

"Harry...enough. Let's go to bed."

"I thought you wanted to start planning. We've got a world to win."

"I want to go to bed."

"I guess we're both pretty beat."

"I'm not tired. I've just got to take care of you, that's all. You gave me another glass of Armagnac."

"Ah, yes. I almost forgot."

"I didn't forget. I'm an honest politician. I stay bought."

82

FROM a column by Bobby Mulloy in *The Daily News*:

...so Tuesday's announcement gives us the oddest couple in city politics.

While Sommers was facing the media gang in committee room four, standing in the glare of the TV lights announcing that she had decided to run for mayor, Fred Englander, the developer, was in the crowd, just a foot away from her.

And in the midst of telling us that she is in favour of non-profit housing, neighbourhood protection, a freeze on transit fares, group homes, and more open government, Sommers let drop that she also supports a new city concert hall.

"We need a showcase for our cultural diversity," was the way she put it. "It shows we're a world-class city."

The word in City Hall is that Englander is 100 per cent behind Sommers. With the money the developer and the concert-hall crowd can pull in, Sommers ought to have one heck of a war chest.

I managed to buttonhole Englander just before he dashed out of City Hall, and I asked how he could support the woman who fought developers on so many apartment rezonings.

Englander said, "The city needs leadership now and I believe Mrs. Sommers can provide it."

After the press conference, I went out to Alcamo headquarters in the west end. Alcamo is operating out of what used to be a bakery, and you can still smell fresh bread. There were stacks of lawn posters with Alcamo's handsome face on them, and a big bulletin board that took up most of one wall. Pinned up on it were the names of people who have volunteered to go out canvassing.

Municipal elections don't really start to heat up until after Labour Day, but it looks to me as though Alcamo has already got people working in every neighbourhood. There is the distinct feeling of a crusade about the Alcamo campaign.

"I only would have been surprised if Mrs. Sommers had decided not to run for mayor," Alcamo told me. "I think her announcement gives the voters a clear choice. I'm running because it's time newcomers to the city had a mayor who speaks for them."

Bong...end of round one. But it looks like, for the first time in years, we are going to have a knock-'em-down, drag-'em-out fight for mayor of Toronto.

83

"WHEN I'M FEELING sad and lonely, Mother Mary comforts me, speaking words of wisdom, let it be...let it be..." Annabel Warren sits beside Dane Harrison, holding fiercely to his arm. The Beatles song they are singing together stirs so many memories, the old peace movement, her ragged hippie days on Yorkville...

Dane and Annabel and Annabel's son, Paul, have just spent a week in a rented farmhouse east of Toronto. The speedometer on the Harrison station wagon says they are moving at barely forty miles an hour and they haven't even got down to Highway 401 yet. Dane said they could beat the Labour Day traffic by getting away early, but even these old concession roads in the country are already packed.

Dane doesn't really mind the slowness. He is in no hurry to get back to Toronto. Tomorrow he will have to face Harry Margulies and say, "No," finally and decisively. Dane has been waffling all summer, but tomorrow he and Harry will begin their regular monthly lunches again, and Harry wants an answer. Well, Dane cannot do what Harry has asked him, indeed almost begged him, to do. Dane simply cannot take a leave of absence from his job and run Victoria's mayoral campaign.

Dane is not one of those naive souls who still insist that politics can be separated from urban planning, which is, after all, mostly concerned with setting limits for developers. Of course, planning is intertwined with politics. But the planner must never actually become a politician. A planner must never be the instigator. That is the lesson Dane learned from the disaster of the Hanover Street Mall.

Dane Harrison never set out to be an urban planner. In fact, it is the last thing he ever imagined himself doing. But now that he's here, he's going to do it properly. The proper role for a planner is to give advice to those elected to wield power. And then get out of the way and let them make the decision.

So Dane must make Harry understand that, even though he thinks of Victoria as a good friend, Dane cannot be seen as favouring one elected official over another. If Victoria lost, or even if she won, Dane would be compromised. He would be known as part of a clique. His advice would be seen as tainted. His usefulness as a planner would be destroyed.

Annabel leans against his shoulder, and together they sing the old Phil Ochs song, one of their favourites, as they take their place in the line of cars creeping up the cloverleaf to climb on to Highway 401.

"Call it peace or call it treason...call it love or call it reason...but I ain't a marching any more..."

In the seat behind Dane and Annabel, Paul Warren stares gloomily out the car window. It is not the prospect of returning to school that troubles him. The summer has dragged on long enough, and he will be happy to see his friends again. But the beginning of school always means a visit to Kernohan.

This time the doctor wants him to come into the hospital for three days. He says it is just for tests, but Paul can tell that Kernohan thinks he is getting big enough for the operation that will finally cure the weak spot in Paul's heart. When he was a kid, Paul longed for the day when Kernohan would say to him, "Yes, the time has come." Now, Paul dreads it.

He has become a good hockey player, and last year he played tackle for the Pierce Park Spartans. This fall, if Kernohan clears him again, Paul is going for quarterback. It's what everybody expects, and Paul kind of wants it too. But he also wishes there were some way he could get out of it.

On the afternoon school closed for the summer, Paul and six of his friends lugged a case of beer to a house where the parents were both safely out working. The boys drank and talked all afternoon. They agreed that they had learned more, and changed more, in grade eleven than they would have ever thought possible. In the fall, when they all go into grade twelve, they will be ready to take over the school.

But Paul knows that his own position in the group depends on his being a jock. He is pretty sure no one would be interested in him—they probably wouldn't even like him—if he wasn't good at sports. So if he wants to be part of the gang that is going to run the school, Paul Warren had better be out there, playing football and hockey.

But Paul doesn't care about sports any more. He doesn't want to keep going to football practice every day after school all through September and October and then, as soon as football's over, start getting up at five in the morning to go to hockey practice. Paul has to concede he doesn't know what else he would like to be doing. He is just tired of sports.

But as long as Kernohan and the operation are still ahead of him, life is not complicated. He has to keep up with sports because he must be in good condition so he will be able to get over the surgery quickly. But what if Kernohan tells him this is the time for the operation? This Labour Day, Paul Warren feels himself being drawn relentlessly towards a series of decisions he is not ready to make.

The water spreads out in erupting ripples, then the head of Devorah Ishmaeli breaks above the surface, gasping for breath. She pushes the goggles up onto her forehead and swims over to the motorboat she had anchored close to the rocky shore. What a delicious day. Devorah has Pine Lake all to herself. All the other cottagers have loaded their cars, put up their shutters for the winter, and returned to thc city.

Devorah has been spending a week up at her father's old cabin, and she has not really decided yet when she will go back to Toronto. After an Israeli kibbutz where everybody is always on top of everybody else, the Muskoka woods, so empty and peaceful, are like a drug. She cannot get enough of being here. Devorah has gone swimming every day, puttered around the silent, mysterious inlets in her motorboat and, in the evening, built herself a roaring fire and worked on jigsaw puzzles.

Shabbos came and went. Devorah told herself she was going to drive over to one of the nearby Jewish summer camps and take part in whatever kind of Saturday-morning service they were having. Instead, she went for a walk in the woods on Saturday morning and tried to think about nature. And she is not being careful about what she eats. Devorah is not consciously violating Jewish dietary laws, but there is no way she can be certain of the purity of the food she has picked up in the Huntsville supermarket.

Devorah feels herself suspended in time. When she talked last to Moshe, he told her not to worry about the baby. The people in the kibbutz nursery are looking after her very well. Moshe sees the baby in the morning and spends every evening with her. Stay and get things settled for Gideon, Moshe said. Then you can come home.

Moshe's voice sounded faint and angry over the long-distance connection. It did not sound like a voice belonging to anyone Devorah knows. She promised dutifully to stay in the city until Harry signs the adoption release paper. But if Harry does not give in soon, Devorah is not sure she will have the strength to go back to Israel.

A soul-satisfying crack and the little white golf ball goes arcing into the air. Peter Dagenham remains holding the gourd-shaped driver upright like a sword, watching the ball disappear for a moment into the white sun and come down again. Then, satisfied that his drive has landed well short of the winding creek and that he will have a sensible approach shot to the green, Dagenham hands the club to his caddie and sets off with his partner, Fred Englander.

Fred, he is sure, must appreciate being here today. This is the first time the developer has ever been on the Elmwood course, even though his home overlooks the fourteenth hole. Dagenham feels a bit like a master of ceremonies. You see, Fred, this is one of the rewards that public service brings—an afternoon on a rich, green sanctuary right in the heart of Toronto while the rest of the world is still out there, crawling home through the miserable Labour Day traffic. Not too many years ago, it would have been unthinkable for a Jew to step on to the fairways of Elmwood—no matter how rich or important he might be.

But Fred Englander is something special. Everybody concedes that his financing package for the concert hall is brilliant. People are being told that the building will cost $149 million. The concert hall committee is asking the government to put up $99 million, and then the committee will raise the additional $50 million themselves with a high energy, public campaign.

However, the actual construction cost of the new building will be just under $100 million. The additional money will be used for an endowment fund. If Fred Englander's plans work out, the government contribution will pay for building the new hall and the endowment fund will pay for operating it. But what if the public campaign doesn't bring in enough money to maintain the concert hall? What will the politicians do then? Well, as Fred has explained at confidential meetings of the concert hall committee, there is no way on God's green earth the government is going to let this wonderful new showcase for Canadian talent—the pride of Toronto—go dark and close.

To get the political side in motion, Fred got Victoria Sommers to endorse the concert hall, and he has been working hard to get her elected mayor. It's a parlay, Fred says. To get something as big as the concert hall going, you have to get money from all levels of government—the city, the region, the province, and the feds. But they all like to hang back, waiting for the other guy to make a commitment. So Fred's alliance with Victoria Sommers will, if she wins, nail down the city's share, and then the other players will have to kick in too.

Peter did have some misgivings when Fred explained how he was going to start raising money from the private sector. Fred almost emptied the committee's treasury to take an option on a twenty-acre site near the old port. The concert hall wouldn't need more than a quarter of that land, and Fred said he was going to start selling off parts of it to guys looking for places to put up condominiums. Being right next to the beautiful new concert hall would make these high-prestige locations.

Peter Dagenham thought, Oh yeah, this is where little Freddy Englander takes a little for himself. But Fred, as usual, was way ahead of him. Fred said, in a full Concert Hall Board of Directors meeting, that the concert hall would get killed if Premier Developments were seen to be building anything anywhere near it. Fred wouldn't even allow any other Jewish developers to buy land. He went to the new, upcoming Italian developers—the "tylainers," Fred calls them. Peter Dagenham is pleased to tell people that Fred Englander is as clean as a hound's tooth. And one of the smartest businessmen it has ever been Peter Dagenham's pleasure to know.

He's a pretty good golfer too. He's figured out the tricky, split-level sixteenth green, and his putt, a twenty-footer, breaks just when it looks like it's going too far, and rolls downhill into the cup. Fred lifts his head and smiles gleefully. That's his fourth par of the day and unless Peter Dagenham pulls his socks up on the next two holes, Peter is going to be paying for drinks when they finish this round.

They move onto the seventeenth tee and have to sit on the bench while the foursome ahead drives off. From here, they can see the sprawling old white clapboard clubhouse that is so distinctively Elmwood. Peter Dagenham decides the time has come.

"You know, Fred, you're so close to this place you really ought to consider joining," Peter says.

"I don't know when I'd have time," Fred says. "I already belong to Oakdale."

Oakdale, Dagenham knows, is the original all-Jewish course in the west end of North York. It's quite a nice place; Peter Dagenham has been a guest there himself a couple of times. But what he is proposing now to Fred is something more than just joining a golf club and he wonders if Fred fully understands it.

"You know, Fred, since you started this concert hall business you've made a lot of friends in this place. Some of them have been saying to me it's time I got you to join old Elmwood."

Fred Englander looks amused. In fact, Peter Dagenham has the distinctly uncomfortable feeling that if Fred were not such a naturally polite person, he'd be laughing out loud.

"You think that's why I'm doing the concert hall?" Fred asks. "So I can become a big shot?"

"No, of course not," Dagenham says quickly. "It's just that...well...a lot of people have got to know you, Fred, and we'd like to have you with us."

"I appreciate the offer, but I'd just be wasting the membership money; I'd never get time to play here." Fred says. "And if anybody asks, you tell them I'm doing the concert hall just for fun, Peter. And because I like the kind of shows they're going to put on there. So let's leave it at that, okay?"

Harry Margulies said they should be smart and wait until evening to drive back into the city. The cottagers would all be home by then because they like to get in early and start getting the kids ready for school. But here it is ten o'clock at night and Harry is being held down to fifty miles an hour. Harry's snappy little BMW is just one more set of headlights on Highway 401, coming into the city from the west. Victoria leans against his shoulder, sleeping contentedly. They have been out at the Elora Inn for the weekend, and Harry's strategy for going back late allowed them to take one more walk around the old-fashioned shops in the town and to have a quiet supper. Most other guests had already left. Harry and Victoria had the dining-room to themselves. They sat, holding hands, at a window table and looked out at the Elora Gorge, where floodlights illuminate the Grand River tumbling wildly through the gigantic rocks. Tomorrow the world begins again. Victoria starts campaigning in earnest, and Harry has a full desk waiting for him at Carlton and Boggs. Who knows when Harry and Victoria will have this much time alone again?

J. Arthur Quinn had planned to spend the Labour Day weekend enjoying the sun and the small wooded island he owns up north, in Georgian Bay. But he has spent all Saturday, Sunday, and Labour Day itself, in his corner office, being chilled to the bone by overzealous air-conditioning. But at least he has made a political point. The younger lawyers have seen that the old man who still wants to run the firm is working just as hard over the holiday as they are. And, Quinn is sure, they have noted the darkened door of Charlie McConnachie's office.

Not too many of these young fellows are full partners and will be able to vote in Quinn's favour. But they can still talk, and a buildup of favourable gossip will be helpful. Harry Margulies has assured him of that.

Quinn has been looking at Harry's proposal and savouring it. Like everything Harry does, this is thoughtful and contains something for everybody. It should be enough to keep McConnachie at bay. But old Charlie can be a kicker and gouger too, when he wants to be.

Over this long, tedious weekend, the thought has often occurred to Quinn: why me? Who appointed Jackie Duhamel, the poor, awkward farmboy from Nova Scotia, to preserve this old Upper Canada law firm? He is an old man with a bad heart. Why not just get out? Who appointed him to save these fools from their own greed and cupidity?

Because…he has done well here. Carlton and Boggs let Jackie Duhamel become "The Mighty Quinn." The system has been good to him. So as long as he is still around, J. Arthur Quinn will work to keep the system going. Maybe that makes him the kind of old fuddy-duddy conservative he used to despise. If so, Quinn can live with that thought. He knows he is simply paying a debt. Sammy Englander would have understood. Quinn wishes again that he could still have lunch at United Bakers with Reb Shmuel and talk about business and the state of the world. But so many people, like Reb Shmuel and old Windy Boggs, who were once so important in Quinn's life are gone now.

It is almost midnight. Quinn peeks out his office door. Only two other offices are still lit up. He has shown the flag enough over this long weekend; he ought to go home now. Lord, he is tired. When all this is over he is going to grant himself a long vacation. Maybe he will go to France and make another tour of three-star restaurants. The doctors would tell him such indulgence could be suicidal. But what the hell? What's the good of being at the top if you don't enjoy your life?

Turning up Bay Street, Quinn feels suddenly afraid. He is the only person there. At this hour, at the end of Labour Day, the financial centre of the country is empty. The enormous office towers block out the light of the moon and stars, and the sidewalk of Bay Street is as dark as a cavern. Surely no mugger would bother coming down here at this hour. But how can Quinn be sure? Quinn becomes aware of how narrow his own experience is. The city is full of people now who are crazy beyond his comprehension. He begins to walk more quickly. The clicking of his heels on the cement sounds like gun shots. Quinn is almost running, clutching his thick attaché case to his side. He shouldn't be doing this, not with his bad heart. But he can't help himself. He sees a light. The upper windows of the Simcoe Club are glowing. Sanctuary is only a few feet away. Quinn is panting now.

Quinn becomes aware of a loud bang. He can feel it run like an electric shock into his chest. A shower of tiny lights is falling over downtown. Then another bang. And another. The sky is filled with a cascade of pretty pink and white little fires. Quinn feels foolish. He pauses at the door of the Simcoe Club to catch his breath and enjoy the spectacle. The fireworks are coming from the grandstand of the Canadian National Exhibition. They are celebrating the last day of the great fair and the final hour of Labour Day. Turning his key in the great black door of the Simcoe Club, Quinn reflects that the Jews are right about time, as they are about so many things. The end of summer is really the beginning of the new year.

84

THE TROUBLE with people in politics is that they are too damned cynical, even the so-called reformers who gather around Victoria Sommers. Fred Englander watches them in action at the beginning of September and decides he had better start getting into things a lot more himself, even though, officially, he is still responsible only for fund-raising. But somebody has to do something, because it's clear to Fred and the concert hall committee that Victoria is going to get killed on election day—and their concert hall will die with her.

The signs are there in black and white. Fred commissioned a poll, four hundred telephone calls placed the weekend after Labour Day. The results showed 41 per cent of the voters would pick Alcamo, while only 29 per cent would choose Victoria. A frightening 30 per cent have no opinion at all.

The shaken campaign committee decided Victoria needed to develop some new positions. When Fred told Peter Dagenham about it, Peter laughed and said, "You'd think Victoria was a hooker." Sitting quietly in a corner of Victoria's City Hall office listening to the campaign committee in action, Fred decided there was more truth in Peter's smart crack than he realized.

Take the way Victoria's brain trust handled the controversy over non-profit housing. Since he did the non-profit project in Scarborough that earned Premier the right to build Eton Towers on Cotswold Street, Fred has done three more non-profit projects and he understands how they work. Most people pay "low-end-of-market rent," which usually means they have a job of some kind and are reasonably stable. Only about one-third of the people in a non-profit are real down-and-outers and take handouts from the government.

But many city homeowners still think all the people who live in non-profit housing are on welfare and must be muggers, drug addicts, and prostitutes. So they don't want non-profit housing anywhere near them. And even though they have always admired Victoria Sommers for helping to stop the Berryman Expressway and standing up to developers, they'll turn on her if they think she's pushing housing projects on them.

The campaign committee decided that Victoria should say Toronto has taken more than its fair share of non-profit housing. It's time the suburbs and the outlying regional municipalities, like Durham and Mississauga, started accepting some too.

So Victoria is not backing down from her commitment to non-profit housing, not one iota. But she is also delivering a coded message to Toronto homeowners. She thinks non-profit housing should be built out beyond the city's borders.

Victoria's position paper on the concert hall says opera is no longer an élitist entertainment, and she is insisting one-third of the tickets in the new hall be offered at affordable prices.

Fred nearly hit the roof when he heard that one. But they explained to him that Victoria was not saying her support actually *depended* on affordable ticket prices. All she wants is to make sure a few places are kept for those poor, starving students who really love music—even if these have to be only standing room. Mr. Englander can live with that, can't he?

When it came to group homes, at least, Fred expected Victoria to come out swinging. Victoria had told him privately that group homes were the reason she was running for mayor. Fred had felt a renewed respect for Victoria. After all, who has suffered more than Fred Englander from people trying to lock up their neighbourhoods? Fred felt that he and Victoria agreed not only about the concert hall, but about basic principles too.

People should have the right to live anywhere they want to.

So Fred was astonished when Victoria's position paper said she was in favour of *controlling* group homes. No more of this spot rezoning that allows them to pop up anywhere. Group homes should be licensed by the city and made to keep 1,000 feet away from each other.

It was, again, a double message. People who favoured group homes would know that Victoria was really on their side. But people who were afraid of group homes would also understand that, as mayor, Victoria would not allow their neighbourhoods to be overrun.

Marlene and her husband, Steve Bukowski, the social worker, a couple who looked as though they never got out into the sunlight, spent whole days composing these position papers. Fred said the papers were very good, but he didn't think people would be very interested. The campaign committee thanked him and ignored his advice. It turned out, though, that Fred was right. Marlene and Steve planned to release one position paper a week so that Victoria could get steady exposure. The media guys turned out in force for the press conference on non-profit housing, but all Victoria got out of it was thirty seconds on the 6:30 city newscast and 3.7 inches on the city page of *The Daily News*. For the press conference on the concert hall, the media crowd was smaller and much younger. Fred could see they were sending green kids now to cover Victoria. And all she got out of it was a small mention in Bobby Mulloy's column. Fred decided the time had finally come for him to speak up.

"I may not know much about getting people elected," he tells Victoria's campaign committee, "but I've sold a lot of houses in my day. And one thing I've learned is, you've got to be absolutely honest with people. The public are not stupid. They can tell if something isn't right the minute they hear it. So you've got to believe yourself in what you're saying."

They thank Fred for his concern and set to work on their next set of position papers, more day care, holding down property taxes, and building more public transportation. Fred can see these reformers are incurably arrogant. Priests and ministers have been lecturing people for thousands of years. How much good have they ever done? Yet the people around Victoria still think they can get her elected mayor by delivering sermons.

Fred gets together with concert hall supporters and they form the Committee to Elect Victoria Sommers. All by themselves, they raise money for an advertising blitz. Fred Englander takes it upon himself to personally supervise the campaign.

The first big newspaper ad comes out on October 9. A full page shows Victoria in a delicate but businesslike white dress, standing in front of a group of businessmen, all in dark suits. There, smiling and talking, and looking as though they have been caught unawares in a moment of great fun are Tommy Lee, president of the Chinese Canadian Professional Association, Mel Swarbrick from Green Flag cabs, Gerry Campbell, president of Meadow Lark Homes, Neil Ward, chairman of Neil Ward Real Estate, and at least twenty others—including Peter Dagenham and Fred Englander himself. The copy says simply, "People who care about the future care about Victoria Sommers."

The next ad, which takes up huge billboards all over the city, shows Victoria in a white blouse and string of pearls, but this time wearing a red blazer with a city crest on the breast pocket. People who are familiar with downtown joke that Victoria looks like one of the tour guides who take people around City Hall.

The ad agency has brought together a tall, muscular black man who looks like a basketball player; a woman in a sari; a Native Canadian with his hair in braids; a Chinese man in a business suit; a Japanese woman in a kimono; a couple of curly-headed, swarthy guys in heavy sweaters who could be Italian or Portuguese; a hook-nosed, coffee-coloured woman who Fred was told comes from Chile; a fair-skinned woman with slick blonde hair who represents Scandinavia, and white people in general; a Sikh in a turban; a French Canadian with a red toque; and, at Fred's insistence, a dark, sensitive young man with a black skull cap and the traditional long curls hanging down the sides of his forehead.

But the best part, the touch that Victoria herself thought up, is the child at the front. His name is Lonny and he's obviously a Mongoloid idiot but so sweet-looking your heart goes out to him. Victoria has her arm protectively around the boy. Again there is only one line of copy: "Victoria Sommers, a mayor who cares."

The concert hall, Fred's personal stake in this campaign, is given the place of honour, the television ads. Victoria is shown looking at the architect's drawing, walking across a stage, visiting an opera rehearsal and the ballet school, and promising the performers she will work to give them a home where people can enjoy coming to see them.

The private poll taken two weeks after the advertising campaign begins shows that Victoria has, indeed, gone from 31 to 35 per cent. But Alcamo has gone to 44 per cent. His message that it's time the new immigrants had a mayor of their own is getting through. And there are barely four weeks left until election day.

85

THE LEAVES are just beginning to turn. From where he is standing on a hill in Eglinton Park, Dane can see daubs of vivid red, orange, and golden yellow leaves replacing dark green on the branches of the maple trees of north Toronto. He really must try to get Annabel and Paul up to Algonquin Park on the weekend. The air is colder up north of the Muskoka lakes, and the fall colours will be glorious. But right now, he should be concentrating on the football game on the field below him.

Dane has become something he would have laughed at just a few years ago, a football father. But why not? One of the rewards of being a deputy chief planner in charge of a whole section of the city is that he doesn't have to account to anybody for his time. So why not come up to Eglinton Park if nothing much is going on in the office? The Spartans' coach is trying Paul out as quarterback this afternoon. And Paul, even though he never asks, does appreciate it when his parents take the trouble to come and see him play.

He has the ball again. Two ends from the other team have broken through the scrimmage line. Paul is moving to the left, desperately looking for a receiver. He decides to run it out. More of the other team have broken through. They have white sweaters. They drag Paul down. They are all over him. The whistle blows. The boys in the white sweaters pull themselves up. The red Spartan sweater is still lying on the ground. The other boys are turning to look at Paul. The coach is coming onto the field. Dane begins to run down the hill.

As Dane describes the scene later that day to Harry Margulies, his whole future flashed in front of him the way a person's whole past is supposed to flash in front of them, just before the end. He saw himself a broken, bitter, solitary old man.

"I could've kept Paul off the team. He came to me this year to sign the papers. I asked him how things looked. He said everything looked okay, but he didn't think he would play next year. He was delivering a message, Harry, only I was too stupid to pick it up. All I said back to him was, 'If this is your last year, make it a good one,' and I signed for him. If I wasn't so fucking wrapped up in myself, I'd have said,'So if you don't want to play football next year, why are you playing this year? Don't you like it any more?' That's what he was trying to tell me. He wanted to quit. But he needed my permission. He's been playing football because he thinks that's what we want him to do. If I'd said, 'No, it doesn't matter any more,' he'd have given the whole thing up. How the hell am I ever going to tell any of that to Annabel. Paul could die!"

They are walking around City Hall Square. Dane couldn't bear to stay in the hospital any longer. Kernohan came out and told Dane and Annabel that, as far as he could tell, Paul's heart was going to be all right. There were signs of strain around the weak spot in the muscle wall but, so far, no haemorrhaging. He's going to keep Paul in intensive care overnight so he'll be under constant supervision. In the morning, Kernohan will take more X-rays, run more tests. If there's no more damage than they've seen so far, Paul should be able to go home.

Annabel insisted on staying on in the waiting-room. Even if she can't see Paul, she can at least be close to him. Dane tried to get her to come home, and she told him he should leave if he wanted to. Dane sat down beside her and held her hand. But then he began to feel that she didn't really want him there. Dane was in the way. He found a pay phone in the corridor and called Harry Margulies.

"Annabel still treats me like an outsider. Even after all these years. It's not right. I raised Paul. I'm more his father than anyone else is. You know how you'd feel if something happened to Gordon."

Harry suggests they get something to eat. They have been walking around the square for over an hour and it's starting to get dark. Dane says he's not hungry. Then, what about going for a drink?

"I don't want to take up your whole night, Harry."

"I've got nothing on, Dane. It's all right."

"I'm really glad you're here. I thought you'd stop talking to me."

"Good Lord, why?"

"Because of Victoria."

"Don't be an ass, Dane."

But the truth is, Victoria was hurt and angry. She talked about all the times she had worked with Dane and how she had defended him after the disaster of the Hanover Street Mall when everybody else on City Council wanted to nail his hide to the wall. Victoria said she didn't understand how Dane could say "no" to her now, when Victoria needed him so much. But Harry doesn't go into any of that. He tells Dane only that Marlene, who used to work in Victoria's office, and her husband, Steve Bukowski, have taken over the campaign. Dane shouldn't worry. Victoria's doing fine.

"Let's go over to the Long Bar," Harry says. "It's closest."

86

HOW LONG the telephone has been ringing, Dane cannot say. The ringing merged with a very involved dream and it seemed to take forever to realize that the sound was coming from outside of himself. Now he cannot even remember what the dream was about and he is standing with the phone stupidly in his hand.

"Mr. Harrison? This is James Kernohan."

Why is the doctor whispering? Where is Kernohan? Dane looks down at his wrist. His new digital watch is flashing in the darkness of his tiny bedroom: A.M. 2:11:26

"Mr. Harrison, can you hear me?"

"Yes, I can hear you. What's going on? Is everything okay?"

"No, it's not. Paul's haemorrhaging. We're going in. I've ordered the room ready and the people. Anaesthetist'll be here in a couple of minutes. Krishna Bhokar, best in the business."

Dane feels his chest tightening. He is awake now but he it still resisting what Kernohan is trying to tell him.

"I just saw Paul," Dane says suspiciously. "I was there this afternoon."

"I know. He was fine all day. I just came by now, just to check. He's losing blood. The hole's small. If it was big, he'd already be gone by now. Probably smaller than a pinprick. But we can't take a chance. It could blow any second..."

Kernohan leaves it hanging, but Dane now understands, clearly, starkly, what the doctor is telling him.

"Thank you for calling," Dane says. But what's the point? Get on with it! "Do what you think is best, doctor."

"Mr. Harrison, there is something I have to say to you. I wasn't supposed to be here tonight. I was on my way home. I was with my curling team. Our monthly dinner. There was a lot of booze. I had a lot to drink."

"Oh, Jesus," Dane says.

"I've called another heart man. Herb Applebaum. Good guy. Knows his stuff." Kernohan is talking too fast now. His words are bumping into each other. "But I should do it. I know Paul. Been with him from the start. I know this procedure. Better than anyone. I should do it. But if you want Applebaum, that's okay. Herb's good. One of the best."

"Oh, Jesus," Dane says again. His own head is still aching from all the beer he drank with Harry Margulies.

"You've got to tell me what you want, Mr. Harrison. Right now."

Dane holds the receiver in his hand, waiting for a sign. He should wake Annabel. But what would Annabel know more than Dane does? It's got to be Kernohan. This other guy may be a genius, but he's a stranger. Kernohan has looked after Paul since Paul was a little baby. No one could care more about Paul. It's got to be Kernohan.

"That's fine, doctor," Dane says, in the measured tones he had used earlier, as though by sounding confident himself he could exorcise the last residue of drunkenness in the surgeon. "You do the operation yourself. That's what we want."

"Dane, thank you."

Kernohan sounds like he is crying. How the hell is he going to perform open-heart surgery? Dane thinks Oh, no! Stop! I've made a terrible mistake! But before he can get the words out, there is a click, and

Kernohan is gone. Dane is alone in his silent house.

He returns to the bedroom. Annabel has always been a restless sleeper, and now, in the middle of the night, she has wriggled free of the bedclothes. Her thick white shoulders are bare; her face lies heavily against the pillow. Dane longs to wake her up and lie down beside her. This is a time when they ought to be clinging together, sheltering each other. But how will waking Annabel help Paul? Let Annabel sleep. She will need all of her strength in the morning.

Dane goes down to his den. This room in which he once took so much pride now seems to mock him. There is the solid oak schoolteacher's desk and the old-fashioned oak bookcase with the windowed doors that slide up and back, all treasures that he and Annabel found in their trips through antique stores and flea markets. When they found this little two-storey row house, an old working-man's cottage just up the street from what had once been a tractor factory, Annabel said it was perfect for them. She has spent endless hours stripping paint off the wooden sideboards and putting up striped wall-paper to give the house what she calls "a perfect Edwardian look." The small square house with its long rooms is just the right size, Annabel likes to say, for three people. God save him from what will it be like if there are only two people here. Dane sits down at his desk, flips on the brass gooseneck lamp, and starts going through the items on the agenda for the planning board meeting. It's going to be a long night.

87

ANNABEL wakes up slowly, reaches out, and is pleased to discover she is alone in the bed. She lies still, straining her senses, and is soon rewarded. A delicious smell is drifting into the room. Dane must be down in the kitchen, making coffee. Bringing her coffee in bed is one of the nice little things Dane does for Annabel.

She really must be kinder to him. When these days of worrying so much about her son are past, Annabel promises herself, she will make amends to

Dane. When Dane came home late at night and reached out for her, she started to move towards him but discovered that he was reeking of beer, and she turned away.

There was a time, and it was not so long ago, when she would have opened up and taken Dane into herself no matter what condition he was in. Annabel was pretty sure that last night the time was ripe for baby making. But then again, she can't be sure. Annabel has stopped keeping track of her insides as closely as she once did. She is no longer so sure that she wants to go through raising another child. And she certainly no longer feels she must always be there when her man wants her to be. When Annabel is upset and frightened, she doesn't want a smelly, befuddled man pounding away at her.

It sometimes amuses Annabel to reflect that the apple didn't fall far from the tree after all. True, she ran away at sixteen and did more dope and balled more boys than her mother would have ever dreamed possible. But Annabel's life now is not so different from the one her mother lived when she was Annabel's age.

Annabel's mother stayed home because ladies didn't work. Annabel stays home because she doesn't care about money and Dane has assured her that what he earns is more than enough to support their modest lifestyle. Annabel's mother volunteered for the Junior League because, she said, it was fun, and because people who have been privileged in life should help others. Annabel puts in three afternoons a week at the Peter Rabbit Play Centre because she says the welfare moms who come there are victims of the system. Annabel's mother took piano lessons and sang in the Rosedale United Church choir in order to improve her appreciation of music. Annabel is taking a university extension course in educational philosophy in order to improve her mind.

One of these days Annabel is going to go home and give her mother a big hug. But right now, she just wants a cup of coffee. Damn Dane. He has got into the morning paper and forgotten all about her. Annabel turns herself out of the bed and pulls on an old tartan bathrobe. Most likely Dane is punishing her by not bringing the coffee up to the bedroom this morning. Well, Annabel can't be too mad at him.

Dane is at the kitchen table. Annabel is surprised to see he is already fully dressed—shirt, tie, and the neat blue suit he likes to wear for planning board meetings. Dane has the thick planning board agenda on the table before him, but he is not looking at it. He is just staring ahead of him. Annabel goes to the stove and pours herself a cup of coffee.

"Dane, I'm sorry," she says. "But if you come on smelling like a brewery, you can't expect me to feel very romantic."

"They're operating on Paul," Dane says quietly. Annabel stands by the sink, frozen, waiting for him to go on.

"Kernohan called last night. Paul was haemorrhaging. He said they had to do it right away."

"Oh my God!" Annabel cries. "Why didn't you get me up? What time did he call?"

"Two-thirty. Three, maybe."

"Dane, for God's sake! It's seven o'clock!"

Dane turns to her. He did not realize how much time has gone by.

"I thought about it," he says. "But then I decided it would be better to leave you. How would it help Paul to have two of us sitting here, going nuts?"

"You had no right!"

Annabel thought she was so safe. She has tried so hard to be a good person. Surely in return the gods ought to protect her. Now she knows for sure something her mother didn't know. You are never safe. Everything you have can be snatched away from you in an instant.

"I'm going down to the hospital," Annabel says.

"I can't take just sitting there," Dane says. "I'm going to the office. Call me as soon as you hear anything."

Annabel wants to say to him, Come with me today. Please, I'm going to need you today. But instead she goes up to the bedroom to get dressed.

88

A SURGEON'S MIND should be clear as a beam of light. But James Kernohan's mind is murky with fury at himself. Why in God's name did he tell the kid's father he'd had a few drinks? A surgeon has to concentrate everything he knows, everything he has, on one sublime purpose—saving human life; instead, James Kernohan has placed his own life in the hands of another man. If the kid goes, Dane Harrison will come after him; Kernohan himself would do no less. It won't matter a hoot that Harrison gave his consent knowing the condition Kernohan was in. He will want retribution. The world will hear that James Kernohan walked into an operating room half-drunk—more than half-drunk if the whole truth comes out.

This has been going on too long. Kernohan can sense the people around him beginning to wilt. The wall clock reads 8:37. They have been at this nearly five goddamned hours. The energy is gone; the room is flat, stale. At the beginning of a procedure everyone is high, pumped full of adrenalin. Kernohan will match the heart team he has built up against any team in the world. But muscle and bone and the synapses of the brain have their limits. Who knows that better than doctors? Kernohan pulled his people out in the middle of the night. Now it is day, bright sunlight is shining somewhere out there, and they are still locked in this freezing, blood-spattered room.

The kid's arteries and veins were too small. He looked mature because playing sports has given him a good build. But he's too young. He should not be in here. It has taken hours and hours and hours. For open heart you have to detour everything, hook all the pipes up to machines and bypasses. It is like trying to clear a dry spot in the middle of a jungle in the midst of a typhoon. Arteries rolled off Kernohan's instruments again and again and again. Veins shrank back into their boggy hiding places.

But now the heart sits bare and dark red, as dry as it's ever going to be. The kid is waiting for him. They are all waiting for him. Oh, God look at it, worse than he ever dreamed. Nobody will ever be able to say Kernohan shouldn't have gone in. But now its time for the patch. Straightforward stuff. Easier than closing a skate slash from a hockey game. But Kernohan finds he has no strength. His arms are clumsy, wooden—puppet's arms. He has never felt so tired in his whole life.

Kernohan's fingers are beginning to tremble. He can't make them stop. Desperate now, he offers up a vow. If God will give him Paul Warren, he will never touch another drop. He has made that promise before, of course, and gone back on it. But his job is saving human lives in terrible circumstances.

He could never keep going if he couldn't take relief from the bottle now and then. But this time Kernohan means what he says. If God will let Paul Warren live, James Benedict Kernohan will never go near the booze again. That's doing it. We're getting there. A stitch at a time. Nothing to get excited about. Kernohan begins to hum to himself. Someone is tapping on Kernohan's arm. His concentration is so intense he doesn't even feel it. The fingers grip. Krishna Bohar, the anaesthetist, and his eyes above the green mask are terrified. The dials. Kris's goddamned dials are sinking back. Kernohan cries out, "No!" The dials keep falling. The child is dying under his hands. Kernohan's rage crashes against the tiled walls: "No! Damn you! No!"

89

ON ENTERING the elevator that will carry him from the parking garage under City Hall up to his office on the nineteenth floor, Dane considers whether he should tell his colleagues and the politicians he will be seeing today about the strain he is under. He decides it would be wiser to say nothing. Everybody would be sympathetic, but later they might use it against him. They'd urge him to rush to the hospital, and then Dane might find himself being expected to do little favours for people he doesn't like because they were kind to him when he was having personal difficulties. The fewer debts one owes in City Hall, the better.

Dane studies his taut face in the mirrored walls of the elevator. The rosy cheeks, proud accomplishments of his week on the farm, have faded. His skin is taking on again its customary, translucent, City Hall pallor. His ghostly image bounces between the mirrored walls, growing smaller with each iteration, until it becomes so small, Dane cannot even make himself out. He is just a sliver of colour on the way to infinity. But Dane is suddenly aware that he is not alone. This is impossible, because he can see clearly in the mirrors that there is no one here but himself.

Daddy, I'm tired. I want to come home.

You have to go back, Pauly, Dane says.

Daddy, I can't make it.

Yes, you can, Pauly. Go back.

Oh, Daddy, I'm so tired.

You have to fight, Pauly. You can do it. You're going to be fine. But you have to go back now.

Dane feels Paul slipping away from him. The lights flash the number 19; Dane has reached the first of the three floors occupied by the planning department. The silvery doors open and he steps out. It was the first time in all their years together that Paul ever called him "Daddy." Dane turns around and marches right back into the elevator.

Annabel is at the far end of the waiting-room. She is talking to Kernohan. The big red-haired doctor looks too serious. But when he sees Dane approaching he lets go with a foolish, happy grin. Yes, Paul's fine. He's going to be okay. He's still out. Dane and Annabel can come back and see him tonight. But the heart looks terrific. Beating like a little baby's. Dane begins to cry. He can't help himself. Kernohan puts his arm around him. The doctor puts his arm around Annabel too. The three of them are holding onto each other and crying together.

Dane takes Annabel home. Before they go upstairs to rest though, he calls Harry Margulies.

"How's Paul? Is the kid okay?"

"He's fine, Harry. They did the operation last night. Paul's in great shape."

"That's wonderful, Dane. I'm really happy for you."

"Harry...does Victoria still need a manager?"

"We're doing all right, Dane. Marlene and Steve have got everything under control."

"Harry, if you still want me, I'm your man. I'll get my leave of absence in the morning and I'll be in the campaign office by the afternoon."

"I'll come by and see you there. Thanks, Dane."

Dane smiles to himself; Harry is too smart to ask for reasons. Probably he already knows. But what does Dane Harrison have in the world? Annabel, Paul, a few friends. He will bind these people to him. There is nothing he could be doing that is more important than that.

90

FRED ENGLANDER did more for this concert hall crowd than anyone ever did, and now they have turned on him and made him an outsider. And the worst of it is, they don't even know what they have done. If Fred tried to explain the hurt they are inflicting right now, they wouldn't even begin to understand.

Tonight is the formal unveiling of the model of the new home for the opera and ballet companies and the symphony orchestra. The premier of Ontario himself has come, pulling in his slippery wake half a dozen beaming cabinet ministers, and orbiting around them, their moon-faced aides and sexy secretaries. Mayoral candidate Victoria Sommers showed up early to work the room and get herself photographed with important members of the Concert Hall Committee.

The evening started with a big-chested soprano in a green velvet evening gown standing in front of the buffet table. Her number had a lot of that high-pitched ha-ha-ha stuff that scrapes on Fred's nerves. But the other guests all standing around with their glasses of champagne applauded enthusiastically.

Then came the ballet dancers. Fred had wanted a chorus of a good dozen or more, just to make the point that it's really the dancers, Fred's people, that the concert hall is being built for. But they told him there wasn't enough room and he'd have to settle for a couple doing a *pas de deux*.

They were enough though. The two of them were beautiful. The reception was being held in the rooftop bar of the Sutton Place Hotel, and the dancers performed against the long windows with the whole night sky for a backdrop. An early November snow was beginning, and white flakes as big as pie plates were drifting by.

At the end of their number, the two dancers, a guy in a black jacket and white tights and a girl in an old-fashioned white tutu, bowed to the audience and then, coming forward to the buffet table, they pulled the cover off a model of the concert hall. Then, while the crowd applauded enthusiastically,

Fred Englander suddenly began to feel he was in the wrong place. What had seemed only a vague idea in the plans he looked at earlier was now crudely, painfully obvious. At least to Fred it was.

The model was over four feet high. It stood in a place of honour, surrounded by platters of pink lobster claws, and liver pâtés as dark and rich as loaves of chocolate. Fred himself chose the menu and picked up the bills because he wanted this reception to be first class. He never dreamed that he would stand in the middle of it, feeling like a little boy again, frightened and alone.

The model showed that the concert hall was going to be two buildings. The inner one would be a box that would be the actual auditorium. The outer building would be all of glass, and the space between the inner and outer buildings would be the lobby and public space. It was the shape of this outer building that shocked and sickened Fred Englander.

The glass shell has a high, steeply sloping roof, tinted by gold leaf. The roof is supported by rows of gold anodyne pillars that the architect, a plump Englishman with a lad-dee-dah accent, calls "flying buttresses." There will be broad stairs leading up to the front. The front will have six sides, creating what the architect says is a "public pavilion" leading to the doors of the auditorium. People will be able to look up and see in the glass tower above them the gold bells of a carillon that will be rung on state occasions.

The shape of the outer glass building will create within the concert hall a feeling of "reverence for art" the architect says. Indeed, "reverence for art" could be considered to be the theme of the whole building.

While everybody is cooing over the model and enjoying the glamour of the bright television lights, Fred Englander slips away to the bar. He finds there what he had been hoping for: Harry Margulies. He had wanted to talk to Harry alone, but J. Arthur Quinn is with him. Well, Quinn has always been a good friend to the Englander family.

"Harry, tell me something: Am I being oversensitive or does that thing bother you, too?"

Harry studies the concert hall model. He can see nothing wrong with it. It looks quite attractive, really. But Arthur Quinn begins to understand what is troubling Fred. Quinn, after all, grew up a Roman Catholic.

"I think they were trying for a classic European opera house," Quinn says. “But you’re right, Fred, what they’ve wound up with looks more like a cathedral. The front could pass for the front of Notre Dame.”

“Yeah, that’s what I think too,” Fred Englander says. His seriousness surprises Harry and Quinn.

“Well, you know what they say, Fred,” Harry says. “Art is the new religion.”

His humour does not amuse the developer.

“It’s not my religion,” Fred says grimly. But he decides he had better not go any further, not in front of all these people. He moves away and leaves Harry and Quinn alone.

“Poor Fred,” Harry says. “Who would have dreamed? I think he’s really pissed off.”

“He’s got a case,” Quinn says. “He raises all the money for them and now he finds out they’re building a church. You know, I think culture is replacing patriotism as the last refuge of the scoundrel.”

“Victoria likes it. That’s what matters,” Harry says. “Let’s get back to the office.”

“All right, I’ve had enough of this place too...Harry, your ‘ex’ has been after me. She thinks I should have a little talk with you.”

“The line forms to the left—after Doreen’s mother, my mother, my brother, my uncles and aunts, the butcher, the baker, and the ushers at the Royal Alex. Doreen’s got half the city phoning me.”

“Are you listening to any of them?”

“No fucking way.”

“Good for you,” Quinn says.

91

THE SNOW has become thicker by the time Fred Englander noses his long black Cadillac up the steep slope of the Sutton Place garage and north onto Bay Street. The windshield wipers strain against the heavy white flakes spiralling down on the city. Fred feels safe in his car. He has become rich enough that not even the forces of nature can reach him if he doesn't want them to. But security does not ease his loneliness. He wonders what would happen if he went to Peter Dagenham and said, Peter, I want a big six-pointed Jewish star of David worked into all that glass in the front. Peter probably wouldn't even mind. He'd say, it doesn't bother me, Freddy. When you've been running things for a thousand years, you can afford to be generous. It's only when you're an outsider that you realize how much is being taken away from you.

Fred thought he was coming from one direction and Peter and his people were coming from another direction and they would meet in the middle, on the neutral ground of art. Now he sees there is no neutral ground. They bring all their own history and religious trappings with them. And they expect Fred to join in with them, thank them in fact, without a murmur. He can just imagine what his father, Reb Shmuel Englander, would have said if somebody had told him art is religion. Even Fred, who is far from being devout himself, could tell Peter Dagenham that watching a ballet is nothing at all like praying. Old Mr. Englander would never have had anything to do with this new Concert Hall. But his son, Fred, cannot walk away from it now without leaving people to think that he's a miserable, paranoid little shtetl Jew afraid to go out into the big world. The goyim have got Fred Englander by the throat. Some day, Fred is thinking, the Jews in this country are going to pay a terrible price for believing they have been accepted as members of the white Protestant élite. Fred Englander is already paying part of that price.

At a red light, Fred studies the people waiting for a bus. They look thoroughly miserable. Their cheeks have been scrubbed raw by the cold and they are wet from falling snow. Fred Englander reflects that he has not ridden on a bus since he was nineteen years old. Suddenly he realizes that the woman turning towards him is the ballerina who danced for the reception on the roof of the hotel. She doesn't look very glamorous now. She has an old khaki scarf wrapped around her head, and her nose is running.

He pushes his Cadillac through the gathering snow and opens the passenger door in front of her.

"Can I offer you a ride?" Fred says.

The woman stamps her feet against the cold and turns away. The best defence against scumbags like this, she has found, is to pretend they don't exist.

"It's all right," Fred says in his friendliest, most reassuring voice. "I'm Fred Englander, chairman of the Concert Hall Committee. I'd be happy to give you a lift."

She bends down then and sees that, indeed, he is familiar. This is the guy who made the introduction for her and her partner. He must be a fan, and fans are usually all right.

"Thank you," she says. "I'm freezing." She slips into the car seat, shaking snow off her like a dog emerging from the water. Fred pulls away from the intersection and watches out of the corner of his eye while she blows her nose, loosens her scarf a bit, and settles a large denim carrying bag between her legs. Fred can just see a bit of the white tutu sticking out of one corner of the bag. She sinks back in her seat, luxuriating in the warm air being blown over her by the car's heating system.

"Now, where can I take you?" Fred asks.

"The subway'll be great."

"That's only a couple of blocks. It's such a miserable night. I'd be happy to take you home."

"No, it's okay. Just to the subway."

"Are you sure?" Fred says. "I really don't mind. I was very grateful to you and your partner for coming out for us tonight. I'd hate to think I was responsible for you getting a bad cold."

"Well," she says hesitantly. "I live way out in the Danforth. Logan Avenue."

"Perfect!" Fred says decisively. "I'm just a few blocks above there. I can drop you off and cut right home."

The Danforth is to the east and Fred lives directly north of the hotel. It is going to take him hours to push through the snow-bound, crawling traffic to drop this girl off and then make his way home. But at least he can do something useful for somebody tonight. "That was a pretty good gig," the dancer says. "We got a couple of glasses of champagne. But all the food was gone. Would you believe it? By the time we got dressed, that big buffet was cleaned right out."

"We'll stop for something," Fred says. "I'm terribly sorry. I should have had them put aside a plate for you."

"No, no, no," the dancer says in a rush. "I didn't mean it like that. I've got lots of stuff at my place. Just take me home."

But then she is sorry she has spoken so quickly. Her name is Lois Keast, and a strange, smokey possibility is beginning to present itself to her. Why not? she is asking herself. Who's going to stop you?

When you have spent your days in rehearsal halls and your nights performing or going to watch other people perform, you have just about zero contact with the outside world. Even the ballet fans are remote. They turn up for big functions like tonight, but you always have to be careful what you say to them. Fans have mysterious ways of influencing who rises and falls within the company.

Still, there are girls in the company who manage to cultivate special friends—uncles or "sugar daddies," as some people still insist on calling them. There isn't too much talk in the changing-room about how these arrangements actually work, but you can certainly tell what's happening when everybody gathers after the winter break and most girls are sniffly and overweight from having been home with mother while a few girls turn up looking skinny and tanned, and start carrying on about how great the weather was in the Cayman Islands.

Lois has always considered dancers who do this to be inhabitants of a country she doesn't even want to visit. But now she turns and begins an animated conversation with Fred Englander. She's not making any commitments—to herself or to anyone else. Lois is not doing anything, really, except enjoying the comfort of a big car on a stormy night and talking to a loyal and interested fan about what a dancer's life is really like.

She finds him rather sweet. The man doesn't know anything. He sounds genuinely shocked when she tells him how many hours she has to spend working out in class every day and he is absolutely dumbfounded when she tells him about the "treatment." Well, most fans know, or they damned well ought to know, how Alice, the artistic director, will pick some girl right out of the school and give her starring roles for a year—parts like Giselle and even Odette in Swan Lake. Alice says it's because she has to keep giving the fans new faces to make a fuss about. But most girls who get the treatment can't handle the pressure. Lois tells Fred she is personally lucky because she survived her year in the spotlight and stayed on as a principal dancer. A lot of girls burn out and leave the company.

"I never dreamed that kind of thing went on," Fred says, shaking his head.

He's quite good-looking, really. Lois notes that Fred has even features, ruddy, outdoorsy skin, clear brown eyes that are probably quite warm when you are looking at him face to face, a silly little moustache, and neatly trimmed brown hair that has only a little bit of grey here and there. But, Lois asks herself bluntly, could she really go to bed with this guy? It would be a strange experience, no doubt about that.

Would he expect her to love him in some way?

Lois has had one great love in her life and one person who was wildly in love with her and very nearly convinced her to actually marry him. But they're both long gone now. Lois has been alone for a long time. It seems to her that if she is ever going to get out into the world again, she will have to get somebody to take her there. She didn't plan any of this, but why shouldn't she hold herself open to possibilities that come along? So when Fred drives up to the house where she and a friend have the top floor, she casually invites him up so that the chairman of the Concert Hall Committee can see how dancers really live.

92

FRED ENGLANDER has been a loyal husband. He has loved Estelle and he would never do anything to hurt her. But now he is thinking, why not? This would just be collecting something that is owing to Fred Englander. They used him to get their goddamned concert hall. Is he not entitled to get one of their people in return?

"My roommate's away this weekend," Lois Keast is saying. "She sleeps on the couch. It's a fold-out bed, really. It's comfortable enough."

"I'm in the development business," Fred says. "I can find you something better than this, believe me."

"Well, we'd certainly appreciate that," Lois says nervously. "But that's not the reason I brought you up here. So many of the fans, the people on the committees and all, think dancers are really doing all right because we've got the union and our pay has gone up so much in the last few years. But everything else has gone up too. Sally, she's my roommate, and I had to hunt for months just to find this place. And we can barely afford it."

She retreats into her bedroom to, as she says, get out of this wet stuff, and Fred is left alone in her front room, still standing in his fur-collared overcoat and his black Homburg. Through an open door, Fred can see a bathroom with an ancient iron tub. The girls have done their best, taped travel posters and movie posters to the sloping walls and filled up a bookshelf with porcelain figurines and stuffed animals. But the attic still looks more like they are camping out than living here. There is an electric space heater in the corner. Fred can well imagine how cold this place gets in the dead of winter.

Lois returns, carrying a bottle of sherry and two glasses on a plastic tray.

"I'm afraid this is all we've got," she says.

"That looks fine," Fred says.

She has changed into blue jeans and a heavy, knitted green sweater. Now that she is unwrapped from her winter outfit, Fred can see she is really quite pretty. Her eyes are large and dark. They're Lois's best feature. Her face is small and sharp, and her long black hair falls straight down. She is so thin and taut that if you saw this girl walking down the street and you didn't know anything about her, you'd still guess she was a dancer. But Fred is reassured to see she has the beginnings of a middle-aged double chin. In the darkness of the car, he had been afraid she might be as young as his daughter. He could not have handled that.

"Here's to the concert hall!" Lois says, raising her glass. "It's really wonderful what you people are doing for us."

"Thank you very much," Fred says, returning the toast. "I hope you feel the same way about it after we get it built."

"Say, you know…," Lois says, as though the thought has just occurred to her, "I really am hungry. I've got some bacon and eggs in the fridge. Would you like some? I've got a bottle of wine too."

This is the moment. If Fred says yes, he will be here into the night, and any night after that he wants. She is nervous and she's scared, but she brought him up here, so this must be what she wants too. So why not?

They'll both be getting something out of it. She'll get some attention and help, which she obviously needs. And Fred Englander will get to thumb his nose at Dagenham and the concert hall crowd. He will show them that Fred Englander has not been fooled; he's known all along what their little culture game is all about.

Fred leans forward. He holds out his hands. Lois Keast comes to him, as if on command. It is like a dream. His lips touch Lois's. Her lips are soft but icy cold. Fred tries again, putting his arms around the girl more firmly. He presses very gently down on her lips. That's a little better. But he can feel her fear now. And trembling through her fear, he can feel Lois Keast's determination to see this thing through.

The dream is over. Fred sees clearly what is being offered to him and he does not want it. Oh no, Fred Englander does not want this at all.

This is too much like going to Artie Quinn's office and drawing up a contract. But Fred Englander is not all business. He does not want everything in his life to be a deal.

"Thank you for inviting me in," Fred says, stepping back from Lois Keast. "But I think I'd better go now. That snow is really coming down."

The girl looks hurt and bewildered. Fred feels terrible. He can't think of a way to explain to Lois that his rejecting her isn't personal. He is really trying to do her a favour. But she looks as though he has slapped her face.

"Listen, Lois, you're a lovely person," Fred says quickly. "And if you ever really need help, please call me. I'll be very angry if you don't. But right now, I think it's the best thing for both of us if I just go home."

Then he is crashing down the stairs. Old Man Englander used to say that the highest form of mitzvah is when the person on the receiving end doesn't even know that help has been given. Not that the old man lived that way himself. If he gave away a nickel, the whole world heard about it. But Fred has just performed a couple of the highest-grade mitzvahs. He has saved a young woman from wasting her time on an old man. And Fred is giving Toronto a new concert hall that he himself will never feel at home in. If there really is a reckoning, if God really does open the book of life on Yom Kippur and measure the sins and good deeds of human beings, then it should be recorded that Fred Englander has already done more in his life than his father, Reb Shmuel Englander, ever dreamed of doing.

93

I'M VITO ALCAMO *and I need your help. I'm Vito Alcamo and I'm running for mayor. I'm Vito Alcamo and I'm going crazy out here. I've got long underwear on, but I'm still freezing my ass off because I have to stand in one place to hand out these leaflets in front of the subway station. If I had any sense, I'd go back to my nice warm bed. I'd go back to my nice warm wife.*

The last poll showed him seven points ahead of Sommers. That still ought to be enough to win. But there's only a week to go. If Sommers keeps gaining, she could pass him. She's brought in Dane Harrison, and everybody knows he's one of the best campaign organizers around. If Alcamo got Dane to work for him, they'd say he was going to turn the planning department over to the developers. But Victoria does it and it's all right because she's a good person and God is on her side. When Vito started this, it was just another challenge. Now it's a cause. He doesn't just want to beat Victoria Sommers; he wants to save the city from that sanctimonious, double-talking bitch. So a poll not covered, a meeting missed, even a couple of votes he didn't get because he was tired and didn't come out to a subway station one morning, could make all the difference.

Vito has the sense that the campaign has slipped beyond his control. People keep making decisions he knows nothing about. The all-important fund-raising committee started with his campaign manager and best friend, Al Spinelli, and a few of the neighbourhood storekeepers. But then the Italian builders and dry-wallers and sewer contractors decided that if Vito Alcamo had the balls to be the first Italian to run for mayor, they would rally around him. Vito warned these new fund-raisers to send back cheques from anyone who could get him into trouble later. But does Vito know what they are doing? Does even Al Spinelli know? Suddenly the campaign has money for non-stop radio spots, billboards everywhere, and all kinds of TV commercials. Stand over here, Vito. Read this script, Vito. Smile, Vito. Look like you're happy.

Vito would just like to know where the hell Al Spinelli dug up the sign crew. They lounge around the campaign office, looking like the kind of hoods you cross the street to avoid. They've got tattoos on their arms, for God's sake. Whenever a campaign worker finds someone who says yes, they'd like one of those nice signs—a picture of Vito and Gillian and their two little girls with "Vito Alcamo, a mayor for all the people!" on the bottom—the sign crew rushes off in the pickup truck and hammers it into the front lawn.

But Vito knows for a fact they spend half their time pulling up Victoria Sommers's signs and making off with them. Vito asks people to vote for him, and they tell him they've seen his boys stealing signs. It's not a big offence, and the boys are not going to jail if they get caught, but just think of the bad publicity. Listen, Al, Vito warns his campaign manager, that sign crew could kill us. But Al says, Don't worry, leave everything to us, and hands Vito his schedule for the day.

So Vito does what he is told. He is up, bathed, shaved, and halfway into his first pack of breath mints by the time the car comes at six-thirty to take him to the subway stop he is to work for the early rush hour. He goes "mainstreeting" in the morning, sticking his head into stores, shaking hands, talking to the owners and managers, trying to get them to take a sign. For lunch there are always speeches, usually businessmen's associations and service clubs, the Downtown Business Council, the Beaches Kiwanis, the Bloor Village Business Improvement Area. In the afternoons, the slow time, Vito is out visiting the aldermen who have pledged to distribute his leaflets, maybe going out with some of their canvassers; suppertime he spends out knocking on doors again; evenings are for speeches and more all-candidates meetings—sometimes they race him around to four and five meetings in a single night.

Ambition alone couldn't drive him to this. Yes, he wants to be the first Italian mayor. Yes, he wants a good job and he wants to bring home lots of money to Gillian and his beautiful daughters. But what he wants more than anything else is for his people, the children of the immigrants, to take power. Victoria and her kind have had their own way long enough. Now it is time for Vito's people to remake the city in their own image. It is their right. And Vito Alcamo is going to win it for them. Or kill himself in the trying.

94

THE MEETING has been called for eight in the morning so the partners can deal with McConnachie and this merger business quickly and still have the rest of the day to work for the clients who, after all, pay the bills for Carlton and Boggs. J. Arthur Quinn says he wants only coffee for breakfast, but Harry insists they both have their regular—bran flakes with "gunk," which is actually chopped fruit and yoghurt spread over top of the cereal.

"It's just another meeting, Arthur," Harry says. "We're going to walk away with it."

Before the bowls of cereal arrive, Quinn takes out a little white plastic bottle and drops a nitro pill under his tongue. Harry watches him in the mirror facing their stools in the Coffee Shop.

The look on Harry's face surprises Quinn. He is becoming so used to these little necessities that he forgets the effect they have on other people.

"Don't worry, Harry," he says. "I'm going in for the full triple bypass—new pipes, new plumbing, the works. I've just been putting it off until this business with Charlie is out of the way."

"Well, then, let's get it over with," Harry says.

"You're right. Once more unto the breach." Quinn gulps down the last of his Earl Grey tea and insists it his turn to pay for breakfast. Together they take the elevator from the underground mall at First Canadian Place up to the offices of Carlton and Boggs where the nineteen men and one woman who belong to the firm's Management Committee—one-third of Carlton and Boggs's senior partners—have already begun to gather in the board room.

Quinn sets his briefcase on the long pine table and pretends to be studying important papers. Harry gets himself a fresh coffee and begins working the room, shaking hands, asking about kids, exchanging bits of gossip. Quinn is making a pitch today, so people leave him alone. The politics are being handled by his floor manager, Harry Margulies. Harry has just heard, he tells a couple of the heavies in corporate law, that J & R is looking for somebody to handle the Consolidated Tile deal; we should be able to get a piece of that at least. The corporate guys appreciate the intelligence. They will get on the blower as soon as this meeting ends.

When he was first invited to the Management Committee, Harry was in awe of the firm's inner circle. The wealth and power these twenty people manipulated every day seemed almost beyond imagining. But now he knows his colleagues as people no better than himself. Some are humorous, some are sour, some drink too much, and more than half of them are divorced, or at least separated. But in spite of their ordinariness, Harry Margulies is still proud to be counted among them. There is a fierceness to the lawyers at Carlton and Boggs. It is one of the few major firms with a "no relatives" rule. No matter how brilliant a partner's kids or nephews and nieces may be, there is no way he can ever bring them in. The firm has missed some fine lawyers over the years because of the "no relatives" rule, but as old Major "Windy" Boggs, the founder, used to say, "When a client comes in, he knows that the lawyer he's talking to is there only because he's the best in his field." The major's portrait, painted in a romantic simulation of his mud-spattered First World War artillery uniform, hangs behind the Management Committee chairman, Robert Dale, as he calls the meeting to order.

"I think we'll ask Charlie to speak first, since he's the one who got us all together," Dale says, with his clipped, Rhodes Scholar accent.

McConnachie does not waste time. He has done his homework, lobbying up and down the partners' aisle, and now he wants to touch on only a couple of important points and make them aware of one small change in the proposed merger. Taking in Azevedo, Fong and Quemoy will give Carlton and Boggs a presence in the rapidly growing suburbs and make the firm a power in the expanding field of immigration law.

The only change is in the numbers. Azevedo, Fong and Quemoy have twenty-four senior partners. Originally, they asked for fifteen of these to become senior partners in Carlton and Boggs. Now they want eighteen members of their firm to be entitled to the full financial rewards that go with being a partner in a Bay Street firm.

But that shouldn't be a problem, Charlie says, because the merger will generate more than enough business to recompense the new partners.

The old partners are not so sure. Looking around the boardroom table, Harry Margulies suspects that if the vote were taken at that moment, Charlie might well lose. Maybe Harry and Quinn have jumped too fast.

Well, it's too late now. Dale calls on Arthur Quinn, as both senior managing partner and "leader of the opposition," to make his comments.

"I agree with just about everything Charlie has been saying," Quinn says.

Old lawyers like these do not show surprise openly. But the boardroom becomes deadly quiet. The partners turn to McConnachie, who is playing with a letter opener and keeping his eyes down. Harry is pleased; he and Quinn have gone over this many times and it's working like a charm.

"I started off opposing this merger because I didn't want to see us turn into a factory and I still don't want that to happen. But I've been doing a lot of thinking this fall and I can see there is rhythm to the life of cities. A law firm like this has got to be part of that rhythm or we'll die out.

"We are in the business of serving barbarians. They swoop down from the hills…or they trickle in from the farms…or they pour out of airplanes that come here from every corner of the world. They all want to make their fortune. We get rich helping them realize their dreams.

"And when these barbarians have entered and sacked the city, they pause and look around and they see that a lot of what was already going on here was pretty good and they want some of that too. We help them get it.

"You could look upon a city as a great machine for civilizing peasants and barbarians. We are part of the civilizing process, and that is the true source of our wealth and power.

"So it is obvious we should merge with Azevedo, Fong and Quemoy. And not just for the excellent reasons Charlie has presented to us but because this merger will give us the jump on our competitors on the street who may not yet have understood what we understand.

"Indeed, I believe we should go even farther than Charlie has proposed. They have asked for eighteen full partnerships, we should make all twenty-four partners in Azevedo, Fong and Quemoy full partners in Carlton and Boggs. Yes, there is a danger that the pie will be sliced into too many pieces at the end of the year. But, by giving all our new partners a full share, we are providing them with the incentive to increase the overall size of the pie.

"So let us take them all into full partnership and let us give them the eight seats on this Management Committee they would be entitled to.

"But—and here I differ slightly from Charlie—let us not give up our civilizing function too quickly. We have all worked very hard to get where we are and we have been shaped and changed by this experience. I think we should offer the same opportunity to our new partners.

"So I am going to suggest we create an executive for the management committee. It will consist of five members—the managing partner of this firm and two people he suggests, along with Mr. Fong, who I understand is the managing partner in his firm, and one person he selects. This executive committee would essentially set the direction for our new firm, but it would have a horizon—three years. By then, any lingering difficulties should be cleared away and we can proceed comfortably into the future as Carlton, Boggs, Azevedo, Fong and Quemoy."

Harry can see that Quinn's long speech has cost him dearly. His face is drained of colour, and his forehead is damp. But Harry can also see that other members of the committee are pleased with what they have heard. The scheme Harry developed for Quinn has something for everybody. The newcomers will get to Bay Street and start pulling in big money right away. But the shock of merger will not be too great for the older members of Carlton and Boggs. Their old friend, J. Arthur Quinn, will control the direction of the firm for at least another three years. And, for Quinn, that will be long enough to move people he wants into positions of power. Then he can retire, knowing the firm is in good hands.

Dale calls for the vote, and approval for the merger is unanimous. They have created the second-largest law firm in Canada.

"I think we can call this meeting adjourned," Dale says. "It's almost eight forty-five. We all have work to do."

"Just one small item more," Charlie McConnachie says. "We don't have to settle this here, but I think we've definitely got to get it in motion."

Most of the partners turn impatiently towards McConnachie, but a few are looking out the window or down at notepads they have been doodling on. They are McConnachie's people. Harry realizes that whatever's coming next, this is the moment McConnachie has been waiting for.

"I think we've got to turn this thing over to the Promotions and Compensations Committee right away," McConnachie says. "I mean we're taking in twenty-four new partners and we have to decide on how everybody's going to get compensated." Harry looks down at Quinn. His face is white, and there is a small, bitter smile fixed on his lips.

"Speaking only for myself," McConnachie goes on, "I think we ought to downgrade seniority. Maybe do away with seniority all together. It's not how long you've been with the firm but how much you're doing for it that ought to count.

"And...," McConnachie says, looking down the table, facing his colleagues in a forthright, manly style, "I will be frank with you and say that I think billable hours ought to be the only consideration. The more money you bring into the firm, the more money you take home at the end of the year. Period."

It is all beautifully, painfully clear now. McConnachie has used the merger to make a fatal thrust at Quinn. Harry knows—and the others will soon know too—that Quinn has fewer billable hours than some of the firm's junior associates. The old man has not been well and he has been relying on a few old developer clients he has had for years. When the others realize how little hard cash the great J. Arthur Quinn brings into the firm, they will never let him stay on as managing partner.

But there is no way Harry can oppose McConnachie's proposal. It sounds too reasonable and fair. The Management Committee gives its approval without even any debate. Dale moves adjournment and the meeting breaks up.

Quinn stays seated, looking a little stunned by how quickly events have moved. Harry comes down the table to commiserate.

"Don't worry about it, Arthur," he says. "I think I can get myself appointed to that Compensation Committee."

Quinn lays his hand on Harry's forearm. His fingers grip hard.

"Hospital," he whispers. "The ticker again, Harry."

95

THE RECEPTIONIST at the front desk wants to call an ambulance, but Quinn won't hear of it. Whatever else he has to endure, he is not going to be carried out of Carlton and Boggs on a stretcher. He orders Harry to get the nitro bottle out of his inside jacket pocket. He swallows one, waits a moment, and then clutches Harry's arm and pulls himself erect.

Together, they make a stately progress towards the elevator, which is, thank heaven, only a hundred feet away. Lillian, Quinn's ancient secretary, is holding the door for them. She steps into the elevator with them and rides to the ground floor. She has a cab waiting, and a Carlton and Boggs charge slip in her hand. But Quinn sends her back. "I need you up there," he croaks. "Cover for me, Lilly."

She is obviously hurt at being sent away when she is needed most. But she dutifully helps get Quinn into the car and then withdraws, as the old man has asked.

"I'll call you, Lilly, as soon as I know anything," Harry says. Nothing more is needed, not even thanks. Lillian leans forward to squeeze Quinn's hand, closes the cab door on the two lawyers, and returns to the offices on the sixty-fifth floor.

Quinn leans back against Harry. Harry holds him upright, squeezing his shoulder as hard as he dares.

"Sorry, Harry. I guess I should have gone in for a refit when they told me to," Quinn whispers. "Stupid, eh?"

"Yeah, Arthur, stupid," Harry says bitterly. He feels like he is going to cry. "Fucking stupid."

Quinn says nothing more to Harry until they reach the hospital. What is the old man thinking about, Harry wonders. The wife he split with over thirty years ago? As far as Harry knows, she remarried and moved out to Vancouver. Is Quinn thinking about the daughter who lives in San Diego? The son who lives in Edmonton? How many years has it been since he saw either of them? Or maybe he's thinking about his years at Carlton and Boggs. Or about his miserable childhood on the sheep farm in Nova Scotia. Harry Margulies realizes he knows very little about J. Arthur Quinn's inner life. Yet, who has loved him more?

At the emergency entrance to the hospital, Harry has only to say one word, "Heart!" and they are all over Quinn. They have him on a stretcher and they're already hooking him up to instruments as they race down the corridor with him. In an instant, the frantic hubbub is over. Harry is standing alone in the emergency ward, trying to focus on the woman at the desk who is brusquely demanding details about the cardiac patient Harry has just brought in.

"His name is J. Arthur Quinn." The woman begins typing out the forms.

"He lives at the Simcoe Club. On Bay Street. I don't have his OHIP number, but they'll have it at our office. He's sixty-four years old, I think. He's a lawyer..."

96

AT SIX O'CLOCK, Dane Harrison has already let himself into the dark campaign office. This is election day. Dane has worked from eight in the morning until eight in the evening to get people out of their homes for Victoria Sommers. Dane begins going over maps of city wards and lists of campaign workers. He has an idea how to win the game today. But it means a frightening risk.

There are twenty-two wards in the city, and each one has three or four places where people can vote—church basements, the kitchens and livingrooms of private homes, the lobbies of apartment blocks and office towers. For every polling station, Dane ought to have three people throughout the day. One should be inside, keeping track of who comes to vote and feeding the latest information to the two outside workers, who will go knocking on doors. Dane knows that even on election day, it is hard to get people to do more than a four-hour shift, so he should have at least a thousand campaign workers to cover the city properly. He will be lucky if he gets even half that many.

Volunteers will call in and be told where to report. There are whole neighbourhoods where Victoria will have nobody at all. The maddening, terrifying question is: where will the troops Dane does have do the most good?

It makes sense to work the downtown and midtown wards where ratepayers are still well organized and the New Democratic Party has its roots. These are the neighbourhoods where canvassers have compiled the longest lists of people committed to Victoria. But Dane would have to ignore Sommers's supporters in the outer, immigrant wards, where Alcamo is strongest.

Dane Harrison wants to send Victoria into the big office at the front of City Hall with the kind of majority that will make other politicians fear her and do her bidding.

Dane is gambling that middle-class homeowners who have said they support Victoria don't need to be reminded to get to the polling booths. Victoria's been their champion for years, and even if they are nervous about group homes, they like the concert hall because they think culture is good for people—especially for their own children, for whom they want the very best.

So why not send his people into the outer wards where Alcamo is strong? For the people out there, Victoria is her own media image. They wouldn't allow one of their own women to be such a public trouble-maker, but they respect these qualities in a remote Anglo like Victoria. They like the way she stands up to the big shots.

There is no way Victoria is going to actually win any of the immigrant wards. But if Dane can cut down the majority Alcamo wins by—and if Victoria does well in the centre of Toronto—she will have the majority Dane wants for her.

He is taking one hell of a chance. If that midtown vote doesn't hold up, Dane could blow months of work in a couple of hours. The Campaign Committee, if Dane took the trouble to consult them, would be horrified. They play politics the modern way, by numbers. Dane Harrison still plays by gut instinct. He knows he is right, that's enough. Besides, Dane Harrison told Harry Margulies he would look after Victoria, and he is going to keep his promise. These are the things politics is about, instinct and loyalty.

Vito Alcamo is going to vote *en famille.* At eleven in the morning, he sits in his kitchen, waiting for his father and his sister, Francie, to arrive. His wife's mother is already there, making coffee and laying out platters of shortbread and coffee cake, the products of her indefatigable baking. Gillian is upstairs, getting the two little girls into the red velvet dresses that have been bought for this occasion. Vito loves his daughters in these outfits. They look like little Edwardian children.

Al Spinelli, his campaign manager, has alerted the media. All newspapers, all radio, and especially television, stations, have been told that candidate Vito Alcamo will be voting at Fulham Street Baptist Church at 11:30 this morning. Let the whole world see that, on this day, when he risks everything, Vito Alcamo has the support of his whole family.

Being a politician, Vito has discovered in this election campaign, is a means of keeping faith. Running for mayor has given him a chance to show his respect for "the first wave" of immigrants, those sturdy, driven men who came in the 1950s and took the first pick-and-shovel jobs they could find and bought pickup trucks and then houses, and raised families and, in some cases, went on to become millionaires. So many times Vito has heard one of these old timers say that if he had to start over, if he lost everything to the Jews and the cake eaters, he could pick up his shovel and start again. Vito expects to win today, but if he loses, there will be no tears and no blaming anyone. Vito Alcamo will pick up his shovel and start again.

Storekeepers come to the windows and smile as the Alcamo party passes by. The day is bitterly cold, and Vito and his family are wrapped in long scarves and red toques. Some people on the sidewalks wave; others fall in behind the colourful party of Alcamos. It becomes a bit of a parade. The cameramen start up their lights and machinery when Vito and his people are still a block away from the church. Vito proudly calls his name to the returning officer, a wispy little woman sitting in the Sunday school room under a lithograph of Christ crucified: "Vito Tomasso Alcamo." He goes behind the cardboard screen to mark X in the circles on the ballot. Newspaper photographers flick blinding strobe lights at him. Vito pushes his folded ballot into the little slot at the top of the ballot box. The powerful lights from the TV crews bathe him for the moment in pure, shadowless glory.

"I am proud to be the first Italian running for mayor," Vito says. "This is a great day for all ethnic people in the city."

The Alcamo party heads back to Vito's house, but Vito is not with them. Al Spinelli has pulled Vito away, and now they are in a rented limousine, heading downtown to Mr. Dill's, a smart downtown singles bar and steak house. Al has rented the place for the whole day. Vito will stay there until the polls close and then he will have his victory party. People will come from all over the city to have a drink with the next mayor, gorge themselves from the buffet tables, maybe dance a little to the Nimbus Jazz Quintet, whom Spinelli has also hired. If visitors are lucky, they may arrive when the next mayor himself is sitting in with the group, playing on his old high-school clarinet.

This easy-going, laid-back affair is actually a bit of strategy designed to mislead Victoria's forces. They have tried to set up a city-wide organization. To Al Spinelli, that is madness. Toronto is too big to try to cover every poll. Vito is relying on friends and allies on City Council. Other aldermen have been handing out Vito's literature and talking about him on the doorstep. They know their own neighbourhoods, and they have the campaign workers. When they push to get out the vote for themselves, they will be getting out the vote for Alcamo too.

Meanwhile, Vito's old buddies in the St. Cuthbert's Liberal riding association have set up Liberals to run for City Council in the downtown and midtown wards, where Victoria is strongest. These people are up against well-established reformers, and they don't really have a chance of winning. But they might do well an election or two from now, and it has been pointed out that, by doing a kamikaze run now, they are getting their names before the public. They have been provided with money for campaign offices, organizational advice, and even some campaign workers from the Liberal party. The dummy candidates are going to make sure that the votes they pull for themselves on Sommers's home turf are also Alcamo votes.

There is even a dummy candidate in Victoria's old ward. Her name is Dorothy Bester and she is fanatically against group homes. The boys in Vito's campaign office call her "the battleaxe," and Spinelli has to keep scolding them to make sure they don't let the nickname slip out in public. But even Spinelli has to concede the woman does, indeed, look like a battleaxe—white-haired, cement-faced; mean in thought, word, and deed. It's hard to imagine what the woman would be like in the sack—if, indeed, anyone was ever crazy enough to want to screw her.

But never mind, Dorothy Bester's energy is phenomenal, and in the confusion that spread through Victoria's home ward after she decided to go for mayor, Bester seems to be pulling in a lot of people. There is more hatred of group homes than Victoria ever imagined. Spinelli is pretty sure Victoria and her people have not figured out how Vito's team is playing this election. And Spinelli is not going to do anything on election day that might alert the other side. Victoria has some old pros working for her, and they know how to move their people around quickly. So Vito Alcamo and his key people will be seen whiling away election day with a day-long party. Politics, Spinelli is discovering, is just like business. You make a plan and you carry it out—a step at a time.

The sun has hardly been a presence and now it is going down. Victoria Sommers rolls over, groggily picks her watch up off the night table, and cries out, "Oh, my God!"

It's after five! She was supposed to be at Exeter Street Public School polling booth at 4:30. Dane sent notices to all the media people. No! No! No! Victoria cannot believe she has done this to Dane—and to herself. Maybe Dane can get some of the press back. She charges from the bed and finds herself half on the floor. Harry Margulies is holding onto her ankle.

"Ow! Stop that!"

"Where are you going?"

"Leave me alone! I have to vote!"

"Why?"

That is the stupidest crack Victoria has ever heard. She twists and turns on the floor, struggling to get her ankle away from Harry. He is too strong for her.

"Harry, please, this is no time for games."

"Yes, it is," Harry says dolefully. "This is the last time we've got."

He lets go of her. Victoria rolls awkwardly onto the floor and stands up. She looks down at Harry. He has turned to her, lying on one elbow, chin cupped in his hand, gazing embarrassingly up at her. Victoria has only her panties on. She was supposed to be taking a quick nap. Dane had them rushing all over the city, encouraging campaign workers, and Victoria said she was starting to wear down. So Harry took her to his house for a bit of a rest. Now look what they've done!

Victoria's mind races ahead, picking out the telephone numbers of her campaign headquarters, composing her excuses to Dane, going over the suits she has stowed in Harry's closet. Which one would be proper to be photographed voting in? The Harris tweed? The royal blue wool? Her own trademark white blazer?

Victoria stops herself. Harry's right. She pulls up the tangle of blankets and sheets and slides in beside him. One vote more or less isn't going to decide the future of Victoria Sommers—even if it's her own vote. But how many more free hours like this will she ever have? Politics is the art of making choices.

It is 7:40 and there are still two more possibles on the list the campaign office handed to Trevor Billinghurst. But even if he can get these dubious Sommers supporters out of their warm kitchens to vote for her, it would likely take them more than twenty minutes to get their winter coats and boots on and trudge to the polling station in the next block. The election does not go one minute past eight o'clock.

Trevor decides to make the calls anyway. He will finish this job, even if the campaign organizers have sent him out on a fool's errand. Trevor is in the western reaches of the city; continental railway tracks slash arrogantly across the local streets out here. This is a neighbourhood Trevor has hardly ever been to before, even in his cab-driving days. It's a patchwork of tiny, cramped wooden slat houses that were thrown up half a century ago for the stockyard workers. Most houses need paint, and they all look as though a strong wind would blow them over. Trevor knocks on the first door. The sudden light is blinding. The little house smells deliciously of frying onions and potatoes. But Trevor is not invited to cross the threshold. The stocky little man with suspenders pulled over the greying top of his long winter underwear says, "Politicians are a bunch of crooks." He slams the door. "You know something, Mister," Trevor says to the empty porch. "I agree with you."

Then Trevor stamps his feet and sets off for his last call, seven houses down the street. It is a frail elderly woman with a fringe of downy grey hair on her cheeks. She looks like a shrivelled-up tennis ball. She can hardly speak English. What on earth does this poor little old lady think Victoria Sommers is going to do for her? But Trevor doesn't press the question. He helps the woman on with her coat. Trevor is practically carrying her by the time they get to the house on the next block where the ballot box has been set up on a white porcelain kitchen table. It is 7:58. Trevor marches down the hallway, thinking that if Victoria wins by one vote, she'll owe her victory to him.

Trevor's feeling of elation lasts until the votes are counted in his poll. He had 62 Sommers' supporters on his list, and he managed to get 54 of them out. But when the votes are counted, Alcamo has still carried the poll by 206 votes to 87. Nobody expected Sommers to do well out here, but Trevor thought she'd do better than this. He calls the results down to Victoria's headquarters and asks the girl how things are going. Better in other parts of the city, the girl says. But Trevor can tell from the hesitant sound of her voice that she is getting worried.

He'd like to go home, fill a tub with hot water and a tumbler with scotch, and just lie back and relax. But he has promised to go down to the campaign headquarters and pick up Vivian, who has been sent out to a Greek neighbourhood in the east end. So Trevor points his car downtown.

An election is the one chance ordinary people like me get to put a boot to the behinds of people in power. I wouldn't give this up for anything. If you said to me, "Trevor Billinghurst you have a choice, you can help look after this poor, cold, hungry little child or you can go in there and drop your piece of paper in the box," I'd go cast my vote and let the little bugger freeze to death.

97

"HELLO? Gordon?"

"Dad? Is that you?"

"Yes, it's me. We don't seem to have a very good connection. How are you, Gordon?"

"I'm fine, Dad. I'm going into the air force."

"You're too young still!"

"It's just camp, one month. They give you training so you're prepared when you go in."

"Are you sure you really want to be a pilot?"

"I'm going to try for it, Dad. But there's lots of other people want it too."

"Gordon, I've been talking to your mother."

"Yeah, I know."

"I want to hear it from you. Do you want me to sign the papers so Morry can adopt you and you can be Morry's son? Is that what you want, Gordon?"

"Well, I'm kind of worried about them. They're sure something's going to happen to me when I'm away. This will make them feel better."

Harry feels relief. This is turning out to be easier than he dared hope.

"So you're doing this for them? Is that it? Are you telling me the adoption is your little gift to your mother and Morry?"

"Sort of. I never thought of it like that. But, yeah, I guess you're right."

"I see...well, then, I guess I can help you do what you want. I'll call your mother and sign the papers for her. Just one thing, Gordon. You may be 'Gideon Ishmaeli,' from now on, but Harry Margulies doesn't stop being your father. And if you ever need anything, you know where to find me."

"I know, Dad."

"And you keep calling me 'Dad,' eh?"

"You bet."

"I might be over in the spring. If I can get things around here cleaned up a bit."

"I'd like that."

"Well, goodbye, Gordon."

"Goodbye, Dad."

Harry replaces the receiver. He sits there quietly, acutely aware of the deep breaths he is taking. He has planned the actual making of this telephone call very carefully. He has come into the office early in the morning so he can catch Gordon before it is too late in Israel. And now he has a desk full of work in front of him so he will not just be sitting there brooding after Gordon's voice has faded away. There is quite an interesting and difficult subdivision proposal up in Markham that the new people have brought him. The merger process is just getting under way, but the land-use lawyers from Azevedo, Fong and Quemoy are already coming to Harry as the canny old man.

They should only know that Harry goes up to the hospital every day and talks over their problems with J. Arthur Quinn. But that's not going to last much longer. The bypass operation has been successful—Quinn's surgeon calls it "the eighth wonder of the world"—and now Quinn is almost ready to come out of the Mount Sinai. He's starting to talk about going back to Nova Scotia and buying the old family farm. Harry has been chosen to deliver the firm's retirement offer. All things considered, Charlie McConnachie has put together quite a generous package.

Still, despite all his planning ahead, Harry is finding it difficult to settle down to work. The sun is fully up now and the light is bouncing off the upper floors of the downtown skyscrapers and pouring into Harry's office. He feels a bit let down. It's interesting to speculate...what would he have done if Gordon had said No, don't do this, don't let them adopt me? Harry had pretty well made up his mind to give in to Doreen. He could not see himself engaged for the rest of his life in an emotional tug-of-war over Gordon. He'd have lost in the end, anyway. Possession is nine-tenths of the law. Who knows that better than a land-use lawyer? Harry will sign the papers and give Doreen and her new husband their final ten per cent.

But there are powers in renunciation, too. By giving up now, Harry is sure he has made a good impression on Gordon. The boy will never think of Harry Margulies as somebody who tried to hang on to something he wasn't entitled to. Maybe, someday, Harry is sure of it, he and his son will be close again.

He reaches for the telephone to call Victoria.

98

FROM a column by Bobby Mulloy in *The Daily News.*

> I can now answer the question so many people have been asking since election night. What did Victoria Sommers actually say to Vito Alcamo when they ran into each other in City Hall?
>
> I am sure most of you saw those dramatic pictures on the front page of *The News.* Alcamo had just finished going around to be interviewed by all the TV and radio people who set up shop in the City Hall rotunda on election night, and he was on his way out the main door when Sommers came in. She was being hustled along by her handlers. The guy clutching her right elbow, the one in the homburg hat and the coat

with the fur collar, was Fred Englander, the developer whom a lot of people—including me—think is much too close to the new mayor. He was trying to hustle her past Alcamo, but Sommers insisted on stopping to talk.

In the first photograph, Alcamo looks grim, like he's just managing to hold himself in. Sommers looks terribly apologetic, as though she's just done something awful and she ought to be telling everybody how sorry she is. You see her reaching up to touch Alcamo's cheek and you remember that the two of them sat next to each other for six years on City Council. Then Sommers leans forward and whispers something in Alcamo's ear. Then you see Alcamo straightening up with a big smile on his face.

The talk around town has been that Sommers offered Alcamo the top staff job in her office. And that actually makes a lot of sense. Sommers won because the old anti-developer, anti-expressway crowd finally came through for her. But she still drew only 53 per cent of the vote. That's not enough to scare anybody. Sommers is going to need all the friends she can find on Alderman's Alley.

But from what I hear, Alcamo's going back to teaching, and Sommers is going to offer the top staff job to Dane Harrison, the number cruncher from the planning department who saved her campaign.

No, what Sommers actually whispered in Alcamo's ear was this: "It wasn't your turn, Vito…Next time."

Alcamo apparently took her words of condolence so seriously he is already working the phones and lining up support for another run. My advice to him is, "Vito, don't quit your day job."

When you've been around City Hall as long as I have, you've seen a few mayors come and go, and they all have one thing in common. They all say they have just a couple of things they want to accomplish and then they'll leave and make way for somebody new and fresh.

Then they try to hang around forever. Once politicians get a taste of real power, they go after it with a compulsiveness that would make a heroin junkie blush.

The first item of business, at the first meeting of the new council, will be electing four aldermen to serve on the powerful Executive Committee. Sommers is already raising a few hackles with her high-pressure lobbying. The four-person slate the new mayor is pushing includes…

EPILOGUE: NEW YEAR'S DAY, 1980

ONE OF THE customs that has grown up in Toronto is the New Year's Day party that follows the New Year's Eve parties. So all afternoon on January first, one can see groups of laughing, exhausted people with shining faces travelling from house to house, sampling egg nog and smoked salmon canapés, and greeting old friends. Politicians participate by holding New Year's Day levees for their supporters. The levee Victoria Sommers is holding today is a special treat. Victoria is the first reform mayor the city has had in a quarter of a century. She has invited all the people who helped her get into office and all those who have supported her throughout her political career to come to her suite of offices in City Hall and say hello.

Dane Harrison is walking across City Hall square. He has his arm around Annabel Warren. With them are Trevor and Vivian Billinghurst. The Billinghursts took an active part in Victoria's campaign, and Dane and Annabel have renewed the friendship that began when Vivian lived with them in a commune. But suddenly Dane stops. He has noticed Harry Margulies among the skaters on the City Hall rink. Dane goes over to talk, and the others follow. Harry greets them all warmly but refuses to join them in going up to Victoria's levee. Dane moves close and talks to Harry confidentially.

"Harry, Annabel's expecting. We're going to do the number. Will you stand up for me?"

"Absolutely. I'd be honoured and delighted," Harry says. "Just one thing, Dane. Does the best man get a chance to prove it?"

"Not on my time," Dane says. He wraps his arms around Harry and hugs him, and kisses him on the cheek.

"You okay, Harry?"

"For sure. You guys go ahead, I'll be along."

Harry rejoins the skaters circling the rink to the sound of the tinny waltz music. Ta-ta-ta-tum...ta-dee...ta-tum. Some skaters want to be graceful, and others are interested in speed. It suddenly occurs to Harry that the pattern the skaters make on the ice is something like the insight into the meaning of life that came to him so many years ago when he lived on Landrigan Street. Clusters of skaters form and break apart, and new groups are created. The skaters are like atoms bumping into each other and exchanging energy. But Harry does not feel sadness for them, as once he might have. He has learned a thing or two since Landrigan Street. People are not just bits of matter floating through the universe. Human beings have memory, and that makes all the difference.